MARK CHRISTENSEN

ALOHA

A Novel

SIMON &
SCHUSTER

NEW YORK
LONDON
TORONTO
SYDNEY
TOKYO
SINGAPORE

SIMON & SCHUSTER
ROCKEFELLER CENTER
1230 AVENUE OF THE AMERICAS
NEW YORK, NEW YORK 10020

DESIGNED BY PEI LOI KOAY

MANUFACTURED IN THE UNITED STATES OF AMERICA

10   9   8   7   6   5   4   3   2   1

LIBRARY OF CONGRESS CATALOGING-IN-PUBLICATION DATA
CHRISTENSEN, MARK.
ALOHA: A NOVEL / MARK CHRISTENSEN.
P.   CM.
1. HAWAII—FICTION. I. TITLE.
PS3553.H718A79   1994
813'.54—DC20
94-13789
CIP

ISBN: 0-671-87023-8

FOR LAURIE, SCOTT, KATIE, AND MATT

DECEMBER

I watch the Wall. CNN. Day-old hits of Frank, a special witness, with members of the House. They buy the obvious: buildings grown not built, all cars driverless, civil rights for machinery, children vaccinated against stupidity, and new immune systems $1.99 off the rack at Wal-Mart, but because my brother is so successful at what he does, which is everything, there is jealousy, even skepticism, when Frank says that we have left a century deranged by its hoped-for dooms and undoings and that in our new millennium cretins will make fortunes patenting duplicity, saints will disappear, and God will quit.

The house doesn't get it. And the minority whip, the white-faced publisher/embezzler/congressman with the lopsided hairdo who CNN says will either be dead or president by 2008, drags the Proteus explosion in, waving a list of "killed," supersizing casualties, talking about "a city morgue worth of arms and legs, heads and torsos ripped up and left floating in the ocean," and demanding that Frank explain "how some shotgun-waving cowboy could build a rocket the size of the Empire State Building and have it launch and blow up before anybody at the dee-oh-dee or over at State had ever even heard about it."

My brother, inventor of, among other things, "The New Age Sawed Off," ignores this and just listens while the whip says Frank signals the end of the nation-state, that corporate feudalism will eat us alive. Not getting a rise, he says that God may have stopped making geography but since Frank obviously hasn't, if the New Island works, perhaps he will favor the world with another Southern California, blow it right up out of the Pacific as well, and that—who cares—even if it is a disaster it can't be any worse than the one we've got now.

Then one of the Drunk Pundits, the fat wizard with the pumpkin head, boots up: "I knew Frank Crawford when he was in the air force and nothing but a Stage Door Johnny at Soviet Rocket Command in Pervomaysk. This numbskull's got an IQ of about 180, all the money in the world, way too many ideas, and way, way too much time on his hands. He was dangerous then and he's lethal now."

But Frank, who says the Constitution guarantees us a free press but not a responsible one, could care less. He replies we know too much but have learned too little, and if the deep thinkers hadn't been asleep at the switch we'd be on Mars by now. My brother is high inside and promises the New Island will be a big success.

A square mile of magma, money, and fax machines, it will ooze from the ocean thirteen miles off the Big Island of Hawaii and, as home of 700-plus plaque banks and booking centers— and as an only-a-few-holds-barred resort—be an ultimate tax and regulatory haven. And, given its location right outside territorial waters, it won't belong to the United States but to us.

Because Frank is such a big businessman (maybe the biggest), and because our fresh century has given him so many opportunities, starting our own country seems to be a way to go, and because I've had a hard time getting my own life started (because of braining Owen Cathcart, etc.), the New Island is very important to me.

Frank has to talk to Congress or the House because what he's doing is so consequential. It represents far more than just the New Island. As it was wrong to have bulldozed and chopped down our world in the old century, so it is worse to submit ourselves to the random vacuities of nature in the new. It's time to replace the natural order. Which has led one congressman to call him a "sorcerer" (making me the sorcerer's apprentice, I guess), and though the process of making the New Island will be no more mysterious than the principle of sticking a straw in an orange to get the juice, people are desperate for something to be afraid of. (Even Roberta is skeptical, wanting to know how well I "know" my brother. We're not going out to get tattoos every other Saturday night, but I'm around Frank at least a week a year. Enough to "know" him.) It has been a tough row to hoe.

Although like most great ideas, this one is simple. The math is second grade. A thousand new acres and, assume in 2010 dollars, each acre worth $4.5 million. A conservative estimate. Nothing compared to downtown Tokyo, never mind Waikiki. That's 4.5 billion in Frank's back pocket right there. Triple that if the island really catches fire. Cost of creation is nothing compared to profit potential. Sure, mining for magma is more expensive than drilling for oil; to concoct a 1,000-acre island with a mean elevation of 200 feet above sea level we'll need access to three cubic miles of lava.

But an underwater varicose vein of molten rock lies close by. And all Frank has to do to make it hemorrhage paradise is speed up natural geologic evolution by 300,000 years.

Eight hundred million dollars down—plus the cost of the build-out: plants, beaches, a golf course designed on his death bed by Robert Trent Jones, office spires ten times the mass of the pyramids at Giza—once it squirts from the sea. But it'll be worth $50 billion easy.

Nauli. The Little Island. Christmas morning forty-six miles south/southwest of Honolulu under a sun close enough to touch. Frank has given me an Apple handheld, no bigger than a book, but with room for a life of days. On the thick green grass under the eaves, I listen to Bye Bye Master's "All the Answers," the beach before me white as snow. A shark slides through the quaking waves beyond the surf. It is beautiful here. Frank has rained a benign caustic across the sand so that, so to speak, the outdoors will not show its dirt.

Saying grace at breakfast we count our blessings: that money is never a problem, that no one in our family ever dies until they are killed.

It will be sad to leave. Frank, who is thirty-nine, grew up on Nauli and I was born here. Before my dad could copter my mother to Honolulu, I'd erupted thirty feet from where I sit. My mother's blood wrecked $400 worth of Brown Thomas Irish linen sheets. Getting up, I scroll the newspapers. A blind item in the *Star*: Frank is buying a new house in Kahala for six million three.

More of my brother on the Wall, his hawk's face twice life size. Frank, who loves truth and hates cant, says the reason for America was to ravage a continent, the job is done, done well, and the next America will be the England of the future, a welfare state for starlets and coatholders, lounge act to the world, the only thing we will make is entertainment and deals, and so what if the ChiComs have hot-rodded the Rust Belt, or if Bedouins make billions hawking chain saws in Pittsburgh, the old line is true: the fact America still lets Americans anywhere near an assembly line only speaks to the depth of our delusions. Besides, just for the record, plenty of our best stuff, be it Howard Stern or the F-15E, is already here. Indeed. Frank has reaped a fortune ransacking the twentieth century, ragpicking media and readapting technologies. He was among the first to win big off the collapse of the Soviet Union, realizing it's not who loses the war but who wins the peace. And forget the T and A they throw on the Wall: that he's put Costa Rica on lay-away or hatched a Spielbergish scheme to recreate Picasso, Shakespeare, or Ed Big Daddy Roth. The story of Frank's success is simple: bartering Western culture for Eastern science, he's attracted everybody from mohole men—elite geologists—to half the big brains from the Energia Heavy-lift Rocket Program. That's where the real action is.

I watch the news: ethnic cleansing in Beverly Hills; Korea using its EconCol Oakland as collateral to buy Chrysler back from the Italians (concurrently, the issue of foreign nationals buying lock, stock, and barrel the public properties of an American city has gone to the Ninth Circuit Court of Appeals); and all the republics of the former Soviet Union that had nuclear weapons on their soil have tallied up their warheads and come up 2,113 short.

Stepping outside, I walk the slope of the green lawn to the white beach. Weird clouds are on the horizon, evolving in clear patterns, as if the sky had developed a mind of its own. The shark is still out there. Christ. I need my camera. Our family has been here since 1902 and Frank wants me to take pictures of everything before we go. Creative, he has rebuilt the old palace, not quite the way it was, but the way it should have been.

Frank, who says civilization is only the art of saying no, has preserved the royal residence—home of the gods, demi-gods, demi-ghosts—and preserved the ruined village too. Blackened sticks stab and lean up from the dirt. Fire left the village timbers busted down to nearly readable shapes, V's, N's, I's, T's. The fire occurred after my ancestors arrived with their new ideas and just a touch of dengue fever. It made the king crazy and he lost his head to a .51 caliber buffalo gun in a battle over before it began.

Not long after, my great-great-grandfather signed the ninety-nine-year lease that is about to lapse. Tomorrow Nauli will be returned to the state. But our house will go with us. Frank is having deconstruction men take it apart and copter it to Honolulu.

This morning I packed family photos. Pictures of me on the beach, small at twelve—perched atop my surfboard, brave as a butterfly, sitting in the water outside the break at Sunset Beach—then skinny at twenty on the beach with a stewardess who knew more about my father's money than she knew about me, and finally in a newer picture where I've finally filled out. Looking okay, I guess, though looking like I'd kill you for a dollar as well, gazing into the camera with that big-eyed, whacked-out Crawford family stare.

Frank's attorney Tom Weire arrived at noon. Through the open and about to be unhinged doors to the lanai, I heard the burble of his boat's old Grey Marine diesel and watched the *Phoebe Zeitgeist*'s long mahogany hull lope off the white caps into our lagoon.

Now Weire is in the gym with Frank. Their voices float over the clank of free weights. Something is wrong with Crawford & Hona. The basis of the partnership is not complicated:

Frank thinks up what needs to be done and the Honas go do it. But I think there are misunderstandings. Frank is talking about his database. He is honest but Syntyrsystym/Monolithic Memory is very invasive—it collects information so well that, in its hands, a dog could win the Pulitzer Prize. It is worth protecting and I hear Frank say if the shit comes down he wants to copter it offshore.

We need another island and if, say, the United States throws a hissy fit about being junior partner, he will make our new one by himself. Regardless, Frank is taking the pink slip on whatever we blow out of the ocean. Ninety-nine years is no joke, but my brother is in the empire business for the very long haul.

JANUARY

After the sky cooked, the wild cats went blind, and I wake to their cries below. Six live in the crawl space beneath the apartment and at first light they slink and stagger out through the bushes and weeds. I've put scraps out, milk too, but doubt it's doing any good. Roberta found two dead ones back by the washers and dryers last week, flies whizzing around cat eyes whiter than cream.

I brush my teeth, pull on an old BAD RELIGION/NO CONTROL T-shirt, and walk downstairs and to the ocean. The beach already has had its visitors—hardly anyone suns at midday anymore. A hot wind blows offshore and the sand is warm as skin. I say the words

MISS UNIVERSE
pink & blue
hydrangea buds
imbued
enfolded by the ocean
walk & shimmer

weirded out
her labia
caress themselves

3 of the judges
notice. 2 give
extra points

but Frank has changed the code again and I have to kick open the door at Less Nervous. Jan and Dean's tavern. Good news, my new camera sits unstolen behind the bar. Frank hates cookie cutter trash and gave me a custom $3,500 Nikon for Christmas. He wants me at Big Store reading his new Apple Mind, but Demi-God Software says it's in paralytic psychosis, so I get stuck wiping drunks off the floor instead. Jan and Dean let the gone sleep where they went. The doyens of Piss Pop; Drastic Plastics, bug addicts, and Icicles. Plus a bunch of Frank's Maui ranch hands he flew to Waikiki for the New Year. Last night we had three knockdown dragouts during the Sullenaires' set, and the police were in and out like birds popping from a cuckoo clock. Finally: a squack attack from the Clit Club. These women are vicious, but don't know how to fight. They throw pool balls.

Less Nervous is a cave and it takes me a moment to see Mrs. Whim sitting in a corner. A black blonde who—if it's night and she's made up and moving—can stop a clock. But Mrs. Whim, still and in the light of day, looks like Ozzie Neusome in a fright wig. Three words from her and I see that the Real Mad she popped at the witching hour is still doing its work, that she remains light-years inside herself, her face still quaking from nightmare orgasms and whatever else $200 a bug has brought her.

I ask her if she remembers who I am and her face splits with a smile. "A boy."

"No," I correct, "a man."

Still insane, she grins, "Nah, jus a lil boy."

She shouldn't have been left here all night. I went home early and didn't see her on my way out and, because she remains in a state where she'd doubtless just as soon jump off a building as cross the street, I know I'd better walk her down to Doc in a Box.

Mrs. Whim says she's hungry. I offer to buy her breakfast and minutes later, after she has remembered what breakfast is, we go. She teeters down the street under a hard flash of sky, carefree in spike heels and a weightless red dress cut off at the crotch.

We pass two rock-faced Korean guards standing in front of the First Unification Bank. Both carry nine-millimeter Disney Bulldog "crowd management" machine pistols. The Bulldog "sprinkles" 700 rounds per minute and is little more than an eighteen-inch magazine that, at its top, has a grip, trigger, and firing chamber. In the wake of the Ccrash, Honolulu is where America's new fortunes are being made—last night a Mexican tampon lord came in dressed in platinum—but not everyone is jumping with joy.

An old Chinese janitor in khaki shorts squirts water from a garden hose over the sidewalk, the water rolls between the guards and is cool on my bare feet. Mrs. Whim, flapper from space, totters on, past the burned-out Hyundai consulate. The whole building coughed across the street last week in a blast of *plastique*, exploded by Korean nationalists mad because their country is now a company. Mrs. Whim, oblivious, walks down a sidewalk blackened by a tongue of ash that shoots to the middle of Kalakua. I'm worried about her, the mind is not a snow tire, and when I ask what she wants for breakfast she says fish ice cream. At the International Marketplace, I sit her down at a picnic table by the Breakfast Nook, order fried eggs, Portuguese sausage, a waffle. I drink Aztec decaf wondering what she'll eat when a wild-haired boy I know from the water comes up and wants to borrow $40. When I return from the ATM, Mrs. Whim is carefully vomiting egg and waffle into a napkin, then she coughs up more, and suddenly my coffee is foraging around at the back of my throat and, yeah, it's time to get her to the hospital. Where the nurses don't know what to do. They understand Ice: Everest, K-2, all that, but Real Mad is too hip for the room. I say it's a virus not a drug and the sickness it brings is full-blown schizophrenic dementia. Have sex with Hitler or go to Mardi Gras on Alpha Centauri and pray the cockroach in the corner who is the Virgin Mary doesn't say your toddler is Lucifer and must have his tender little throat cut.

They put her to sleep. I walk back past the guards at First Unification. The latest figments. Frightening. But it is no longer just the New Moonies. Since the Ccrash, every other bank and big retail operation in Hawaii has got Bulldogs out front.

Our machine's broken, so I stop at the gothic wood edifice (palace to half the queens in Honolulu) that is Do What You Look Like for ice. Dewey is in Mexico and Ronald Sousee, Dewey's manager—a huge brown local who is fat enough to have breasts—doesn't want to give me any, so $20 for a bucket full of frozen tap water.

I cross the street, plastic pail in hand, and I see Hanna and Sis, the ancient Swedish au pair girls who live in the apartment above me. They are beautiful tall old women, sisters—though time has made them twins. They are standing by the kicked-in front door of Less Nervous, waiting for their breakfast. They have an illusion—that I own this place. I nuke scoops of Nutrient Slush left over from the night before and I am taking the plates out of the microwave when Vince, our bartender, walks in. I ask him about the till. He pats a curl of greasy black hair off his forehead, says *comme ci comme ça*—after he paid the bands, $190.

Perfect. Outside, a pink primordial sky, a sky that CNN says has not been this way for a billion years. $190. At this rate we'll be gone in a month.

2 JANUARY

Frank is moral and hates this. Think-tank trash who know nothing about catastrophic failure or 783,000 gallons of liquid hydrogen slammed through a frozen witness valve at 65,000 psi, but everything about playing to the cheap seats on C-SPAN, are, out of nowhere, claiming triple the actual number of deaths. Now a Senate select committee is going after our subcontractors—Rockwell International, General Dynamics, Data V—tracing the Proteus's rocket motor parts all the way back to their ingots. Frank says that if it goes to trial they'll drag us into depositions before March 1, so I should write down what I remember about the launch.

Well, the rocket blew up. Beyond that, what I recall is nearly missing the explosion. The weather had been crazy, wind ripping the water to breakers high as a house. They planned to launch right through the eye of a class three hurricane and my heart had been trying to beat its way out of my chest for two days straight. An hour before they torched the rocket off I fell asleep and then all I remember is Frank's hand too hard on my arm, gripping me awake. I got out of my bunk, wiped my face and chest with a towel. Even then the air was a wreck. Way too hot and even at sea I'd wake up covered with sweat that felt like bacon grease.

I walked a companion way past the launch crew at terminals. They looked like men crowded into a video arcade. I climbed metal steps to fast salt air, saw my grandmother at the rail in jogging shorts, and heard the flashing red lights and low concussive thunder of helicopters racing away from the gantry and over us on the *Gogol*.

Then a boy's fever dream of science fiction shot to life. Just before the rain began crashing out of the sky and in the fans of the gantry lights, before I could hear it, I saw the rocket rise from the rolling water. The Proteus was so big it was almost all I could see, rising in a dawn of its own creation. Tall pink clouds switched on at 4 A.M. and a blast of rocket light appeared at the center of the horizon. Hard billows of steam jumped around the floating gantry and yellow jets of light shot from the ring of solid boosters. The sound so loud that it rippled the air and, wham, there was an awful glare far brighter than even our current sun.

Now I fly alone in Frank's new Cayuse Proto. The helicopter passes over the launch sight and below I can still see the black circles of booster girdle—huge submerged rings that held the Proteus's first stage in place thirty fathoms down.

The Cayuse passes over the *Gogol*—former pride of the Soviet Navy, an 800-ton antisubmarine corvette. Beamy, its white hull measled with rust and flying the flags of three republics, it has an old 1980s-era trainable/elevable multitube rocket launcher on its stern from which Frank's Russian mohole men have fired guided cameras across her feathery wake. The ship cruises at ten knots; its fan of cameras trail behind, scanning the seafloor for manganese nodules.

The Cayuse swings toward Frank's Magma Farm, accelerating so hard my palms are corrugated where I grip myself by my corduroy-covered knees. I don't like this much. There is no pilot, Frank is flying the Cayuse from the ground, only a passenger—me.

Surf appears frozen off the black beaches of the Big Island. We have had another recent accident, at Frank's Geothermal Heat Farm. With an asterisk or two, Frank is as normal as

Main Street and the explosion alarmed and embarrassed him.
I load my camera. Frank wants pictures from the air. Over
the steam fields, heat wells rise like oil derricks from the jungle. One just blew at Christmas, throwing up hydrogen sul-
fide in puffs like an Indian smoke signal. The idea was to drill
into hot rock, pump water down the hole, turn it to steam
for the turbines, get the power and get the money. But something went wrong.

3 JANUARY

Cuffed and stuffed. It was get out of the car, get on the ground,
spread your hands and legs. After which a cop with a knee in
the small of my back grabbed me one wrist at a time and
slipped the cuffs on my fragile extensions while the other one
told me I had the right to remain silent and anything I said
could be shoved up my ass. Then one of them pulled me up
off the ground by the elbow as if it were the handle on a suitcase and put my face to one of the few brick walls I've seen
in Honolulu while—for some reason—they radioed for backup,
which took forever to get there. A tow truck was lifting the
front of Jan and Dean's '56 Ford off the ground when the second black-and-white pulled up, its red, white, and blue riot
lights exploding silently off and on all over the top.

In the back of the black-and-white, going downtown, I say,
"Listen, all I'm asking is: What's the problem?" The cop who's
not driving says, "Read the warrant. Unauthorized possession
and transport of a regulated and dangerous substance."

"Warrant? Where? For what?"

Nobody gives me anything, but the cop, who has an angry-
looking black mole on the back of her neck that may put her
underground, says, "Charges filed by the Federal Interstate
Commerce Commission, the Nuclear Regulatory Commission, the State of Hawaii, the FBI, and the Federal Airline Security Commission."

I say, "I'm not in possession of anything. What do I possess?"

"A muffler on that old Ford," the other beefed-out lady cop
says, "that's not worth shit."

✳

In some decade of middle age, Lieutenant Vorhaggen is mixed-race, probably mostly Japanese. But big almost to fat and sliver-eyed and, with his cowboy shirt, he looks country and western. In his white-walled office, he reads out loud, "Reckless endangerment, assault with intent to kill, one count, no *two*, of attempting to elude, two each of trafficking in unregistered weapons and stolen goods, wait—oh, *excuse me*—four counts and one each of felonious assault." He holds up the papers. "This is a real page-turner."

I explain that it's water over the bridge, all pleaded out, and I had to spend six weekends sweeping leaves at Kapiolani Park, see a psychotherapist, take a few pills, and that was it.

He says, "Lucky man," and I say it was horseshit anyway. Vorhaggen gets up, walks to a water cooler diagonal to his desk, pulls down a paper cup, draws water, and says, "Four auto wrecks in three years, six, seven . . . eight citations. Two license suspensions. Possession with intent to sell."

I don't say anything and he says, "Your father was the builder. The American International, the Pacific Bay Hotel, the Imperial Inn, the Diamond Sands Mall. The proposed megamall on Kaui."

I say, "Yeah," and he says, "What do you do at Less Nervous?"

"Bounce."

"That's all?"

"I cannot serve the public."

He looks at me.

"It's my probation. The liquor commission won't let me bartend."

"Your brother Frank. The Air Force Academy. A big career coming right up. What happened?"

I say, "He got booted out of the air force for trying to start World War III."

"Oh yes," he says, "that." He picks up a piece of yellow paper and slides on a pair of black-rimmed glasses whose lenses look as if they have been cut in half and lost their tops. "A man on the fast track. U.S. Air Force Academy; B.S., civil engineering at age twenty; pilot, F-111 Squadron, Upper Heyford, England; SAC school; flight leader, FB-111 Squadron; graduate school, MIT; White House Fellow, National Security Council; senior USAF SIOP planner, Joint Strategic Targeting Center, Omaha. On track for bird colonel before retirement. Project engineer, Proteus Heavy-lift Rocket Program. CEO, Crawford & Hona Construction." Vorhaggen lifts the half glasses off his eyes. "Tell me about the big rocket ship."

I say, "Which big rocket ship?"

He says the rocket ship that killed so many people and I tell him he probably knows more about it than I do.

Vorhaggen's phone rings. He picks it up, says yeah, and then tells me: sit tight. So I do. For an hour. When he comes back he wants to know about Frank's big drills and I tell him nothing he probably hasn't already seen on the Wall. That Frank had bought a number of huge old Soviet mining tunnel drills and was going to use them to drill, basically, down instead of sideways.

"To do what?" Vorhaggen asks.

"The obvious," I reply. "If you want an endless supply of heat energy, all you have to do is drill about fifty miles down to get it."

"And these drills run themselves?"

"He gave them heat sheaths and ran them on turbines run off steam generated by water poured down the hole they've already drilled. When it's hot enough, and the turbines reach maximum horsepower, you turn them into electrical generators right there in the ground."

"And solve all the world's energy problems forever."

"Well, solar, oil, conventional hydro power would become irrelevant, yeah."

Vorhaggen taps his fingers on his desk. "Maybe a mi fine idea."

"Maybe a mi fine idea worth about $50 trillion," I say, then ask to see the warrant. He reaches into his front pocket, pulls out a wad of dollars, and chucks them on his desk. I ask what's that for and he replies cab fare, and that by the by, I'd better get the muffler fixed. It turns out there is no warrant; it was all a big mistake.

Frank says all things are knowable, simply many unknown, and maybe this is part of that: an afternoon downtown with notaries and lawyers, wand scrawling the monitor of an Apple World-Write, signing documents. I'm buying or selling 130,000 shares of General Motors class-H stock, but I can't tell because Frank's notary is in a hurry and I have to sign a lot fast. Page after page pops up on the screen. Finally, eight million shares of Magma Farm stock are gone in return for a cashier's check made out in the sum of one cent.

I ride the elevator down, rubbing my eyes. Last night at Less Nervous, Jan and Dean let Icicles and Drastic Plastics network their highs in the Nancy Spungeon Room. Walking coat hangers. Touchy too. One of the Drastic Plastics wanted to trade lunacy for a sex act and the recipient of this wish, offended, pulled a Hot Stick, sent a bolt of superheated hydrogen into the guy's head, and the stink of burning hair still hangs in the room. The cops were there and at midnight a liquor dick came in to complain about things I was already way too tired to even understand.

One cent? I get off the elevator, go outside. The notary's building is new, in the financial district, and sits across from one of the huge new Japanese superblocks. Post-mall architecture. Wild. They take regular city blocks two to six at a time, rip everything down, and build one huge integrated structure, with a mall, hotel, and about a million square feet of new office space.

Two balding Generation X types in old golf shirts stand beside a bucket with a cardboard sign above that reads *Alms for nameless scum,* and I drop in a five, then jaywalk Shit Street and buy a newspaper. A blind item in the *Star:* Frank's buying the frequency band and is out to own the airwaves. I call him from a facefone on the corner. He says not to worry, the one-cent business is just a tax trick. Frank is not at his desk, so with just a chair on the screen, it is as if I am speaking to an aura or a ghost.

4 JANUARY

Darkness at noon. Roberta's in the women's john going to high school with her Apple when I tell the old guy, "It's simple: we don't subscribe to Budweiser as if it were *The New York Times,*" and from the bathroom I hear her squawk that

she can find the contract if she has to. But Mr. Uda, an elderly bowlegged local, doesn't get it. "Why is it there is no
money? Jan and Dean says there's gonna be money."

"There's no money," I say, "but way too much of your beer,
and we're not paying for it until we use it."

"You gonna pay," Mr. Uda says on his way out. "I got a contract for sixty kegs a month and I got guys."

The world happens around Jan and Dean, rarely to him.
Usually it happens to me instead. Kegs are stacked up the
walls in the Nancy Spungeon Room, and two mokes outside
want to unload thirty more.

Teenage Roberta remains in the can with her Apple Scholar
finishing a trigonometry test. I can't see her—Less Nervous
has been here forever, probably created in a primordial time
before there were windows—but her voice is clear. She wants
to know what Frank wants me to do, and when I say fly to Celestial City, I hear her say, "Fly into a war. Stupid, Crawford."

A little Japanese guy wearing a black T-shirt that reads
across his goose neck chest WELCOME TO MY NEW IN-
FORMATION comes in and asks to see the big black dick
go into the little white chick. I think I've just heard the best
in new bad English before I realize he's talking about the
Crude Rude Lewd Really Stewed Almost-Nude Mini-Dude.

Top new cracker tech—the Crude Rude Lewd Really Stewed
Almost-Nude Mini-Dude is a foot-tall holographic bearded
black man who, when the Japanese guy slides five dollars into
the machine, runs out, starts swearing, gets an erection, and
masturbates on the bar top. "That's all?" Japanese man asks.
"Where's BJ from Miss Universe?"

I say we can't afford software for Miss Universe yet. I hear
the toilet flush. From the Nancy Spungeon Room, where I
still can't see her, Roberta asks, "What's Frank giving you?"

"Enough." The Japanese guy looks cheated, the Crude
Rude Lewd Really Stewed Almost-Nude Mini-Dude has run
back inside the machine.

"Double the 'enough,' Crawford," Roberta says, walking
toward the bar. "It still isn't worth it."

I reply that it is, by a lot, and Roberta—who dislikes Frank's
foretellings of the end of books, drive-up involuntary incar-
ceration, and civilization doomed by no more war—says, "You
know, the sexiest thing about you, Crawford, is that you're

fairly stupid. I wouldn't trust your brother any farther than I could fly."

I look down at her. Bright black hair cut short, long eyes and long red mouth, she told me last week a smashed doctor from the California Society of Reconstructive Surgeons came in here and suggested that, by means of the lost wax method, her breasts could be used as templates to provide True North for top Hollywood boob jobs.

"Roberta," I tell her, "you don't know Frank from Adam."

And she doesn't. This is a simple job he'd do himself, but my brother, who is tracking down the end of creation, says Demi-God Software says his new Mind may be blown. Frank wasn't asking the machine for cosmic consciousness, just for it to think.

He's having a knockdown dragout with the Baby Bells and until his Mind's back on line he has to hang by. He wants me to pick up film packed in an Oman Egg for the telescope at Amer-Eye where they are now beyond galaxies beyond quasars and have reached pure plasma. That's the miracle of the new film, he says. It will allow Amer-Eye to photo things that are less objects than auras. All I have to do is fly the Egg back to Mexico City so Dewey Hona can sneak it through customs to Honolulu.

But when I tell Roberta this she says, "Stay put and I'll give you a kiss." That might be fine, she's a child—ten years younger than I am probably, I'm not even sure she has her driver's license yet—but she has the biggest and most beautiful mouth. Yet the way she says this isn't too attractive. "Crawford," she goes on, "use the complete unexpurgated version of your micromind and think about this: you haven't the foggiest what Frank is actually doing."

What Roberta doesn't know is that the best part of this deal, the thing that will keep me safe, is that she's right: I have no idea what Frank is really up to. My hole card is, in fact, that I don't know jack shit.

I'd like to make Roberta clear on this, because she worries about me and also because she doesn't understand our family—Frank could be happening on another planet for all she cares—and it pisses me off. But when I walk into the Spungeon Room and look among the Love Machines, I see she is, as if by magic, gone. I go outside, finger a *Star.* The headline is that a nice piece of Romania has been bought by Germany for a song. Inside Less Nervous, I hear the sound of mokes unloading all that Bud.

5 JANUARY   *Celestial City*

Fifty thousand dollars COD. Boom, I'll get in and get out. Frank loves freedom but hates confusion so that, while he's pretty much just given me the names and destination and turned me loose, what I have to do is very simple: deliver sealed envelopes in exchange for an Egg.

Easy. Still, I'm not naive and know this could be asking for it. Two years ago I got arrested smuggling crazes into China and Frank says that, so far as I'm concerned, picking up and delivering the Egg is make or break, but the trip in is more or less a snap.

Leaving Less Nervous was easy—Vince claimed he just got fired from his job as child molester at the Wailuku Day Care Center and told JD he could work double shifts, my hours plus his, and the next thing I knew it was Honolulu–LA. LA–New York. New York–Frankfurt. Frankfurt–Kiev. Kiev–Novosibirsk. With a six-hour layover in Magnitogorsk. A freezing desert. Then ten hours rattling into the horizon on a train to Semipalatinsk where a twenty-dollar bill makes me Christ Come Back in a dining car with three windows smashed at their tops to sooty stalagmites. More hours in a ZIL army truck loaded with oranges infected with mold that looks like ash and vegetables that seem in the force of a supergravity—all flattened out in the back next to wet boxes of Turkish cigarettes and Japanese VCRs. I'm chauffeured by a fat man with red eyes who keeps a pistol between us on the seat. Goats make better roads.

Oh yes, and there is fighting here. We pass four burned-out halftracks on our way into town. I spend the night with a family of brothers who wear brand-new AntiWeight Nike Cross-Trainers. Young astronomers and technocrats, and their dad. Friends of Frank's, I guess. It's hard to tell, because all I speak is street-sign Russian. They live, it is explained to me, "out of the war zone" and seem consumed by some kind of Reagan-era yuppie materialism. It is a big house, nice, some fine old furniture and a lot of appliances—at least four TVs, three stereos, and a bunch of toasters. If I didn't know better, I'd say their decorator was a fence. One wall is dominated by a large crucifix and hanging from its nails is a tortured Christ as big as a midget. When I arrive the father is asleep on the sofa, his mouth an open square. One of the brothers, Avek, a little older than I am and already balding, takes me next door to where he and his wife have bought a "condominium" from their bank, McDonald's, that has a toilet in the living room.

He asks me about my "purpose." I explain that Frank is certain that with the film I take with me in the Egg, Amer-Eye will be able to photograph, so to speak, nothing. To record the perfect void beyond the edge of the universe.

Avek seems oddly uninformed. "Where is Amer-Eye?" he asks.

"The telescope? On Mt. Klu." I look at him. When he blinks, I add. "Klu. As in, 'I have not got a.' On Maui."

"And what is Maui?" On and on. His understanding of twenty-first-century America is a stew of fact and absurdity: he believes that the USA is now so wildly prosperous that even the honest can get rich, that the CIA is run by the Center for Disease Control, that women are being bred for beauty and nymphomania, that a new AIDS virus has infected 50 million.

We go with his four girls downtown. A police state has become a flea market. The big ex-government grocery by the town square is having a special on potatoes, turnips, Soviet light infantry uniforms, and hashish wrapped in gold foil–like big pieces of Godiva chocolate—offered by a clean-cut boy in a New York Knicks warm-up jacket who asked to buy my shoes. Spidery little gnomes, Avek's daughters forage the place like a pack of wild animals.

The area where Celestial City is, Avek says, was inhabited by only nomadic Kazakh Muslims before Stalin built a gulag in the foothills below the observatory. After the Germans invaded he exiled Volga-Deutsche here—descendants of Germans who had lived in Ukraine for 200 years but whom Stalin didn't trust. Years later Nikita Khrushchev came to America, saw all the corn, figured corn was the answer, and exiled thousands of Russians and Ukrainians here as part of his nitwitty

Virgin Lands program. Finally, Avek says, Brezhnev decided
to make this a science city crowned by the Geozin Observatory. Though the telescope has six-meter mirrors and is bigger than the Hale, the observatory was in fact a beard for the
military. The real science was weapons science.

Created by a community of displaced ethics who hate each
other's guts. Avek describes it as "a cancer that lives inside a
body already sicker with an even more serious disease."

I ask how he met Frank and he says Lawrence-Livermore;
he spent four years there before repatriating as part of a Clin-
ton administration make-work nuclear weapons program for
Soviet rocket and bomb scientists—a submarine-launched
nuclear rocket torpedo that, if exploded, would destroy life
in twenty-five cubic miles of ocean while avoiding "blue on
blue," the danger of the detonation killing the crew that
launched it.

Strangely, something in this explanation says to me: go
home now. I ask what that had to do with astronomy and he
looks as if I asked, why are you a homosexual? He says it's all
numbers, one is cousin to the other. We walk down the street
into a place he says used to be a high school. Its gymnasium
is now a store. It's piled high with only six or seven products.
Anti-Weight Nike Cross-Trainers, Teflon-coated aluminum
cookware, the reinvented nightmare toys of my childhood
well identified in English—The Uncanny X-Men with Wolver-
ine Motorcycle and Pedal-Powered Transformer Face and Re-
tractable Claws. G.I. Joe Eco Warriors Code Named: Cesspool,
Sludge Viper, and Toxo-Viper.

I ask where all this stuff came from and Avek says this is
only a fraction of it, the deal was complicated. But bottom
line they traded away a forest to the Japanese.

This does not quite answer my question and I feel suddenly a million miles from anywhere. Avek is not large, has a
child's neck, and I feel like—for no good reason—grabbing
the nape of it, slamming him up against a wall, and telling
him that if he fucks with me, he'll be dead.

Avek says, "Let's walk to the progress," and we go to
the mini-mall whose construction has been delayed by a
135-millimeter cannon shell. He is telling me that his brother
just got a McSecond on his condominium when I see a girl
in a wheelchair. That's it, a chair with wheels. A cane chair
axled under its seat and tipped with bicycle wheels. The girl

is teenage, sarcoma lesions leech off the sides of her face.

These people are living in the last three centuries all at once. We walk back toward the house, stop to see another of Avek's brothers. A computer programmer, he lives by himself in a shotgun shack without even indoor plumbing. His mattress is stuffed with straw. But he's got an Apple with enough memory to hold the Library of Congress. He runs it off storage batteries connected to a generator made out of an old Fiat 128 set up on blocks out back.

I'm going to the observatory for the pickup tomorrow. Then I'll be gone.

6 JANUARY

Night. A delay. I've moved to a hotel. Bad news outside unless you like war in the streets. The Fascist Party of God has voted down democracy in the Separatist Nationalist Legislature and somebody has mounted a set of twin fifties on the corner and tracers are whipping into the City Park. An incredible racket. What they are shooting at besides bushes and trees, I have no idea.

Avek doesn't show, the phones don't work. This is the end of the world. All I can find in English is *The Guinness Book of World Records*. An old paperback copy, I can lift its brittle pages out one by one.

I sit in my room with the twenty-five-pound newborn baby, the world's loudest screamers, women who wear beards made of bees, and failed Sufis with fingernails as long as garden hoses. The electricity goes out at dinnertime. I write in the nervous light of a kerosene lamp fueled by what smells like old motor oil. Its flame sends a veil of black smoke to the ceiling where it pools and eddies across the plaster.

7 JANUARY

No fighting today. The Snipers Union has gone on strike and there has been a sympathy walkout by the New Marxist Mongol Irregulars, the unit responsible for machine gunning the boulevards.

I've been moved to a brown room that offers a view of the

"celestial" side of Celestial City. Silver rockety buildings stand before me, streamlined and dented and dirty. It is like seeing a city from the future, but from an old future. Reconstituted lard appears in English on the room service menu. The sidewalk is littered with balls and cigars of dog shit, and trash covers the streets. Anarchists have stormed the garbage dump. A black flag flies above mountains of refuse and a guy with a bazooka guards big old compactors.

Lunch at the Murder Without Bloodshed Instant Coffee House. There is something liarly about Avek. Yesterday I asked about flying out of here tomorrow and he could not answer a question about the airport because, "Bad English. I cannot understand." But here today, before we order, he pats his round stomach, shakes a Camel straight from an almost full pack, and says, "Appetite suppressant of the gods."

Over latte that tastes like the back of a postage stamp I tell Avek get off the dime, I want the Egg. This won't be as simple as smuggling kidneys. Because the film is so sensitive, it will be packed in protective lead shields and weigh, inside the Egg, maybe 400 pounds. I tell Avek I want a critical path and perhaps he doesn't understand because his mouth warps and his eyes narrow suggestively. "So you want money and we keep the Egg. I get you some. ECU? Dollars? How much?"

I ask him what he's talking about and, as if he were some sort of instant amnesiac, he looks confused and doesn't seem to know.

We walk Main Street. Muslims, a lot of people whose teeth are gold or gone, old horses, bare rock mountains in the distance that look far closer than they are, and some heartbreaking whores, but who has the nerve? AIDS and fundamentalism have finally collided. Bundled-up old ladies, vapor drifting from their mouths as thick as cigarette smoke, stand in lines that don't move. Like a bunch of palimpsests waiting for the latest impression.

Avek speaks to me but the only words I can really recognize are "don't worry" and "bureaucracy" and "tomorrow." I see Japanese men in fat red-and-green parkas flash by in two Range Rovers followed by tough-looking copper-faced soldiers carrying automatic weapons in the back of an open GAZ six-by-six. Avek, suddenly far more understandable in a way that really pisses me off, says the local militia is in bed with the local tourist bureau to provide armed guards for foreign fishing parties trekking out of here into Tannu Tuvu, the Mongolian-populated Russian Autonomous Region beyond the Altai Range. He says it costs the fishermen only $500 a week for four army escorts. I ask if this is a bargain or a swindle and Avek says it depends on where you want to fish.

It's tomorrow. Though I can see the observatory from here—it has the shape of half an egg on the side of a bare rock mountain that can't be twenty miles away—Avek says there is no need for me to go there. "We will come to you," he says. He doesn't show for hours so I'm stuck taking pictures of stone buildings that seem to have grown straight up out of the earth.

We go to get the Egg. Supposedly. Avek says it has been moved from the observatory. Helicopters circle above like wasps at a picnic. Below them sits an enormous paved lot filled with army tanks. All for sale, their turrets are whitewashed with numbers Avek says are prices represented in both dollars and the new ECU. To pay for the junk designed decades ago to blast its way through the Fulda Gap. Some are behemoths—old T-10s—the size of small houses. They look racy, even streamlined, but black creeks of oil wend between their tracks and the mud guards on one are so rusted that I pull them apart like a cookie. Avek says they leave the hatches open at night and cats live inside.

Then he insists on taking me into a showroom that's really a big barnlike warehouse where I see another kind of tank entirely. At first I think it's incomplete. It has no turret, it looks decapitated. Just a massive hull with a cannon mounted externally across its top that's as big as a telephone pole. Painted metallic flesh, fresh as a new penny, a T-84, the most advanced armored weapon in the history of war and part of a shipment of thirty-two headed to an Arab emirate. But if I want one or a hundred, Avek says there's a guy here who can cut me a deal. I ask him again: "Where's *our* guy?" And Avek says out back.

We walk to a building that looks made out of mud but inside has furniture popped fresh from *Architectural Digest*— neo-Bauhaus. Avek takes me into an austere Formica-paneled boardroom that has a floor-to-ceiling, high-definition TV screen on its far wall. There he introduces me to a man, about fifty, with a tall face and hair that has been clearly sewn in rows across the top of his forehead. We stand before a table on which there is a squarish sharp-angled rifle that looks like a space-age two-by-four.

He begins to talk with enthusiasm, and on the HiDi screen words appear in English

VELOCITY MORE THAN
TREMENDOUS
EXTREME KILL

but I understand only the aura of salesman. Then a young woman comes in. She wears knee socks and a blue blazer. She speaks London English and says what I am seeing is an example of the never introduced Soviet advanced combat rifle, a weapon "100 percent more effective than your M-16-A4."

She says it is designed to double first-round hit probability using flechette ammunition. Darts. Three zip out each time you pull the trigger. Darts that altogether weigh half the NATO 5.56-millimeter standard round, attain superhigh velocity and a "superflat" trajectory. She says the cluster effect of the flechettes, each with "very favorable soft-target lethality," can make a hit out of what otherwise would have been a miss and assures me that if the rifle isn't my meat, not to worry, they have much, much more.

On the HiDi screen the rock blushes, goes white, explodes— hit by what is described to me as an electric ray gun. A leftover from Soviet weapons research that, so it is explained, unfortunately would require an hour of New York City's electricity to obliterate a single tank.

Then it is down to business: Flaggens, Fencers, Flankers, Flashlights, Fishbeds, Floggers, Foxbats, Foxhounds, Fulcrums. Brewers, Blinders, Badgers, Backfires, Blackjacks. Everything from old fighter aircraft to strategic bombers cataloged by NATO code names on the HiDi screen whose computer English translation system has finally begun to work. I am told that all are available COD at one eighth the cost of comparable NATO systems.

I like being in the wrong place at the wrong time as much as anybody, but the novelty of this is beginning to wear off. I say, "I don't know what I'm here for," and a towering plain-faced man wearing a suit and shoes so nice that he seems owned by his clothes says if I don't, he does. I reply he's mixed me up with someone else. He says, "No you've got you mixed up with someone else." Introduced as "the cryptographer," he speaks English like the Beach Boys used to sing, his words high and nasal: "Take your pick. Battlefield lasers, better than your MIRACL system, that will blind seeker-heads of incoming laser-guided missiles, blind troops in the field, blind you name it. Psychiatric services—drugs, personality alteration, will fix everything from politics to booze." Plus a "bacterial acid" that can eat through the activated charcoal of the toughest noddy suit and today's special: labor camp dogs—wolves inbred with rottweilers and Dobermans during the Brezhnev re-Stalinization period and trained to be "coursers," to guard the perimeters of prisons and mental institutions without handlers. Dogs like Alger Hiss. Dogs so smart they can figure out who belongs in and who belongs out all on their very own.

It's the goddamn Fourth of July out there except instead of ladyfingers and sky rockets it's howitzers and 20-millimeter cannon shells. This is not going as I planned. Avek is in my room, it is dark, he's handed me some kind of old Bolshevik six-gun and says, "They're coming." Coming for who or what? Talking to Avek is like talking to someone in a bad dream. Asked about the Egg he speaks in a Möbius strip of words made out of "soon" and "stay cool" and "let me worry about it." Today when we went to lunch—so-so goat and chocolate milk shakes—I got forceful and noticed that across our table my hand had grabbed the furry collar of his coat. I told him I wanted the Egg and wanted out.

Avek said, "Tomorrow," and that besides weapons, the one thing they have is a surplus of dairy products. I asked what'll go in the shops once the mini-mall is complete—ice cream and nerve gas? And he said, "No, all the nerve gas got snapped up by the Iranians ten years ago."

Here in the dark Avek says that "only a boring number of people actually get killed." Later, also in the dark, Avek says he's happy—it's his wedding anniversary and his wife gave him a microwave, a Stechkin machine pistol, and a subscription to *Vanity Fair.* I sit on the floor, revolver in hand, feeling scared, angry, and, when after hours no one shows up, cheated. In the morning, when everything outside stops, I shoot three holes in the door and the bellboy gets upset—the door was 300 years old, I have splintered important iconography.

Outside, on the street, the twin fifties killed a kid, blew through shops before ripping off the top of a tree in the City Park. The boy does not look dead, he looks like a live angelic boy lying on the dirt, frozen in time, with his left eye bitten away. His cheeks are flushed, his other eye open, looking at me. Avek says the war is over for the week.

Waiting. I play basketball by the riverbed. The river got dammed away in a hydroelectric project that left lightening-shaped cracks in the ground big enough to fall into. Avek's little brother and his friends are sketches. I can't tell if it's adolescence or malnutrition. We play horse for money. I can dunk a basketball blindfolded and have good fun: I scream foul on every shot and it's a blast to lose $280 in an hour and a half.

9 JANUARY

Hertz. An outpost of the bright, clean, and corporate, built of rectangles of red Formica like a big house of cards, it sits next to the new Scientology center in the building that once housed the Communist Youth Center. I told Avek I'm not waiting any longer, that we're going up to the observatory to get the Egg right now. I rent a little Japanese beer can and drive toward the high stone mountains on a road made of tar and dust.

Avek, whom I suspect now is a loser, allows it was not smart to go down to the river, that during the 1950s it served as a "waste disposal system" for the *yadershchiki,* the "nuclear

weapons guys," and even recently a gamma ray detector placed
on the bank only twenty kilometers upstream read 1,500
micro-roentgens per hour. Ninety times normal level. Alarmed,
I ask if that is enough to kill me and he shrugs. "Nah. Just
leave you sterile."

When we arrive at the observatory I see horses out front,
their reins lashed to wandering strings of a barbed wire fence.
The pale egg of the observatory itself is still a mile away. A
mahogany-skinned guard stands next to a boxy old Toyota
LandCruiser. He wears Levi 501s, has a handlebar mustache,
and carries a revolver in a holster hanging to his knee.

The Wild, Wild East. I explain who I am. He reaches into
the LandCruiser, pulls out a cellular, and minutes later I see
a flag of dust coming from the observatory. Another mahogany-skinned cowhand drives up in a kind of buckboard
with an engine at the front. I'm pointed back into my car and
motioned to follow.

There appears across the observatory's broad curved exterior only one small door. We are ushered into a tiny anteroom
on whose walls are lithographs of old men from some antiq-
uity. Softly and far away I can hear the sound of Grofé's *Grand
Canyon Suite*.

The inside door to the anteroom opens and I am face to
face with a large nearly elderly woman. Her face is pale, looking as if talced for the grave. Her chest is looped with rosaries—
a little brass cross hanging from the bottom of each. She and
Avek talk and all I can understand is that their conversation
is not pleasant. Then she disappears and at the other end of
"On the Trail" returns with a piece of paper. The letterhead
is in Russian but reads in English. *We do not sell film. Thank
you, O. L. UTSKOI.*

10 JANUARY

Under a re-godded sky I heard a muezzin calling for the fifth
prayer of the day from a minaret as I gave whomever whatever—an astronomer, a fat-chested sparrow in an elegant old
three-piece suit gone fuzzy at its creases who looks like the
owner of a sick bank. I've got a truck coming and want this
to be a memory.

We sit by the door of a church. Stations along its walls are decorated with medieval psychomania. Each scene depicts a lively cruelty. Humility stabbing Pride. Truth tearing the tongue out of Falsehood's mouth. The gluttonous force-fed toads and rats. It is here that I get what I came for. A gold Egg that Frank has sent ahead. God's strongbox, oval and no bigger than a beer keg. Its skin titanium laid over a shell of tungsten carbide, laid over a shell of nickel chromium armor plate, laid over a laminate of cloth made of thread from spider silk, fiber ten times the strength of steel.

I want to just get up and go, but roped to my pew by this gumbah's curiosity, I explain the "spider fiber": genetic material is removed from a spider's glands and grafted onto a piece of DNA, which is placed into a bacterial host—which produces the artificial silk, organic Kevlar. It is woven into the back of the nickel chromium steel alloy to provide the central hard case.

I should have stopped there, but this guy wants the whole drill, so mesmerizing myself with the sound of the Crawford family spiel, I explain in a voice too loud for a church: invented by my grandfather, its two halves are milled to the 1/10,000 of an inch so the egg appears a single piece. Its lock is voice-coded, the metal acts as a diaphragm like a "gertrude" underwater telephone on a submarine and receiving the correct words by the correct voice—neither of which I have—it will pop open. "But," I tell him, "if someone tries to get inside without the code, the Egg can 'understand' and, if worse comes to worst, will get mad—not the way I would get mad, but more like a cockroach would get mad—and incinerate whatever it has inside, or even, depending how it is programmed, blow itself up."

Just then, I see that I have been had. I should have just taken the Egg and left. A truck drives up, but not mine. Four militia get out and, like the mokes with the Bud, load up the Egg, and before I can do anything it's gone in a dirty cloud of exhaust.

Avek says it was a change of plan due to the sudden gaslessness of local airliners. The airport is closed to civilian flight, he says, so I won't see the Egg again until the airport at Kiev.

Dinner with the cryptographer in a pillbox. It has windows not big enough to crawl through. Inside, cane-backed leather chairs and tablecloths that look like silk bedspreads.

He stands when I arrive. His grey head almost to the ceiling, he leans across the table and pours brown liquid into a glass. "Flinni," he informs. Whatever Flinni is, I wouldn't light a cigarette near it. When I drink, he sits so slowly I wonder if he has arthritis.

The restaurant is crowded. Vaguely western faces hover in candlelight. Flowers stand on tables between people who have a well-dressed but worn-out look: like unemployed royalty. We are served maroon slabs of meat he says has been genetically "grown" as beef muscle in a lab.

Avek said "break bread" with this guy if I had any questions. And I certainly do. I ask, "Why was I separated from the Egg?"

And he replies, "Controls. We have more than General Dynamics, more than Hughes. We know about you and who you are even if you don't. Even the Egg you are flying away with has controls. No one can get at the film inside until I wire to Frank the codes."

I say I wasn't supposed to get separated from the goddamned thing and he replies that he loves America and have I read *The Snow Leopard?* I say in college. He opens a wine bottle with a corkscrew he has on a big pocket knife. "What I would like is sell just one MiG-39. Just so you could try it out. Your ATF—the YF-22? Take two YF-22's, cut a wing off each, and weld the two fuselages together, you can have the MiG-39. So powerful it can hang in a vertical stall for thirty seconds at 80,000 feet."

One thing is certain: I'm not doing what I think I'm doing, I'm doing something else.

12 JANUARY

Shot by a tank. Running. I see parts of the street jump up. I put my hands to my face and feel a stinging sleet. I was with Avek down by the twin fiftied City Park asking why the Egg was trucked away from me. We were sitting next to girls huddled four or six to a table at the Murder Without Bloodshed

Instant Coffee House. Avek's English was on the fritz again. One girl has beautiful eyes, though her hair falls in such big ringlets it appears to have been curled with cans. Avek revealed in a sudden clear confidential hiss of complex nouns, verbs, and adjectives that some are so desperate they'd start a family in exchange for dinner.

Later I was thinking about this, walking in the twilight past women wearing head-to-foot chadors, as Avek, twirling a mustache as thin as his eyebrows, asks, "You have seen, by any chance, inside the Egg—really inside it?"

I start to shake my head and see at one side of the square a mob of old-fashioned skinheads in white T-shirts and Doc Martin boots. Somebody has a sign that seems to say—I can't read Cyrillic for shit—MOPPING UP IS LOCAL GOVERNMENT.

The Pamyat Dinner Club, Avek says. One of these guys, drunk I think, walking like he's on the deck of a ship, comes up. He's got hair all over his face that extends down his throat in a dusty fuzz and is carrying a carbine with a clip hanging off it as long as a horse cock. He wants something. And I'm wondering how much this'll cost me when I see lights far down the street, at the bottom of a grey silk sky.

They flash blue and white and come at us, trailing a black cloud. Exhaust. A T-72 tank owned by a militant liberal faction of the former secret police. A cop with a twin-forked beard rides its turret yelling at dinner club members who are fading back from the street. I hear something cracking off like cherry bombs. It's the drunk with his carbine. Next, pieces of the street are splashing up in front of me and now I'm picking bloody slivers of grit out of my hands with Polish tweezers. I'm getting out of here.

13 JANUARY   *Kiev*

A ZIL again. The train again. Then Novosibirsk–Kiev, Kiev–Frankfurt. With customs somewhere in the middle. Scary. Because I'm not Joe Blow from Federal Express nurse-maiding sable jackets to Saks Fifth Avenue. I'm getting paid a bundle to slip God knows how much super–high-tech film out of a confederation that doesn't want it going anywhere.

And now I don't even know where it is. At the airport in Kiev I have two vodkas straight up and, high on panic, go to the office of the Ministry of International Trade and Customs, ask for who I've been told to ask for, and tell a dark man wearing an old red-striped power tie that I have to see the Oman Egg, that it's packed in lead, can't be opened, that I'm carrying film that has to be protected from cosmic rays, damage by airport security X-ray machines, gamma rays, UV, visible light, infrared signals, door-opening radio frequencies, millimeter wave and microwave radar, and that it's supposed to be here and I have to check it out right now.

He says, "Okay, okay, okay, okay. Export license and end user certificate."

I hand them over. He looks them over, says more okays as he flips through them. Who knows what he knows or thinks he knows about this. He makes the gestures of conversation—waving his hands, shrugging, nodding—all without actually saying very much. Finally, he asks me what I'm doing and for some reason I say becoming a businessman instead of an artist. Still, he's friendly enough and friendlier still when I hand him a sealed envelope given to me to give to him from Frank. He takes me about a quarter mile out on the runway and shows me, and with great pride, the An-124 Condor in which the Egg will make its transatlantic flight. A plane so big I'd kill myself from the fall just jumping out of the cockpit. He tells me it will fly in a pressurized, heated cargo bay along with nuclear reactor components—the shell of a containment vessel bound for Hona Nuclear in Mexico City. When I ask to see the Egg itself he says that will be impossible, then explains why in a language that I know I was never meant to understand.

14 JANUARY   *Dawn—the Sky*

Kiev–Frankfurt, Frankfurt–Mexico City. Over the Atlantic late at night when I know we are on *nobody*'s radar, I have a premonition that the An-124 will not be there when I arrive. The scraps of whatever is calling itself Aeroflot are in the hands of a holding company in New Jersey and who knows who is really in charge. I go to sleep and wake up at dawn, air-

phone Dewey at his office. He tells me to forget the Egg, that
the Egg takes a back seat to a far bigger issue, that Crawford
& Hona, the longtime partnership between his father and
mine, is coming apart. "What are you flying, brudda?" he
asks.

"United." A Boeing Jet Town. It's like being aboard an airborne Dodger stadium. Eight hundred passengers, Christ.

"Well, count yourself lucky if you're not served a subpoena
before you hit the ground."

Out the window I see we're flying above clouds that are
pure white and look hard as stone.

Noon—the Sky

There's going to be trouble, trouble, trouble, trouble with this
and I'm going to end up fucked, fucked, fucked, fucked.

8 P.M.—Mexico City

It's nothing but a dangerous way to kill an animal for a reason that isn't even meat, and as soon as he says before anything else that he wants to take me to a bullfight, I know I'm
really in deep serious.

Ex–golden boy Dewey, a former one-man supermarket of
vice and good times, who once told me the Hell's Angels de-
nied him membership on the grounds he was a troublemaker,
is supposed to meet me at the airport. I've known Dewey all
my life. My father met his father Lewis on Maui when the island was paradise instead of a shopping mall. The Honas, our
only neighbors, lived in a house below where my father built
ours on the side of Mt. Klu.

Though Lewis was a direct descendant of a Hawaiian king,
a look out our living room window down the hill revealed the
Joads' move West. The Honas' house had plank walls with
tufts of insulation smoking out around the door jams and a
corrugated steel roof scabbed with rust. Dewey's mother Maye
was a pillow-thighed blonde who raised sunflowers and smoked
Benson & Hedges out by their swimming pool. When I was
four or five I asked Maye about their big basement window.

Coors beer in bearish hand, she told me it was a sliding glass door to hell.

Maye Hona and my mother were friends, though what they had in common I'll never guess. The raunchiest thing about my mother was that she was a Catholic. She had come from a creative background—her grandfather invented condominiums—and was from such a good family that I'm lucky my blood clots. Maye called her own family a litter and, so the story went, had "customers."

The relationship between my father and Lewis Hona was easier to understand. Though my dad was already heir to a huge construction company, it didn't hurt that Lewis, robin's egg Hawaiian blue blood, had talked his cousins, uncles, aunts, nephews, nieces, in-laws, grannies, and granddads out of 22,000 acres of prime Maui real estate by offering them shares in developments he thought might actually be a good idea to build someday.

Lew Hona and my father used the real estate to leverage an empire. After Brazilian rain forests were chopped down, they sold the government "City Kits," which *The New York Times* called "infrastructure à-go-go." Crawford & Hona packaged entire new municipalities—sewer, electrical, roads, and all municipal services—even school systems and police departments. Their out-of-nowhere towns were designed to grow up to 50,000 in population. They would corral "anchor" industries and big retailers—GM Assembly, Sears Roebuck, whatever. Supposedly they made so much money so fast even now nobody's had the time to count half of it.

My father was the visionary and Lewis Hona the boss. My dad dreamed everything up and Lewis rammed it through. Lewis was huge, had the muscles of a gorilla, yet did not live a healthy life. Think of the Terminator gone totally to seed. For Lewis, literature was the phone book and a good time was to break somebody's neck.

South American oligarchs like that in a man. And Crawford & Hona was a big and unblemished success until the Proteus, by ten times the largest rocket ever built, put a hole in the ocean. Now that my dad and Lewis are gone, management of Crawford & Hona has fallen to Frank, Maye Hona, and her oldest son, Dewey. Like my father and Lewis Hona, Frank and Dewey are different. Frank is an idealist, a straight arrow, who, until he flunked out of Armageddon School, was a pilot in the air force. Now he is what my father was, the one who invents their businesses.

Big, wool-haired, ram-faced Dewey is supposed to be what his dad was: under-boss. And that's how he started. Back when Crawford & Hona was knocking the city down to make room for the superblocks, I worked for Dewey. I'm good at wrecking things—and I'd set charges on job sites. Dewey lacked formal training but was an idiot savant at blowing things up, and we torched off buildings, houses, hotels, half of Honolulu. But after his Maui Wowie ranch burned down and took his neighbor's barn with it, Dewey spent six months pulling weeds out of the rutabaga patch at the state prison farm, and I think he lost heart.

At the airport Dewey is late. He arrives in a dark suit, his curly pale hair trim. He is tan, and looks old enough to be presidential. The first thing he asks is, do I want to go downtown and see the great Juan Desoto awarded an ear.

"I hate bullfights," I say. "Where is the Egg?"

"Brudda," Dewey replies, "I've got the manifest, but the Egg's not in the plane."

I hear this and just walk. Words work at the back of my throat but won't come out. What a place. The Mexico City airport is a crowded city made out of jets, escalators, confusion, and dirt. I say, "What happened?" and Dewey says, "Nothing, that's the problem." He's got a limo waiting. I see my long dark reflection expand and pull apart in the black mirror of its wide flank. It's a new quarter-million-dollar Mercedes that Dewey's mother just bought, and when I get in he says, "Not too shabby for an old kidney peddler, huh?"

I'm on Mars. We drive off. Dewey's Soviet Doberman, Alger Hiss, sits beside him on the back seat like a good high school date. The limo glides across a sea of concrete. The tail of the An-124 looms toward us, tall as the mainsail of an America's Cup yacht. Its huge rear delivery doors are open. A containment vessel big as a building rests at a tilt on the plane's cargo ramp. I ask why everything is so filthy.

"Strike," Dewey says.

I say, "What?" and Dewey says the local air freight and maintenance people just went out on strike so, sorry, the Oman Egg is just one of a hundred things he has to worry about.

We walk up the ramp into a cargo bay the size of a warehouse and I talk to the Russian yuppie pilot and Ukrainian proto-punk crew chief. Nobody knows what happened to the Egg.

I grab Dewey's cellular, call Syntyrsystym, am patched through to Monolithic Memory. Frank's voice says he'll call back. As the crud of the city rises around us, I ask Dewey what he's been up to and he replies that lately helping his mom lose her shirt in the nuclear reactor business is about all he's had time for.

Though Frank says that Dewey's problem is he's more clever than smart, I can feel the chickens coming home to roost. A twenty-year mind-bogglingly successful partnership down the drain. God.

15 JANUARY

Loud cars whiz out of a low-lying poison mist that makes seeing three blocks down the street a miracle. Through my window only the tallest buildings stab above the murk. I'm at the elegant old Geneva Hotel in the Zona Rosa. Mexico City is a bus garage. Here nobody cares about the ozone layer disappearing because the smog is so bad that UV rays can no longer get through anyway. I take a cab out to Hona Nuclear, formerly Crawford & Hona Nuclear, formerly Quinn Nuclear. Corporate headquarters was in Los Angeles before the company got booted out of the United States because it couldn't account for a ton and a half of uranium hexafluoride yellow cake that had been shipped by rail from the old Quinn Nuclear facilities in Bakersfield to the new Crawford & Hona operation in Oak Ridge. This was three months after government sensors discovered Hona Nuclear had set up an electromagnetic isotope separation facility near the Gulf Coast in Tampico.

Now, removed from the clutches of the NRC, the rule at Hona Nuclear is that there aren't any.

The blocky, sprawling industrial park was built with Korean light-metal money, but all according to time-honored Mexican tradition: beautiful, dramatic new buildings knifing into the smog with people breaking the windows out of them before they're even finished. Hona Nuclear is, however, unscathed and unprepossessing. A two-story slab of concrete facing the street, a single steel door.

A breeze. Hot, used smelling air—as if it had just been pumped out the back of a vacuum cleaner—knocks my hair in my face. I stare into a camera that matches my retinas to digitals of my retinas. The steel door slides open and I am in a large windowless anteroom where two supermen sit behind a four-million-pixel flat color display. They carry sidearms that look like ray guns and tell me to sign in. I am handed a wand and write Tod Crawford within a rectangle on the screen. My face at twenty-two appears on the screen, then is aged to match the passage of three years.

They see I am me and another door slides open, this room leading to a lobby, also windowless, surrounded by a moat. Big Japanese goldfish glide in loose schools under its surface. There are, I have heard, pipes at the moat's bottom that will flood the room flush to its ceiling in ninety seconds.

Dewey comes down, I follow him past windowless rooms, most with a guy and a computer in them. Major machines, APA French-Cambodian superbootlegs, all the power and speed you can eat and on their screens nothing but numbers. We go to his office.

A picture of his dad, Lewis, is on the wall. Black hair and a confident slash for a smile. When he became a partner with my father, he was the only alcoholic Hawaiian prince with an engineering degree that I have heard about, and was project manager for the Big Eye binary gravity bomb, a so-called air-delivered chemical factory, able to lay VX/Soman gas over a third of a square mile.

Invented by the Germans during World War II, Soman was deemed too deadly for "safe" combat use.

But not too deadly for Lewis. When Big Eye went off, the Soman attacked the synapses in the lungs and heart. The body strangled itself. Big Eye was to be dropped along with 500-pound high-explosive bombs designed to rip away protective clothing and create "window" lacerations and flesh wounds. Big Eye was Lewis Hona's pride and joy, and when the government canceled the program, Lewis quit his company to throw in with my dad.

Now Lewis is dead and Hona Nuclear is in the hands of his wife, Maye, and his oldest son, Dewey, who has gone from running a bar in Waikiki to this: riding herd over a bunch of thirty-five-year-old American technocrats who wear $80 haircuts and jog ten miles a day and an even bigger bunch of émigré Russians and Ukrainians and Eastern Europeans who have faces the color of a sidewalk, but who could write *Ulysses* out in atoms on the tip of a flu virus. Everybody pitching in trying to figure out how to make billions in the new century with nuclear technology so unfairly maligned in the old.

Dewey says he's going liquid, turning all he owns into gold or electrons. He says he can hear my brother tick, and that the reason Frank had me fly into Mexico City and not direct transpacific from Vladivostok was because he can fix it with customs and Frank can't. Fix what is the question, but I don't ask it. Then Dewey says, "Talk story, how's Robert Vescoville?"

I say, "What?"

"The New Island."

I tell him, "Beats me," and he says, "Frank wants to get rid of me and I'm just first on the list. If I were you, brudda, I'd get yours while the getting is good."

At the hotel a message from Frank: Come home with the Oman Egg or don't come home at all.

16 JANUARY

Dewey says the Revo/Evos claim the atmosphere is melting; in two years all that'll be left is Keith Richards and smoke alarms, and the Kennedys are blasting a refuge under Palm Beach. "Good deal for us." He pulls behind a bus that is throwing a twirling worm of exhaust to the street. "On the invitation it says $10 million to get in the door, caviar and oxygen on the house."

The Revolutionary Evolutionaries believe that, spurred by excessive radiation, life on earth has been slammed into fast forward and is evolving at one thousand times the normal

rate in a way that is crazy and completely out of control.
Dewey says they are so naive and optimistic it's enough to
make him sick.

He is taking me to lunch up above the city in ... The village is stretched out along the road. Dewey's wearing a T-
shirt and jeans, and I can see the old long curving scar under
his right bicep, the result of a high school game of chicken
he and Frank played more than twenty years ago on Maui.
Nobody chickened out, Dewey's GTO slammed through a
guardrail and tumbled sixty-five feet into the Pacific Ocean.
Dewey, I guess, still has no luck in cars. He tells me he recently hit a drunk Mexican on the road right here and that
"the poor bastard popped off my hood like a chip shot."

We eat outside at a little chalk white cantina—tongue
tacos made on tortillas soft as cloth—by one of my dad's abandoned old cement mixers. A relic from the Mountain Highway project. Propped high up off the ground on tar-streaked
railroad ties, its engine is gone and below the windshield a
ganglion of wires and hoses hangs off a harness in a ponytail.
The driver's door is open and I read the faded *CRAWFORD
CONSTRUCTION. We Serve You Right.* As a boy I can remember my thin father working on this truck right here, back
when he was planning to blow a "second" Panama Canal
across Nicaragua using nuclear-tipped charges that would take
out nothing but granite and Sandinistas.

I ask how much longer he'll be in Mexico and Dewey replies,
"Not long. Weeks, days. Me, here, bummahs." He says he's
not the same guy his dad was. "If it's perverted or illegal it
usually makes sense. The nuclear power folk come close, brah,
on both counts. But this shit—"

Dewey waves across the road. Behind a high-wire fence are
lines of Crawford & Hona earthmovers, forty of them, lined
up side by side in a truck park. They used the blades three
years ago to punch a six-lane freeway right over the top of the
mountains but the government got into money trouble, de-
faulted on construction bonds, and all our equipment has
been sitting there ever since. "Whadda we gonna do with all
this crap?"

I say I don't know, sell it off.

Dewey burps, wipes his mouth.

"Your brother pisses me off. Last year I tell him, 'Frank,

I'm in deep,' and he says, 'Sign here.' I do. I make 'im manager of my part of the Crawford/Hona trust. Makes sense—
I figure better Frank than my mom." Dewey takes a paper
napkin, balls it in his big fist. "Cuz with her I am, give or
take, her favorite piece of shit. So I sign with Frank. Now I'm
wondering what's happening to all the money."

Mexico City is spread out below us. There is so much smoky
crap in the air that it appears the whole place is on fire. On
the drive back to town Dewey asks again what was in the Egg.
And when I say, "Film," Dewey grins his flashy grin and says,
"Yeah."

When I go back to the hotel the concierge looks at me like
I'm dirty and says I had visitors. Police. My room has been
carefully sacked. The papers for the Oman Egg are gone, along
with my airline ticket. What have I got in my wallet? Two
hundred sixty dollars American and a half-dozen credit cards.
I'm getting out of here.

17 JANUARY   *Mazatlán*

Twelve hours on a bus full of chickens and crucifixes.

I've checked into an old hotel the color of a grocery bag.
My birthday. Twenty-five. No sleep. In the middle of the night
I get up to use the bathroom. On the wall above the toilet
someone has scrawled READ THE BIBLE. ADULTERERS
WILL BRUN IN HELL. E. TAYLOR. R. REGEN. ZSA ZSA,
ETC. In the mirror my face looks cracked and unearthed.
Lines have formed at the corners of my eyes. In the hall a girl
with tangled blond rags of hair and a smeary mouth pops out
of a room and asks me for $100.

At dawn the empty streets smell like piss, fish, and gas. I
go to a restaurant, sit at a table, wait, but nobody shows up.
I'm so tired my head keeps losing its balance on my neck. Finally, an old man with whiskers hanging off his chin like pieces
of string walks in and sets a box down before me. Wires coming out of it, and he offers to sell me an electric shock.

• • •

18 JANUARY

This is what I'll do: find my grandfather. Oman. He made our fortune reinventing building construction. Scheduling. On a big project, A has to be done before B, and if it's not, C, D, and E come in way behind schedule. Excavation, foundation, subelectrical, concrete, the iron workers, all that. My grandfather invented three-dimensional job plotting. He threaded everything into such an exact order that he could low bid almost any job he went after. He also got into Japanese steel real early, as well as skip welds on girders, high-strength bolts instead of rivets, post tensioning, tilt-up slab construction, cinch and expansion anchors. Look out any window in Honolulu and you can see the result—the base line of the whole thing was Oman Crawford devising the critical path.

He rules our family, and perhaps because I'm the baby of it, I'm his favorite, and when there's a problem, like there certainly is now, his house is the place I like to be. Only, there are so many of them. Houses, that is.

Down by the docks rain spits out of the sky, heavy and vertical. Water vomits out of the gutters. A wind comes up and blows the rain in rippling sheets across the swaying line of boats and ocean. When it stops I hire a big launch and help the owner stow great sagging rolls of tarp. His engine blubs and crackles and my eyes water from the exhaust. The sun appears as a white flash in the sky. Clouds move and separate. We get going.

19 JANUARY   *Cabo San Lucas*

The boat ride. I bought a copy of the *International Herald Tribune*, interested in a story about scientists saying that the earth's life systems, because of the drastic devolution of the atmosphere, have begun wild mutations. Soon we will see cockroaches as big as mice, primitive weeds growing ten times normal size and at three times normal speed.

Decks and moorage slid by glistening and steaming as if laminated with smoldering glass. I sat back by the transom to finish the story, the paper rattling in the breeze. When we cleared the slips and the 15-kph buoys, the guy pushed the throttle forward and the boat stood up. The newspaper whipped out of my hands and exploded in the tumbling V of

our wave—whirling rectangles of news took moments to settle on the ocean and disappear.

The boat was really moving, making a bumping, clapping
plane over the chop. Half the day later I saw Baja, snaked with
mist. We passed a sailing yacht. Two small children leaned
over its rail, genderless, their features obscured by long hair
and identical mirror-lensed sunglasses.

Cabo expanded in front of us, the water below was clear
above a brown mottle of coral and weeds thirty feet down,
strewn across pale sandlike pieces of a jigsaw puzzle.

20 JANUARY

My grandfather's home in Baja is on the beach ten miles north
of Cabo. Security mistakes me for Frank, and when I tell
the truth—no, I'm just Frank's younger brother—they won't
let me in until I convince them with fifty dollars of my last
seventy-five.

The house is old, ancient even. Made by missionaries in
the 1700s, then updated by my brother Frank so that—white
and with great arching columns out front—it ressembles Zor-
ro's hacienda.

My grandfather is not there. The phones are gone, and the
house is empty except for paintings, chairs, beds, and guns,
and looks knocked around. The only thing that seems untouched is in the garage: Frank's drag boat, V. If it goes fast
and you can drive it, Frank does. And last summer he had
V—a chip of fiberglass cradling an 1,800-horsepower V-16 Al-
lison aircraft engine—running up to 265 miles per hour before the prop cavitated, the engine blew up, and the boat
sank. Frank loves risk but hates waste and so, instead of aban-
doning the boat, he had it raised himself. And now, returned
from smithereens, it takes up one side of the garage, better
than new.

21 JANUARY

No money, but a Jeep. My granddad's. I drive into town, walk
along a new broad avenue off the beach, and try to kite a
check at my granddad's bank. It's a building that, with its

great curved roof, seems to have been built in the shape of an idealized mailbox.

The cashier tells me they have no record of Oman Crawford at the bank at all. Which is impossible. So what I have to do is hawk one of his lesser oils—Francis Campbell Boileau Cadell's *Green Shutters, Cassis*—to a gallery that won't give me a dime until they can get an appraiser in on Tuesday, and when I get back from this second trip two Mexicans in shiny shirts and sports coats stand by the gate. Cops. I can smell it. Time to go. I don't have any of his phone numbers, but I figure I'll find my grandfather in California at Newly Formed Materials and crawl straight under his bed. Two cans of gas in back and what's in the tank of the Jeep. Mexico isn't big on my credit cards and I roll into TJ on vapors. Jagged brown hills carpeted by junkyards and shelters and shacks made out of cardboard boxes and packing crates.

There's a line at the border. A toddler tries to sell me a ceramic Jeffrey Dahmer. My alma mater. Way back when, sitting right here, my tires packed with kidneys, listening to New Order on a CD, waiting not to get caught, then through customs and on to Chula Vista, where the doctors would remove the kidneys from my tires, and away. But now it's dicey. The Jeep's tags are expired, I have to show ID, they find my pills, and though I say the Antiswaq are prescription tranqs, they do an info rip and I figure now it'll pop out: the never-ending story.

But no, by magic the computer voids. And by more magic what has to be the dumbest ATM ever pops for $300. I drive north, check into a Holiday Inn in Long Beach where, in the dim of dusk, I stand in the parking lot and see the beady white lights of Crawford refineries and the red flowers of their flaming burnoffs tumbling wildly up to a dirty lavender sky.

22 JANUARY   *Long Beach/Wilmington*

There are rolling neon green dunes of some sandy chemical, a beach of it, dumped out in the yard behind a high cyclone fence next to the twenty-five-story, corrugated aluminum–sided NFM Crawford & Son Building A here amid the great silver stacks and pipes of petroleum jungleland north of Long Beach. I say the words *Death before nostalgia* and the fence lock slides open. Building A is triangular in front, like a huge peaked roof with no house underneath it. The building is old. There is a chessboard of windows, stories tall, at the center and top of that triangular front. During the 1970s, secret government research that shot beyond black to lightless took place inside. Models for nuclear pulse rockets that would move through space at hundreds of thousands of miles per hour by detonating nuclear warheads in "blast theaters" at the aft of the ship.

It was here they tested the Proteus. Eighteen strap-on solid rocket boosters, each the size of a Minuteman ICBM. The ultimate Big Dumb Booster, the Proteus was simple as a bomb with a computer on top and created to do just one thing: put big weight in the sky. To be able to launch Disneyland or the Grand Coulee Dam into low earth orbit. To carry a whole Freedom Class space station in a single launch and "factories" as well, to return to the moon, mine the lunar rock and use the minerals for manufacturing purposes so that eventually, I guess, everything from washing machines to CD players might one day literally start raining right out of the sky.

Now I'm wondering once again: Granddad, where are you? And why is no one here? It is beyond strange. This is a facility employing at least sixty people doing God knows what and getting paid well to do it, too. Now nobody. I peer through a dusty window with its inch-deep magnum glass and see the long snakes of fat chain, each link heavy as a baby, hanging from high above, each with a big hook at the bottom and drooly with oil.

Not a place that welcomes visitors. The door is three-inch mil steel and the code is complicated, something, I guess, from one of my granddad's favorite poems. I say the words

If I could only live at the pitch that is near madness
When everything is as it was in my childhood
Violent, vivid, and of infinite possibility:
That the sun and moon broke over my head.

I hear the high whine of an electric motor and the door slides open and I slip in. The place is huge. How much money did they sink in here—a billion? Easy. While the Proteus used heavy lift technology around since the Apollo program and the old Saturn 5, it cost a fortune. Though Tom Weire says there was so much government black money in it, that "so far as Crawford & Hona's investment went, it never even touched principal." Amazing, given the mass of the thing. The central "aquaboosters" were each the diameter of a baseball diamond and when the first stage blew up they were passing six times as much water per second as Niagara Falls. Except it wasn't water exactly. It was flaming steam, the byproduct of the combustion of liquid oxygen and hydrogen.

After the explosion at sea launch, just before the program collapsed and was abandoned, Frank's engineers ripped out the back of the building and the concrete under it to test the rocket motors inside. The blasts from the cones of the apartment-size nozzles funneled the blast through silica-sided troughs, each trough as deep as a fair-size riverbed, out three sides.

The rocket motors were the biggest ever made and many of the components are still here, like a junkyard from a future that never happened. Steering gimbals—horseshoes of titanium fourty feet wide—still hang from the ceiling five stories up, bathed in sunlight that cuts through the big grid of busted-out glass skylights. Result of a bad accident.

It was six years ago yesterday that Frank had engineers fire an entire first-stage assembly, put x million pounds of thrust through six nozzles. The air inside backheated and blew windows designed to take cannon fire point blank 2,000 feet straight up into the California sky.

Unfortunately, that was just the first act. Rocket motors are tested horizontally but Frank, because of the danger to the refineries, went vertical. A great safety idea, had the ground below the flue not been soaked by a century of hydrocarbons. The earth caught fire, cooked the road behind Building A to a shimmering tar lake, then torched off Exxon Western Heavy Chemical.

The fire was flameless, but fried the air so the silver Exxon buildings looked like rippling mirages until they went up in huge flowers of yellow and red. The blaze could have torched off Long Beach, if it hadn't hit the 10 Freeway. Somehow no one was hurt, it was a Sunday and the Exxon guys had booked, and Frank, who is daring but not reckless, had done this test by remote, but Building A was never the same. The tremendous lift of the rockets had moved the whole structure off its foundation and broke into a storm drain/water runoff, so now a creek runs through the back of the building and over the base of Silica Funnel South.

I walk back there. This is very strange, not only is my grandfather not here but no one is here and the whole huge place looks more than vacated. And for a moment I feel like I've lost my mind. I'm blank. I can't figure out why I'm here. What's happened to this place? I knew, didn't I? Grass and weeds, blackberries and alders have sprouted all around. Animals are in here, frogs, squirrels, lizards, even rattlesnakes. Didn't my grandpa say Newly Formed Materials has become a zoo of how Southern California used to be before people like him came here with their industry and dreams and colossal refineries and rocketships and greed and hair-raising myopias and really fucked it up. Didn't I know that before?

There is a message at the hotel from Frank: Be at the house in Tahoe tomorrow by dark.

I rip my suitcase apart and go through my clothing. How could he have known where I was? A que, that's how. I don't know how he plants them, doubtless couldn't find one even if I did. It frightens me. Frank is hands on, and when things go south it's trick or treat. Sometimes he forgives and even lays out a morale-boosting bygones-are-bygones reward, like my Triumph cafe racer after I got arrested for assault with a deadly. Other times, like when I got arrested for the hot kidneys, he hits. Two broken ribs that I can still feel with any deep breath.

23 JANUARY

Morning. I look out the window down to the parking lot. A chubby man in a golf shirt is crouched behind the Jeep, as if sizing up a putt, but writing down my license number. He got into an appliance pastel four-door sedan and, tires chirping, was off. I'm gone: I pawn my money clip and, three twenties in my jeans, drive.

Tall woods. Fir trees with limbs like giant green feathers. Dirty snow in blobs and slabs across the yard. The largest private home in Nevada. A ski lodge built beside no mountain. At ten I'd lie on Frank's bed with a stopwatch timing the speed of thought, while downstairs in the stone-walled living room my dad wined and dined and mined top spooks in nukes with dreams of a fission world.

No sign of Frank. No rent-a-Mercedes or BMW outside and all the high windows are dim with dirt. At the front door, I say *Screw your courage to the sticking place* and walk in. The house is built on a scale that tells me life is temporary but our home here is not impersonal: in the master bedroom I can smell my parents in their clothes that still hang in their closets.

No Frank, and no granddad either, but at least a place to sleep.

The house is run down and this is eerie: My grandfather has tended to all the homes near the coast forever, so why not now? The shake roof is furry with moss. Its eaves hang over the house like wings of a prehistoric bird and the shingles are the color of shadows. The whole spread could have been designed by Frank Lloyd Wright and assembled by orangutans. No door or window is identical or built to standard size and you could hold the Soap Box Derby on the living room floor. In my old room, above a list my dad put up of the hard-science courses I'd be taking in college, there remains a sign reading BITE BACK. Frank put it there when I was in fourth grade and he'd just graduated from the Air Force Academy.

In the living room, from the beam that divides the ceiling, hangs a model of the three-engined Sentinel 5000 Radar Airship. Designed by my father, the Sentinel was the largest nonrigid airship ever built, a 2.5-million-cubic-foot-volume "super blimp" that could remain aloft for thirty days and had an advanced phased array radar able to track anything from low-altitude cruise missiles to airborne dope dealers.

It was here, in this big wood-and-stone room, ten years ago, that my father had asked me what I assumed my future with Crawford Construction was to be. He was not thrilled to hear that my ambition was to stuff our fortune into a fire hose and blast the cash across the barrios, slums, and ghettos of the world and then retire at twenty to a tree fort, a poor but validated thousandaire.

The phone. It's Frank. I say, "Where are you?"
   "Right where I need to be."
   "Where's Granddad?"
   "Right where he needs to be. Where's the Egg?"
   "I lost it," I say, and explain.
   Frank's RX: "Go back and get it."
   I say no and ask him why would the Mexican police have
gone through my room.
   Frank replies, "You better be gone by the time I get there,"
then hangs up. I drive out to the lake. It is beautiful, endless,
burning with cool green color, fiery and calm.

Granddad right where he needs to be. What does that mean?
I don't know what to do and the fear I'm beginning to have
gives me too much energy so I go skiing and get caught on
top in a dry sandy snow. Clouds float down, everything goes
white, and I ride down with six others in a big cat. One guy
has a compound fracture, blood Rorschachs through his yellow rain pants.
   I buy a hot dog. Food at a ski lodge should be at least as
good as food in prison but the hot dog isn't. The best thing
about it is the wiener looks impressionistic.
   I call Terry Pow, my probation officer. He says I could be
arrested for traveling and what can he do, fake my urinalysis? I do this every month—urinate in a cup. To prove I'm on
drugs. When I got beaned for assault, to avoid jail I agreed
to take Antiswaq, a medication I hate. Pills that make me
sleepy and nervous at the same time.
   If I don't take the test it's back to three hots and a cot so
I tell Terry that I could fly back tonight (how, I don't know)
but he says it's too late, the horse is out of the barn.

After a shower, I look for ques in the mirror. Though even if
one were on me, fifty-fifty I couldn't see it. Each que is an
organic but not self-replicating life-form only about 100 times
the size of a conventional bacterium. An integrated circuit

that works as a series of microchips. Its soft parts are silicon-based and its "skeleton" is gallium arsenide, so each que's nervous system is semiconducting. Alive, they look mechanical—like Apollo lunar landers. Where the cockpit would be is the tiny homing device. They land on your skin and dig in like a mite, then beep out signals to a satellite so Frank, with a monitor, can track me anywhere.

I paw my shoulders in front of the mirror, looking like a paranoid pipehead—and the truth is, I don't even know if ques exist. If my brother has a fault it's that sometimes it is hard to separate what he's done from what he says he's going to do. Still.

I'm strong and if Frank wants to shake it up I won't wait. Two ribs are plenty.

24 JANUARY

Someone was in the house last night. I fell asleep downstairs and woke up to the sound of the ceiling crackling above. Footsteps, someone walking across the old wood floor of the living room. I got out of bed and felt my way to the closet and snapped on a light. Frank keeps a .45 down here someplace but I couldn't find it, so I crept up the stairs carrying a tire iron instead. But the house was empty and, miraculously, all of the doors and windows still locked. Whoever it is was slick and it makes me sweat to think about, because it was as if no one had been there at all.

25 JANUARY

There is a dismal vacuum made of godlessness in Nevada, even in Tahoe, where you can return to California by crossing a street. Under the big red snow-topped sign that reads in letters tall as men, "The Trend Is Your Friend," is Frank's new Big Break. I have found a nice old 35-millimeter Minolta in the garage and, until I am kicked out, take pictures inside. Frank has mated computers, the stock market, and casino gambling. At Big Break, people, the elderly mostly, "ride stock waves" on computers that track the stock market second by second and pay off, if you sell on a "cresting" wave, in silver dollars like a slot machine. When the old men and women win, and coins avalanche from their Apple Midas Threes, they are unblinking to their good fortune. They do not rejoice or, any of them, look around in wonder and glee as if to search out and thank their genius benefactor.

Back home I'll blow these faces up until the features are shapes. I'll print a piece of a mouth or ear or nose. It looks good and seems a nice substitute for a real idea.

26 JANUARY

Frank's dum-dummed the shells, plus shot back through time to reinvent black powder—added nitroglycerin or some damn thing—and the .45 really raised a stink. After it is all over, the basement smells like a fire in a dynamite factory.

This time, when the ceiling crackled, I didn't wait around. I had the pistol on my bedstand, turned on the lamp, chambered a round and at what sounded like a step above my head—I emptied a clip, slammed in another, and emptied that, so on and so on, five in all.

But when I went upstairs. Nothing. Nobody. But what a mess. The shells put fifty some holes in the living room floor as big as baseballs, and splintered the oak to kindling.

28 JANUARY

Good luck and then something very bad: I'm getting another come-hither look from the cops.

I don't know what to do for money, am bouncing off the walls and so confused I accidently get a job. Through a friend I ran into in a bar after I went to the chief of police who said, "Let's make a deal: get out of town right now and I'll get a floor guy and a finish carpenter in there, bill your brother direct."

The friend, a fellow former junior high school lounge lizard at Maui Golf and Country, introduced me to a newspaper editor who hired me after seeing the pictures in *Photo* of my girlfriend after the wreck. There's Jeanie. A smile so big and blood dripping off the poor guy's face into the deep **V** of her cleavage. I wrote "itinerant billionaire" under Previous Employment on the application and it's a new life.

Work. Just another SUN RISES MILLIONS GO TO WORK WIFE SWEARS HUBBY NOT GAY county-wide daily. The picture editor still lives back in the group-and-grin days when you had a speed graphic with an on-camera flash and no matter what, when you needed a picture of somebody, all you did was stand them up, focus, and zap.

I walk into the office right after lunch and see my friend, the chief of police, talking at my new desk with one of the reporters. Chances are there's a warrant out for me in Nevada and by this time tomorrow I will, once again, be holding a mop and bitching about the government decaf. I ought to just bolt.

One good thing though. I hit the end of a pay period, get $320, and at one of those little casino bars where you can watch Elvis eat a ninety-nine-cent top sirloin at three in the morning, I meet a girl named Ann Teal. Tall, pale, ripply, raw wood–colored hair, no makeup, she wears a plaid housedress, sandals, and a man's tweed jacket.

I'm not short or tall, fat or thin. I'm in good shape, have a good face, but except for skin dark as a Comanche, if you saw me on the street you'd probably just think: sell me a Volvo. Still, often things go well for me. I tell Ann Teal about my life doing bush league nuclear targeting. Her head tips. "What's that?"

"Paint by numbers stuff, mostly," I explain, "picking out cities and missile sites and radar stations and command-and-control centers."

Her brows lower, as if to protect her eyes from the sight of a lunatic. "You're in the service."

I say no, but that I've seen the new plans for the end of the world and how the lost Egg is, I'll bet, Pandora's box cubed, and wherever it is, is the last place I want to be. I tell her I don't want to sleep at home for all the obvious reasons. She's impressed and takes me to her house in an old Saab painted blue with a brush.

Everything seems inevitable, as if the night has been mounted on railroad tracks. She waits tables in Tahoe and lives on the bottom floor of a tiny duplex. Living room, bedroom, kitchen, can. A futon under a table-size painting of peaceful pastel blobs. A nice painting. She tells me she worked double shifts three weeks straight in order to pay for it. Then, as if I had asked her to dance, her elbows are on my shoulders.

She says, "With respect to the institution," twists off an engagement ring, sets it on her mantel. I hadn't noticed that. She takes Seen Cleans from a blister pack, the needle raises a red ball on her wrist perfect as a pearl. No plaque for us. Who'd've thought the letters NEG would prove an aphrodisiac more erotic than any perfume?

The moment to clear some brush. "Your boyfriend won't he dropping by, will he?"

"He's in Park City."

I ask what he does for a living and she says, "He was on the Nevada State ski team until he blew his knee out."

"Is he nice?"

"In a please and thank you way." She pulls her hair back and makes a pony tail with both of her hands.

"He's not kinky if that's what you're asking. The worst he's ever done is to say when he was drunk that he'd love to sit here in that chair and watch me suck off a really cute guy. Would that be cool for you?"

"To what?"

"Have—make love to a girl while her boyfriend was watching?"

"No."

"How about the other way around?"

That takes a second to compute before I shake my head.

"So what would you like?"

Some privacy. She pulls her dress off over her head. "What do you do?" she asks. Stare, I think. What beautiful breasts. Her skin is as white as wedding cake. "Did I ask you that?"

"I work for my brother, and work in a bar. In Honolulu."

"What's your brother do?"

I play to the cheap seats. "A lot of things. He's one of the richest people in the world."

Her touch has an electric kindness. She has a vinegary-sweet smell of picked flowers—and a weird sense of (I hope) humor. She says her beloved's added fantasy is to have a "funky leather stud" in their honeymoon suite to "join in" on their marriage bed. I ask if she thinks that's a good idea and she sighs, "Eric is very male."

Very nuts would be my take, but she is wonderful and in the morning she gives me a goodbye blow job so sweet and wholesome Norman Rockwell could have painted it and stuck the picture on a Hallmark greeting card.

Twenty minutes later she's jangling keys waiting to take me back to the Jeep. A rescue in mind, I ask her to come out to the house and she says, no, she's flying up to her mom's in Portland for two days. When I move to kiss her goodbye— we're standing in the parking lot in front of the bar—she says, "Better not advertise."

I climb up in the Jeep and say I'll see you when you get back. She grins. I feel heat, then she tilts her face up into the cab, kisses the corner of my mouth and says, "Why?"

29 JANUARY

It's black as the void, I feel I'm nothing and nowhere, and then rising from my bed I hear the phone ring. It's Frank calling from some area of the night to say Dewey stole the Egg. I ask what for and Frank tells me he'll ask the questions. I reply this is ridiculous, I have no power, no control, have been treated like a messenger boy, except I've never even seen the message. I say nobody'd wreck an insanely profitable company to steal film he has no plausible use for, and Frank says my encyclopedic ignorance always amazes him. "Tod," he tells me, "Dewey's blowing us off." I ask why and Frank replies, "It starts with R, ends with K, and has ATFUC in between." Then he tells me I've got three days to go back to Mexico City to get what's ours. I ask how and he says, "Grease Dewey if that's what it takes."

What's on the block? Two billion dollars, three, five, ten? A buck ninety-nine? If Frank and Dewey and Dewey's mother claw the whole thing apart, what am I going to end up with?

Bats are in the house, they swoop down from the ceilings— wild black rags. I go into the dining room. It's like a mead hall and cold as snow. I go into my old bedroom, paw through my drawers for a sweater, and find a picture of me at age three or four, in a cowboy hat and crying. My open mouth takes up half my face and my mother is holding me in her arms in a way that suggests she wished she weren't. My parents could have been my grandparents by the time I was born, and I grew up feeling like the esteemed guest who would never leave. By two I was a bee in a bottle, I had temper tantrums so bad my favorite first memories are of the stinging relief of the cold showers I was popped into to make me shut up.

I was dosed sane on Ritalin and while it wasn't hugs for breakfast every morning I think I was loved and I did okay though certain things stick out, like: in eighth grade a teacher told my mother I was "a brilliant student in a school that doesn't exist," able to read and draw anything that wasn't assigned, and could do any task as long as it was irrelevant.

I go through my dresser. I don't know what I'm looking for but whatever it is I can't find it. All that turns up, aside from an old high school annual—*Tod Crawford: Tennis, Golf, China White*— is a book of my old rent receipts. We've got a lot of commercial real estate—110,000 acres give or take—about Fresno spread all over. After it didn't work out in premed I collected rent for Harmony Trust, our holding company for apartments. Heartbreaking credit histories. It's light-years between what people earn and what they can pay. Single parents raising kids on oatmeal, MTV, and Cheesewhiz. Try making it on two grand a month take-home—and pray ACME Livelihood is good for major medical while Mom is fishing her Spam, diapers, and last month's *Elle* from a drop box behind the Pic n' Sav.

Three months into the job I felt guilty because, overdue rentwise, I was only $30,000 in the hole. And that was before the Ccrash when people were burning each other's homes and businesses. By then I was into hot organs. I don't believe in laws or the power of the state, but I know people have it tough, especially with hospital costs, and I was running kidneys of Mexican donors across the border for surgeons to use to save the lives and money of their patients. And if I was poor, I'd get hip. If I was the masses, I'd drag guys like me out of our mansions and ax us to round steak.

Carpenters in the house all day. The floor is ripped out, I can look down to the basement bed where I have my bad dreams through a rectangular grid of two-by-eights. Thank God the carpenters—two brothers with ponytails, Indians maybe—are hip. Instead of money they take paintings—W. R. Spencer's *The Carlisle Castle* and Helen Frankenthaler's *Mermaid's Song*—right off the walls.

Jan and Dean calls with news the cops came looking for me and have ripped our apartment a new one, that he can't keep Less Nervous going alone, and if I'm not back soon he'll fold the tent. "The cops had a search warrant, Fauntleroy, and you better kiss my ass for telling them you were still on the island."

I can see my breath in the living room, even the ghosts in this place must be freezing. I go downstairs to relight the pilot light to the furnace. On the wall in my dad's old study are the pictures from "Face Lift" that got me a double truck spread in *Photo* when I was nineteen. My big splash. My mother's face before, during, and after. Left side, right side, full frontal, ten photos each in three horizontal strips. I look at her eyes tired and dark under her delicate brows, the skin that curtains under her chin, then at the bruises and black worms of suture and blood that made her young at fifty-eight. Wondering why I haven't done shit since takes away patience I need to ignite the pilot light and I get angry about Ann Teal.

She should be back. I drive up to Incline Village. It's little and her duplex was in the middle of it but why can't I find it? The pills is why. I go home, look in the phone book. But no Ann Teal there or in information. I can't sleep. I need somebody. After it has been night for a lifetime I go in my mother and father's room, to their bed, to find them among the sheets.

No police. Spooky.

30 JANUARY

No joke, the sky has had it. Sheep are going blind in Argentina, while plants and weeds mutate to crazy trees in Chile. I have been assigned a miracle. A deity is to walk the surface of the

Truckee River as a publicity stunt for a religious sect moving here from Miami. Since the Ccrash, Messiahs have been crawling out of the woodwork. This latest is scheduled to drop out of the sky, but short on spaceships, he and his flock show up in VW vans. The congregation, ordinary in golf shirts and slacks, watch as he gets the wheels of a Dodge Power Wagon buried to the hubs in mud at the river's edge, then walks into the water and shows himself to be as buoyant as a stone. I waste two rolls of Tri-X on this craven nitwit, leave, and get fired. No surprise. I work hard, am good at what I do, but for some reason bosses don't like me.

I head home, whip the Jeep up into the long tipped-up U of our driveway, and see under the shadows of the firs a pale four-door sedan, à la the one from Long Beach.

Maybe this is just a stiff from the gas company, but I've been chased before and my philosophy when I think I am is to get going and keep going. Because I've decided I'm not going to jail again. We've got houses everywhere and I'll ricochet all over the country if that's what it takes.

FEBRUARY

Forget Ann Teal. That's how it goes and my only question is:
Will it happen to me? Will my blushing bride have just played
"Taps" on some barfly's heater five minutes before she glides
down the aisle to take our sacred vows?

My granddad has got another house in Brentwood so maybe
that's where he is. I try to call ahead, but I've lost the number and it's unlisted and now I'm on the road back to Los Angeles, in a town made out of a Burger King, liquor store, tavern,
two gas stations, and three motels. From where I sit I can see
the on-ramp to Interstate 5, the freeway back to Mexico. So?
I could go back to Mexico City and get killed chasing after
the Oman Egg. Frank would appreciate the servitude but he's
had his thumb on my cowlick long enough.

Sitting here in the Jeep on the graveled roadside I see that
I have been enveloped in a buzzing dust of tiny flies, they
pepper my forearms. Forget it. I drive into Los Angeles and
call Jeanie from a Pizza Hut. Her phone rings across the ocean
but there's nobody home.

LA. Granddad's house in Brentwood. Tall and grey. Every
house around has lawns manicured like putting greens but
his grass is as high as summer wheat. He's not there and I'm
beginning to wonder if he is, any longer, anywhere at all.

One of the French windows is shattered in place, the glass still there in a transparent jigsaw puzzle. My sister Diane, who married a college teacher and is off enduring death by casserole at the University of Kansas, left $40 in a piggy bank in the dining room. Which I take. As well as, sadly, James Rosenquist's *Electrons Dance in Space*. Once removed, it leaves a huge pale rectangle on my granddad's bedroom wall. I pawn it at the new Mask of Smiles in Westwood—there is, not surprisingly, the sticky issue of ownership—and all I can get is a grand and a half.

7 FEBRUARY

I've got blotches all over my arms and the sides of my back where I thought I saw ques. Imagination or flies, I get sick of this, so finally I just call Frank. One in a million I get through. The skip-coded registers on the secure phones are mounted on the roof and are fouled with bird shit so conversation is scrambled and staticky—it's like talking to Marconi transatlantic in tongues. I tell him I'm flying back to Honolulu and he says if I do I'll regret it until the day I die.

8 FEBRUARY

Aerospace is gone, Rockwell's hanging on threads, and McDonnell-Douglas still has a P.O. box somewhere. Fifty-five thousand unemployed are living in the street. Otherwise LA is great, especially if you're into avocados, traffic, and people who don't read books.

In the LA *Times* this morning what do you know: Crawford & Hona Refineries just got fined $1.3 million for not supercharging their burnoffs. Frank was quoted saying we're doing the city a favor, the ozone layer is so shot Los Angeles is going to be forced to repollute its air or everybody will die of malignant melanoma twenty years before the smog gives them even half a chance of catching lung cancer.

I'm going home. If Frank wants to shake it up, he can try it at the airport.

• • •

The jet goes up in the sky. I go through proof sheets, the pictures of the houses in Celestial City look like the kind that have "Motivated Seller" written under them in real estate magazines, and only a couple of shots are even worth developing. A stewardess who has rusty hair and a leering, fresh-faced wholesomeness gazes at a picture of a Celestial City car wreck—a great big Cadillac cut in half by a utility pole, some old apparatchik in his American battlewagon dead over the steering wheel—and says, "Ick."

I get off the jet thinking I should get her name but don't. It's late afternoon and I'm looking for Frank when a man in a suit says something to me. He is with a slender birdlike woman. They look very clean, almost evangelical, like the people who sell *Watchtower* door to door, and for an instant I think these two are here to remind me my subscription has lapsed. But instead, the guy, who is thin and wears old-fashioned granny glasses, is asking me if my name is Tod Crawford. I say yeah, and he shows me a document that looks like a passport and says he's with—though I'm still not sure—the Department of Energy.

Then the woman wants to know if I am familiar with the Federal Witness Protection Program. And the guy, who has translucent blond hair and looks young and almost frail, asks if I've been served. Served what? A subpoena. I say no and he looks at me as if, yes, I have sinned, and says if I'd like to talk to him just call, and he hands me a card that says:

J. Gary Beane, Special Investigator
Nuclear Waste Management Division
Department of Energy

Then they are gone. I stand there. No Frank, thank God. It's so hot and humid that I can see the reflection of my face in my forearm. Home at last.

On the way from the airport I see towns of people living under the freeway overpasses. Somebody has sprayed LOVE KILLS in beautiful luminous green letters all over. Frank says society is separating away into its true component parts, the poor getting poorer while the lucky sons of my class and generation wait around for their parents to provide them makework jobs as fat cats, movie moguls, and U.S. congressmen. I pay the cab, get my prescription filled at ABC Waikiki Pharmacy, and walk by Mask of Smiles. A new show. The painter is Rubin Kole, an artist who has finally done the obvious: his paintings are his signature. "Rubin Kole" signed across any canvas in oil, chalk, watercolor, a million different ways.

I go back to the apartment, go upstairs, say *The secret to life is that it stops,* but the door won't open. I try the old *What fresh hell is this?* but nothing. Angry, I smash a deck chair through the glass vents that cross the top of the door and let myself in.

1 1   F E B R U A R Y

Dawn. Light seeping over the apartments. Palm trees. The phone. In bed I pick it up and hear "Brudda." I say, "Who's this?" Somebody says, "A kotonk died on my flight. Collapsed in the aisles on his way to the john. The stewardesses stuffed 'im in with all the lunches and dinners. Feature that. One minute you're bee-bopping on your vacation and the next you're folded up in a frigerator. Know what, you're not going to last five minutes on the street."

I say, "Dewey."

"A big fat Jap. I don't know how they did it. Cops are wise to you, brudda. Step outta that apartment and it'll be a race between God and the law who nails you first."

"Where's the Egg, Dewey?"

He says, "The life of da bag man. You kill me."

"Absolutely, brah, I brought it back. Yeah, and it's stashed in the cooler at Do What You Look Like." Then he laughs and the sound he makes is a legitimate ha-ha-ha.

I get up, grab wax and two wadded dollars off the coffee table, and go into the bedroom across the hall where Jan and Dean is sweating in his sleep. Books are stacked everywhere and on the wall above his bed, there is a poster of a grinning skull in Special Forces attire with the words SPEAK ENGLISH OR DIE in yellow letters below.

I push open the glass sliding door to his lanai, pick up a surfboard, and lift it carefully, quietly, and thread my way back out to the living room.

On the coffee table I can see a note in Jan's blocky script: *Call Lt. Vorhaggen HPD 435-9923 A COP, FAUNTLEROY— HE'S CALLED 3 TIMES.* Outside it is cool and getting lighter. I go downstairs and pass a man wearing pendant earrings and a dress. We say, "Morning."

Next to the carport a black rag erupts from the weeds, squirts toward me, and looks up. One of the wild cats, his left eye gone to milk. I've forgotten to put food out.

Behind a line of old houses, new hotels, and palm trees, the Yamamoto has half the sky. Forty stories, the new hotel stretches across three blocks, all the way to the beach. Just behind it, its sister ship, the 8,000-room Fuchida, is in the first stage of construction; there is a four-square-block hole five stories deep to hold its foundation. The Japanese conglomerate building these hotels bulldozed a block just to create parking for the construction crews.

Down the street, Samoans are in the trees. I hear what sounds like three or four lawn mowers, look up, and there they are, up in the palms with chain saws cutting back the long hanging fronds to their stumps. Like half the other vegetation on the island, the fronds have dried out and catch fire willy-nilly. In the paper some sob sister from the Environmental Protection Agency said if the atmosphere continues to degrade, the whole island may just spontaneously combust.

The Samoans are big mokes, like pro wrestlers. They start the chain saws on the ground, then pull them up on ropes. Rising, the chain saws fart puffy grey clouds of exhaust into the air. Samoans are an ancient long-ago people. I think they don't know too much about chain saws or poisoned air. Those things are just random trash from the present. Junk to use or endure while you get money to keep civilization off your back so you can nut up and have a good time.

Still half in my dreams, I see Frank and police everywhere. I walk by the white Catholic church, under its row of spiked dormers, hear the muffled cadence of the litany echo from behind closed doors. Mass: I'm trying to recall the names of the rest of its parts when I hear a crash like a cannon shot and see that around the corner Dewey Hona's weed-eater brother, August, is in a huge crane swinging a wrecking ball into the Palms Hotel, a building next to Less Nervous. Jan has the last of the old Waikiki saloons, lately better known as Patron by the Slice because of a bloody Hot Stick fight we had in there six months ago.

The hotel next to it, the Palms, is being razed by the Honas to make room for a very large new hotel Maye Hona has her infarcted heart set on. Vines of rebar twist from the wreckage, rooms are exposed in a pale quilt of wallpapers and ceramic tile. Dust floats over across the street to Dewey Hona's nightclub, Do What You Look Like. Vince the Queer, up early too, is standing out front, his lips at the ear of a boy.

Across Kalakua Avenue, the beach is washed smooth by the tide and pocked only by a single string of footprints that run parallel to the water. A guy I know from somewhere with long, white blond hair combed straight back, and wearing baggy yellow trunks, stands in the lapping shallows waxing his board. He says, "Sup, Crawford? I thought you were in jail," and then, unbelievably, as if I am someone else entirely, asks if I want to help him rob a jewelry store.

I set Jan's board in the quaking shallows, then paddle on my stomach, feeling the rough waxed surface of the board on the muscle and bone on my chest as I move my arms through the water, sitting up as the waves rise, break, and splash over me. A girl is gliding down the face of a wave about fifty yards to my left; her board is just a drop of fiberglass. She jerks up and down the face of the rolling wave as though she is weightless.

Good water. I'm still inside. On the shoulders of the break the waves swell and roll under my board. There are six or eight other surfers on the break. The ones in the pocket at the center paddle with quick jabbing strokes to catch waves before they feather and come crashing down on top of them. The sun is rising and feels good. On my left, faraway, spiking from the horizon, I can see the tops of the long pipes, the huge concrete forms that will shape the New Island. Stonehenge at the bottom of the sky.

The drilling will begin soon, a half mile underwater with the mohole men boring holes a quarter mile through coral and volcanic rock. But first Frank must finish building the concrete forms and put them in position on the sea floor so the lava will build up rather than spread.

The mohole men told Frank that to get at the lava he'd have to use nukes. But Frank did pressure studies and realized that conventionals, shaped right, could do it. All he had to do, basically, is set them off like beads on a string.

A wave breaks in front of me. There's an offshore wind and my face is sprayed with mist from its crest. I see the next one loom and move my arms through the water. The board rises up from behind. I grab its rails, hop up, and swing the nose away from the high-curving wall of water that was the face of the wave.

I cut up and down across it until it falls apart and then I move back out through the chop and wait for the next swell. Little rollers, then the first wave of a big set shadows up. I inch backward on the board. A guy next to me strokes landward slowly. I can hear the wave crest but do not look back, instead dig my arms deep in the water, paddle in long, quick strokes.

It is large, then overhead, moving, a long falling wall. My board wells way up high on the wave's lip. My arms stab once more through the water, I jump up, take the drop, and, wham, as if out of the sky, some guy swoops down on me from nowhere. I cut back, the board knifes into the face of the falling wave, pearls, trailing, for an instant, a swirl of bubbles. I'm in the air. It's like falling off a two-story building and the wave crashes down on top of me.

Twirled and bounced softly off the coral bottom, I wait for the water to let go, and slipping back up, feel the tiny rush of air bubbles brush my skin as I come to the surface. I break into the air, take a breath, and wipe the hair out of my face.

It's calm. The wave is still rolling to the shore in front of me, much smaller now. Out at sea, there are no more swells. I put a foot down to see if the water is over my head. It is. People on the beach are dots of color. I swim shoreward and see Jan's board, floating upside down, its yellow skeg like a shark's fin. I paddle in, and leave the water with bright red strings twining down my legs. Coral cuts. The surfboard may be over. There's a gash in its rail as big as a piece of pie. The dry sand above the tidal wash is already hot and gets hotter as I walk away from the water to the public showers and rinse off.

I snap off the spigot, wander out, and see a pretty girl on the sand. A flag of blond hair and milky skin that with the atmosphere blown you don't see out that often. She's very pale. It looks as if someone has sucked her blood, but in a very alluring way. She is wearing a satiny Esther Williams–style one-piece and platform sandals.

Mokes in zoot suits, Titas in bellbottom hip huggers— half the island is celebrating some spot in our just vanished century.

Her glance ticks to me, and my, what eyes. 3-D, a whole world right there and I think, why not just walk up and offer her an engagement ring. Because I have possibilities. Women like me—once I even caught nonspecific urethritis from a Miss Young Hawaii—so who knows.

It takes me a moment to remember what I should do next: which is walk the hot sidewalks to Najami Bar-B-Q to get chicken for the cats. Najami's is one of the few of the old ma and pa restaurants in Waikiki and they give me chicken scraps for a dollar a bag. But when I get there the glass front door is locked. I set the surfboard skeg down on the sidewalk, cup my hands around my eyes, and look in. The place has been gutted.

Boy. I walk home to the apartment. It is still early and quiet. Jan and Dean's pink-and-white '56 Ford convertible sits under the carport, listing to one side. The windshield is broken where Jeanie kicked it from the inside with her boot heel and cracks spiderweb around a dime-size hole below the rear-view mirror. The white Naugahyde upholstery is split and torn, the body rusting out along the rocker panels. Jan left the keys in the ignition. He wants the car stolen so he can get the insurance.

Our neighbor Tony's boat sits in the arbor between our apartment houses, rising above its eight-wheeled trailer like a new Noah's Ark. He has painted the hull a yellow so bright it seems to make light of its own. Tony is a Turkish skinhead who believes Christ has already come back but accidently died in his swimming pool. He speaks little English and the most complicated thing he's ever said to me is Brian Jones died for your sins.

Tony is a house painter. With his shaved skull and the red bumps that dot his white unmuscled arms and legs he looks like a man who has just been deloused. He lives across from us with his Swiss hippie chick wife and their three boys, big-eyed, milk-skinned stringbeans, all under twelve.

Tony built the *Ajax* for Armageddon. God told him to do it. Days before creation is set ablaze, Tony will know and he'll pile his children aboard, roll the *Ajax* down Paokalini Street and into the Pacific. There could be something to this. I've gone to the horse track with Tony. There God told Tony which horses would show. I've bet on God's picks and won every time.

So when the End is near, maybe Tony will know it, and sailing away will be the thing to do. Nevertheless, he has punched so many holes through the hull for auxiliary exhaust, bilge, and electronics that once the *Ajax* is put in the ocean I'm afraid it'll be about as seaworthy as a Cheerio. So I helped make it watertight, laying enough fiberglass around the fittings of the hull to build ten surfboards. I don't know where he's going or what I'm doing but he's taking the kids with him and it's a very big ocean.

I go upstairs. And there, in the apartment, Roberta. Her short bobbed black hair is now streaked with locks of neon red, but I see the same long bright eyes and vivid mouth. Pretty bare feet on the coffee table, her butt is perched on the edge of my black director's chair, an old paperback copy of *Within Normal Limits* upside-down on her lap. She is wearing a bikini top and Levi cutoffs cut so short the flaps from the front pockets descend below the ragged hem.

She says, "You're back."

I ask what happened to Najami's.

Roberta sticks a precisely manicured finger into a cup of pink yogurt. "Dumb shits lost their lease to Namura Incorporated. The big Japs eating the little Japs. In the paper it says they own more land in Hawaii than America does."

She sucks her pink finger. Roberta tends bar and sings occasionally at Less Nervous and has a thin wire of a voice I can sometimes hear three or four blocks away.

She's from a broken home—her mom is in Condo Repos and her dad is a Polaroid she's got stuffed in a box someplace. Jan and Dean has a crush on her chest and Roberta spends a lot of time here. She is watching the Wall. On the screen the Three Stooges are as big as gorillas, filling an aristocrat's mouth with cement.

"Crawford," she says, "a fun job for you." Eyes on the Stooges, she puts a yogurt-dipped finger to the red petal of her lower lip. "Knock me up. I need the cash." When I do not reply, she says, "$5 million for fifteen minutes. Anything you want to do from—" She gazes at her rubber watch. "Let's say five before five until ten after. As long as you take a shower first. Did you get the money?"

"What money?"

"The $50,000 for the Egg."

"I will," I say.

"You got burned. How do I know that, Crawford, how do I know?"

I ask, "Where's Jan?" and she says, "Going potty." I carry the board back through his bedroom and set it out on the lanai.

In the bathroom Jan and Dean is in front of the mirror, bearded with shaving cream. He wears only canvas swimming trunks. He is hairy, thick chested, has a big nose and the blinking eyes of a baby bird. His thinning black hair corkscrews away from his head, as if to represent the detonation of his skull.

I say, "A guy dropped in on me. I put a ding in your board. A bad one."

He says, "The least of our problems." He sets the razor to the top of his cheek and cuts a rectangle down the foam, then puts his razor under the tap. Water eases a white eel of foam off its edge. "The cops were here three times while you were gone."

"Why?"

Jan seems to be staring himself down in the mirror, black little eyes on black little eyes. "You tell me, Fauntleroy. And guess who tore the place apart. What were they looking for, anyway?"

I say I have no idea.

"Unreal," Jan says, cutting another rectangle down the foam. "They came in with bags and took all your shit." He runs water on his razor. "Stuck everything in little plasticine envelopes, carried it out, and brought it all back two days later."

I go in the living room. Everything looks the same. Roberta

asks if Frank knows I'm back. So he can come kill me. I say
not yet, go into the kitchen, open a can of chili, and let its
lumpy, red-brown essence slump into a pot. Jan rarely fingers
anything but the heartiest, most basic grocery. Nothing with
a shelf life below 2,000 years. I look at the glop and realize
I'm not hungry.

Still, not knowing what else to do with it, I heat the stuff
up, put it on a plate, go in, and sit on the couch. The fabric
feels good on my bare back—providing as it does both itch
and scratch.

Jan sits down beside Roberta and begins to lace up his running shoes. Watching, she says, "JD's having three girls over
here for an orgy." Then: "Get 'em over here, Jan. And just before you whip out the Crisco and ben wa balls, give me a
buzz."

Jan stands up, says, "Zip it girl." He has scars, large splashing ones, as if someone had heaved molten metal across
the top of his chest. He claims he was the only officer to be
fragged by his own men during the war with Iraq and, as a
Christian Scientist, refused to let the medics patch him up.
Aside from aspirin and chemotherapy, Jan says medicine is
voodoo. Last year he fell off the lanai drunk and broke his
arm and wouldn't let me take him to a doctor. I had to set
the bone myself by trying to remember how they did it on
an old St. Elsewhere and I imagine the pain was so bad it nearly
killed him. But Jan is tough, he never said a word, and though
his wrist has lost most of its mobility, he's never complained.
He says that's how God wants his arm to be.

He punches up Harriet Morsel's lilting "Bye"—an all-drum
lullaby, different—and I watch as he then disappears into his
bedroom. A moment later he bolts out screaming what the
hell happened out there, his goddamned surfboard is wrecked
for good, and then—pulling from the air what he just heard
from Roberta—he says he can't wait for Frank to show up
and kill me dead.

1 3 F E B R U A R Y

Alger Hiss has left a crucifix of turds, one crossing the other,
in mint condition behind the pool tables for the liquor dick
to see before I did when he came in right after I opened. The

dog was in here last night with Dewey while I was up to my ears with pissed-off-at-each-other "Agent Orange made me rob the liquor store"–type Vietnam vets here for a memorial service.

Then another squack attack. Bikedykelesbopunks from the Clit Club, three of them who had pulled up on new carbon-carbon Harleys and who were led by a big busty number in crotchless toreador pants, claimed the nutrient slush we served them had been eaten before and started throwing the admittedly vomity-looking stuff all over the place.

Roberta said she'd about had it. If Jan and Dean didn't start paying her more she was going to quit. While I was gone she bought an old Volkswagen from her old boss when she was comic book queen at Good Stuff Junior. The car looks half digested, its convertible top is confetti, the seats have holes that show the floorboards. She got it for the price of its parking tickets but it's going to cost money to fix and she wants me to dig up $3,000 to help. One good thing though: No Frank. Maybe if I just stay here he will exist across the island from me, separate forever. Going back to the apartment, I check my mail. A micro CD from Whore School, *Tricks of the Trade*, and a note from *Photo* re: my casino pictures; the answer is no. Unless I want to end up seventh banana at some fourth-rate ad agency or spend my life taking pictures of ex–brat packers for *Geezer Beat Magazine*, I've got to get something going. Quick.

We fix the board. I put the nose on the edge of the couch and prop the tail on the seat of a director's chair. Jan spreads newspapers under it, most from a therapy group newsletter he gets whose pitch is life isn't so immoderately fucked as to be unbearable. I take a handsaw and cut a line on either side of the gash. Jan cuts a new wedge of Styrofoam, sands it to fit, takes a square of fiberglass matting, and lays it over the foam. We pour a syrup of clear glass resin and catalyst over the top. Jan smoothes it with his fingers; he concludes, "Surfing's a damn rude sport."

Roberta says, "I let JD touch my breast today, didn't I, Jan?"
Jan says zip it. We are on our way to Big Store.
"I didn't let him touch both. Both is for next year. We'll
progress. New Year's Eve we'll have actual sexual intercourse.
Lights off, sheets up, missionary position. Good fun, yeah?"
Jan parks the Ford by the shore of an asphalt sea and we
push shopping carts through canyons of laundry detergent,
tires, and frozen fish. Frank must be making a mint. "Gimme
your card," Jan says as we get in line, the carts stacked high
with food and liquor. Weeks' worth of restaurant supplies. I
look up to a ceiling so wide and high you could fly an airplane
in here. Frank says his Hyper Mart on Maui, geared to the
needs of the post-Yuppie, "New Stupid," will be so large he'll
close the loop and become the controlling consumer force in
the Hawaiian Islands.

I hear a noise and look to the turnstile. Jan is pounding on
a Big Store credit machine. "It ate your ANYTHING card!"
he says. "Frank had the machine eat your card."

Outside it's only ten but so hot already the new blacktop
is soft. Cars stretch everywhere and it takes ten minutes to
find the Ford. Jan has a new bumper sticker slapped on the
back that reads SAVE A DOG—EAT A CAMBODIAN. "I'm
a walking time bomb," Jan reminds me, putting his fore and
middle fingers to his head and wagging his thumb. I'm not
too worried though, figuring my roommate and mentor is still
far too tentative for oblivion.

14 FEBRUARY

Roberta is bold. Because what can she be? Seventeen tops,
fifteen would be a better bet. But when the liquor dicks came
in for the umpteenth time last night and one finally had his
synapses aligned well enough to ask the obvious—How old
are you?—she whipped out a perfect set of 3-D ID that said
she was 22 and went coolly apeshit when the guy asked her
more than two questions about it. Nevertheless, one of these
days, the city is going to add two and two.

This morning I catch Alger Hiss—who traces his lineage,
according to Dewey, to the Soviet attack dog program but
who is, according to Dewey, "a virulent anticommunist"—

dancing through our garbage. The Doberman's eyes lock on mine. The dog has heaved trash all around the old beer kegs out back and, as I approach, looks at me as though he is not a dangerous animal but a thoughtful man.

I go inside.

Blow brother Vince—half bull, half rooster, big chest, little legs—has greased-back hair and lips the shape of a small fat heart. He is already behind the bar. He asks me if it would be cool to throw an end-of-winter bacchanal—nothing but a breakfast really, Fruit Loops and Zombies—for his chapter of Rump Wranglers Anonymous.

I like Vince. Though Jan calls him Pitcher in the Rye he really is good with kids. And he too has been to war. He tells of ambushes gone incredibly haywire, ream jobs solicited under rocket attack. Given the current phantasmagoria, after a while the lyric simplicity of his faggoty bullshit seems more real than what I am seeing in front of my face.

Namely, the middle class. Icicles nutting up. Morons.

Inside Less Nervous at sunset, two moms sit at the bar showing me pictures of goo-faced toddlers. They are nice women who've been heated and re-heated so many times that their faces are melanoma farms. Then one of the lovely old Swedish au pair girls, Sis, glides out of the Nancy Spungeon Room. Like an ancient Tinker Bell, she's a dreamy cobweb, but not doing well. For she's so scared she's peed on herself. A blob swells below her crotch, browning her diaphanous beige dress in a long sinking streak. She looks down as if she has, magically, sprung a leak.

Her humiliation seems to give her resolve, her face congeals, decades fade to show a girl. She says, "How could they do that?"

Do what is the question and, walking past the Love Machines, the answer is: perv in public. One of the Icicles, his head shaved, his jams down around his hairy knees, says he and his partner just got married so butt out. I look at the other guy, who could have been the young Jackie Kennedy if she were a man, and say, then you and the missus take your act down the road, and the shaved-headed one pulls a carbon-carbon Hot Stick. Not good news—Hot Sticks are about the only stupid thing Frank's ever done. He designed them to replace stun guns. A bladder of hydrogen with an electric wick, hit it and, boom, a three-foot sword of superheated hydrogen. This guy pops it, flames the sleeve on my T-shirt, then groom and groom sprint down Kalakua.

Less Nervous. Unreal. Somebody spraypainted ACTION KILLS FEAR across the front doors in letters as wide as tire tread. Jan and Dean hasn't taken care of anything. The toilet in the men's room is yellow and oily with old urine, and the dishes in the dishwasher have mold growing on scraps of food three weeks old. I feed Mr. Real. Jan's fish. An Ariwana who lives in a tank above the bar beneath the case of the bomb. Mister Real is mostly head and his head is mostly jaw and his jaw is mostly teeth. Long white needles, maybe a hundred of them. I fed him a bag of goldfish and goddamned if he doesn't nearly rip off my fingers as I'm dropping them in.

I've got to take care of this place before it takes care of me.

15 FEBRUARY

Have you ever worked in the service of a foreign government or in concert with foreign nationals to plan the use of or to procure nuclear weapons? "No." *Have you ever been involved in the procurement of nuclear weapons for anyone for any reason?* "No." *Have you ever planned the use of nuclear weapons against the citizens or properties of the United States or its allies as defined by the Oslo Agreement of 1998?* I don't want to get within a light year of that one. "No."

This again. Amateur hour. I'm innocent, give or take, but it's scary. Vorhaggen's office. He called, said he wanted to show me something important and now the wispy-haired, sickly looking DOE guy is there, staring at me, his eyes big and watery behind his glasses. Vorhaggen says, "Just after Christmas you were transporting something for your brother, bringing that something back to Honolulu."

I say that would have been a violation of my probation.

"So how was your flight?"

When I do not reply, Vorhaggen says, "Frank sends you hither and yon, all over on errands he's either too busy or scared to do himself."

I ask just exactly what it was he wanted to show me and he pulls out a folder and says, "This. I'd like to read, if you don't mind, a psychiatric evaluation made of you in wake of the first incident. The author is Wallace Rice."

I say, "My psychotherapist."

He reads: "Textbook passive-aggressive. A sweet kid, but wackier than seven hundred bucks. He rationalizes his violent activities so thoroughly he believes in their rectitude himself."

I say, "What's the point?" and he flips me a quarter.

I say, "What's this for?" and he says, "Your phone call to your lawyer. You're under arrest."

I say, "What for?" and he says, "How does treason sound? If you're lucky you might even get a Valium with your lethal injection."

A cell, pale cream walls, a cot, and a sink. Passive-aggressive, right. To the cops passive means a guy who can get on a city bus and ride three blocks without tearing out the throat of the guy sitting next to him. To the police aggressive means a guy who comes home, finds bikers raping his wife and killing his children, and says, "Now stop that." It's all meaningless. I'm about as passive as a hand grenade and as aggressive as a May fly. But I have to play to the cheap seats so Wally can claim I wasn't responsible for whatever it is everybody needs to think I did.

Just after dinner—coffee, peas, chicken, and mashed potatoes that were actually very good, to the extent that I wonder why the coffee in the Honolulu jail is better than the coffee at the Honolulu Hilton—I get a roommate. A horse-faced black man in for traffic violations so complicated they take an hour to explain. Then he tells me how when he got married he and his bride dropped six tabs of acid on their honeymoon and visited the snake chamber on a Hopi Indian reservation. It blew her circuits and she split on him, headed for San Francisco, and changed her name to Brother Dorian Sylvanus. He didn't see her again until six years later when he discovered her, tin cup in hand, giving a lecture against animal vivisection in London's Hyde Park.

Tom Weire, attorney at law, dressed in a white linen sport coat, his face looking less tan than cooked, says, "I thought you were dead. Good thing you're priced to move." Weire says they were trying to set my bail at $500,000 and what happened?

I say, what kind of film could I be carrying that would involve me in treason? Weire says no kind he knows of. I ask why I'd be asked all those nuke questions and Weire says, "The good news is the police are tiring in fantasyland and the bad news is you don't know the half of it. Gimme five minutes and I'll return you to the wild."

We go to his office. A maze. Everything's white. Even the rugs. Weire is a good guy. About thirty-five, dark hair, eyes set close together. Five nine, maybe 150 pounds, his skin is a bright dark red so at first you don't notice that blood vessels have begun to surface and break on the sides of his nose and top of his cheeks. He has the quick movements of a bird and perhaps because he talks so much he reminds me of Heckle and Jeckle, the cartoon crows.

With a two-million-dollar house on the beach in Kahala and a flat stomach when he thinks about it, Weire credits his success to the fact he can't tell right from wrong. He came to Hawaii while in the air force working for the judge advocate corps. His specialty is influence peddling and wheel greasing and he portrays himself as just another chipper minion of business as usual. He's been Frank's attorney for years.

He says he's way too busy, greensheeted to the moon, that he's being sued for malpractice by some hypo who says he's a part-time Puerto Rican for the FBI. Then he wants to know why I was after the Oman Egg and when I tell him for $50,000, he says, "Frank was paying you $50,000 to play messenger boy? To carry film?"

"Yeah. I wonder who actually owned it."

Weire squares his tie and says that's not the issue, that I worry about the wrong stuff—"You're the guy who steps off the boxcar at Auschwitz and says, 'Bitchen showers, but too many heebs.'"

I say I need some money. Weire says what's some money

and I say the $50,000 Frank isn't going to pay me, in order to buy our way out of Less Nervous.

"Why not just leave?"

"Because I spent all my pocket trust last year rebuilding the bar and buying the Love Machines and redecorating the Nancy Spungeon Room."

"Why not just take the Love Machines and cut your losses on everything else? Just get out of there."

"Because I don't own them, that holographic shit costs a fortune—I put in $30,000, Maye put in $45,000 and she has the pink slip. To get the title to the Love Machines so I can sell them I'd have to pay her $45,000. Plus I owe her for the shitty job we did using her money to redecorate the bar last year, hanging the A-bomb and stuff, and she's mad because I wouldn't sign a lease."

"So you need the $50,000 Frank promised you to pay Maye off so you can grab the Love Machines and beat it." Weire laughs out loud. "Talk about curing cancer with aspirin. Crawford, do the math. If you owe her $45,000 for the Love Machines, and owe another God knows how much in back rent and even more for the redecorating, she's not going to let you just pick up and go. She's gonna keep you pinned to that place like white on rice."

"Maybe she'd just square with Jan and Dean."

"Give you title and let you sell the machines? You get the machines, she gets Jan. That sounds cool. Jan, psycho Disneyland, as collateral."

I say, come on, he's just a little manic-depressive, and Weire replies, "Face it, Jan and Dean isn't *together* enough to be manic-depressive. Crawford, a stupid question—but this old lady is rich. What's $50,000 from you one way or the other?"

"She says I owe her, she's had a couple of strokes. Maybe she fixates."

"Why not get Frank to pay this off?—No, wait! I'll answer that one. Frank doesn't exist to solve your problems. He told me that. Wait a second." He picks up his phone and says, "Let's get this from the horse's mouth." He dials, waits, says, "Jan. Guyfriendbuddypal you owe me money. Your divorce, remember?" Then: "No, we're not a large impersonal firm, we're a small impersonal firm." Looking to the ceiling he offers, "Arbeit macht frei," and then to me: "You and I, we'll go and see what the old lady wants. Doubtless the world."

Her hair looks made of yellow wires and her voice is hoarse.

"They should never have launched in that weather. It was raining so hard you had to put your hand over your face to breathe. When the thing blew up it was the sound of hell exploding. It sent out a wave that was huge and haystacking. I was afraid of going over myself. My Lewis, a sailor of years and years, yelled, 'We have had it.' My stomach was gripped with that beautiful acid of fear. I saw your mother hanging onto the railing, her knuckles white as a star.

"That rocket ship was the first thing your brother really fucked up. And there'll still be hell to pay for it."

We are in Maye's office at the top floor of the Continental Hotel in Waikiki. It is dusk and twenty stories below, the beach recedes toward Diamond Head in a long smoky curve.

"That New Island scheme of his." She puts a sausage finger to the window and says, "Look at those things." I do. The long pipes. Their eight-story concrete forms rise in the sky in front of Pearl Harbor in a way that suggests giants have landed among us.

Maye doesn't look well. Her ankles are as thick as her neck and she has bad psoriasis sores on legs smeared white with salve. "What could have possessed him?" she wants to know.

She listens to my explanation, says, "My God," and then, for some reason she asks what I got in trouble for in Mexico the first time. I say kidneys and ammo.

Then she tells me about the hotel she'll build across from Less Nervous. Fourteen hundred rooms using x thousand feet of seismic steel, y thousand tons of concrete, and a forest of teak.

I say wow and she pulls open a desk drawer and lifts a stack of papers so thick they make her old hands shake from their weight.

"This," she says, "is a phone bill for $562,991.37. For one month, Haole boy. Frank's got a gizmo in a vault out at Big Store that hums, chirps, and says 'my my' now and then, that's not human but bills through my office and, according to what I see here, spends twenty-four hours a day calling up every bank in the world."

I am listening but looking at a model of her hotel mounted on a table next to her desk. It was built big but now it is bigger. It has expanded to the size of a superblock and it appears it will occupy the space now—my, oh, my—occupied by Less Nervous.

"Tod," Maye says, "You know nothing about facts. You just gave me your version of Frank's island and you do not understand it. Not the engineering of it, the cost of it, or the why of it, nothing."

"Yes, I do." I'm looking at her model. Yes, definitely, she'll need our space.

"You tell people your grandfather invented the critical path method. That, sonnyboy, he did not do." Suddenly she lets loose a lung-retching cough with so much force to it that it is as if she is being kicked from the inside. Her face brightens, pales. She reaches for a tissue, puts it to her mouth, and for a moment wears the tissue like a mask. What's the critical path got to do with anything?

I ask her if she is all right. She says, perfectly.

She says she remembers me as a boy, that I was considerate, lonely, then she adds, after coughing again—but softly— "You don't know who you are or where you came from."

"Maye," Weire says, "deal for you: Give the kid $50,000 for what he's got tied up in the bar and let him out of there."

"I got a better deal for me: he gives me $100,000 for what I've got tied up in that piss bucket and I agree not to sue him for vandalism. Meanwhile I want this boy right where I can see him."

Seeing me, I assume clearly, she says, "Tell me: What's your brother really up to?" Maye's old moonface is bloodless and littered with the shadows of leaves from a plant she keeps in a pot by her desk.

And when I say I don't know, she says, "Frank's running that crap shoot he calls a construction company like a Ponzi scheme. He's not buying down his debts and the way he's hanging money out everywhere he's bilking himself out of millions. The New Island is a spoiled brat's pipe dream, and the way things are going, sonny, you'll be on Shit Street with your palm out by Easter."

I stand there, looking at this bigger model. Frank says it doesn't matter if you're Jesus Christ or the Bitch of Buchenwald, all it takes to make it in this world is one great idea. I think I've got mine.

Maye has more things to say, but I have to take a leak and I leave Maye with Weire, go down the hall to the men's room happy to be pissing outside the immediate bracket of her muse.

16 FEBRUARY

Mask of Smiles. No originals. The Batlatters sell one of nothing.

I peer through the gallery's window at photographs framed and containing no images, only degrees of dark and light, and see myself going hat in hand to Robin and Rickie Batlatter. They are big, young, dark, more like a confident and athletic brother and sister than man and wife. There's something unsettling in their strapping androgyny and their taste: the work they show is either very slick and nonthreatening or just bombastic and wild and, at best, incomprehensible in an interesting way. Masks of Smiles in New York, LA, London, you name it. The Batlatters make careers.

I walk into Less Nervous under the evaporative air conditioning above the front door. Nozzles above the door spray water in a cold stream over me as I enter. Behind the bar, Roberta, plucking beer glasses out of the dishwasher, says Frank just called and he's coming down for a heart-to-heart. Perfect.

Less Nervous should be a gold mine. Instead, wedged amid Waikiki's angular hodgepodge of huge new superhotels and leftover nightclubs and convenience stores, it remains an idiot miracle of indecision. Above me, a skylight. Its wire-meshed glass is opaque with dirt that casts a dilute slab of light on the bomb that hangs from the ceiling on thick link chains that look like they came from some long-ago nightmare century. The bomb is empty, the shell of a Little Boy like they dropped on Hiroshima. Jan and Dean has spelled out TO BELIEVE IS TO CARE. TO CARE IS TO DO, in black duct tape across its gray metal hide. On the walls there are paintings. Most by artists who have abandoned the real for the abstract due to poor hand-eye coordination.

Two chubby, white, marshmallow-legged tourists sit at the bar, fingering wine coolers. Fingering is Frank's best idea, it makes cash nothing and removes a last physical impediment to purchase—namely reaching for your wallet—but they are not registering on Jan's Apple Midas. When they pick up the glasses, their fingerprints are supposed to register who they are, what they've got in their credit accounts, and subtract the price of wine coolers, but I can see from here it's not happening.

This place is a mess. Jan and Dean has left his dirty laundry, most of his clothes—plaid swingeasies, a half-dozen T-shirts, and a couple pair of jeans—on the pool table. Maybe half of what he owns. His life could fit in a box.

"Good fun, Crawford," Roberta chirps, her big eyes bright. "I fired the Bud mokes."

Behind the bar, under a sign that reads BEER, IT'S NOT JUST FOR BREAKFAST ANYMORE, is the rest of Jan's estate. Ten kegs of unpaid-for Budweiser. A reliable sucker for almost any kind of sales pitch, Jan has bought tons of restaurant equipment over the years. But now he owns only what he sells.

"Guess what else?" Roberta asks, "Frank's on his way down and I could tell by his voice on the phone that when you two meet, Crawford, it's going to be fun to watch."

I sit at the bar making constellations—Pegasus, Orion, the Big Dipper—with pocket change. Fucking Frank. I should be here turning the Black Hole of Honolulu into a money machine or, at the very least, figuring out how to con the Batlatters into a show for me, so I can start a real life. Failing at that, I think about clothes. I have no sense of property. I lose them or loan them out and forget to whom. I need to learn how to own things.

Beside me Celia Berger picks up her pitcher of beer and pours. She hasn't finished what she's got and there's an inverted explosion in her glass. Celia's orange hair is ratted to a circle and her hands are so dirty you can see her fingerprints. She's our garbage woman, has a face I'm sure used to be pretty, and claims to have had sex with famous men. She drops by afternoons to bend Jan's ear and to listen to the two of them, you'd think they were trading all-star whore stories with Taki Theodoracopulos at Xenon.

I walk over to the open front doors and watch the breakers off Waikiki Beach swell up and collapse on themselves.

After minutes I see Frank coming. His Zero whips off Kalakua in a silver jolt and I listen to the alternate mutter and roar of its engine as he parks out back.

When he comes in he stares at me with headlight eyes. "What are you doing here?"

I say, "Not violating my probation."

"Didn't I tell you to stay on the mainland?"

"That's not your business."

He says, "My business is what I pay for. Come on."

He moves past me to the front doors. Frank is tall and made of angles. His face is striking enough to be in advertisements, though in some light it looks like a stone sculpture carved out and buffed too fast.

Ambitious, he takes up a lot of space in any room. I'm not big on standing too close to him from a childhood fear of being unexpectedly hit. I grew up thinking that if Frank said the sun was going to blow up tomorrow, best go buy a pair of Ray Bans.

I follow him out to his car and he says, "Get in."

The carbon-carbon Zero is gorgeous. Rebuilt from the ground up, it resembles a stiletto melted over four wheels. He's doubled the horsepower and removed all the emissions equipment. He says having catalytic converters on a race car makes as much sense as wearing a G-string in a nudist camp and when he gets tickets because the car can't pass smog he tears them up and forgets about it. Frank pretty much exists above the law.

The car screams east down Kalakua, down Paokalini, and down the Ala Wai Canal and into the hills, where Frank says, "If whoever went through your room in Mexico City was the cops then I'm a girl, but if the cops are after you, forget about it. It's one thing running all over Lake Tahoe and LA, but you won't last three days on the street in Honolulu, buddyboy."

I ask, "Where are we going?"

"You figure it out." He twists the steering wheel in his hands as we whip through a tunnel above Kailua. "You got a weakness," he says. "Zero judgment. What are you planning to do?"

"Help Jan and Dean with the restaurant."

"Dig up the corpse and force it to move its arms and legs."

"A corpse sitting on one of the most valuable pieces of property on earth."

"What's that supposed to mean?"

"It means I saw Maye's model of the new hotel she's building—she's supersizing it—the east side will be extended right over where Less Nervous is now."

"So?"

"So what if we stay instead of go?"

Frank downshifts. "You don't know who you're dealing with." The exhaust crackles as we decelerate toward the first traffic light in Kailua. There we are. Below the hulk of Puu Konahuani, a green and dark steaming jungleland which as a boy, I'd imagined as the last secret place for lost lizards and reptiles, the monster iguanodon and duck-billed anatosaurus. I know where we are going now. On the horizon I see a huge mushroom-shaped cloud that could be a freeze frame from a thermonuclear blast.

My brother says, "Let's call things by their right names."

We are still in the Zero, parked in his driveway. His property overlooks a curving expanse of cream white beach. Waves bump up suddenly, crest, and detonate to white foam at the shorebreak. The water is blue-green and transparent for sixty feet.

"Less Nervous is garbage. First of all, Jan's got nobody in there but a bunch of hopheads chewing on each other's knuckles. Second of all, if you two think Maye Hona is going to sit still for this—because, spare me the details, but I know what you're thinking—Jesus. She's a thug and her sons are worse."

Frank rubs a small blemish on the side of his dark neck as if it were delible. His hair is dry, straight, and combed back, a cut suggestive of motion. We look alike, though he is taller and has lines around his eyes that could have been put there with a knife.

"No," he says, "what you do is go back to Celestial City for another Egg. And this time you get it back."

I get out of the car, go in the house. Outside, its stained-wood walls are grey and veined with bright long curling plants. A tendril of one has grown to a question mark around the front door.

Inside, I smell the perfume of rough-cut wood. My brother pulls off his black cowboy boots, drops his shirt on the couch, goes to the bar, and shoots water into a glass. His chest is white, his arms brown to a line above his elbows. The tan on his forearms looks like a pair of long brown gloves.

The house is normal but without bedrooms. I follow him down the hall into his office made out of the den. A window, floor to ceiling, fronts a beach so close it looks as if a high tide could slam water across his carpet. Cross-stitched on a sampler hanging by the door are the words

It's not who you know
or who you blow
but who you beat
and who you eat.

Frank wants to know if I'm taking my medication and when I ask what difference does it make he says, "Two years' worth if they haul you in for a urinalysis."

He is going through his desk drawers, looking for something. Above this desk is what appears to be an abstract oil painting of an amoeba. It is, however, a schematic of the island of Oahu, the place where we live, and it is measled with tiny dots of red, each representing a piece of land owned, leased, or optioned by Frank. The red dots are everywhere. With the exception of the Bishop estate and a couple of the other Mukka Mutha landholders Frank is the biggest player on the board.

I follow my brother out to the garage. Frank can go from Alias to robot right here, design a chassis on the monitor and instruct the steel Chassis-Maker to build it on the spot. Tom Weire says computer and machine are going to apply to the graduate school of mechanical engineering at MIT, and maybe even join a fraternity.

Frank says the words *The family is a court of justice that never shuts down for night or day* in front of the door and it opens, putting a wedge of light on another two of his cars, a red P4 Ferrari powered by a supercharged Ford F1 racing engine and a 1964 Ford lightweight stocker in which Frank has installed a turbocharged 502 Chevy V-8.

The reason we are here is that Frank's hobby is collecting Red Chinese money. By the box. He lifts a crate of it to his shoulder and takes it back outside to the Zero.

We drive to his office. At Big Store Frank says *An age is over when it has exhausted its illusions* and titanium doors slide apart. All the locks in Frank's universe are coded audible. A system my dad was working on when he drowned. He takes the crate of yuan notes, tells one of his managers to turn it into dollars, and we go upstairs. His office is large and almost empty except for a desk and the stuffed corpse of his beloved double-crown winner, Shining Path, standing on its hind legs.

Frank is a cartographer and has redesigned the world, replacing the outdated system of longitude and latitude with a modern grid of his own. On grid 1999 rests the "epicenter" of what will be the New Island. The result of Frank having simply noted, again, the obvious: that just south of the Big Island lies an underwater canyon, its floor less than a mile below the surface.

I don't know the details—(In Maye Hona's office it was insulting: She said I wouldn't know a mango from a papaya, a rocket from a bomb, that all parts of life—biology, geology, geography, law, language, space, time, the spelling of the street on which I lived—were a complete mystery to me. Yeah, what I know and what I don't know is very important to me, but liarly Avek et cetera notwithstanding, that's ridiculous, and what made it worse was that she did not say it in an insulting way, but as if she cared for me. It was like my state of mind was a scary disease)—but there is a geologic hot spot whose ceiling is only a few hundred or thousand feet below the surface of one canyon ridge or on the canyon floor. Frank discovered this by accident reading an *Audubon* story about a weird colony of underwater life that flourished wherever the lava was closest to the surface. So all he did was hire some divers and send them down to take the temperatures of the ocean bottom in the area and, sure enough, it was five to twenty-two degrees warmer there than anywhere else.

Then he added two and two, hired more divers—Russian mohole men, who set off an explosive, timed and measured the shock wave, and determined that a huge vein of magma was bubbling right along there only about 1,300 feet below. From there a new paradise is about to squirt.

Frank is macro, not micro, hates bureaucracy, sycophants, and coat holders. The only people in his office are those in the photographs on his long walls: pictures of our male lineage back to my great-great-grandfather, a carpenter who came to Hawaii by way of Australia and waited ten years before meeting a white woman—a six-foot-tall missionary schoolmarm from Seattle—to marry. His only son established the island's fist lumberyard and his oldest boy, my great-grandfather, realized that while Hawaii was expensive the sky was free. Expanding the lumberyard into a construction company, he built the first buildings in the Hawaiian Islands above ten, twenty, and finally thirty stories. As well as most of the military housing out at Pearl City, Hickam as well. His son, my grandfather, went into the U.S. Army Air Corps.

Frank has a photo of my grandpa with Ed Teller and Stanislaw Ulam. My granddad served with the Twentieth Air Force. As an advisor on Curtis LeMay's staff, his studies convinced the general that the Japanese had no effective small-caliber antiaircraft weapons. His discovery led to the low-level fire bombing of the Japanese mainland by B-29s. After the war he was hired by Los Alamos and got the idea to levitate the cores of the primary fission stage of a hydrogen bomb. Instead of having high-explosive lenses pushing directly on the bomb's core he figured why not levitate the core and line the lenses with tamper material made of beryllium, so on detonation the tamper hammered the core, requiring much-less-high explosives. He filled primary cores with glass beads containing tritium gas, boosting the weapons' power and making their yields adjustable.

When my grandfather left the air force he returned to Crawford Construction, but it was my father who really made it boom. In 1978 he put up more square footage than any other private construction firm in the United States.

There's another photo on the wall, taken years later, of my granddad and my father standing by a drawing of his Proteus launch vehicle. It is massive—lots taller than a man even at one-thirty-second scale. The Proteus was to have been their crowning achievement. It was a sea-launched, three-stage rocket eighty feet in diameter at its base, many times the size of the Saturn 5 rockets that put us on the moon, and able to launch Kansas into low earth orbit. The main boosters on the first stage were fueled by liquid oxygen and hydrogen—their combustion created an immense jet of pure steam. Strapped around the first stage were eighteen solid-fuel side boosters. The picture was taken after my granddad had supervised completion of a plan for a manned Mars mission. A plan that would have used the Proteus as its workhorse.

The first-stage explosion at the rocket's launch changed all that. Just after huge white light ploughed sideways in the sky I was coptered off the boat. The next day when Frank showed up at the house in Kailua where I'd been left with the maid, I got the news. I knew their sailboat had been closer to the blast than the *Gogol*, and when he came through the front door I asked about Mother and Dad. When he didn't say anything I asked if they were dead and he said, "Sure."

In our family each first son does more than the last and Frank is doing the most. He took over after my dad drowned when the Proteus exploded. On one side of his office there is another row of pictures. Frank a quarterback in high school. Frank with one of his hot rods—Sudden Death, a 1949 Ford. He used to race before he went off to the Air Force Academy. In the photo the front fenders and hood of the car have been removed. Sudden Death cradles a blown and injected 454-cubic-inch Chevy V-8 on its skeletal frame. It looks delicate, but isn't. Frank had built structure all around the front end so he could take a head-on at 120 and survive. There are three other pictures. Frank in uniform at the Air Force Academy and at the war college. Frank beside the stealthy fiber-epoxy-bodied Have Slick air-to-ground "shotgun shell" missile: he was its program element manager at the Pentagon; it could fly at Mach 1.6 and drop 1,200 pounds of "submunitions" along a twenty-mile track. And a new one: Frank in khakis beside Joe Dozer, a machine designed to bite buildings apart at the base the way a beaver cuts apart a tree.

He sees me looking at it and says, "Twenty million dollars' worth of licensing fees right out of Tokyo's pocket. The real world. Meantime, you're pissing off people I do business with. We're partners with the Honas in endless deals."

"I want my money, Frank."

"What money would that be?"

"The money due me from the will."

"*I* am the will," my brother informs. "We're in league with the devil and I'll fix him. But it'll take time and not Less Nervous."

Huh? I watch as Frank reaches to the console on his desk, calls up his Mind, then continues.

"When I first met Jan and Dean he was fifteen and dripping his acne into a cheeseburger at the Kahului Burger King. He hit me up for $35 to start a biotech business and blew the money on a .38 instead. Then he spent a couple of years running around telling people he was being followed around by CIA agents disguised as his parents."

I say Frank and he says don't Frank me. "I've been subsidizing his romanticism for twenty-five years. Enough's enough. One of these days you'll go home and find him chewing on his washcloth and screaming for the Mothership. I mean, explain to me: How can you own a nightclub in the middle of the biggest tourist trap on earth and still do nothing but lose money?"

I start to say something and Frank puts up a hand. "Only if you've got the touch of shit. You gotta learn to tell the difference between opportunity and chump change. I'm not the Tooth Fairy. I pay you good money just to keep your head up your ass and you can't even do that. So I think it'll be off to Heaven, where at least I can keep track of you nine to five."

I say, "No way. I hate Heaven."

"Then you fly back and pick up another Egg."

I tell him, correction, I'm going to get the Honas to pay Jan and Dean and me good money and Frank says, while I am wondering what it would take to kill him, "Fat chance. You haven't got the guts."

17 FEBRUARY

August bites. And afterward, not an hour later, Dewey comes in and says, "Brah, I want you gone."

I say, dream on. "If your mother wanted us out of here she shouldn't have sent your brother in here with that lease."

"Which Jan refused to sign."

"Three months ago. He sure as shit signed it this morning. August did too. Right here. All three signatures. Jan's, August's, your mother's. Seven years, Dewey. Your mother wanted us, she's got us."

"So you and that brain cell Jan and Dean extort x number of dollars from my mother, then you can lose Frank too. Makes sense. The only question I have is: What'll it take you to vacate?"

I shrug. "A million cash?"

18 FEBRUARY

Teenage Cut Grunts from Second Battalion Special Ops Nine Corps egging them on, Kuzaki fistfight in Japanese, toe to toe, punching each other in a fresh vicious Oriental boxing style and screaming before I can lay in with a pool cue and—whack! whack! whack! nine from the sky—get everybody to relax and listen to reason.

This should be easier than it is. All we have to do is whatever it takes to get tourists from Two Car Garage Minnesota through the front door to buy beer for ten times what we paid for it. The lease agreement is unambiguous, the Honas would have a better chance of putting a K-Mart in the Vatican than they do of putting a superblock on this property so long as we meet our payment schedule. But Jan and Dean is circumspect: "Dewey's not going to fuck around. We're going to end up with our butts floating off our bones on the bottom of the Ala Wai Canal."

At ten we had Harriet Morsel on synth and Jan paid Gas House $500 to asphyxiate the crowd. Roach exterminators by day, Gas House pulled up in a mail truck with Kill Kwik written across the back, ran hoses inside and then it was sit or drop. They leech oxygen out of the air or pump cyanide into it, I don't know which and Gas House won't tell me. They fear patent infringement. It was good fun, but we're not doing it again.

A sun-fried touristy girl, wearing so much mascara it looked like a butterfly was perched on the bridge of her nose, hit her head on the bar and Roberta and I had to take her down to Doc in a Box. The crow at Admitting was nasty, told us we'd have to wait, and Roberta said, "Unbitchify your minimind, this girl could have a fractured skull." The nurse said go sit down and Roberta said, "Get her a doctor or I start screaming," and the doctors got rolling, but all in all last night I got three hours' sleep. I was out in the water at daybreak.

I've got a new undingable carbon-carbon six-finned/razor-skegged Bad Magic long board and paddling out I could see more skyscraper forms of long pipes down toward Pearl Harbor. Preparations to create the New Island. It's amazing no one thought of doing this before. Tap into that right and we got a whole new place. Frank says maybe worth *more* than $50 billion. He says $50 billion may be just our cash up front. In fact, that if $50 billion were to be all we got, it wouldn't be worth his time to do the paperwork.

The outer breaks at Twos and Threes range from flat-as-a-floor all the way up to gentle, and inside Queens is a lumberyard, the waves formless and closing out, and I'm out of the water an hour after sunup, walking warm sand looking across Kalakua at the ACTION KILLS FEAR graffito scrawled over the front door of Less Nervous when I hear a somebody shouting my name. It's Roberta, shiny brown legs slashing out of the shorebreak. Pushing black wet hair behind her ears she trots toward me. "Biggerize your brain," she instructs. "I swam halfway to Queens shouting after you and you never even heard me." I let the weight of the Bad Magic rest on my hip and say, "What are you doing out so early?"

Roberta slips fingers under either side of the elastic hem of her bikini bottom, lifting the fabric to reveal slivers of slick white skin, and then she lets the elastic snap back. "Work for me next Friday night," she says. "I've got tickets for + = + at the Shell."

I say, "Let me think," and she steps back and says, "Crawford."

Roberta is evolving. The pale fabric of her wet bikini bottom is cleaved at the center. Her crotch has let's continue the race written all over it. I say sure, and she says Kaptain Krunch at my house if you want. I say maybe, and she's off. As she retreats I see fine commas of down on the slick hollow of her back.

More young Nine Corps Cut Grunts belly to the bar in red berets and full camo gear flashing phony IDs with a new Humvee trailering a six-warhead Soviet mini-MIRV parked out back. I need more sleep. Because I think, I hope, that was a dream. They come in in full camo gear, young, mean, some kind of new special forces—and I have to deal with them.

They are arrogant, loud, and too well exercised. And what's scary is now—since the army either unionized or failed to unionize, I forget which—you can rent them the same way you'd go to a garden store and rent a weedwhacker or a lawnmower. Big construction firms on the mainland are supposedly hiring them up by the platoon for security on inner city "reurbanization" projects and the only big issue is what weapons they are allowed to carry.

Oh well.

Vince is stuck working a double shift at his new day job— towel boy at the Aerovapor Steam Baths—and tonight I'll have to work four 'til closing. The Ice Age is wearing on me. Last night some dribble-chinned mahu congratulated me for beaning the Kuzakis and asked how do I defend myself. I'm five eleven and weight 165 pounds. If I ever waited to *defend* myself around here I'd be dead in a week.

19 FEBRUARY

First light. A ribbon-cutting ceremony at the Kamkua cemetery. Though Frank is big into Unisom/Microsoft, Capital Cities, and whatever is left of NBC News, he says our future may be less with information than with the dead. We stand before a long rolling carpet of grass that pales in the bright early-morning fog as the hearse rolls up. Inside, my psychotherapist Wally Rice's father, Vernon, the first of an entire population to be biointerred. Vernon was high inside in "Big Science" and the service has attracted communication and defense people.

Wally—a jumpy, loving man—is with his older brother, State Senator Bill Rice. Bill has TV hair and looks like a two-by-four but he's crafty. Frank finessed Bill's expansion of his district to include half of the neighboring district as well, so they are friends. And Rice, who would like to be president of the United States but who—because he's currently under investigation by the attorney general's office for racketeering, conspiracy, extortion, money laundering, and election fraud—may have to gerrymander his ambitions (fat cat seems to be his goal of the moment), is looking to my brother for seed money to slide private.

Frank makes good use of his time so the funeral is attended too by a delegation of TV executives from Tokyo. Frank is making "beyond lifetime" deals with the Japanese media, he's got money up front for hit series from people who haven't even been born yet.

Also there are members of the board of Deutsche Aerospace. In the nineties, my brother was the first to turn the hunted into the hunter in a way pilots had been trying to do since the invention of killing men in the air. Flying a Rockwell/Deutsche Aerospace X-31 over Edwards Air Force Base, he aimed the jet straight up to the noontime sun, then jerked it over on its tail. The air slamming against the plate of its undercarriage threw the plane into a stall and Frank rolled the X-31 over, aimed the nose to the world, and came screaming back in the direction he'd just come from, all within a turning radius of 200 feet.

Frank is a bunch of the money behind the "commercial" application of the plane—his great idea: (A) Dumb it down. Make the controls no more complicated than those from Nintendo. Make it "drive" like a car. (B) Tech it up. Go biomimetic. Use post-Egg technology to create armor out of rat's teeth—rods of a calcium compound embedded in the fibrous protein collagen so that it would take God's own fist to knock it out of the sky.

Wearing dark glasses, Frank speaks only briefly. Before a gory rising sun he reminds the bereaved that the twentieth century was a disaster, that aside from TV about all anybody got out of it was penicillin, pantyhose, and Adolf Hitler, then he remembers Vernon Rice as a visionary's visionary. The deceased, in a simple black coffin, is planted in the ground.

Planted is, I guess, the word. For neither Rice nor the coffin will be buried for any eternity. My brother is also a bunch of the money behind the basic ashes to ashes, dust to dust "deconsumption," based on a virus that will turn Rice's remains to soil. The dead, because they keep taking up more and more space, represent what Frank has defined as "high-end consumers in reverse."

The first big new important market of our new millennium.

After the final interment, Frank talks with a well-dressed old Soviet, who buys a lot of syndication stuff—reruns, mostly. Over there in the former republics, the American Oughts are too hip for the room. TVwise Ukraine, Russia, Kazakhstan, et al. are late 1970s early 1980s cultures, and the guy wants to cut a deal for *Miami Vice*–type shoot-her-or-fuck-her-or-I'll-change-the-channel dressy violence stuff, and Frank, who respects the dead, says enough is enough and copters us home.

Wally is strapped in back.

He's still upset—he really loved his dad—and he does what he usually does when he is upset, he tries to go to work. "Tod," he says over the blast from the rotors, "how've you been sleeping?"

Wally, who has a booze problem, provides one-stop shopping for sanity, and he's not greedy. With money so crazy now and everyone being into barter, in a pinch he trades me trans-actual analysis for vodka zombies. Back when I could still serve the public I would stand behind the bar at Less Nervous layering red, green, blue, and yellow liquors in a tall glass in front of him while he asked me questions like: "Why is it you are afraid to get out of bed in the morning?"

Now, out of sorts, tears still in his eyes, he asks me to describe my dreams.

"Mostly," I say, "they are nightmares."

"What about?"

Frank swings the copter up in the air, rotating the tail as we ascend so that, looking down at the grass and palms, I have the momentary illusion that the world is spinning out of control.

"Usually," I reply, "about being hunted down, trapped, and about to be killed. Sometimes, though, just about having my fingers, hands, arms, feet, and legs chopped off."

"Who does the chopping?" Wally wants to know.

"Usually I do."

"Frank?"

"What?" my brother asks.

"What kind of nightmares do you have?"

"Am I paying you for this?"

"I'm just asking."

"I don't have nightmares," my brother allows, "because I do not dream."

20 FEBRUARY

In our baggy chrome cloth swim trunks, walking down Paokalini, Jan and Dean and I are going to break into Roberta's. A clapboard hutch, part of a fourplex, a short picket fence surrounds it. The fence's bare wood is mottled here and there with cracked and curling strips of ancient white paint. Four-by-four posts rotting, it relaxes toward the grass. A baby is crawling around the weedy oblong front yard, its legs and arms jerking like a filthy mechanical cherub.

We walk, as though we belong here, across the little front yard. The roof far overhangs the walls and lavender wisteria blossoms fall from the eaves in flames. It is like looking into the burning mouth of a cave. A pie-faced girl steps down from the porch and picks up the baby. She's about ten and wears a brown dress or smock. Her hair hangs in strings.

The other half. These people weren't doing a shoddy imitation of poverty like Jan and Dean and me. This was the real thing.

Jan just got an eviction notice for Less Nervous and seems to think it means something. Now he's looking for his gun. Roberta's got it, she took it home after he lost his license to conceal. Jan is still angry with the city, upset because the police won't let him carry a Colt Python stuffed in his underpants anymore now that he really "needs" it.

We go around back where Roberta lives in an apartment she shares with three other girls.

"Tell you something," he says as we walk into the shadow of the side of the house, "you better get your Egg money from Frank. We gotta pay rent."

I try to look in the square window of the fourplex but it is opaque with dust. Someone has written a review of a local radio station—KPOI SUCKS—through the dirt. At night it's like hanging by the monkey cage at the zoo during a full moon.

Jan tells me we should have brought a screwdriver but when

we get to Roberta's door there is no breaking-in to do. It is open. I say, "Roberta," but there is no answer. She's not there. The room smells nice, it has a perfumy scent I can't quite recognize.

The walls are lined floor to ceiling with paperbacks, everything from *Cannery Row* to *Come Back, Dr. Caligari*.

Jan starts rooting around, looking for the revolver. He finds it under Roberta's little pallet of a mattress.

He holds the Python up between us. It is big. "When the Honas start fucking with us, guess what, Fauntleroy?"

Jan needs to live in a world of threats, and when I tell him that the Honas' eviction notice is worth about as much as a bunch of counterfeit Confederate money, he replies, "Try this on for size. One round from this thing—it goes through the guy, goes through the wall behind him, shoots through a wall across the street, and blows the head off a lady reading *TV Guide*."

As we are leaving, I recognize the perfume. It is the smell of books. Most of them doctor-related. I slide one out. *The Essentials of Surgery Illustrated.* Key disembowelings. Roberta has vowed to become the me that I didn't: a medical student.

Jan and Dean puts a hand on my arm. "If you don't get the Egg money, Fauntleroy, we're fucked."

When I reply that paying the rent is not my responsibility but his, Jan is enraged. "You're just hiding behind the skirts of me not knowing what I'm doing."

"What does that mean?"

"If we lose Less Nervous you'll say it wasn't your fault."

21 FEBRUARY

Jan and Dean has bet heavy on hallucinations. He has bought the latest in expensive lit vids and sex machines and the latter riles people up. Some yo-yo sneaked in with a Hot Stick and sent a flaming rod of hydrogen crashing into the bottles above the bar, it was a goddamned lightening bolt and three tourists were cut by glass and two of Frank's mohole men— just a couple a guys peacefully pounding down vodka zombies and staring at Mister Real—got burns across their chests and arms that looked as big as shark bites.

A terrible day yesterday. As usual we were short-handed. Because of my record I cannot serve the public, all I can do is bounce—check ID and prepare the Nutrient Slush.

Lunch was okay, tourists and the university crowd eating, playing the new lit vids "Uncle Vanya," "Ball Four," and "The Story of O" in the Nancy Spungeon Room. But by midnight I was trying to separate a bunch of Frank's Russian mohole men—engineers here to build the New Island and not getting an excellent first impression of the Land of the Free— from sex-machined Drastic Plastics who had gone insane.

It's depressing. We should have a gold mine. A goddamn 3,500-square-foot nightclub in the heart of Waikiki beach. If I can't launch a life off an opportunity like Less Nervous, what is wrong with me?

I have to get something going. I'm afraid I'm reaching the unbreachable limits of my abilities photographywise. At Mask of Smiles the Batlatters accuse me of throwing a tantrum when I say they were not interested in artists but just overpriced illustrators and stunt men after they said they wouldn't give me a show because why buy a pig in a poke?

Leaving, I walk a block then just stand on the corner, defeated, a barely tethered buoy in a river of Japanese tourists. I finger a newspaper—there's a blind item in the *Star:* Frank's attempting a leveraged buyout of the nation's blood supply.

I eat breakfast on a picnic table outside at the Marketplace. White rice, fried eggs, and Portuguese sausage. One of the Batlatters—I'm so confused I can't remember which it was— said I was nothing but "a slick vulgarian."

The sun is on my back, too hot. Fifty-fifty the earth is falling from its orbit. I walk down to the beach, walk the flat glassy sand washed by the foamy white skirts of tidewater surging to the shore, past a man on the beach who has long wet hair tied back in a ponytail and is gouging the ominous, primal signs of the Zodiac into the sand with a stick. I ask if he'd like to sell it.

He looks up and says, "Five bucks." He's sunburned and has delicate blisters on his shoulders. Like soap bubbles made of skin.

I'm not some alienated artistic type who goes around scrawling 666 on the side of shopping malls, but I like things I can use to protect myself so I give him three dollars, all that's in the pocket of my trunks. It's a fat wand covered with raised lines that leave marks on my palms like peace symbols or chicken tracks if I grip it too tight. I play with it, dragging and stabbing my name into the sand, sit out on the beach until I see my shoulders are maroon and I feel myself about to cry.

22 FEBRUARY

White and alone on a plain beneath the misty wrinkled grey-green Kalini Mountains, the slaughterhouse has risen like a cathedral. Meat for the New Island. Workers stand on scaffolding four stories high. Inside, narrow windows cut light into slabs and, looking up, I expect to see some old bearded dervish hanging from a pulley painting creation between the steel ribs of the ceiling.

Frank is macro and designed the place to kill 800 cattle a day. He has discovered an essential truth to cattle ranching: lobotomy. By severing the frontal lobes of our cows and feeding them mindless in pens, they have become what they should have been in the first place: meat machines, veal forever.

Conveyors stick like tongues from vast service bays that await the trucks. I can see the future carcasses gliding forward, throats cut and ribboning red. But a problem. Frank has a crane with 180 feet of stand pipe hanging from its hook and only 200 feet of boom to maneuver with, so the thing is just hanging upright next to the building. It must be laid down into this trench but he's only got twenty feet to play with and the field supe is saying he's nuts, the crane will tip over into the trench and he'll never get it out. Ground starts to break away under the crane's right front outrigger. Dust jumps away from the side of the trench. The crane is sinking.

But what Frank does is brilliant. He has a cherry picker—an old flatbed truck with a boom, line, and hook on the back—hook on the other end of the pipe to pull it up so it hangs between the crane and the cherry picker like a long toilet paper tube from two pieces of string. He then has a monster D-9 earthmover drop its blade over the counterweight of the crane, over its butt end, to hold the chassis in place. The cherry picker swings the pipe around and the crane operator—half out of the cab and ready to jump—sets the pipe down. It's amazing. Thirty men standing around going, "Fucking-A."

Five minutes later Frank says to go out to Blue Villa.

"Which," I ask, "is what?"

A condo, he informs, that Crawford & Hona is putting up on the North Shore. "You go out there Thursday, wipe everybody's nose, wrap up the sewage and the drywallers. Get washers, dryers, stoves, and refrigerators in as soon as painters squirt the place. Then Blue Villa goes out the door. We get our money, the Honas get theirs. You run the crew. Finish it so I can get a broker in there."

When I do not reply, he adds, "Blue Villa or Heaven, it's up to you."

I say, "Wouldn't August be running the crew?"

"Not anymore, you're the guy. If he doesn't like it, hand him his lunch pail."

We walk around the great churchlike structure. It's beautiful, unreal. Frank shakes a Marlboro out of the pack in his shirt. "You know the part about me I like best? That I'm almost never wrong."

23 FEBRUARY

I'll give her this, she pays attention. Roberta, with her berry lips and teeth like sugar cubes, stands by Frank's aluminum lozenge of a horse trailer, telling the Fed Ex handler that this isn't a mare any God ever made, when Anastasia, her black eyes as big as eight balls, bolts down the ramp. I'd've been flattened if Roberta hadn't yanked me back, so next I'm on my butt looking at this crazy Russian horse clip-clopping on the runway, her steel-shod hooves flashing over the asphalt like a bunch of butcher knives.

The animal is beautiful, boiled down, and useless as a ballerina. Frank's having us overnight her to the Southwestern States Arabian Show and Sale in Scottsdale. Sadly, Anastasia hates to fly. Roberta, who is great at controlling wildness, has her by the reins and manages to swing her to the loading ramp on the Fed Ex C-5, but, long neck whipping out like a rattler, she bites a loader in the shoulder on her way up, and it's water into wine Anastasia gets more shirt than skin.

Roberta looks angry enough to cry. "You don't put twenty-foot leather reins on a horse like that. It's a dangerous mutant."

"It's not a mutant." I say, "Without the reins you couldn't have got her into the plane."

We walk into the terminal. Roberta glances back at me. "Crawford, your mind is a compact unit. That horse was made in a laboratory." In the airport lounge, she promises, bet on it: one day Frank will get so much going inside of himself he'll explode and if I want to spend thirty years waiting around to get rained on by his blood and guts, that's up to me.

Below us, jet fighters sit parked on a concourse. Deutsche Aerospace partnered with Wal-Mart Ordinance and, using Frank's money, is selling X-31s complete with air, tilt, and cruise, fighters easy to operate as the latest "No Exit" lit vid, so that Third World pilots two generations out of the trees can, as they just have over the Sudan, blow four new French Mirage ATF's out of the sky while losing none of their own.

"A handy example," I say, "of why maybe I should toe some kind of line. Unless I want to be out on the sidewalk."

"You are already," she says.

The waiter appears. Roberta, who credits me with only several of the five senses, says, "The pig is all that's good," and when I order fried wonton she tells the beanpole standing between us, "That's not what he wants, bring him the pig."

24 FEBRUARY

At dawn in the water I'm caught by a cross current. As if behind the surf there was a river running over the sea. I was pulled down to the beach by the Ala Moana Shopping Center. There a bearded brown cherub told me a mad God now rules the ocean.

I walk two miles back to Waikiki. This is where the future

is. Moving west from California and taking a breather here in the middle of the Pacific Ocean.

A cyclone fence that looks like a high strip of gauze boxes the sidewalk in front of the smashed-up Palms Hotel. Sunburned, my skin feels stiff and papery. I stop at Less Nervous, Roberta is already inside, scrubbing blood off the floor with soap and a pillowcase.

I ask her what happened and she says, "Last night. This idiot." The pillowcase is white and brilliant pink. "Weren't you here?"

When I say no she says Jan and Dean owes her for 56 hours and that if I agree to threaten him she'll tell me something strange.

We lock up, walk home by way of the Yamamoto. Out front two reedy whores stand like lost fawns that have wandered out of the woods into a lumber town. Except instead of a lumber town the Yamamoto is, in one huge building, a chunk of Japan.

"Crawford, how shitty would something you knew about Jan and Dean have to be before you would get rid of him?"

"Is that," I ask, "what's strange?"

"No," she replies.

We stand under the marquees for *Rawhide Life* and *Hip Teen Angst*. The shops have American products—cowboy clothing, burgers, wall-length videos of Elvis and Meat Is Murder, and the help is American, but the customers aren't. Because of our crime and violence, if you're not Japanese you need a pass to get inside. This way Japanese tourists can go to America without having to visit it.

The whores teeter on stilt heels in front of the White Gallery. Mr. White, né Hiro Maniguchi, is out front elegantly cadaverous in white linen shirt and black cotton slacks. He is so small that, standing beside him, I feel like Godzilla. He has a sense of humor. After addressing me as Gaijin-san, he asks me if Roberta is "your baby."

Hiro went from Top Ramen Noodles to Lobster Bisque in less than a year. There are fortunes to be made here. All you need is a formula.

He asks me if I have any good new pictures and my lie that I do makes me weightless. Roberta and I get going. "Crawford." She takes my free hand. "I met a guy at the Iliaki this morning who looked like Albert Einstein. He offered me $5,000 to come up to his room. Where he said, 'You'll never be touched.' "

Roberta is wearing Jap flaps, but I am barefoot. I tightrope the shadows cast by the power lines and then walk carefully along the sidewalk, staying on the lightest section of concrete and shifting the Bad Magic from under one arm to the other. "So?"

"I think he's into pictures. He said I had the second best body he's since he's been here and that's two months."

I shift the Bad Magic under my arm. It has autogyros in it and weights as much as a TV set. "What happened with the first best body?"

"She told him to go fuck himself. That's what he said she said when he asked her. Do you think I should do it?"

"Do what?" We walk by the canyon created for the foundation of the Fuchida. Honda Worldmover bulldozers are squaring the corners, pushing around tumbling slews of crushed coral and rock. Dust rises from the hole in ribbons of pastel smoke. "Go up to his room? What if Albert Einstein has a knife or a gun?"

"Look at this," Roberta instructs, gazing into the colossal hole that will soon fill with the huge hotel. When it is finished, most of the suites will be reserved by Japanese. Frank says the Japanese envy America for its bold irrelevance and the reason so many are here is to have good seats to watch Rome burn, but that fiery collapse is contagious and it will incinerate them just as it incinerates us.

At the next corner I walk a white painted stripe that defines the crosswalk. But then there are no more shadows or painted crosswalks or even pale sidewalks and I have to move over hot pavement from one patch of grass and sand to the next, trying to keep the feeling of pain in my feet and out of my head.

Finally, we reach the shade of the apartment's covered carport. Roberta is still thinking about Albert Einstein.

"$5,000 is $5,000," Roberta says.

"To you, maybe." I flip the little door open on our mailbox and find a single envelope inside, addressed to me. Enclosed is a check made out to Zen Rents for my March rent. These checks, mailed by software at Frank's bank, come at the middle of every month. Realistically, I don't think Frank has any idea I could, or would ever have to, actually take care of myself.

Roberta is gone, upstairs I guess. In the arbor, weeds twirling up around the wheels of its trailer, stands Tony's ark. Its hull the brightest yellow I've ever seen. Yesterday he told me the end is near. I aim the Bad Magic up the stairs. I'm paying for the window, though breaking it was almost Jan's fault.

While I was gone he changed the words on the lock from *The secret of life is that it ends* to *The killer awoke before dawn. He put his boots on* without having my voice code in its memory.

Roberta and Jan and Dean are inside watching the Wall. A new Liberty Mutual/Budweiser da-da-mercial. Dead celebrities, morphed alive by Unisom–J. Walter Thompson. I like Ernest Hemingway and Charles de Gaulle as much as anyone, I just don't want them getting drunk and selling me term insurance in my living room. I hit search and get porno. Above my head, the tip of a dick, big as a steamer trunk.

I'm trying to lose this crap just as the Thrash Catholics, Pius X Principle, boot the screen. A woman's ground zero, as tall as I am, flashes away and her moans are drowned by the rip chords of "Ave Maria." The red words I GAVE YOU A DIAMOND, YOU GAVE ME DISEASE, *Pius X Principle* scroll across the twat. A latest bootleg. Local bands without big labels buy energy and blow their message across a channel. Cheap advertising.

There is a flowery insertion as the answering machine makes its panicked mechanical scream, then a voice: *Lieutenant Vorhaggen. Tod, a chauffeur or a bench warrant, your choice.*

I ride my motorcycle downtown. It's an expensive machine—Triumph's first café racer, and I shouldn't have let it sit outside. It doesn't track right and feels like it's shaking itself apart. The seals have gone to dust. Smoke and oil as thick and black as boiling licorice leaks from the head. The color worries me because I think when I poured the oil in new it was a syrupy red.

Instead of going to the cop shop I figure better safe than sorry, so I go to Bernie Elgin's Bike & Car on Kapiolani, where I see Frank's Zero is up on a lift.

"What's it doing down here?" I ask, looking up into the serpentine geometries of suspension, differential, and exhaust.

Bernie, a small, buck-toothed Australian, says, "The transmission gets lost, doesn't shift right, won't shift to high gear when it's supposed to. The car can't handle its own technology."

Bernie used to be crew chief for Jeff Andretti, his hobby is rare motorcycles, and he has been Frank's mechanic for years. "The engine has no distributor, everything works off a computer that takes its cues from the vibrator dampener at the end of the crankshaft. The computer won't even cue in unless, when the starter motor turns over, the crank starts turning at exactly the right rpm. Which it almost never does.

"It's also got a heat problem. The rear end is a barrel of snakes. You got headers, mufflers, intercoolers, there's no room back there. It'd be great if you could put the exhaust system in a trailer and tow it behind you."

Okay. At least I get oohs and ahs over the bike from the shop rats. Bernie says it'll take six weeks just to get parts. If he can find them. He asks me where I got the bike and I say from Frank, and Bernie says to get it inside "yesterday." So I figure I'd best forget the cops and go home and I'm surprised when, at the corner of King and Bishop, two squad cars appear and rip me right off the street.

This again. Cuffed and stuffed.

Now I sit at a long wood table, staring at the wire mesh threading the glass in the square window that is face level at the middle of the door. A conference room at HPD. The cop with a lazy eye and coathanger shoulders says to me. "First time's a charm. Whadda we got: Lucifer or just another hapless bystander?"

Another cop—big, brown, squared off, wearing a suit the color and almost the shape of a cardboard box—says, "He says he's not Greg Felt but Frank Crawford's brother."

The skinny one wants to know why Greg Felt has my picture on his driver's license.

"The picture isn't me, check my fingerprints."

One eye drifts toward his nose. He asks what was I doing
with Greg Felt's license and I reply that people leave their ID
in the bar all the time, that I probably just picked it up, and
he wants to know if I know Felt is wanted in three states for
aggravated assault and he wants to know what I do at Less
Nervous.

I reply, "Bounce."

"No bartending?"

"I cannot serve the public."

"Your girlfriend, Jeanie, worked for Frank. What happened?"

"She's on vacation."

"What's the deal up at your brother's office, Tod?" the big
brown cop asks. "I go up there and it's a ghost town. It looks
like he doesn't even have a secretary."

"Frank hates bureaucracy."

The skinny cop smiles. His face is tight against its skull.
"I'm late for the revolution. Condos, dead people, mindless
cattle, wacky buildings. Jets made out of rodents' genes,
cheapo cereal, and diamonds at Big Store. Tell me, does all
this shit actually work?"

"Have the cops been following me?"

"The guy's a financial wonderland."

The big cop says, "I never even heard of him."

"Are you kidding? He's been all over the Wall—Hang 'Em
High period Clint Eastwood as told to Scrooge McDuck. Dig
it: this clown's blowing an island right out of the ocean. I
flunked geology at Hilo Community—so I can't figure it. He's
gonna blow a tunnel through the thousand feet of basalt or
concrete or whatever God's got going on down there. How's
he actually gonna *do* that, anyway?"

"Explosives," I reply.

"Danny," the skinny cop says to his partner, "the guy's a
trip. He opens a cemetery that's only got one grave, the rest
of what was the boneyard, voilà! thanks to Frank, a golf course.
A virus turns the stiffs to mulch so a graveyard becomes a
country club."

"It's not that crass," I say. "It just saves a lot of land."

He hands me a document. Says, "Read it."

SUBLAUNCHED BALLISTIC MISSILE (SLBM) LOADOUTS AND REQUIREMENTS.
S-N-6, MOD 1/2: 1 × 1.1-MEGATON SRV (SINGLE REENTRY VEHICLE)
SS-N-6, MOD 3: 2 × 220-KILOTON MRVS (MULTIPLE REENTRY VEHICLES)

AIMPOINTS	REENTRY VEHICLES	DELIVERY VEHICLES
CENTRAL PACIFIC ISLAND TARGET EX. HAW. IS.		
KWAJALEIN ATOLL, MARSHALL ISLANDS:	1 × 220-KT MIRV	SS-N-18 SLBM #1
MARSHALL ISLANDS INT. AIRPORT, MAJURO:	1 × 220-KT MIRV	SS-N-18 SLBM #1
WAKE ISLAND:	1 × 220-KT MIRV	SS-N-18 SLBM #1
JOHNSON ISLAND:	1 × 220-KT MIRV	SS-N-18 SLBM #1

HAWAIIAN ISLANDS, GENERAL
HIGH-ALTITUDE, ELECTROMAGNETIC PULSE
PRODUCING AIRBURST 5,000 M/ABOVE OAHU

"That's it?" I ask.

"A page is enough. It's Frank's. Familiar?"

"I want to make another phone call. Where's my motorcycle?"

"Tell me about Heaven."

I say, "It's an acronym for Heavy Engineering something or other, a think tank for Strategic Nuclear Planning."

"So how could you," he asks, "at the time a twenty-year-old college dropout and convicted felon, have a special-access Top Secret security clearance?"

I ask again to make a phone call.

"You worked under an assumed name, a series of assumed names."

"I worked for my brother. He knew who I was."

"Your brother was in charge. Why would the feds fund a think tank run by a former air force officer who violated several national security acts?"

I ask what they are going to do. The skinny one—who has that fatless look some guys get just before they go down with full-blown AIDS—says, "Squeeze you 'til you squirt."

I'm thinking oh my oh my when I hear the quick clicks of metal cleats on the back of boot heels down the hall and there's Frank, face pinked under his tan, wearing a pale, unvented grey suit and looking like a carnivorous bird. He says, "Somebody start talking."

The big brown cop puts a hand on my shoulder. "This one got pulled over for excessive noise, exhaust, and presented a driver's license belonging to a man who has violated the terms of his parole." They go around about that and then the evangelical little DOE guy with the translucent blond hair from the airport appears with an older cop, Al, who seems in charge and knows Frank. The skinny cop nods toward me, says to Al, "Mister Man here was carrying the license of a felon. He himself is currently on probation. If he wishes to call an attorney—"

Frank points to me. "Is this who you thought he was or not?"

The skinny cop says, "No, apparently not. What I suggest you do is call your attorney—"

Frank put a finger to the bottom of the guy's throat and says, "Fuck you. You got the wrong guy. And Al here isn't going to let you get away with it." Frank takes me by the arm. "We're out the door and if you don't like it, shoot us in the back."

Frank is too hip to be hip, hates being recognized, doesn't fly commercial, and needs an executive jet. So we get hung up at the airport and are late to a Monolithic Memory meeting at Syntyrsystym. Men and women hang like paintings on a wall in Frank's office on a grid of new flat-pack high-definition television screens. TV monitors no thicker than the *Mona Lisa*.

Frank is finishing construction on a huge undersea tunnel across the Bering Sea. Built by Russian mohole men and stretching between Siberia and Alaska, it will transport natural gas into the United States at supersonic speed. Frank tells his managers that hard resources are the key to the twenty-first century, that we must get ready for a dive to make the Ccrash look like a gold rush, that soon Park Avenue matrons will be panhandling Bowery bums, that now is the time to dig in for the long haul, and that to do business with someone all you have to ask is, "What do you want?" Concentrate on the big things and the small things take care of themselves. He is offering Hawaii's 400 top employers $1.05 back on their dollar to issue 50 percent of their employees' paychecks in Big Store credits. He says everybody he has asked has signed up so far.

Afterward, I enter Frank's new Mind, close the door, sit down in the perfect dark of unconsciousness, say the words *Wake up* and it does. The dark pops to new life in the form of a many-colored planet dotted with uncountable holes. I insert myself, maneuver through a tunneled maze, say the words *The revolution will not be televised,* and I'm in the main info dump. Ideas and information appear alphabetically on a vast grid. I fly between them, select, lock, and see the access: READ AND FEED. I don't have the code.

An old-fashioned Soviet-style nuclear attack on the islands, that's *incoming.* Where did the cops get that? To take my mind off the obvious, I do a new LOAD. The target is the hardened fabrication plant in Yongbyon, North Korea, where plutonium is milled into cores. I'd've cooked it off with an SLBM but Offet won't backfit a Trident packed with an earthpenetrating warhead. So I suggest an F-117 using a 100-kiloton mod five B-61 laser-guided gravity bomb. But Frank's Mind says it will kill more people than Panasonic Fire & Casualty will pay for. Oh well. Back in the saddle once again.

25 FEBRUARY

It is the most beautiful boat I have ever seen, as perfect as a wish.

At the Ala Wai Yacht Club, by the water and under a white-hot haze, a big mirror-skinned sun truck pulls the *Fauxpas* atop a long mesh steel floor of a lowboy trailer onto the dock. The planks make crackling sounds under the weight.

Incoming. It makes no sense. Except, doubtless, to Frank and, unfortunately perhaps, to the Honolulu police. The HPD are relaxed but wily, confident too. No one got shot in the back but I know the other shoe is about to fall.

My brother, who says the secret to his success is that he's never had an original idea in his life, says, "Congratulations, you just got hit by the lucky bus."

He says, since its creation, the weight of the universe has increased tenfold. Out of nothing. And that if I want the chance to help discover why, I better be ready to pick up another Egg.

Incoming. What can he be doing? The possibilities sweat three dollars' worth of starch out of the ice white Mexican wedding shirt that hangs, at this early morning moment, like a wet rag off my shoulders.

Frank says no Egg, no end of the universe. "If you don't dumb down," he says quietly, "this will never stop, your life will be yesterday times forever."

Then he says all that is lacking is the film. All I have to do is go back to Celestial City and pick up another Egg.

"It's too dangerous," I tell him. "Way too."

I look past him, avoiding the glare from his lighted eyes. Frank is putting a sixty-foot racing sloop with an eighty-foot rigid "spider fiber" mainsail into a slip. As soon as the *Faux-pas* is rigged, within an hour or so, we will sail to the site of the New Island.

"I need a use for you," he says. "You wanna stick by, go out to Blue Villa and get it squared away. As new boss. August squawks and he can pick up his lunch pail."

My job?

Frank says that were he not in a knock-down drag-out with the Baby Bells he would do it himself. It's pushing dirt with a World Mover. "Easy," he informs, "to start it you just say *Honey, I shot the dogs* and all you have to do is throttle, pivot, and float the blade."

When I say I've got to work with Roberta, Frank does not reply and when I ask him where Jeanie is he says that he'll make it simple: "I don't care who your girlfriend is or how tight you wear your pants, but the tail does not wag the dog." For the first time I see, like trails of falling stars, streaks of white in his hair.

I figure I might as well go for the belly laughs, "I want my money. And not just my rent."

Frank says that's not the point. "There's a billion dollars

at the end of this particular rainbow. And that's just the opening act."

Trying to remember which rainbow, which act, I hear Frank say what he means is go get another Egg. And maybe I should consider this. For my idea of a real-world career stretches before me only in the vaguest way, like my grade-school paper route extended to the infinite.

"If you want your $50,000," he says.

The trailer has cherry pickers fore and aft. Mechanical arms lift the sloop to the air and—in one motion—set the white hull down in the water. Frank is disciplined. Until work chewed up all his time he forced himself to relax by building boats. For Frank the building was more enjoyable than the sailing but he no longer has time off so he has hired professionals to have the fun for him.

And they did. The boat is fantastic. A sliver, its superstructure a smoked-glass curve, its sail ten sails—plates of spider fiber louvered one on top of the other, putting enough surface to the wind to push the *Fauxpas* to 60 miles an hour. It has no keel.

Because once out on the ocean the *Fauxpas* puts out boneless arms for balance. The boat is unique. So to speak, alive.

The highway to the airport. The old Ford's convertible top down to a night sky of countless stars, under a sky so clear we could be in outer space, Roberta and I have our hair ripped by the wind.

Something is wrong with the *Fauxpas*, so Frank has had his cigarette boat, the V, Fed Exed from Baha. We're late, I'm moving. The red needle on Jan and Dean's Ford quivers to ninety. But by the time we get to Honolulu International everything has been taken care of. Frank has left the keys to the Zero at the Fed Ex office, with word for me to drive it back to his house, where they've moored the boat and where he'll pick us up.

The Zero is unreal. Frank had Bernie ant-hill the drivetrain, everything is new. Including fly-by-wire steering and a computer-controlled transmission with sixty-four forward speeds. On its radio I pick up the New York Philharmonic playing "Hot for Teacher." Because the speakers are built throughout the fabric of the car's upholstery, it is like listening from the orchestra pit.

A long day. Frank's developing a language for the New Stupid. His idea: for a billion of the world's postliterate consumers knowing how to read is bringing the mountain to Mohammed. So he has devised a "trade" language based on binary "Yes," "No," "I love it," "I hate it," "How much does it cost?" and after we couldn't get the *Fauxpas's* ten sails to take wind Frank said, fuck it, called same-day delivery, and went back to work.

Roberta is following me, the Ford's headlights are starry eyes in the rear-view mirror. Going over the mountains, I boot it. I'm going 55, but the Zero's rear tires break loose and the speedometer whacks from 55 to 130 in a heartbeat.

I wheel into his driveway, get out. Barefoot, Frank's grass is prickly under my feet. Tendrils of odd vegetation, their vines as thick as my wrist, are growing around my brother's house at amazing speed. The question mark around the door has evolved to an elaborate scrawl that seems nearly precise enough to read.

Lights swell down the street to the racket of Jan's old Ford snarling up its gears. Its tires crackle over the gravel into Frank's driveway as Roberta skids to a stop. Waiting for him, she chews gum and blows bubbles, pink balloons. She says Frank is a one-man circle jerk and if I'm smart I'll stick with Less Nervous, because it's the only real thing I've got.

My brother drives up in a minivan. Frank unfurls, his face dark and his white T-shirt bright under the luminous evening sky. He holds up a *Star*, there is a blind item on page three that says he is collecting the credit histories of everybody on earth. Going inside, he tells me, "I want you on an airplane."

It's windy. We walk around his house, across the cool sand of the beach to the dock where the long low V is moored next to the jetty.

Roberta's fingers lace between mine. She breathes, apropos of I'm not sure what, "Horse shit."

I climb down into the boat. It's different. Now its cockpit is as big as a bedroom. Frank, at the throttles and wheel, has to muscle through the surf, and even past the last break the waves crest, their white faces smashing over the bow. I'm soaked. I say I want to know how much I have coming from this estate.

Frank says no wine before it's time, that right now he's going toe to toe with the Baby Bells and says he's putting the frequency band on lay-away, which will do for us what the Gutenberg printing press did for the New Testament.

The V's supercharged V-10s are screaming and I have to shout. "I don't care about that, I care about my money."

"It's yours when I say it's yours." Frank throttles back and under a crescent moon he asks Roberta if she and I are an item.

It is almost light as day and I see Roberta's long wolf eyes widen. "That depends on what he gets and when he gets it."

"You go to school?" Frank is slamming into the rollers. Waves are crashing over the bow. The sea looks made of metal.

"Electron High." She slips an Apple Scholar out of her jeans. She too is soaking wet. "Mi-fine campus, yeah?"

It takes an hour to get to the site of the New Island and when we arrive I'm puzzled, it just looks like more angry ocean to me.

In the dark before morning at Big Store Frank shows us mansions, Ferraris, and airplanes that pop out of nowhere, holograms that present products too large or expensive to be easily stocked. Products to appear before consumers immaterial, as palpable only as a notion or a dream.

26 FEBRUARY

"He's poison," Roberta says, scraping the front door of Less Nervous. "Gutenberg Bible, my butt. Lose him."

"And lose a fortune."

"Crawford, your mind is mucho miniature. We're going to have to use a router on this thing."

"We don't have one. So what's the answer, Roberta?"

"You and me." She wipes her forehead. Her pretty blunt brown face is glassy with sweat. "And this." She indicates a Less Nervous that looks as if it has been painted with mud.

ACTION KILLS FEAR is still on the front doors and won't come off. The paint has bled into the wood. "The problem with the answer," she says, "is that the answer is owned by a nut."

We are still scraping when Jan and Dean gets off a bus from downtown. The bus, a long new slab of white with an advertisement

Better SEX ORGANS FOR BETTER SEX ACTS

MORPH UROLOGY

displayed across the back, leaves Jan standing on the curb, angry because after I retrieved it from the police, I pushed my motorcycle upstairs and into our living room. He hangs a sign that reads NUTRIENT SLUSH, ALL YOU CAN STOMACH $4.99 and calls the liquor commission. I watch him, surrounded by the luckless array of dirty dishes, broken furniture, standing there on the phone, his hair volcanic, playing the world's saddest song on the world's smallest violin, and when he's done the liquor dick says the computer says Jan has two other tickets outstanding.

He gets off the phone and says he wants to book Millions of Dead Cops.

"What is this, the club cabaret at Leisure World?" Roberta laughs. "Those guys are on walkers by now."

"Plus I'm booking Shit," Jan says, "for the weekend."

"Shit," I say, "costs money." When I ask how are we going to pay for them he tells me I'm the most middle-class clown he's ever met. And, boom he's out the door.

Roberta says, "You've got to start taking charge of things. We can handle Jan."

A thought. All he seems to have the energy for is to chase women and mismanage his business in his spare time. But what can I do? I don't know the terrain of his manias and I'm not sure he does either.

Roberta goes into the Nancy Spungeon Room under her new and, I guess, ignored sign that reads USE A FUCKING KLEENEX and begins wiping cybergasms off the Love Machines.

Franks shows up at midnight with his new Mind hanging

off one hand like a lunch pail. Unfortunately, we've got stadium speakers by Killer Bass for a Loving Race going at eleven on the ten scale, plus a lot of colors. Purples, greens, yellows, and reds spill and leap across the bar, the tables, the cut grunts, Kuzaki, Icicles, bikedykelesbopunks, and virgin nymphomaniacs. Now that hardons are the world's top murder weapon, half the women who can't figure out how to turn queer are going crazy. They come in, get drunk, scream, and fight.

In any event, it would have been hard to read it. Frank's Mind. He wanted to show me the latest iteration of the New Island, put it all over the room, but tonight that isn't possible. For Jan and Dean has spent $2,000 on a Prototechmindhouse laser light show bound to eat the door. Roberta says Jan's mind is a city of intersections where all the green lights overlap for thirty seconds. She points to the house specialty: Nutrient Slush. A stew. Tasty, mysterious. $4.99 for all you can eat. But he orders it in fifty-gallon drums from Syntyrsystym and has never figured what it cost per serving—probably more than he's selling it for. He books bands at a loss figuring to make his money back on beer, which isn't happening, and in no time we'll be lucky to still have lights and electricity.

Face facts: Roberta should be running this place and I should be running Roberta, she's smart and disciplined—if anarchists take over Honolulu she's a shoo-in for chief of police—but she's young and I can control her . . .

Onstage the Additional Oswalds, who look like they spend their days hung up in closets, sing *I'm going to heaven in a flash of fire, with or without you.*

Frank hands me airline tickets. Colors jump, fall, and whiz off his face. I tell him we're not leaving this place unless the Honas pay full bore and he says, "Good luck."

I'm trying to be careful, to steer a middle course. I've done another LOAD Frank's quite happy with—a tit for tat 170-kiloton "neutralization" of the Pakistani nuclear research facilities at Islamabad and the Indian test range at Rajastan by means of ALCMs fired by B-1Bs flying out of Diego Garcia. But Frank's angry about the Egg. Chances are nothing will come of it, but he warehouses his beefs and I don't want a bad job to come back and eat me alive.

I've just fed about a hundred goldfish to Mister Real when

three Cut Grunts in their camos—bare headed, their skulls shaved and tattooed with a crown of thorns—push through the crowd.

One shoulders Frank, and Frank, in a way that is almost gentle, pushes him three feet back in a snap. For a moment I think there'll be something, but no. The world doesn't really like to fuck with Frank and the only thing that happens is that he turns to me and says, "All the army is is a bunch of armed bureaucrats. Nothing but a few young hot shots clawing each other apart over promotions and the dregs at the top who couldn't run a war to save their lives."

Jan steps from behind the bar. Shirt off, his scars made raw by a day in the sun, he looks as if he has athlete's foot of the chest. He puts his arm around a mousey, balding man about thirty. Jan says, "We're upping the ante. Screw the Love Machines, it's back to traditional values: Live sex onstage. John Q. Public here is the star. He doesn't look like much but he's hung like the Alaska Pipeline." Public, cheeks paisley, smiles. Jan says, "Roberta. A drink for Frank. A foxmilk martini with a gasoline back. On the house. The real carne crudo."

Frank says, "What are you grinning about? This is a halfwit shakedown. If you think I'll be whipping out my checkbook when Augie Hona drops by to knock your teeth out, think again." Then to me, "If I were you, buddyboy, I'd get on a jet while I had the chance."

27 FEBRUARY

I wasn't born to be doing this. Jan and Dean had set a fire in the ashtray so the buttons on the selector are a melted mess, sagging floorward like watches out of Dalí, and the long silver plate of the Pacific Ocean beside me, I bang on the radio trying to get more than static while driving thirty-five miles out to Blue Villa in Jan's convertible. Cups and bags from McDonald's and Burger King are all over the seats, an old record album, *The Dictators Go Girl Crazy*, lies on the floor ripped in half among a junkyard of old Superman comics—Roberta's severance pay from Good Stuff Junior—their covers bearing dramatic news from the Fortress of Solitude, Ma and Pa

Kent, and Mr. Myxyzptlk from the Fifth Dimension. All that wafts through the radio is something about the Islamic "Center Party" extolling Arab unification in the wake of the East Jerusalem car bombing that just killed two hundred.

Yeah, I should have been out here earlier. Days ago. I drive off the road into a wide gravel ribbon still waiting to be paved. This is not what I had expected. Forget infrastructure à-go-go and mowing down rain forests, forget blowing up rocket ships the size of the Empire State Building, bottom line, the Blue Villas of this world are what Crawford Construction is really all about. Through the company and its subs, my father built more condominiums than anyone else in the world. So, given Frank's description, I know what I'm supposed to find out here. And this isn't it.

The condos are unfinished all right. They sit behind sandy mountains of red-brown dirt. Nothing's complete except the pads. Some of the framing is up, but mostly on just one side, like wood bars on an invisible jail cell. No way Blue Villa is going "out the door" in two weeks. Two months with two crews working two shifts is more like it.

Aug is tilted against a blue pickup truck, sipping coffee out of a fruit jar and scratching a pale blob on his forearm. A pregnant muscle man, his stomach falls over the waist of his shorts and his tool belt hangs off his hip like a cowboy holster. He says, " 'Sup?"

I look around. I remember the land, the big rock bluff that slouches away from the ocean. I say, "You're fired."

He looks at me.

"Don't argue, I'm only passing the word and I'll pay you for the rest of the week."

August says, "You gotta be joking. My mom owns this place."

I say, "Aug, I thought Frank did."

"Did is the word, brah," August amends, raising the jar to the line that makes his mouth. "Pick up a shovel or pick up your car keys." The guy's got a face like a ling cod.

I say, "Gimme your cellular." I reach into his truck, grab a receiver, and dial Frank. Frank says, "Put him on."

Aug holds the cellular to his ear, then his face seems to shrink at the chore of having to listen to Frank on the other end—and I wonder how this is going to turn out. Until now

I've been, so far as I know, actively and continuously disliked by very few people. August is one and no way I want to fuck with him.

We went to high school together at Punahoe. To Aug, history, math, and literature were only the quack mythologies of civilization and school was the weight room, where he'd lift barbells until his arms developed a scary life of their own.

August drops the receiver back on the seat of his truck. I say, "What'd he say?"

Aug burps. "To go to work, hoale boy."

I figure, okay, and we do. We're there to do everything not covered by the union contracts: dig holes for the electricians and move kitchen appliances, but now we lay pipe. The idea, as Frank has explained it to me, is that I must learn the business from the ground up. Reasonable.

By noon it is way hot and humid—drink a quart of water and piss a cup. I'm used to the heat, but something is really going wrong and I am thinking: Reasonable or not, I hate this.

Though the sun is blazing white, the sky is blue almost to black. I get scratched and my skin stings like crazy. We are laying concrete drainage pipe in a trench that has created long mountains of dirt. The trench is five feet deep. Each piece of pipe, sealed with a rubber garter, sits on a bed of gravel. There is a building ordinance that says an inspector must be able to see daylight through each straight line of connected pipe, no matter how long. They guy is coming at five, so we've got to get it done before that. Between six of us, we lay two 200 feet along the frontage. Lifting pipe between us—Aug sticking me with the heavy-bellied female end—he says, "Get outta Less Nervous." And when I say, "Gimme seven years," he says, "Any day. I'm throwin' you out a piece at a time." We set the pipe in the trench and I feel something pop, then hurt, in the middle of my back. "Arm. Leg. Your head last. Promise."

We work through lunch but by two most of the pipe is down and the ptomaine wagon is back, so I go down with another guy and order snack-truck junk. When I pull my gloves off, my hands feel skinned. We get our rice, macaroni, and chicken. I don't want to go back up there.

Sooner or later August and I are going to get into it. Once

I watched him fight a big local kid out at the Yacht Harbor. He battled in fits and starts; it looked as if the lurching brown boy was receiving a chaotic, choppy, upright massage, a spectator to his own beating. Finally the kid just sat down and cried on the grass. Standing over his victim, Aug exuded a seedy vitality that was amazing.

Eating my rubber chicken, the guy, Walt, older and bony, tells me a good unbelievable story about him and Frank parachuting DMSO into Cuba. When I realize an hour has passed I go back up the hill pulling on my gloves again, their insides cold and wet from sweat, my forearms and fingers still cramped with fatigue.

We get back. August's backhoed all the dirt into the trench. I don't think about it until the inspector comes out at five. No light.

We have to dig up and re-lay the pipe. All of it. It'll be time and a half but it will also be right now, August says. Around seven the arm in the backhoe seizes up, so we finish under starlight with shovels and finally by hand. It's like being in the Bible.

August fires me in the dark after I dump a mountain of gravel from a bucket-fitted D-8 bulldozer about two feet from his head.

28 FEBRUARY

Homicidal psychotic loadies. How can you miss them if they won't go away? A freak fight at lunch. It must be the air. Walking into the bar the cold steam from the nozzles above the front door falls across my face but when I touch my cheek it's already dry.

Jan has bought new software for the Crude Rude Lewd Really Stewed Almost-Nude Mini-Dude. We try it out. He runs down the bar top, swills a tiny bottle of scotch, and has sex with a blond "Miss Universe" in ways that are still felony illegal in about forty-five states and, seeing this, an Icicle— one of the Knew Christians—gets pissed off.

Forgetting that the essential truth of a hallucination is that it is one, he grabs after the Crude Rude Lewd Really Stewed Almost-Nude Mini-Dude and his hand zooms right through.

Frustrated, the Icicle tries to steal the machine. Rip it right off the bar top.

I hurt him. No roundhouse rights, no chairs broken over any head. Just a brief, slashing melee sparked by a scared, violent fool who understood only pain and punishment. Usually I have to kick, scratch, gouge, bite, and fight like a girl, but the iron stick I bought from the Zodiac man proved a stitch in time. Whack, whack, whack, nine from the sky and the Icicle was down and out.

Roberta says I've got to do something about this place, it's time to either shit or get off the pot. Waiting for the cop, I go back outside. Not too good news from the sky: it is disappearing. I look up and see stars at noon.

On the Wall this morning CNN said we have entered a time of "terrifying prosperity" and that our new century is being defined by a "free market run amok." I wish it would run amok in here. Jan has booked Voice of Ron, promised him more money than we can pay and, in defense against the consequences of his own stupidity, he goes out and gets drunk with Mrs. Whim. I cannot serve the public so Roberta and Vince have to handle all the food and drinks.

Fortunately, Wally, my psychotherapist, comes in. Wally's job is to like me and he's good at it. At my trial he testified that I was "the prototype of the sensitive young man" and even risked perjury by saying the reason I brained the guy was because I had "no perspective and cannot tell the difference between, say, the consequences of a flat tire and that, say, of ax murder."

Wally's sort of the Sigmund Freud of hanging around and it works. In my very first year we got past "Why did you give the cop the finger?" to "Don't give the cop the finger," and tonight he helps tend bar. Pulling beer at $350 an hour may sound spendy, but at least I'm not paying for it.

The crowd is young and some of them may even be earthlings. Around ten Jan calls to find out if I've been "touching" Roberta and says, "Watch out. 'Cuz I have a Zen indifference to the ends of action." I ask what that means, and he replies, "It means I'm blasted out of my tracks." Roberta's

roommates from her fourplex show up baubled and cleav-
aged, rich girls who've been gone and are about to go again
and Roberta says she's through living with "screamy beach
bims." Still, all in all it's not a bad night. Even though Voice
of Ron's manager, Bob Sex Act, demands $100 more than we
agreed to over the phone. I see promise here.

"Forget Frank," Roberta says when we are locking up, "and
remember me."

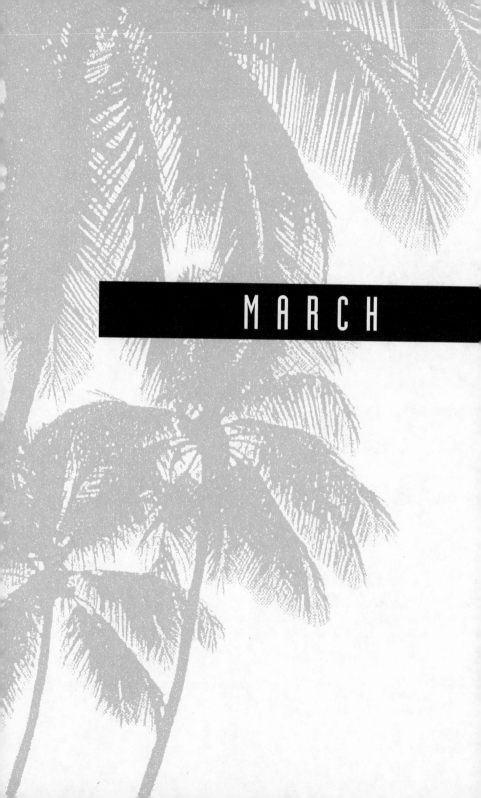

MARCH

Frank's reinventing the wheel again, so I guess we're doomed to make another gazillion. He's going to insert "passenger pods" inside his supersonic natural gas pipeline to create "an underground airline," one twice as profitable as any before it because it will require no fuel. Each "500 passenger pod" will shoot down the pipeline like a message in the old-fashioned pneumatic message tubes they had on the *Titanic.*

I'm flying to Nikol. The elite Russian city of nightmares. Honolulu–LA they show a movie about a hitman for the mob who, a loser in love, tries to get lost in his work. I sleep New York–London and get stopped at Heathrow and bumped for the night.

So London. Piccadilly Circus. The world's first theme park, the theme being friendly, worn-out, tarted-up London itself. Then a hotel. Room service. Dinner. Grey, greasy meat and green vegetables cooked pastel. Wizened carrots, crooked sticks pale and sickly. It's as though while the plants had been barely alive to begin with they cooked them to mush just to make sure they were dead.

Forking this medley around, I wonder about the film I'm supposed to think I'm picking up. How could it work if it had to be protected from exposure by cosmic rays? At some time light has to be allowed to fall on it, and aren't cosmic rays more penetrating than light rays? Maybe the explanation is exposure time. I guess the optical astronomers are willing to risk cosmic ray damage for the short time the film is exposed to celestial light.

Last year Frank cut a deal with the Chinese to exchange licensing rights to American fads for the labor to manufacture the next ones. I flew to Shanghai and, when there was a misunderstanding, I was put in jail. Now I have nightmares in which, through dream logic, I realize the end of the universe is practically right next door.

2 MARCH   *St. Petersburg*

London–St. Petersburg. I am met by a baby-faced fat man at the airport who carries a placard with TOD? written across it in blocky red letters. He drives me north to Nikol. The landscape is a freezing plain of filthy snow. Crooked branches hang from bare black trees like cracks in the bottom of the sky. The first I see of the city are its smokestacks. My chauffeur says they throw 320,000 tons of sulfur dioxide into the air every year. This place is a billion-dollar-a-year mining and refining town, one of the richest places in the country and, due to the pollution, everyone is sick. The city is walled. Wages are so high that markets are almost as well stocked as they would be in an American slum and people from miles around are desperate to get in. We have to pass armed sentries at the gates.

Avek meets me at my hotel. Maybe he lives everywhere. He asks me if I've heard the new $+ = +$. Outside it is snowing ash.

He gives me another Egg. If film is actually inside I'm actually St. Francis of Assisi. In the morning I deliver it to the St. Petersburg airport. I am flying as Greg Felt. When I show my passport to the customs Russian, swear to God, he looks it over then says in perfect southern California English, "Leave the Egg." Which I do.

I cave. I give up. I'm not going to jail for this. Between the devil I don't know and the devil I know, Less Nervous has got to be the way.

3 MARCH   *The Sky*

London–New York I dream of Jeanie. She shows me she has skin on which there are scars so intricate, planned, and precise I can read them. In a room she turns on TV and we watch Frank in high school playing football. He is quarterback and barks crazy audibles: Heartbreak. Murder. Loneliness. He takes the snap, fades back to pass, then bolts forward, squinting through a riot of interior linemen on his way to the white H of the goalposts.

Then Jeanie and I decide to make love. She lifts the sheet off the bed. It fills the air like a parachute, then falls down around us. Her mouth is so full it looks swollen. As if someone has just struck her. Really popped her a good one. Then suddenly she starts screaming for the police, saying her arm is broken, and I wake up hearing the woman in the aisle across from me, crocked silly and yelling at her boyfriend, calling him "une grande et grosse merde" as I finish geysering into my $300 slacks.

4 MARCH   *Home*

Frank's gone, nobody's here. I'm in his empty office high above Big Store. A muscled old man with a swoopy 1950s haircut and a tattoo on his forearm that has grown smeary with age comes in and says he's Ernie Sift here to help build the tunnel that will release the magma to create the New Island.

"But," he says, "you can't set off a bunch of *plastique* like a string of firecrackers and get a viable tunnel out of it. The Feds won't let you do it, number one, and I can't do it, number two. The only way to hit that vein is with a nuclear-shaped charge designed to blow an underwater hole about a mile by a mile. No walk on the beach by any means."

5 MARCH

I go see my probation officer Terry Pow downtown. He says I've got a warrant pending but the judge won't sign it. I ask what's it for. He says who knows and I better just go pee.

6 MARCH

Out of the water and walking off the beach, the Bad Magic under my arm, and dreaming of a nightclub empire, I find a runover rat. The dead rodent's six clawed feet are delicate and clenched like the hands of a starved old man. Its guts have dried to red candy on the pavement.

Still half asleep in some other time zone I walk down to the bar at nine. The weather is out of season and there is an unsettling clarity to the heat unusual for this new bad time.

Less Nervous stands before me, new in my mind. I'm seeing it now not as it is, but as how it will be. For tonight I've booked, on my own, a 90s retro band, 500 Channels of What, and told them no guarantee, but they can have the door. That way we get all the zombies and beer and there is no chance we can lose money.

I feel someone tug at my back pocket. "Crawford, I had a dream about you." It's Roberta, in yellow shorts and a sleeveless grey leotard that covers her body like a shadow. I say *We all live in a house on fire, no fire department to call; no way out, just the upstairs window to look out of while the fire burns the house down with us trapped, locked in it* to the front door. It opens, and right behind us a bunch of Frank's Russian mohole men, divers and geologists off the *Gogol*, come in trailed by a liquor dick.

More bad luck for Jan. The dick finds a drunken Icicle—another satisfied customer, passed out behind the bar sleeping it off from the night before—and wants to know where he can find Jan. Back at home sawing in and out of Mrs. Whim is where I'd look. The guy gives me a $300 ticket.

Roberta says, "The dream you was much better than the you you."

The mohole men order zombies. They've scooped up little magnesium but are gearing up to start work blasting the hole on the ocean floor that will create the New Island. They call it *Novij Raj*, which means new paradise, and wonder why there's no Lynyrd Skynyrd on the jukebox.

After they leave I sit at a table by the door and flip through my ID looking for something that has my real name on it or at least something with a name on it to match one of my credit cards. Because to finance what I have in mind for Less Nervous, credit is what I need.

"Crawford," Roberta puts her cheek by my shoulder, "in the dream I was Miss Universe and we were about to do the unspeakable. And then you took off your jammies—and

I didn't know guys ever got made like that. You looked down at yourself and said even God goes south once in a while. It would keep you out of the army though, yeah?"

I say, "Roberta, you want something?"

"We need to break into Jeanie's."

"Why?"

"Because it's the right thing. To find out what happened to her."

I hear, "How you? How you? I fine." Buddy Walsh and his wife. Both straw-haired and looking like kids, except up close their faces are a million years old. Their usual breakfast is hard-boiled eggs and Diet Cokes but this morning they order the special.

In here, the days of the Mr. and Mrs. Buddy Walshes of this world are numbered. Roberta stands behind the bar with her back to me, cooking their omelettes on the grill. Nudged here and there with a spatula, the still-liquid centers wobble as she drops tufts of grated cheese over them one at a time.

Roberta wants to know when Jan is coming in. I say beats me and she tells me she's bored shitless. To demonstrate this state she yawns and stretches, her sensual kid's body arched, breasts pushed flat against the grey fabric of her leotard. She puts a paper cup under the spigot and brown soda jumps out in violent coughing spurts.

I'm going to take over this place: if it works it works, if not, I have a fall-back position—I can always just kick back, panhandle for a living, wait for Frank to explode, and then go to work ruling the world.

7 MARCH

And why not? Frank says we'll have the Cayman Islands cubed. The New Island will provide a corporate tax, liability, and lack of accountability nirvana worth $500 per square foot per month in office rentals. And that's all it will be, rentals. No outside ownership. No matter what, Frank keeps the pink.

Frank is moral, but you don't have to be the ghost of G. Gordon Liddy to know companies that could host and toast their presidents and unindicted coconspirators side by side. Frank says IBM, Texaco, Kerr-McGee, TRW, Chevron, Sony,

General Motors, Banco Nazionale del Lavoro, you name it, all want in.

We're flying. The dusky ground—Waikiki, Ala Moana, Honolulu—slamming by a thousand feet below, Frank says that the twentieth century—ignoring the warnings of Annie Dillard and Albert Speer and conducted at its end by nothing but do-gooders, hippie chicks, experts, and the media—collapsed around itself, having abandoned the power of progress. He says now an ever-widening caste of the useless will be manipulated by an ever-shrinking caste of the smart. The great consumer booms will follow a squall line created by expanding higher education running into low wages, an economic front created by the brightest, worst-paid talent available. So, by the year 2101, Mercedes will be owned by the Zulus and the president of the United States will be able to trace his ancestors to the Viet Cong and, by the way, where is the fucking Egg?

Frank threads the Cayuse between two buildings. I say I don't have it because who's kidding who? It's smuggling and I'm not dying to spend my emeritus years eating mashed potatoes and fish sticks in some federal lockup.

This should be catastrophe but Frank does not appear even mad. The closest to mad he gets is to say, "Nobody at customs would say that. You're hearing voices again. Are you taking your Antiswaq?"

When I say yeah he says great, because he's got another LOAD. All I have to do is figure out how to best "decapitate" the French nuclear submarine pens at Ile Longue in the Bay of Brest. "Something along the lines of a sea-launched 90-kiloton Tomahawk—no, fuck the frogs, make it 500 kilotons B-61—you work out the details, but patch it to Offet by Tuesday."

I say no more LOADS and he doesn't get mad at that either.

He puts the copter down on a pad next to the roof of the Coliseum and we go see the Waves against Golden State and I sit on the edge of the bench right next to L. Dornier Vetrochuck, our six-foot nine-inch, thirty-four-year-old Ukrainian center. A hobbling repository for four million dollars, his left knee is swollen to twice normal size. The Waves are 22–27 for the season. In the second quarter L. Dornier gets off the bench and shows the fans he's still got his money shot—a strange backassward jumper that puts no spin on the ball, so you can read Wilson on the side through its whole arc to the basket.

Frank talks to Jack Sealy at halftime. Jack's Frank's beard for the team—a big gap-toothed developer who has a piece of gold the size of an ear hanging around his neck. He plays owner for the public and press so Frank doesn't have to take the heat. Frank loves media but hates publicity. He says the only time to be in the newspaper is when you're born, get married, and die.

During the second half Frank tells me the Waves are the quietest team he's ever seen. "They don't talk on defense. There's no on-the-court leadership." Passing at ghosts—the ball crashed into the press tier twice—they seem to be moving in slow motion as if playing underwater. It's not until the fourth quarter that they come back and pull it out 109–104. A miracle, Frank declares, with four starters hurt.

Flying home I tell him about my 1990s night. Five Hundred Channels of What punked but we drew the New Stupid off the Robot Radio ads and though pissed about the no-show, they're a nice crowd; suave, monied, languageless. Three thousand in the bank.

Frank says injuries are caused by too many games and he may force the NBA to cut back ten games a year and that, by the by, it's a good thing I'm so sharp because from now on I'm on my own. He's cutting me off.

8 MARCH

I go up to the university and pick up proof sheets from their photo lab where, because nobody knows me well enough to realize I'm not a student, I have extensive free lab privileges. Then I walk back to the beach and find Jan in front of the Royal Hawaiian lying out on the sand, eyes closed, twisting his head from side to side as if enduring an agony. He tells me he had to use the $3,000 to pay off the liquor dicks and then says he just found $20,000 worth of debts he'd "forgot about" in a box behind the bar. He's got an ace in the hole, however. His ex-wife Barb. He says, "Let me handle this, Fauntleroy. I'm going to hit her up for every dime she's got."

9 MARCH

Barbara Graham is ten years younger than Jan and Dean and lives in a small cottage in Manoa Valley above the university. She is a clean-cut young woman who gets involved with unusual men and every two weeks or so she drives into Waikiki to see her ex. Usually, she shows up either alone or with their two daughters—but this morning she brings a friend along with the girls. I see her Land Rover come down Paokalini Street and park in front of the apartment. She gets out. Thin and tan, in cotton shorts and a long-sleeved man's shirt cuffed neatly at the elbows, she's got the spare, efficient physique of somebody who might one day be launched into space.

The girls spill out after her. Both have their mother's straight blond hair, green eyes, narrow nose, and small triangular face. Jan and Dean's much darker, blunter features are almost nowhere. Then surprise, there's Dewey.

He gets out of the Land Rover on the passenger side. Barefoot and dressed in an old Hawaiian shirt and sailor pants. Alger Hiss slinks out behind.

Jan and Dean is in the bathroom singing *Simolena Pilchard dripping from a dead dog's eye*. Rita, his beach find of the day before, lies on our exploded old couch, asleep. I shake her shoulder. "Rita," I say, "wake up."

"Eat me," she murmurs, flopping halfway over. Her lipstick, still thick and red, looks as if it's been applied with a paint brush. I shake her again. "Eat me," she repeats, peering up at me with one brow cocked as if she's staring through a monocle.

I say, "Come on. Time to split, beat feet, book out of here," not sure she understands words couched out of the vernacular.

Barb and the girls stand at the door, Dewey behind them. "What's shaking?" he says. Jan and Dean comes out toweling his balding head, looks at the woman who was his wife, and allows, "A lot." Going down the stairs Jan reveals that, now that he has become middle-aged, he must get realistic, forget his plans to commit great good deeds, and come up with something more down to earth like, say, the crime of the century. It is time, he concludes, climbing into his ex-wife's Land Rover, to do something very wrong very well.

Dewey drives. Alger Hiss, all teeth and attention, between him and Barb on the front seat. We go to Frank's beach on the North Shore. I sit in back. Dewey's curly blond hair thick as a poodle's in front of me. "Picture this, Jan. Vacate Less Nervous and I save your bacon."

Jan sits in back too, his daughters wedged between us. He says, "I don't deal with you, Dewey. I deal with your mom."

Dewey says, "Mom's gonna die. She's got a heart as big as a catcher's mitt. If she lasts 'til Christmas it'll be a miracle. So, brah, do you and I break out the Vaseline or what?"

Dewey wheels over the mountains and back down toward an ocean that is a glittering plain. We pass one of Frank's huge new hotels, a stacked tier of concrete slabs. Hona hona grass arcs up behind it away from the beach.

Beyond the hotel the road follows an empty beach to a rise of sudden jungle—a high green bluff snaking out of the foothills. At the crest of this rise Dewey brakes, makes a right, and shoots down a weed-rutted cat track. Winding the engine out in second gear, he sends the truck banging and pitching toward the shore, leaves and branches whacking against the windshield. Light cuts through the trees above us in slashes and blobs.

Barb says, "You want to know what he did just before I divorced him?" We are walking over rocks and across a long hot beach headed toward the shade created by our big new hotel. "One day I came home from work early and walked into the bedroom. There he was. Accompanied. This little urchin might have been old enough to get herself a driver's license.

Want to know what he did when he saw me?"

I ask, "What?" and she says, "Well, I'll tell you the second thing first. The second thing he did was to freak. To panic, to cry, to plead, to babble out of his head." She stops walking. We are surrounded by small white doves. She looks up at me and goes, "But want to know the first thing he did?" I nod yeah and she says, "He finished."

Jan, burping for the length of a breath, says, "I took what I knew and Dewey took what he knew and we just added 'em up, try this on for size, Fauntleroy: Frank is covered with blood. You better go find the fertilizer that used to be your Jap glamour-puss girlfriend before the cops do, am I right?" He looks at Dewey, who is looking at me.

"Question, brah," Dewey says. "Where's the will?"

"What will?"

"Your parents' will." He throws a rock down the beach and Alger, going after it, leaves a flash of divots on the mirrory tide-washed sand. "Frank and I, we're splitting things up, and having that will would help—" Dewey takes a drink of beer. "Now that you haven't got a pot to piss in, I'd imagine you'd like to see it too."

Barb and I have just walked back, Jan and Dean says, "Dewey just told me some shit about Frank that would blow your mind, Crawford. Have your pea brain shooting out your ears."

Dewey says, "So Frank's carving this up too. Makes sense."

I say, "It's going to be major, yeah. A development, restaurants, the usual drill." He and Jan and Dean are standing atop an old World War II gun emplacement. Below them is a small beach held in a curve of black moss-pocked rock. A waterfall courses through a **V** at its summit, a glassy sheet that splashes to a perfectly clear pool fifty feet or so behind the bunker. Sperm-shaped lizards dart among the rocks. Jan's daughters are playing at the shore. Dewey says, "Know what I heard? Frank's going broke. His Big Stores are circling the drain and he's spending himself into chapter eleven."

I say, "Tell me another one."

Jan says, "I hate Frank, I really do."

Elbows on his knees, he is holding a long-neck bottle of

beer in both hands as if it were a divining rod. "In high school, the guy fingerfucks my girlfriend at the Kailua drive-in and doesn't even have the courtesy to enjoy it."

Dewey has a Hot Stick. Its handle is as big as a corncob. "Picture this, brah: With this thing you could feed Frank spaghetti, then fire open his tummy just to count the meatballs."

Barb says, "Don't give him that. Jan doesn't need one of those."

Dewey says, "Yes he does."

She nods at this. Her hair, clipped just below her shoulders, sways against her collarbone. She take a menthol cigarette from her blue canvas purse, lights it, waves smoke away from her face. In conversation, most of Barbara Graham's gestures are linked to the rhythms of lighting, smoking, and extinguishing cigarettes. "Put the torch away, Dewey," she says.

He says, "JD, tell me a secret: How's your sex life?"

Jan says, "Same old, same old."

"What's that?"

"Oh, you know, get whoever she is up to the place, pull down her panties, and squirt her full of baby batter. The usual drill."

To protect Jan's ropy blond daughters we have made a tent of blankets. Lying in its long shade JD picks up Barb's compact, sees his face, and says, "I look like an ape."

I ask when he plans on hitting her up and he says, "In good time." The kids splash out of the shorebreak. They look like sprites. Above us Dewey picks his way down through the rocks, bags of beer under either arm, Barb behind. She sits down on the sand, pulls a wrapper off a sandwich, and asks if I was going to marry Jeanie. Jan, opening a beer with his car key, says, "If he ever figures out what happened to her. Jeanie and Tod love each other so much they're gonna have their faces sewn together."

Barb asks me what happened in Mexico and Jan says, "Crawford got cracked for selling Frank Zappa's piss to the Indians."

I say, "It was just business."

Jan says, "Dewey burned him. Tell her about it, Dewey."

Dewey says, "Nobody got burned."

Jan tells him, "Dig Crawford's eyes. They drive the faggots crazy. One look and you can tell if he hates your fucking guts."

Dewey says, "Talk story: Wasn't that girl Jeanie of yours going to be in a *Playboy Holo?*"

Jan stands and whacks sand off the back of his orange canvas swimming trunks. "Who looks at that shit? What did Hugh Hefner know about sex? To him it was just another capitalist gag to sell cigarettes and shaving lotion. Even I know more about sex than he did. Right, Barb?"

We all get a little drunk. Dewey brought a football and Jan says, "Deion Sanders!" and trots down the beach.

I follow him, just walking fast. Dewey waits, cocks his arm, and throws. Jan runs and I bolt after him, our feet slapping into wet sand at the water's edge. The ball goes into the sun and shoots out. I jump and nick the side of it hard enough to sting. It skips out of Jan's hands, cartwheels end over end down the beach, and splashes into the shorebreak.

Jan picks the ball out of the water, wipes it against his swimming trunks, then tosses it back, grinning at the spiral. Barbara, her face expectant, goes after it, thin gold legs churning, looking as though she has somehow reentered awkward adolescence at age thirty-four.

We leave late. Despite being smeared with Dead Man, both girls got burned.

Jan tells Dewey about being in Desert Storm. "I was a Nazi," he says, and pulls a picture out of his wallet. It's a Polaroid of Jan in combat fatigues, bandoliers of ammunition X-ing his chest, a machine gun on his shoulder that he's gripping by the barrel like a deadly baseball bat, a carbine in his left hand, and grenades strung around his body like so many Christmas tree ornaments. "Barb, dig it: The new name of my restaurant'll be Himmler's. You gotta be blond to get

served after five and we check your ID every fifteen minutes."
Then he shrugs and says, "Let's get a move on. The kids are
fried."

Jan whistles a song whose lyrics, if sung, express a man's
indifference to the loss of a woman, and climbing into the
Land Rover he says, "Dig this: We remodel. Concrete floors,
concrete walls, iron bars around the bar. We call it For Dirt-
bags Only, the only place in town where nothing you can do
can get you 86'd." When Barb doesn't say anything Jan says
to me, "She's got the money. Her mom is Martha Stewart."

"Who," I ask, "is Martha Stewart?"

"Only the She-Christ of the Borj-wa-zee." Jan leans into
his ex-wife's face: "Come on, Barb. All I'm asking for is ten
grand to uncook my ass."

"My mother is not Martha Stewart," she replies.

Dewey, driving, says, "I'm offering you $50,000 to vacate,
take it or leave it."

JD says, "Get real." Then to Barb, "You fucking this guy?"

Dewey says, "Okay Jan."

Jan says, "Don't okay me, Barb. Come clean. You fucking
him?" Alger starts barking, his white teeth everywhere, and
Dewey swerves the Land Rover to the side of the road. In one
motion, he reaches back and pulls Jan out of his seat by the
throat.

Dewey says, "Brah, guess what? Nobody is going to uncook
your ass. You're gonna be off that property, gone an' gone
quick. Make sense?" JD's expression is one of surprise. Then
he smiles and spits in Dewey Hona's face.

1 2 M A R C H

Grid 1999. On board the *Gogol* fishing lines hang over the
side like kite strings. Spittle-topped waves smash lazily against
the hull. Twenty feet below I can see grouper, their big mouths
open wide and eyes bulging perhaps from the horror of being yanked from the bottom of the sea, swung to the air, gutted and thrown back as chum for the AK-47–wielding mohole
men who sit on the deck beneath the *Gogol*'s bridge drinking Bud and waiting for sharks. A lot of the grouper have open
sores, purple ulcers eaten into their silver sides and, like the

wild cats, eyes that could be made of cottage cheese.

I sit on a cardboard case of beer, waiting to go down in the bathysphere, reading the *Star*. In it, a story about Jerry Wiler, 86, "a pioneer in the American effort to create a hydrogen bomb that culminated on November 1, 1952, at Enewetak Atoll in the Marshall Islands with the detonation of a device a thousand times more powerful than the bomb dropped on Hiroshima."

The account concludes Wiler is "associated with the effort to create a 'new' Hawaiian island." Frank says if a reporter calls don't say boo. I ask why I'd get a call and Frank says the best thing about me is I don't know anything—that if human evolution depended on the Tod Crawfords of this world we'd still be killing each other with rocks.

Just before the sharks arrive a seagull hangs in the air above the fish guts on deck, wings outstretched as if crucified, and a longhaired red-knuckled mohole man maybe my age who looks made out of sticks lets go with his assault rifle. The brass casings tinkle against the metal bulkheads and then everybody is firing into the ocean. I look down, see a shark glide to the surface, snag a dead grouper, and tip over on its long white stomach, so for an instant it looks as if someone is surfing the bottom side of a wave.

Frank says it boils down to this: Divorce is ugly and to finance the New Island we're going to end up fighting over the billion-dollar table scraps of a ripped-up construction empire. Frank is an environmentalist and he has hired Wally Rice, my psychotherapist, to hot-rod his subconscious at Monolithic Memory, and he has brought his lunch pail–sized Mind with him, so that we can see, at a glance here in the *Gogol*'s ward room, his plan for paradise: a nonpolluting New Island that will host a city of 50,000. Frank's vision is splayed around us. It is spectacular. Nobody has thought this way, he says, since Ramses II.

How will he do it? At first he planned to build a jacket, a

concrete form to contain the lava, ten yards at its base, tapering to one yard at the top, 700 to 800 yards tall, encircling an area 8,350 feet in diameter at base on the sea floor. But that would have been spendy because he'd have to pour a million cubic yards of concrete, even without rebars, at almost $100 a yard. Enough concrete to build a freeway 33 yards wide, a yard thick, and three million miles long.

A chore. So what Frank will do, after he blows the hole in the sea floor to let the lava up, is lower pieces of concrete pipe fifty yards in diameter and a hundred feet tall over the magma gusher. He'll just barge each piece out and lower it on top of the one below and as soon as that one is anchored by the cooling spew of magma coning up around its base, we'll have paradise squirting up all over the place.

Above it, a new city will rise out of the cooling magma, built vertically instead of horizontally. Parks will be created on two huge round elevated plates, so the New Island, in a way, will resemble the Starship Enterprise made out of grass and dirt.

I tell him that the old demolitions expert Ernie Sift had said in order to get enough magma we would have to use a nuclear explosion and Frank laughs out loud, showing teeth as white and perfect as new.

Frank is, in his way, inviting me back to the fold. And though I do not want to stretch too far the old ties that bind, I am not going to be his boy. I ask him what he wants.

"Maybe a baby. Could you and that little estrogenhead, Roberta, come up with one of those? Because you make that fist a hand and you still got a great future." Shape up, Frank says, and I'll have my own suite atop a hundred-story spiral. Be good, he says, and I'll die road-testing show girls at the top of whatever is left of the sky.

The bathysphere is big, I can see that climbing over the *Gogol*'s stern. In the quaking ocean it looks like a cartoon bomb, black and round, except that on top, where the fuse would be, is a hatch. The engineers are going to set off the first explosions to create the "magma umbilical" to form the New Island.

Climbing through the hatch is like climbing down a manhole into a sewer main. Inside it is part spaceship, part men's room at the Tijuana bus station. Mohole men, two engineers and a geologist, have spent a week preparing the detonation. They have somehow plugged the head, their piss and shit has risen to a slurping stew around its rim.

The bathysphere was built in St. Petersburg when it was Leningrad and it rests on tank tracks. It seems the product of two centuries, the last and the next. Its bulkheads are iron, the welds make thick scars at the seams. But the control suite is arrayed with an elegant computer horseshoe of flat plate monitors, sonars, and command equipment. We sit before a video screen two in front, two behind, as if in a car, in seats torn from Frank's old dragsters, secured by five-point harnesses that X our chests. One engineer drives while the other, lips moving, reads a paperback French-language edition of *Dianetics*. The old engineer driving says he spent two months aboard the *Mir* space station during the 1980s. He maneuvers the bathysphere not by levers or wheel but by a hand-held paddle controller like from a TV video game.

The heat vents from the magma vein have spawned a jungleland. We slowly tip and roll through liquid trees, whose trunks and branches part and disappear as we pass. Fishlike pieces of intestine with mouths stand suspended in a school then squiggle away, whipping around something I think is Jack's beanstalk but the engineer reading *Dianetics* says is the line to explosives buried below the ocean floor. Then we begin backing over our own tracks and everything fades away, one light goes out and the other reveals only curtains of silt in the dark. Frank is counting down toward detonation and I hold on to the pilot's seat in front of me, looking at the yellow bulkheads for some way out. I see the sweat I remember on the walls at Heaven but when the explosion goes off we shake a little but otherwise I feel nothing at all.

1 3 MARCH

The cats have disappeared. Their milk has curdled in its pan and Roberta and I crawled under the apartment looking for them, but nothing. I held her hand and she says her mind is in the gutter. Something has happened. Last night Jan came in while Roberta and I were on the couch watching the Wall. We'd walked down to Butt Floss Beach and Roberta, wearing green twine for a bathing suit, had sand white as salt matted to the top of her thighs.

There had been a bad message on my machine: Wally, my psychotherapist, saying a spot of melanoma on his chin had leeched into his jawbone. After that I stared blankly at bad hits on the news: a girl, a surf Tita, had been shot in the water, here in Waikiki, and Roberta—who wasn't quite just sitting next to me but on my lap—was crying and holding me when Jan came through the door.

Jan got mad. He picked up a pomegranate off the coffee table and threw it against the Wall. It made a starry splash and he said if I touched Roberta again he'd shoot me in the head.

Well, Jan can shoot who he pleases, I do want to touch her and she says, "Touch all you want. He's not the boss of me," but that we're in for a really bad time.

Tony promises doom by Christmas and is in the last stages of outfitting his ark. He has strapped clear plastic coffin-size water tanks, two on each side, to the deck of his yellow-hulled sailboat. I guess he's ready to pack up the family and hightail it. Because I believe that he is a better prophet than sailor I have a schizophrenic fear for both me and his kids.

I am in Less Nervous when Dewey comes in and gives us his own personal eviction notice. I tell him that if they want us out they'll have to buy the lease back and it'll cost a million dollars cash.

Dewey laughs out loud. "Legally I still have to give you guys thirty days, but unless you want to end up looking at a picture of your dick on the side of a milk carton you better be gone in nineteen."

14 MARCH

As if she were the star, and it was Take 27 of *Two-Fisted Love Nymph*, I see Roberta in a way that, I'll admit, makes an impression along the lines of a branding iron but that also reminds me that she is planning my world her way.

At dawn I paddle out to Queens. Good water. Waves breaking four to five feet, glassy. This is the hottest spring ever and the ocean is warm as spit. Even though the air right there on the water is cool against my skin. I feel heat underneath, as if I am being cooked from inside.

I walk home barefoot under palm trees that cast swaying islands of shade. I'm meeting Roberta at eight for Trix and when I go back around her fourplex to where her apartment is, the door is open and I hear the shuddery shriek of her shower being twisted off and a minute later she bops out, sees me, and, like a naked wooden maid on the bow of an old schooner, throws her new chest back, says, "Minimind, you're early," then bounces back into the can.

We have the breakfast in her galley of a kitchen. Overlayed in front of the Roberta who is tipping over a box of Trix so the Trix can avalanche into our bowls is the Roberta who was standing before me in a pair of panties as wide as a line and made, if memory serves, out of fabric thin as mist. Wrapped in a white terrycloth robe, she says I have to start acting aggressively if I want my life to point toward success and peace of mind. I tell her that every time I start acting aggressively my life points toward lawsuits and jail.

When I get back to the apartment the liquor dick is in the living room with Jan, who sits on the couch wearing nothing but white swingeasies blobbed with stains—like the maps of pale lost continents—across the front. The guy tells us Less Nervous is looking at $6,500 in fines we cannot possibly pay.

15 MARCH

Apropos of kissing his (our? my?) business goodbye, Jan and Dean sighs and spits. It's four o'clock in the afternoon and the sidewalk in front of Less Nervous is an oven. He wears only his old orange canvas swimming trunks and, allergic to his own sweat, the skin around his armpits is misted with a fine red rash. Last night he got mad because I called one of his ex-wife's lovers an asshole and he socked the bathroom mirror. This morning, his reflection in shards, he'd cut his neck shaving and blood from the nicks has smeared around his throat so it looks as if he has just been hanged.

The state liquor commission has presented him a bill for $6,500 in back fines. Due "immediately or sooner."

I go back inside to feed Mister Real. I pull a rubber band off a plastic bag filled with water and pour in a school of goldfish. Mister Real goes mad.

Outside, the Honas' big crane straddles the sidewalk while the fat black wrecking ball swings into the old Palms, raising spidery plumes of vaporized mortar and concrete.

Roberta says she really wants to make Less Nervous go, that we should forget Shit, phkyrslph, Additional Oswalds, and all of Jan's other Top 40 bands. Jan and Dean's old, we're young. He's the past, we're the future. Roberta says if I want a life for myself it's time to go hardcore.

16 MARCH

At Less Nervous, Vince's mahu friends in cowboy booties from Rump Wranglers Anonymous sit chatting up new safe-sex bondage schemes. Leftist Jan and Dean, wiping down the bar, says all he ever asked from life was to die rich and then he goes home.

Frank has offered, so to speak, to make me second-in-command of the universe. A fate I'd pay to escape if I could get the pink on this place. If we just booked the convention crowd—everybody from Team Prozac to the Sorcerers' Union uses the big hotels to feed their conventioneers—at lunch we could handle three hundred.

By six there's $60 in the till, the sound of a drop hitting the bucket, and two people at the bar: Wally, my psychotherapist—who, thank God for false alarms, has had the cancer plucked from his jaw and, aside from a stitched-up new mouth across his chin, looks as good as new—and one of his patients, some yo-yo in an $800 suit—dapper and plausible, the archetypical madman.

Aug Hona comes just after dark. Lips a line, hair a blond cap hanging to his shoulders. He's got the big blunt body of someone who could dive into the ocean and swim for years. He says, "You guys be out of here by the end of the week."

And when I say, "Dream on," he says that if we are not gone in five days he will stomp my face to jelly, simple as that.

17 MARCH

Dr. Nyung, Frank's accountant, says, "This Frank of yours is a handful. I call him, and talk to machines that converse. I ask them too many questions, they get in an uproar."

I ask what's wrong.

"These stocks are brokered through Syntyrsystym that buys and sells stock for the Crawford Family Trust in some arrangement with Hona Nuclear." Dr. Nyung puts his short hands together in a shape that makes a tepee. "For three weeks Syntyrsystym has been very active, selling off Crawford Family Trust properties in a way that is highly stupid. Big companies, little companies, new ones, old ones, local ones, national ones, all liquidated by Syntyrsystym with no method."

Dr. Nyung is director of "financial software" for Frank's Monolithic Memory, the "file cabinet," the "library," the passive whatever-you-want-to-call-it repository for all of Frank's loot.

Stout for a Vietnamese, a short, shiny toadstool, Dr. Nyung is a cardiac surgeon educated in France who way back when was one of the boat people. The AMA wouldn't let him practice in the United States so he became an accountant. When I was a boy, he and his friends would laugh at me in a way that was flattering. His house was high on Mt. Klu and, cut out of the jungle, had a backyard no bigger than a tennis court. Dr. Nyung paid me $40 to spend 20 minutes mowing it, then got me to lose the money in Vietnamese gambling games he and his pals played on his lanai.

His office is in midtown on the twenty-fourth floor of the Hirohito spire in a new Japanese superblock. He motions me to a computer screen and says, "Active Aluminum. Twenty-six percent on earnings last year but gone at below cost. And look at this: Revco Distributing—in the red but with a lot of quick sale inactive equipment, mostly trucks and new lift equipment, is left untouched. No method. Bell Hauser Burke—they make bearings, a beautiful company, 32 percent earnings last year—Syntyrsystym liquefies it and sells it for scrap."

I ask, "Frank's doing this?" and Dr. Nyung says codes are

doing it. Numbers shoot through the system and make sell orders. Who controls the numbers? He has no idea. He says that the trust appears bottomless, "the money seems to go forever," but it is being devoured willy-nilly from the top "with no method just madness," and I leave his office imagining us sucked dry by a vampire blind as a bat.

18 MARCH

Frank says yes there is a method. Dr. Nyung just doesn't know what it is. He says the system is part of Light + Weight, "bio-light" software he's developed using a nanometer-size protein called bacteriorhodopsin derived from saltwater bacteria. In today's *Star* the mayor of Honolulu has called Frank "a cowboy Strangelove" and the New Island "a lethal hallucination. Space-age banana republicanism at its worst."

19 MARCH

Tom Weire says, "I know you two are practically family, but Dewey's killed people. He prefers Mexicans, but he might settle for a white boy in a pinch." And re: squeezing the Honas for a million dollars, Weire allows, give or take, I'm a real good guy and do I really want to?

I say, "Don't you believe me?" and, fanning himself with his bar bill, he replies, "Sure. Christ knows, kiddo, desperation like yours simply can not be faked."

We are at the Kahala Hilton for lunch by the pool. Old white men play cards under a big umbrella, Mafia guys, Weire claims, who have flown out to sun their scars and chat up Frank about the New Island. Nothing serious, Weire says. They're just curious. Tom Weire has been on a water diet and is thin as a stick.

An afternoon off. Weire's old bathtub Porsche just got out of the shop. An $80,000 concourse-level restoration. Acid bath, the whole drill. Cherry red, it's as clean as a bubble. On his car phone on our way to play tennis at Kamkua Golf and Country he says, "Frank, guyfriendbuddypal, yeah, I know what 200 million means," hangs up, and when I said what was that about, he says, "Hyper Mart. You'd think if some gumbah set out to build the biggest retailing outlet ever he'd understand there might be the odd glitch here and there."

The government claims Frank paved twenty acres on Maui that were part of a national tropical forest reserve. "The Feds want to sue him," Weire says. "America with a K."

Weire says Frank's trying to acquire six trillion cubic feet of Siberian natural gas in exchange for syndication rights to *Starsky & Hutch* and *Beavis & Butthead,* plus all episodes of *Howard Stern and His Asshole Pals* that would otherwise just be beaming twenty light-years toward the Dog Star Cyrus.

I ask him when Frank will set the charges to blow out the undersea tunnel to create the New Island and he says, "You tell me."

We drive up into the shadowy green of the Manoa Valley. His Porsche smells great, all leather and gas, and I am becoming sort of happily nauseated when he says the Proteus has become "an incredible liability problem" because eighteen people died when the rocket blew up.

Rolling my window down, I ask, "Why?"

"Crawford, we're talking about the biggest nonnuclear explosion in history."

I say that doesn't answer my question.

"It was not, quite, a government project and the insurance carrier wrote a manifest about conditions where a launch could take place. The rocket, the gantry system, everything was floating out there when bang, there's weather. Namely, a hurricane. It was use it or lose it and unfortunately they used it but lost it anyway. Christ, kiddo, you were there."

"I don't get it." We are in little Manoa town. I see a sign above the old bank that reads

+ = +
Music by Music

"They launched riding bareback," Weire accelerates away from a stop sign, "with iffy insurance and the carrier refused to pay off. They got the government to pay limited liability and have been crossing their fingers ever since. So you're seeing the split-up of the company. Maye Hona's afraid people are going to start suing their way down the food chain. Your dad's gone, so who's that leave? Her and Frank. Then she looked at this New Island monstrosity and that did it: she wants out."

"So let her go."

"Crawford, it's her hard equity that guarantees the real value of your estate."

"Meaning what?"

"Meaning—how can I put this in a way you'll find most enticing?—meaning that play your cards right and you could become the superstar of the greatest riches-to-rags story ever told."

Under the dark, cloud-smoked mountains of Manoa columns of palm trees planted along either curb bow toward a long black driveway straight and flat as a floor. The pavement is new, clean, and takes us to a clubhouse built before World War II. But not built here. Frank had it coptered in piece by piece from the old Big Island Country Club cum Crawford time shares in Hilo. It's stocky, pink adobe, three stories high. An idyllic Alamo.

Weire parks between a swoopy new red Mercedes V-12 and some caddie's zip wagon and we get out. The fairway before us is a green carpet. Two big, old, pale-haired men in khaki shorts click and crackle by in their golf shoes. Watching the men approach the practice green, I hear, behind me, Weire say, the goys of summer. I ask why Frank would be directly liable for the Proteus and he whistles. "Tod, it was Frank who pushed the button."

I show my card at the clubhouse and we are given a corner court. We knock balls around, rally for serve. I win but can't get much going. Weire does whatever I do. I'm playing myself in a mirror. Deuce, his ad, deuce, my ad, deuce, his ad. A set for me, a set for him. I'm distracted. This is not good news. I ask Weire what he thinks I should do.

He twirls his racquet in one hand. "You got Less Nervous."

Yeah, and we'll be evicted just because Jan and Dean doesn't have the x thousands he needs to make the rent and

I can't do anything to stop it. It's ridiculous.

A fat lady comes out and tells me all whites on weekends. She says my shirt has color in it—I look down. It does, it's pale blue—and I'll have to get a white shirt or get off the court.

At the pro shop it's $65.50 for a white Stefan Edberg tennis shirt that's not even 100 percent cotton. I go to charge it and I'm refused. God damn Frank. I'm still cut off. I ask Weire, "Now what?," and he says, "Use money." Right. I hate money. I don't carry money. He fronts me four twenties.

The next game Weire plays so hard I'm just an angry spectator. The ball goes where I'm not. I say I want k10s on every corporation we own or have investment in, want to know what I'm going to be worth and what I stand to lose, that I'm tired of hearing the estate is none of my business.

Weire says, "Be cool," but I hit one of his lobs so hard the ball is embedded in the mesh of the wire fence that surrounds the court. I have no control, so if I don't take the point off the serve I usually have to settle into a rhythm and pray whoever it is makes a mistake before I do.

"It's kind of like necking with your sister," Weire says. "There are certain things maybe you'd like to do but better not. I represent Frank. I'm bound to act in his interest."

I say, "You mean you can't even show me what I've inherited? Nyung says our whole estate is being cannibalized by Syntyrsystym."

Weire serves and faults, then advises, "Crawford, seek the Buddha mind. When you need to know, you will." He hits a slow second serve and I return it so deep that, thinking it's back, I smack my racquet against the base line. But it's in. Weire's return hangs in the sky. As he scrambles back onto the court, I smash it. The ball hits him in the face, and though I say sorry, sorry, sorry, for an instant it feels great, and holding his head, Weire says, "Speech."

23 MARCH

Frank says America is shot and the problem with the utopians who want to fix it is they have no imagination. On the New Island there will be no laws except death for murder, rape, and theft.

It's ninety-five degrees by noon. The liquor dick came back and cited Jan and Dean for working in his undies.

Then August Hona, trading down Murder for Mayhem, put the wrecking ball through the side of Less Nervous, after which Tom Weire, JD, and I stood outside, an ambulance siren warbling in the distance while JD screamed at Weire to do something.

Holding binoculars to his eyes, Weire says, "I've done all I can."

Aug said he made a mistake; that he was aiming at the Palms and missed. He showed the cops an order to vacate.

Weire says, "Twenty bucks it's Hamms." He passes me the binoculars. Down the street a woman has been hit by a car. There is a broken beer bottle beside her and her head is rocking back and forth with the momentary steadiness of a metronome.

I say, "That's a long-neck Bud. Make it twenty-five."

Jan says, "Weire, you've got the attention span of an ant."

Weire says, "Thirty." Then, "Janguyfriendbuddypal, I've done all I can. The problem is, Dewey's trying to send you a message."

"What message would that be?"

"The more things change, the more they stay the same."

25 MARCH

Roberta, "tired of wiping Middle America's orgasms from Jan and Dean's Love Machines," insists we get rid of him. Maybe she's right. Our crowd tonight is broke bikedykelesbopunks on the crawl from the Clit club plus drunk college kids. Roberta, wearing a T-shirt with the words SMASH THE STATE in black block letters across the back and a platter of empties held above her head like the Statue of Liberty wielding her torch, swings the glasses down on the bar and says, "Guess what whatsherface sitting over there just asked me? She's smashed but it's priceless. Is it true if a guy gives you pearls it's cuz he wants to titty-fuck you and come on your face?"

We do it about a quarter after midnight. The moon lights the rubble around the wreckage of the Palms Hotel and the high cab of Aug Hona's crane. Jan pulls on a pair of rubber dishwashing gloves, climbs into the crane's cab, and cuts the ignition wires. Then he touches two together. The starter motor makes a sound like Donald Duck clearing his throat and the engine burps to life.

The crane moves across the street to the beach, its boom slashes into palm tops. I walk alongside it to the water's edge.

Jan steers the crane into the ocean. Shore chop splashes across its tracks. It rolls deeper and deeper. Water rises up to the top of its tracks and then over its fenders.

He sets the wrecking ball in motion, back and forth, higher and higher, and leaps into the shore break as the ball smashes its own cab to junk.

28 MARCH

"Be an angel," Roberta says, handing me a new tube of Dead Man and turning over on her back. We're at the beach watching August Hona try to pull his crane out of the surf. He's using three steel cables and three winches bolted to a thirty-ton Honda World Mover bulldozer he trucked in this morning. The thing sits on the beach and I've been watching August haggle with the cops over the sound of about six songs on Roberta's new micro–boom box. I guess the city is extremely pissed off.

Roberta says if we get married she's got sex acts on the drawing board that will blow my mind. I glance across the street where Jan and Dean is inside behind the bar at Less Nervous. Roberta has perfect, delicate feet and hands—like feet and hands released from work and gravity. Her mouth and big, hooded eyes are beautiful. Yeah, her jaw is strong and she has a brief boxer's nose that makes her look a little bulldoggy, but still. She bites me on the shoulder and says, "Less Nervous, we've got to get the pink."

Frank calls with the news that on Maui up on Mt. Klu somebody is breaking into my parents' mausoleum leaving trash, puke, and graffiti written in a language possibly new to the world.

Weire was on the Wall last night with the mayor and the man who is both president of the Federal Reserve Bank of New York and head of the Bank of International Settlement's committee on global banking supervision in Switzerland—who said that the New Island would become an "essentially lawless entrepot" for up to 25,000 companies and trusts. The mayor called Frank "a Ted Turner with a double Y chromosome." Weire observed that because the United States was not a signatory to the International Law of the Sea, Frank could do anything he wanted so long as he was outside the twelve-mile limit.

I go down to the docks, park Jan's convertible, and walk to the warehouse beneath the great foam concrete long pipes that will control the flow of lava as it spews out of the ocean floor. The foam concrete weighs only 40 percent as much as ferro and is 90 percent as strong. There are seven long pipes there, each about a block wide and eight stories high. Vestiges of a monster Stonehenge. Beside the long pipes are great matrices of heat-resistant rebar, huge cages of it ten stories high that will be set into the cooling magma in immense inverted carrots that will provide the earthquake-proof foundation for the six 100-story spires where 50,000 fatcats and their coatholders will live and work. Frank says the secret of land use is not to. Most of the New Island's land area will be either a tropical park or Robert Trent Jones's deathbed golf course.

The rebar is like a kid's set of monkeybars that goes on forever and it throws a grid of shadows across the parking lot and across the dull silver aluminum hide of the warehouse. Last week a guy came out with a Parapente—a paraglider and chute—climbed up, and leapt off the top of it.

I walk to the warehouse doors and say the words *The United States, at present, is a country without political ideology, without any intellectual movement, without direction or goal. We are paralyzed by the unadmitted knowledge that we are trapped in a crumbling structure of "mixed economy"—and, while the girders are cracking under our feet, about to collapse, our political leaders are haggling over which rugs and drapes to loot from some rooms for the decoration of others.* The doors slide open and I let myself into the warehouse. It's Sunday and nobody's there. The place is big and full of Joe Dozers. Frank's new machines. Each chassis houses a supercharged Cummins diesel that sits between four independently suspended balloon tires that are taller than I am. Their cabs sit in front of their engines. The driver operates the machine's forward speed and power steering from a single joystick. A Joe Dozer is designed to hit eighty on the road, but the machines' purpose is not rapid transit but destruction. Another lever with a pistol grip controls Joe's big steel mouth—hinged hydraulic jaws whose task is to bite buildings apart in hours. Frank will revolutionize the wrecking trade. A single Joe Dozer can knock apart a decent neighborhood in a week. Twenty Joe Dozers in concert—though Frank hasn't tried it yet—will topple and chew apart the World Trade Center in a day and a half.

30 MARCH

A sizzling little blast of cold. Steel wand in hand, my grandfatherly dermatologist freezes a brown dab of premelanoma skin off at the top of my left cheek and says don't worry, if I stick to 150 he can "harvest these cancers as fast as they grow." Meanwhile, not too good news. Something has been going wrong with the Triglycerin-3 charges Frank is setting to free the magma.

Roberta and I, in Jan and Dean's Ford, the top down to another night of stars, are driving down Ala Wai Boulevard beside the black mirror of the canal, on our way to break into Jeanie's. Roberta insists we must "seriously eliminate" Jan and Dean. When I ask why, she puts her perfect bare feet up on the Ford's pink dashboard and replies, "Because he did something to me."

"When?"

"When we were drunk."

"What did he do?"

"Something with his finger."

I pull up to the signal at the bridge over the canal. The intersection, bathed in yellow street lamps, appears shattered through the cracks in JD's windshield.

"So how do we go about this eliminating?"

"Put a bullet through his head." Roberta says if he's not gone by Friday she's going back to work for Good Stuff Junior. We pull up in front of Jeanie's apartment. When I say I don't want to do this, she says I have to because I'm "responsible" for Jeanie and that we have to "do what's right."

Roberta's B-movie consciousness has told her that "something has happened" to my old girlfriend: It is evidently harder for her than it is for me to accept the fact that I have been ditched—and she, Roberta, is convinced the secret lies here.

But two security cops are standing in the lobby and we have to drive back to Less Nervous.

Frustrated, Roberta wants to know, how can making the rent on the place be such a nightmare?

"I don't know," I reply, in the past, if I needed however many thousands of dollars for something, Frank's software just told Hawaii First Federal to write me a check.

I go behind the bar.

A problem with the bomb. The weight of its casing above the bar has cracked the concrete at the base of the inverted horseshoe of three beams he installed to hold it up. The cracks cross the floor like tiny bolts of lightning. With our luck, if the thing ever comes crashing down it will be on our one good night of the year and kill fifty people at a whack.

Though Roberta wants to go hardcore, I'm holding out for a more conventional Less Nervous and have solicited investors.

Two Kuzaki come in. *Kuzaki* is Japanese for "esteemed young thug" but these are nice guys. They explain the Kuzaki gestalt. Exercise, no meat, kicking ass, and making art. Japan has ordered its people to be creative and the Kuzaki medium is violence. They finger the Crude Rude Lewd Really Stewed

Almost-Nude Mini-Dude who is, since Jan somehow leased $1,000 a month worth of new software, now also shrewd. He strides out on the bartop hand in hand with a tiny "Miss Universe" and tells the Kuzaki that for $500 they can watch him take "this mi fine woman round the world," otherwise he's going back in his box.

The Kuzaki ask if, along with retaining our liquor license, it would be possible to get a permit to fire automatic weapons in here. I reply that in our new century anything is possible.

I have told Jan I'm manager now. He's accepted it gracefully, telling me, "You pay the bills, you can be king."

Just before closing, a Drastic Plastic wearing a purple neon body suit ruptures an eardrum trying to vomit through a straw.

APRIL

Hell to pay. August Hona and Ronald Sousee come in. Round immense, threatening toddlers. Not handsome men. Sousee has a Space Rasta hairdo that has left him bangs hanging from his forehead like little wet cigars. The pale rashes on Aug's big bare arms have been scratched to bloody arcs and blobs. He says, "Tear up the lease and give me $28,000 to fix my crane."

I say, "You mean the crane that wrecked our building?" I am washing glasses behind the bar. Snapping the latch back on the dishwasher, I pull its door open and—bending into the ranks of beer mugs—am enveloped by a burp of steam hot enough to burn.

I say, "Beat it before I call the cops," and he says he'll walk out, take the bulldozer they're using to clear rubble from the Palms, and mow this place to the ground.

I know he can—the earthmover is as big as a 7-Eleven. And I know he will. For a moment I just stand there like a rabbit in somebody's headlights and then I take the iron wand I bought on the street, walk out from behind the bar, and we shake it up. Aug grabs for my throat and I hit him on the head. Hard. I get the same painful vibrating feeling I used to get in Little League when I hit a bad pitch.

But nothing happens. He just stands there. After a moment he says, "God," then he sits down on a table by the door. Suddenly I see the damage. His left eye is defined by blood around the lid and looks as if it is set in a small, crimson-lipped woman's mouth.

The back door is open and outside I see a rat mincing a power line. Then I see Sousee going for the wall phone. I ask what are you doing, and he says he's calling the cops.

August Hona sits there, holding his head. A snake of blood slithers down the back of his hand. He looks like he's forgotten who he is. He watches as my right hand moves forehead to sternum, left shoulder to right. Once again invoking the tired ass of the Lord and wishing I could erase and correct my immediate past.

2 APRIL

At his house Tom Weire says, "Joke for you, Crawford. Mrs. Smith goes to her doctor for a routine blood test. The doctor calls back the next day and says, 'Mrs. Smith, we got your test mixed up with another Mrs. Smith. You'll have to come down and take the whole thing over.' Mrs. Smith says, 'That's absurd. Jut analyze the blood and if they're both normal forget about it.' The doctor says, 'Why didn't I think of that?' and hangs up. But then he calls back the next day and says, 'Mrs. Smith, we have terrible news. We analyzed the blood samples and they're both infected. One with AIDS, the other with Alzheimer's disease. Sorry, but it looks like you've got one or the other.' Mrs. Smith is so shocked she faints. So her husband, Mr. Smith, picks up the receiver and says, 'Hey, what's coming down?' and the doctor tells him his wife has either AIDS or Alzheimer's. Mr. Smith freaks. 'Doctor,' he says, 'what should I do?' 'Well,' the doctor replies, 'this is a toughie, but here's what I'd suggest: Put her in your car, drive her ten miles from home, let her out, and if she finds her way back, never fuck her again.'" Then he says, "Now, what'd you tell the cops?"

I start to think how to say what happened when the phone beeps. Weire picks it up, says, "Frank. Sure. Dewey. Offer him—write this down—a fifteen-year fixed with no negative amortization—*just write it down, Frank*—with a sixty-day full rate lock. Okay, then a Jumbo thirty-year fixed at ten point eight seven five and give him two points flat. Yeah. Bye." Weire hangs up and speaks to the phone: "Please God, don't have him call back." He sweeps papers off his coffee table.

"Okay. The cops. What'd you tell the cops?"

I say not much. They were more concerned about getting an ambulance. I tell Weire that Vorhaggen keeps calling me and I ask who exactly he is and Weire says just some gruff goddamn-it-type German-Jap who's been around forever.

Then he asks who else saw it and I say Wally, my psychotherapist, plus a couple of ghouls from the Sullenaires. I look around Weire's living room. Though he's lived here as long as I've known him, there's little furniture nor much to suggest that he didn't move in yesterday.

I say I called Frank and he said not to worry, the whole thing was a setup.

"You mean he thinks Aug *planned* to have his head bashed in?"

I shrug and Weire says, "Lemme tell you something about Frank. Talk to him and 90 percent of the time he's not listening. He's just thinking of what he's going to say next. What'd you hit him with?" I say hit who with and he says, "Crawford, what's your name, what round is it, who are you fighting?"

I tell him a metal bar. Weire looks vaguely appalled, so I add, "He grabbed me by the throat. He's a whacko who'd kill me in two seconds given the chance."

"An iron bar, Jesus. Are you still taking your meds?"

I say why and he says if I'm not, the DA's office will be all over me. He asks about the dosage, and I say 100 milligrams of Triglycerin-2/Antiswaq a day and, "Face facts, I'm not a monster."

He considers this and says, "What did you do this for?"

I think about that. What scares me is that August was shivering. It was eighty degrees easy and, looking like nothing but a giant child—one eye terrified, the other gore—he was shivering. But I'm average, just like the body representing man on a deep space probe. With better muscle tone but I'm not a 250-pound August Hona, and God won't give me new teeth when an August Hona punches the ones I've got down my throat. When it starts, stop it, is the way I have to look at it.

Still, what I finally say sort of surprises me. I tell Weire I did hit August because I'd rather be sorry than pissed. That no way I'd ever choose anger over regret.

• • •

Re: The New Island. Frank says the program to blast a hole to the magma has gone south. The shaped charges his Russian mohole men are using are only venting into the rock, creating a chain of unconnected holes, but not an umbilical.

Above the glassy wash of the shore break, scouring the top of Jan's board with wax, I hear something. Like someone has blown up a paper bag and popped it. Wondering what it was I see Roberta coming toward me to ask about my dreams.

Jan's got a bright red stripe of blood across his forearm. Dressed in a blue shirt, white bucks, and gold slacks, he looks like an Easter egg. He says he was walking up the stairs to the apartment and the front windows leapt right out in front of him.

The explosion has blown out the sliding doors in back. Jan's bed could have been hit by a meteorite. Mattress crap hangs in tufts everywhere. The glass remaining at the bottom of the doors to the lanai sticks up in jagged towers like the silhouette of a see-through Alps.

Somebody stole my motorcycle and camera equipment. All my proof sheets and film are gone to ash and goo.

Frank drops out of the sky. His helicopter's rotor nearly snaps a power line coming in. He unhooks himself from the Cayuse's harness and steps to the pavement. The blades continue to spin, then slow and sag. The machine's skid struts are scarred by gaudy welds. Frank is making the landing platform stronger, and the Cayuse is evolving; its motor now delivers 10,000 pounds more thrust than the new army SuperCobra.

I tell him that most of my photographs have been destroyed. Jan says this stinks and Frank says, "You got that part right."

5 APRIL

Shirtless, fitting wood to wood, measuring and nailing, Frank says information in the new century science will defeat famine, boredom, and the plague, but—thank God for us—vital knowledge will become so elevated that nobody will know how anything works. Easing a little Mikita buzz saw through a loose two-by-six, he tells me that the good news is that everybody will be empowered; the bad news is nobody will understand why.

Pushing a mop, I agree. A bubbly lava of soap and water rolls out over the floor. The apartment is a burned and busted mess. I put an air mattress on the living room floor last night and it was like trying to sleep inside a cigarette butt.

Frank cuts a board in half. We are rebuilding the wall between the living room and Jan's bedroom. Frank is no saber-toothed fat cat locked away in an ivory tower, Frank is hands on and—so Jan and Dean and I don't get kicked out of here too—he's wowed Zen Rents by offering to repair our damage himself.

My brother asks if I have any Dead Man. His chest is purple and the long muscles in his arms stand in fevered relief. He rubs a white worm of 175 onto his shoulders and says, "I just want to ask you one question. Do you plan to sit still for this or what?"

7 APRIL

I call Panasonic Fire & Casualty. Aside from my parents, I've never lost anything I couldn't just go out and replace. I report what's gone: Everything. I call Bernie to get a cost estimate on my Triumph. He's beside himself. It is as if I'd lost a national park.

One good thing, though, and it's amazing. Frank, working twenty-two hours straight, rebuilt our apartment. Made it simpler, more or less just one big room. Then he "Big Stored" it, coptered in new beds, chairs, tables, two old-fashioned lava lamps.

In return, he has a job for me. Frank says to cover the spewing magma that will create the New Island I must find a cubic mile of sand.

8 APRIL

A bad storm. Roberta and I have driven across the Ala Wai Canal to my lost girlfriend Jeanie's apartment. I park Jan's Ford. No more security cops but solid grey clouds make it dark as dusk at noon. Robot Radio says it's thirty-seven degrees, a record low for Honolulu, and getting out of Jan's Ford Roberta's wet black hair is smashed back against her forehead and she screams above the wind, "You idiot, look out." A door spins from the sky, crashes to the pavement across the street. She grabs my hand and, pushed by the wind, we run across the street. The windows island-side have been boarded up or X'ed with wide strips of masking tape, but the glass doors to the lobby have been smashed, maybe by looters, I don't know. Sprinting up stone stairs and not wanting to be here, I say we won't find shit. In the elevator Roberta instructs, "Gimme your driver's license."

She looks at it and says, "George Van Arrison. Who's he?"

I say nobody and Roberta stops at Jeanie's door, knocks, waits until nothing happens, then slips the license into the crack between the door and its frame and wiggles it up and down. She twists the knob and we go inside. The apartment is furnished in a spare, stylish, Japanese way. Outside above the sound of the wind I hear police sirens.

Shivering, Roberta says, "Swing Out, Sister. Mommy is a Mammal." I see her in the bright light of Jeanie's living room, framed in front of the floor-to-ceiling diaphanous shades, punching up discs in Jeanie's Sony.

I say don't monkey with her stuff and Roberta says, holding up a CD, "Monkeying with her stuff is the name of the game. Whaddaya think we're here for? What's this?"

The Word of God. Catholic Gospels and foreign-language instruction. I'd often go to sleep here listening to alarming questions spoken in English and repeated in French or Spanish. *Take me to the police station. Which way to the hospital? Help me, my arm is broken. Officer, I have just been robbed.* Jeanie wanted to be ready for the worst anywhere.

I go in the kitchen, open the refrigerator. Nothing but a bottle of mineral water and an orange with skin like an old lady. That and a rigid wiggle of long-dried egg yolk in the sink are the only real sign that anybody's actually eaten here. Jeanie's apartment is enchantingly impersonal. Like a very expensive, very tasteful hotel suite.

"Is this what I think it is?" Roberta asks, wetting her finger in a little round-bottomed brass bowl beneath a crucifix.

"Bootleg holy water. She gets it from a nun who has a crush on her."

Roberta peers into Jeanie's second bedroom. The walls are mirrors. Machines that could be robots stand around looking as if they are bored and dying for something to do.

"The exercise room," I say. Jeanie worked out two hours a day every day beginning at 4:30 every morning. A ritual that seemed rooted in the ascesis of an elite no-bullshit organization like the Jesuits or the SS. The exercise made Jeanie strong and fatless.

Roberta goes across the hall into Jeanie's bedroom, pulling open tansu drawers. "What's this?" She picks up three empty envelopes, instructs, "Feast your eyes." Each is addressed to Jeanie, is monogrammed with Frank's office address, and bears his seismographic signature above the address. Roberta says, "She's diddling him, Crawford." I say bullshit, she was doing ads for Big Store. Those envelopes probably contained her paychecks. Roberta says no way he'd send her checks personally, they had to be love letters. "Think about it, Crawford."

I do. Roberta wanders off to the back of the apartment and I stand there, remembering. It makes my chest tight. Good old Jeanie. To this day I associate her image with any number of rent-a-car agencies, interisland airlines, and hotel chains. Her dark skin that seemed in soft focus, as if misted with a tiny atmosphere, her bright black hair and big teardrop eyes. She was a face of Hawaii to the world and her darkest secret was that her grocer parents were Mexican and from Southern California—Buena Park aspiring to Anaheim—and Jeanie hadn't been west of the bait shack at the Long Beach pier until she was twenty-three.

I met her on Frank's sloop while he was below hawking T-cells to Ugandans. She said she sold flame-retardant window coverings made in Singapore. Unreal, I replied, already eager to share her hopes, her dreams, her fireproof drapes. Frank says life is a chemical trick, marriage a burn and love hormones, and perhaps, but this was like falling down a well. The next thing was dinner or drinks, movie or the Waves, Trojan or spermicidal gel.

At dinner she had picked at her food, shopping her vegetables bean by bean and eating little of what was in front of her. She was quiet, said she hoped to go from ads to soaps, so I explained how Shakespeare threw the "players" into Hamlet because he was short a second act, how *Waiting for Godot* was the dramatic fraud of the century, and how my flunking out of premed didn't mean I wasn't going to end up rich, rich, rich, and by the time the sun rose I doubt I had anything left to bestow but blood and bone.

Love letters? I stare at the envelopes. If they were love letters, I'd be relieved. No, this is something maybe a whole lot worse.

I go in the bathroom. Roberta is toweling her hair, looking in the mirror. She says, "First it's the eyes, then the chin. The legs last forever." I say, "Let's go," and she says, "I'll probably hit twenty like a wall." Then, "Be an angel, grab me a Kleenex."

I say, "Forget Kleenex. Let's go before somebody calls the cops."

"Crawford, you should be nicer to me."

I close my eyes. I want out of here. I feel her push past me. "Seriously," Roberta says, "I read a book a week. I get lonely. I masturbate. Play your cards right and I could be the wanton slut of your dreams."

9 APRIL

Strange. A serious misidentification. The bomb case that hangs above the bar at Less Nervous turns out to be not a Little Boy but one even more valuable. It's the shell to the first and only American four-stage hydrogen bomb.

I find out because Jerry Wiler comes in out of the rain. He

is pale as death, and eerie with old age. He says he knew my grandfather from the early H-bomb projects, Mod O and Mod T. He identifies my granddad as "a beautiful man, quiet, modest, a championship-level tennis player," and "a giant in deterrence. I knew your dad too. An angel."

I'm among those who owe their lives to the rhythm method and never knew my father as young. He was forty-five when I was born and almost seventy when he drowned. I like hearing about him. But the old man wants to talk about our bomb.

"That's the case for the Mark 31. The most powerful American nuclear weapon ever made. The trigger alone could destroy a good-size city. It had a primary fission stage boosted by tritium gas to three times Nagasaki strength."

He asks for a 7-Up, then puts a long hand up and touches the belly of the bomb. "Three-and-a-half-inch steel. Probably weighs eight tons. How the devil did you hoist it up in here?"

I explain that Frank had it transported in pieces and then had it welded back together. "It hangs from ten-inch steel beams." I point to the ceiling.

Old Wiler seems shocked. "He had it cut apart?"

"That was the only way to move it, let alone get it in here. The pieces barely made it through the skylight as it was."

"You might as well have cut apart the *Spirit of St. Louis*," Wiler says. He gazes back up toward the ceiling. "I remember your brother as a child. A violent little boy." He takes a sip of his 7-Up. "Your grandpa prepared this bomb's grandfather for the MIKE Shot. I was drowning in flop sweat, spooked it'd fizzle, but your granddad was cool as a snake.

"We blew up a whole atoll. Both of us were in the plane. The bomb was so heavy that when they dropped it out of the B-36 we shot 300 feet straight up in the air." Wiler is hairless, his head a skull with skin. "When Khrushchev came to the United States he brought a scientific mission with him headed by Andrei Sakharov's boss. The idea was to show the Russians what they were up against. They flew him out to Sandia in New Mexico. The bomb was so big—bigger than a Polaris missile—that they had to jack up a B-52 off the tarmac just to fit it into the bomb bays."

"And?" I wanted to get to my father in this.

"And there it was. The Soviet looked at it long enough to

recognize what it was, and tears came to his eyes."

"Because he was horrified at its power?"

"Because he recognized a masterpiece. This baby could blow up the world."

10 APRIL

Frank says horseshit. The crater itself would be less than four miles wide.

Frank's accountant, Dr. Nyung, says that unless he is missing the fine print, I am party to a fortune that makes Bill Gates a pawn broker. But he worries it is all going out the electronic door.

Outside the apartment the rain is crazy. Roberta says the new FM station Robot Radio is run by computer deejays and when I turn on Jan's old stereo a Robot weather man reports that the weather has turned "spastic." He or it is right. Rain is hitting the windows with the sound of a thousand little rocks.

11 APRIL

The sun is hot again. Looking out the living room window to Tony's ark—which is steaming like a huge cup of coffee—I listen to my brother say forget Dr. Nyung and his comic strip autopsy of our family fortune, go get the cubic mile of sand.

The hurricane is over. Honolulu looks cleaned and ruined. The streets appear glistening and new around the million-dollar houses that have had their roofs ripped off. We drive in Frank's Zero, he's had Bernie replace the transmission again, this time with one that is mostly software instead of gears. I ask where I'm supposed to find 1.2 billion cubic yards of sand and he says the yellow pages. Then he says he'll send me to Heaven no questions asked. "No cops, no lawsuits, you just disappear." No thanks. I did that already, right after Frank flunked out of Armageddon School. It was a bad place then and I doubt it has improved.

Downtown with a lawyer who is also notary. I tell her I want my money. Now.

For who knows, I may be on a roll. There has been improvement at Less Nervous. Roberta cut a deal with the top sales computer chip down at Robot Radio to have the words "Less Nervous" played at the end of every song and she no longer wants to "simply eliminate" Jan and Dean, she more concretely wants to have him killed. I figure now that she's kicked her hates and frustrations upstairs to fantasyland, maybe we can all live in peace. Though, maybe not.

This morning she said, "Have you ever felt him? The hair on his arms is like wire. When he stuck his finger in me it felt like I was being raped by a ball bearing with a claw on top."

She claimed she told one of the bigger and dumber Drastic Plastics that if he blew Jan and Dean's head off she'd give him a lifetime pass to the Love Machines.

Driving into Honolulu in Jan's Ford I listened for our spots but heard only a Robot voice tell me that the atmosphere has devolved to the state where soon we can expect "vacuuming." The air will part to allow nothing in, the void will descend to the earth tight and those caught in this vacuum will explode, like overinflated balloons.

The lawyer is sexy. Half Japanese, half Samoan, dressed like a powerful librarian, she wears glasses as delicate as fishing tackle and a woman's idea of a pinstriped suit. Her black hair is pulled back to a bun skewered by a black chopstick and she says, "What money?"

"The money," I reply, "that I should be inheriting."

"You'll have to talk to Mr. Weire about that."

"Who are you representing in all this?"

"The estate."

"My estate?"

"*The* estate. Mr. Weire is representing your brother, who controls the estate."

She says that she is only a "functionary in all this" and that because so much money is involved she prefers to read from a script, and she does. Paper in hand, she instructs me to sign and initial the documents in an exact order.

"So I'm just the corporate dummy in all this?"

"You can call Mr. Weire."

Beginning to feel very angry, I chew a 100 mikes of Anti-swaq, and begin going over the documents.

One relates to Quick Sound which allows you to use your telephone to play CDs on your stereo receiver from a central library. And Fine Print, a system that banks all pertinent information about you—credit rating, criminal record, history of employment—by means of "nonlinear identification"—the hospital footprint taken the day you are born.

"That's what I am," I say, "esteemed corporate dummy."

"Most of this is just tax stuff," she replies.

Trying another tack, I tell her I like the Japanese because they are polite and the Samoans because they aren't. I'm trying to get a rise and lose track of what I'm signing, because while I'm looking at this willowy document cop I'm thinking where am I going to get three trillion pounds of sand.

And between the distractions of the sexy power clerk and the 100 mikes of Antiswaq I just took so I can pee according to the law, nothing wants to compute.

13 APRIL

Long curves of steel rise toward the crane that divides the sky. Sparks from welders' torches roostertail and bounce off ribbing for circular hulls 300 feet long.

At Pearl City, Russian mohole men are building the barges in a dry dock as big as an open-air amphitheater. They are using what Frank calls "high school dreadnought technology."

The 1,200-ton foam concrete long pipes are being rolled on their pallets onto barges that are really just huge steel shells. An instant before the detonation that will bring the magma to the surface of the seafloor, the barges will be pushed into place by oceangoing tugs, the kind that steer the big aircraft carriers in and out of Pearl Harbor.

The pallets are set on steel rollers and pulled by tractors with treads as big as barn doors. The driver sits two stories off the ground above twin jet engines that, despite generating 55,000 pounds of thrust each, can move the pallets at only one and a half miles per hour.

Once the lava begins to flow and the first of the long pipes has been set in place, Frank will have divers wire superheated ionized hydrogen gas "strings" through the rebar surrounding the pipe and leading to the heart of the hot lava flow. That's the secret here. Because with this setup the New Island never has to stop growing. Turn on the hydrogen and the strings reheat the magma and get it flowing again. Want more paradise? Flip a switch and it comes bubbling and steaming right out of the sea. Valhalla on tap, guided to the periphery, so as not to disturb the paradise already there.

1 4 APRIL

I park the car, come in a hankie. Focus. Roberta and I are here to visit Mr. and Mrs. Buddy Walsh. We walk through weeds, go inside. What a dump. Newspapers in foothills up against every wall. The linoleum floors feel like they're made out of chewing gum.

The Walshes' kitchen counter overflows with bread, sliced-up potatoes black with age, and droolie ketchup bottles. The baby staggers around, his face paisley with rashes. Buddy says, "Welcome to the Fourth World. 'Sup?"

"Not much," I reply.

Driving here, we made semi-love. Roberta unzipped my zipper, I unfurled. But her strokes seemed less sexual than abstract, as if what she'd released from the open fly of my Levi's was closer than anything else, a larger, softer, more tubular worry bead.

Roberta is a do-gooder and we are here to save Buddy's baby. Buddy has just got a job selling Fords and is using his commissions to finance a new hobby—heroin. Roberta planned to take his child. To just go in there and get the little kid.

Roberta tells Buddy this has got to stop, that Buddy's son is three and should be learning abstract words like yesterday, tomorrow, and because. She says we're taking the toddler to Children's Services and we do. Just like that. Buddy's so nutted up he thinks it's a good idea—in fact, a wonderful idea—and Mrs. Walsh is "at the grocery store." Leaving, I look at Buddy Walsh and thank God I wasn't born that kind of weakling.

• • •

15 APRIL

Frank wants to know where is his sand and I say I haven't got it, don't know where to get it, and haven't made a single phone call and don't know why.

We are down at the docks in the shadows of the long pipes. They sit on their steel pallets, rolling floors half the size of a football field. The underside of each pallet, lifted to the air, would resemble an abacus. One hundred axles, each fifty yards long, cross each pallet in parallel lines eighteen inches apart. Every axle is strung with 100 steel wheels.

Roberta has a gift for me. A handcuff key she says she got from a cop.

16 APRIL

Frank is understanding, he says he'll get the sand, that the sand was too much for me, that we are going to make the first custom-made country, and that the difference between his world and mine is the difference between two dimensions and three. The sand, he says, will come from Kahoolawe Island, the navy target range. Frank says he has an explosive ordnance disposal contract with the federal government to return Kahoolawe to its original state, which calls for him to comb it for unexploded shells and bombs, and to remove introduced species, mostly pigs and goats. The sand will be his payoff.

Now I watch him ten years ago in *Wheels of Fire*. Roberta and I are at the Kailua Drive-in. The best parts are in slo mo. Frank sliding into the machine, strapping himself into the seat, and pulling the streamlined helmet over his head. Behind him sits a 488-cubic-inch aluminum-blocked Chevy V-8 Keith Black racing engine topped with a GMC supercharger big enough to live in. Frank is attempting to break the quarter-mile time and speed record and his means will be simple: The huge engine blubs and crackles on a standard race mix of nitromethane and methanol. The moment the lights on the Christmas tree descend, he'll hit a switch injecting Triglycerin-3 into the fuel. He'd designed the engine to take twelve seconds worth of this additive before blowing up. All the time in the world.

The lights on the Christmas tree descend. Even in slow motion you can tell he's ripping it up. Monster black dragslicks scream into the pavement. Smoke jumps to the sky and "The Thing" flashes through the traps at 302.26 miles per hour. A quarter mile in 4.78 seconds and then—before Frank can shut it down—the engine blows into the sky 3.28 seconds ahead of schedule.

Roberta and I have gone to see a double-bill, *Mt. Analog* and *New Hope for the Dead*, and this is playing between shows. Frank's more or less the belle of the ball in *Wheels of Fire*, a short about top racing disasters. On the screen "The Thing" disintegrates in a long, skidding smear of flame. Its chassis skips and bounces over the asphalt. The tires and engine burst to bits.

Then there I am. The camera has cut to the starting area below the grandstands where I'm shown with my hands on the side of my head, my mouth big, open, and wobbly—screaming.

The Thing spins to a stop. Men in fire suits swarm around it. Nothing's left but the cockpit. All black and round. Then it begins to hatch like a barbequed egg. Frank emerges, smoke pouring from his silver fire suit. He pulls off his helmet. Not a scratch. Cut to some lunatic slamming into wall four at the Indianapolis 500.

I pop 100 mikes of Antiswaq and Roberta says I better take it easy. "That stuff is the same as Triglycerin, whatever you call it." If I take too much, she thinks, I could actually explode, or at the very least, "end up, Crawford, with a literally blown mind."

It's cool and dark in Jan and Dean's Ford. Roberta sits on my lap, knees roped by the waistband of her panties, ankles manacled by fallen tennis shorts. She tips her head back, arms on my shoulders, legs parted slightly, she allows me brief access to her glassy interior.

Her mouth is at the top of my neck and she says, "Jeanie had the hots for Frank. Really. I saw her with him in JD's when you were getting ripped off in Mexico. You shoulda seen it. She'd smile at him, eyes going bat, bat, bat, saying, 'Tod's such a nice boy,' bat, bat, bat. Are you still a boy, Crawford? Maybe, but what a *big* boy."

I say, "Let's lie down."

"No, and don't come on me."

We sag sideways. Roberta says, "Get that thing away from there. Nobody gets that. Least of all you. Be cool, and I'll make you come on a Kleenex." I hear race cars crash. "Besides, the other'd be too messy, I'd probably bleed green."

1 7 A P R I L

When I hear Tom Weire say that the word "disinherited" can mean a thousand different things I am in his white office looking at a blind item in the *Star* saying that the Waves' Ukrainian L. Dornier Vetrochuk has no mom or dad, that the center was conceived in a petri dish, and that Frank has got the pink on a dormant Soviet genetic engineering program to create man-made men, men tall and strong and armored against the effects of radiation and disease, of which Vetrochuk was an admittedly flawed rough draft. Distracted by this, it takes me an instant to realize that my brother apparently is trying to throw me out of the family.

"It's Aug's eye," Weire says.

"But an eye can't be worth, even if the Honas sued us and won, it can't be worth—it'd cost us what? Point zero zero one of whatever we've got?"

"Crawford," Weire says, "shit mushrooms. He'd just rather be safe than sorry. Afterward, he'd reinstate you."

"So I'm going to lose everything?"

"Don't panic. Or go screaming to Frank. That'll just make it worse."

"So what am I supposed to do?"

"My advice: Make your hellhole work."

I am. No matter what. In for a penny, in for a pound. But Less Nervous is not going to be easy. Last year a genealogist glommed onto Frank and in return for *x* amount of our family fortune wrote a report stating—three generations of Crawford cat burglars in Australia notwithstanding—our family stretched back variously to Leonardo da Vinci and to the House of Roses and I have to wonder, with all that erudite man-powered helicopter/adroit princely garrotting DNA twirling through my genes, why I cannot, at age twenty-five, figure out a way to raise money by a more sophisticated means than panhandling in the street.

Disinherited. Weire breaks what may have been an hour's silence, "How's your new little girlfriend?"

"She wants me to find out what happened to my old one."

Weire, a hand to his still swollen cheek, says, "She left you, yeah?"

"To go to Europe."

"Why?"

"Because she said I was a sociopath."

"So where do I come in?"

"I told Roberta you had access to Jeanie's travel records."

"Jeanie. Jeanie," Weire says. He punches up his Apple Squealer, a holographic display puts names and numbers up in the air between us. Their light is so sharp the numbers are tattooed on Weire's cheeks and forehead. "It says that on December 28, or was it January 28, she flew Honolulu–Los Angeles, Los Angeles–New York, New York–Amsterdam, Amsterdam–St. Petersburg. Then on January 3, or was it February 3, she flew St. Petersburg–Amsterdam, Amsterdam–New York, and boom, that's as far as she goes."

When I say I want to know about the will, he says first things first. He says next week we all meet at Maye Hona's office. He, me, Frank, Dewey, Augie, Jan and Dean. "Maye's fixated on building her hotel. I think she plans on being entombed in the lobby, so get ready to feel the whip." Feeling it already, I ask what it is corporately that Weire does for Frank. "Consider me," he says, "Frank's Vice President in Charge of Thinking. Listen, Maye's going to come down hard on the eyeball issue. The new DA told Vorhaggen he wants you in jail, that you're worth A-1 priority, let's-nail-him-right-now attention."

"Is he a good prosecutor?"

"Crawford, are the jumbo shrimp fresh? He's not bleeding from the mouth if that's what you mean. And you've had priors. You could get twenty years. Worse comes to worst, the question is, guyfriendbuddypal, are you ready to do time?"

18 APRIL

Roberta and Jan and Dean are screaming so loudly and wildly that their words make no sense, except for Jan's inappropriate "Crazy dragon lady little bitch." All I see as I go into the bar, dark at noon, are teeth.

She says she'll "get him," that she's got the Python back, has a silencer, and is potting the revolver off into the sand in her tiny backyard, firing it "TV style," one hand gripping the wrist of the other, through her bedroom window, shooting at her flowers. Roberta won't show me the gun and I think this is fantasy, but the smell of powder seems to have soured the perfume of her paperbacks. I look out her window. I see flowers. I see sand. I don't know.

The sand. Frank's math is completely wrong. We don't need a cubic mile or anything close. I pencil it out: Assume that the New Island will describe a circle with a radius of one mile—the island therefore will cover 3.14 square miles. Assume an average depth of the beach to be two yards—a generous allowance—and width a hundred yards, including the sloping area permanently under the ocean and covered even at low tide. Eighth-grade multiplication—1,750 x 2 x 100—yields a total required volume of 352,000 cubic yards. This is .00645 percent of a cubic mile: 5,451,776,000 cubic yards. I tell my brother that by my lights he is off by a mind-boggling factor of 17,000.

Frank says the issue is not bean counting about sand and soil. He asks if I am still taking my meds and I tell him, yeah, but I keep forgetting: that's how I was unwacked enough to do the math.

We go down the block to see his guys test a Joe Dozer on old buildings beside the Ala Wai Canal that were scheduled for demo but get to be ripped apart by this new machine. I tell him Weire says Jeanie got as far as New York and that that's all he knows. Frank says that's all he has to know.

The Joe Dozer cracks to life. It's a loud cubist *Tyrannosaurus rex.* It bites into the side of a four-story building and concrete, stucco, and mortar splash down on the cab.

I say, "Frank, where is she?" And Frank says, "On vacation." The first building comes down in just a few big bites.

19 APRIL

Frank's poison by her lights and here's more proof: We were, Roberta reveals, living in Tony's ark on an ocean of grass above the bio-interment plot at Kamkua. We had children—Jan and Dean's daughters who we'd adopted—but Frank, standing below by the single grave, needed them for mulch and I said it was okay and that scared her so much she woke up.

The point of this dream, she says, is that she needs to run my life. To protect me from myself. I am at her mom's looking into an open suitcase. "My inheritance," she explains, "from my dad."

Inside the suitcase are nice white shirts and swingeasies.

"Your dad. Is he dead?" I ask.

She shrugs. "I haven't seen him since he didn't show up at my birthday party in seventh grade."

Roberta says the shirts and undies are mine if I need to replace what I've lost. She says we must stick more together and wants to know how much I'll make if the Honas buy out Jan and Dean's lease. I say maybe $500,000 and she grins, "Cut me in for half and guess what I'll do?"

Blow me is the answer.

She'd called from her grandma's to say her V-dub wouldn't start and could I come get her? I drove to Aina Haina—a tropical Levittown; tract houses carpet the hills and when I walked in Roberta had + = + dirging away on the stereo. The smoke of primo Cleveland herb hung in the living room in ribbony layers against a gallery of old Patti Smith and Sex Pistols posters. Eons ago, before real estate, Roberta's grandma was a punk.

Roberta, undressed to kill, nothing but a mini black kimono over her bra and panties, whose pattern seems to reveal *Guernica*, demanded to know, "What are we going to do about us?" And when I said, "Nothing," she replied it was time to tell Jan and Dean what's what and if "You won't I will." I said, "Just keep your mouth shut," and she replied, "You're not the boss of me."

But now she has softened. "That's right, Crawford, my first ever. In the nude, with love, no questions asked."

I say, "A $250,000 BJ?"

Looking into her father's suitcase, she says it would be a bargain at twice the price, "like I said, with love, no questions asked."

20 APRIL

Frank says in the new century energy will be to paper what paper was to gold, that money is just an idea we've all agreed upon and all cash will disappear.

He is hosting an African monarch at his house. Uzis and 9-mm Bulldogs galore. The power lines for his majesty's phone system and trailers for his security people make the scene resemble a movie set where nobody has a camera but everybody's got a gun.

The king, whose kingdom rests above an ocean of oil and who wants my brother to figure out how to get at it, talks about his kingdom as if it is more of a business problem than a country.

21 APRIL

Jan and Dean has gone to the store for beer, garlic, and hamburger and Roberta is in what used to be my bedroom but what is now just a corner of a much, much larger room. Her bathing suit top is unbuttoned in back and it hangs off her like a bib. She's straddling me. The bottom of her bathing suit is on the floor, revealing across her tan hips a perfect pale V. At the bottom of the V runs a soft black slash of pubic hair. She has me in her hand and is rubbing me up against her. She is wet, looking up at the ceiling and smiling. Her throat bucks gently as if she were drinking water.

The game, she says, is chicken, for me to come in her hand just before Jan and Dean, dinner in hand, booms through the door.

At dawn the water is glass. A four-man scull needles across the green mirror of the Ala Wai Canal, its oars putting eight pools in the water with every syncopated stroke. There is no coxswain on board and they row down the canal's center quick and blind.

NBC devoted ten minutes to the New Island last night. Frank doesn't talk to journalists but a geologist from Cal Tech surmised that Frank had drastically underestimated the depth of the earth's crust along the underwater ridge line. The good doctor stated that the New Island was an "impossibility, using even the most powerful conventional explosives."

Revolution. Madam X and her seers got drunk on Fuckup's Milk of Amnesia that Jan and Dean was selling as a breakfast special over the bar for $5 in a liter glass—the cream, booze, and anisette it takes to make each one costs at least $7.50—and I said, "Remember, I'm management now."

Roberta has hung the black flag of anarchy behind the bar above the 200-gallon aquarium that holds Mister Real. I have big hopes, though it has been an awful day. The Ice Man cometh by Less Nervous this morning. Gordon Roth, dressed in Gucci shirt and shorts, is a hairy skeleton. Sooty bruises pocked his legs, a Rolex hung off his pale string of a wrist. Looking like the richest man in Treblinka, he told me he had a new batch of Real Mad popped fresh from the dairy case and did I want to stay awake for a week or two?

I told him to beat it, I had to get ready for Madam X. But in fact what I had to do was go through the bills. Jan and Dean had them in a box, and what they show is that the money is going hogwild into hallucinations. Last night was a pornographic nightmare. He's spent a fortune hot-rodding the Love Machines so apparitions can emerge à la Crude Rude Lewd Really Stewed Almost-Nude Mini-Dude and hang corked into each other in the air above us.

It makes our bread and butter, the Drastic Plastics, crazy. When I came in this morning broken glass covered the floor in starry shards. And today's brunch for Madam X was it. I'd gone down to her office to arrange this ages ago. Talk about all knuckles and know-how. This gypsy has networked the earth, she operates a palm-reading empire, and I had 200 tellers of the future in here at $20 a cheese omelette. We should have made $2,000 profit straight off the top.

I told Jan that was it, I was taking over, and anchored my demand by downing 300 mikes of Antiswaq. Roberta got angry. She hates the stuff. I've told her that it's like lithium, that it has both explosive and calming powers. Just because the chemical could, say, torch off half a city block does not mean that same amount, ingested, could blow my head off. It amazes me that, despite all her medical school ambitions and all her cruises through the *Journal of American Medicine* and *Psychotherapy Today*, she has not run into the word "metabolize" and it points to the scary difference between us: Roberta is a child, I am a man.

23 APRIL

On her roof, seated in a wheelchair with her sons Dewey and August, Maye says, "You know Frank here's crazy don't you? You know he planned the end of the world."

I say there's a big difference between crazy and visionary.

"Yeah, Sonny, but you don't know what it is." She sucks oxygen from a tube attached to a green cylinder as if it were a straw in a milk shake. "Right now, boys, I got just about everything that can kill you but before I go I'll make things clear. Everything you think you own is mine. And you folks can just forget about that shit." She waves toward the ocean. "If Frank tries to create that underwater Tower of Babble with all that pipe it'll make a mess Christ couldn't clean up."

Seated in a white beach chair beside Maye's rooftop swimming pool twenty-two stories above Waikiki, Frank's eyes are leveled to the horizon.

"Frank," Maye says to me, "has problems he hasn't the sense to think about. A big one, Tod, is you.

"Frank," she looks at my brother, "how long does the yes-sir boy become the fuck-you man? About as long as you keep him loaded on tranqs would be my guess."

Weire giggles through his nose.

"As for you." She waves her green bottle of oxygen toward Jan and Dean. "Get out of my building or I sue."

Jan, his thin hair a black smoke, says, "That'd be suing a corn husk."

Maye says unless he wants to die with his boots on, he better get gone and, oh yeah, we're all here all right. I'd gone up to Maye Hona's office with Jan and Dean. She was not there, so, idly, I read her walls. They were decorated with old *National Geographic* maps going brown at the folds and I'd identified twenty-six countries I've been to when she rolled through the door. She extended a hand and when I took it it felt as dry and light as a butterfly's wing.

Beside her, Dewey with his gold wool hair, in a pale summer suit, penny loafers, and no socks sits by the pool, August beside him—his belly stretching the fabric of his Outrigger Canoe Club T-shirt and his eye swollen in a way that scares me, and stitched closed at the lid like the seams of a baseball. Four Kuzaki, two-fisted herbivores, stand by the elevator doors.

A breeze lifts the old woman's wiry hair. Maye drinks more oxygen. She appears to be dying in sections. Her right leg looks mummified, like old leather. Her left leg is swollen and prune black at the ankles. "Tod," she rasps, coughs, "this boy's eye's finished. His retina is so badly ruptured it can't be repaired. I cry for him and—" using a word I take as a threat, "I mourn for you."

She says that facing death, she sought Redemption, but her priest told her the Catholic Church lacked the manpower to absolve her. In the meantime she has, in league with the Justice Department, served Frank a writ to freeze all Crawford Construction funds.

"Otherwise, Tod," she lifts herself up, in a way that looks painful, in her chair. The flowers on her mu-mu are moving, and I don't know if it's my drugs or her technology. "You're the heir apparent. Cuz Frank here is a nut and my boys don't have it." For which she takes much of the blame. "I was a flower child from the love generation smoking so much herb and crack this boy"—she puts a hand on Dewey's leg—"is lucky he doesn't have an arm growing out of his forehead and a mind made of hookah smoke instead of just a fag bar and a mean streak. He doesn't care if it's Miss March or Joe Steamfitter's hairy dirt chute, so he's probably got bugs killing him even God doesn't know about."

"Mom," Dewey says.

"As for Augustus here." She turns slowly to her other son. "What this big fat boy is is the most musclebound lawsuit you folks have ever seen. That's it but that's—" She puts a hand over her mouth. "Enough. So that leaves you. And Sonny, seeing you get whatever I got is not going to happen. I won't let it. Whatever we got, you ain't gonna get it and by this time next week you all are going to be talking to so many accountants, cops, judges, and attorneys you're gonna think shit is Christmas."

Frank, who says nothing during all of this, tells me in the elevator on the way down that for all he cares Maye can sue us to Kingdom Come. "But next time you get in a beef with somebody like that, don't knock their eye out. Do the smart thing."

I say, "What?"

Frank says, "Kill 'im."

Roberta's all wet and her forearms are skinned with sand. She squats above me, drips water on my chest, and says, "Coral cut. Feast your eyes. The inside of me. Look." She is bleeding from a little gash on her knee that looks like a grin. I say she's got da kine figure for a twelve-year-old and she says nineteen-year-old and I say if she's nineteen I'm one hundred and she says I'm one hundred. "You're a little old man, Crawford."

Then she asks me what will I buy when I get my inheritance. A car? A boat? A house? A state? I smear Dead Man on my nose and say sure. She pulls on a neon pink tank top she's made that says FUCK LUST in big block letters across her nice new chest and says she wants me to invest my billions in a T-shirt shop.

I roll over to get the sun out of my eyes and she asks if I think I got anything inside her Tuesday. I say impossible and she says she's going to marry me for my money and she's going to get every last cent.

24 APRIL

Frank says that in the new century fortunes will be held on points that take no space and empires will find their homes in areas no larger than what it takes to hold a thought.

He informs me that the state is going to try to stop the New Island by resorting to the fine print. His barges, the ones that will deliver the long pipes to the magma hole, will be powered by Pratt & Whitney TF-33-P-3 turbofan jet engines. Frank bought 500 of them off old hotel model B-52s oxidizing at the air force boneyard at Davis-Monthan in Arizona. They are before us, being mounted on huge steel grids above the round tail of each barge. If Aerospace had tried something like this it would have cost them a billion, but Frank's doing the whole thing for lunch money. He says a fifteen-year-old could have come up with the idea and any fifty yard-apes with welding torches could have executed it—as about fifty yard-apes are doing now.

But the jet engines have attracted state attorneys who say no way they'll let Frank torch off 500 loud, smoky old turbofans in the city harbor. They'll arrest him instead.

25 APRIL

A cockroach as big as a mouse is scurrying around in the sink when I open this morning. In the paper some biologist from the Revolutionary Evolutionary movement said that cockroaches are growing an average 1 percent in mass per generation. The Revo/Evos claim some roaches will soon be big enough to attack and eat the weakened young of other, bigger scavengers. Like, say, six-legged mutant baby rats.

In her old bed at her mom's house, with her mom out repoing a multiplex, Roberta, naked, says, "Promise not to try to push it in, swear to God you won't, because if you do, I'll scream."

I am ascending slowly and under a black arrow of down, shiny and soft as baby mink.

26 APRIL

The Feds served a writ to stop the New Island all right, but they enjoined the wrong holding company. Using his Mind,

Frank had changed the corporate ID and moved the money hours before, he tickled the ivories on a computer keyboard and billions were gone. He says they can chase the cash all over the globe if they like and never catch it, because our grubstake now zooms fiber-optic cable at the speed of light.

Frank got this, got my handheld, I left it at his house. He read what I wrote, some of it anyway, and who knows what he thought, because pitching it back to me he said satire is just a silly form of hate.

I'm in the apartment, thumbing through a bomb-tattered copy of H. S. Wolf's *Biomedical Engineering.* A relic from my premed experience. An old textbook for a class I was going to take before I ran face first into organic chemistry and got involved with medicine at the more intimate bootleg-kidney level instead.

A diamond-eyed rat scurrying across the road is caught in our headlights, Frank swerves around the rodent and says people never remember what they've done to you, only what you've done to them.

We are riding at night in the Zero. Frank has given the finger to internal combustion, had Bernie install an electric motor from a Japanese bullet train, and has rebuilt the seats so we are laying way back, our spines almost parallel to the ground. He says the Honas must have been the ones who wrecked my apartment. "If they didn't, who did? Mokes. They never change, man. I can remember in fifth grade when Dewey and a bunch of brown brothers pulled me into the girls' john and tried to flush my head down the toilet."

The low lights of the Zero cut narrow triangles up the twisting pavement of the Pali Highway. I ask him why we are doing this.

"A dog that pisses on your carpet," Frank replies, "smack him or he'll piss on the carpet forever."

He says he'd figured I was going to do something on my own. Now that I haven't, he will.

Frank's got the Pop Gun stuffed behind the headrest on the driver's side. The Pop Gun is a brilliant idea. Frank has rethought the entry wound for the twenty-first century. In war death is bad—bury the dead and the dead are gone. No, the injured are where the action is, it takes six people to tend to one injured man, the injured consume lots of resources. By blowing a shallow but massive entry wound the Pop Gun creates minimum lethality but maximum injury. A shotgun with a sniper-scope designed to replace the current-issue Remington 870 Wingmaster, Frank invented the Pop Gun to be the first "multiload" combat weapon, and his original ammo was New Age dum-dum bullets. It was to provide a safer method of crowd control than either the "bean bag" guns used by the Israelis or the rubber "baton bullets" employed by the British in Northern Ireland. It fired a soft and benign antibiotic-laced charge that, in essence, punched the body rather than blowing a hole in it. But the military said the Pop Gun was useless because as a "close assault weapon system" it would conflict with their Advanced Combat Rifle Program and so Frank has upped the ante.

I ask, "Should we be doing this?"

Frank's face is abstracted in the dim illumination of the dash lights. "Consider it already done."

I pull my seatbelt harness tighter across my chest. Frank is hauling. Unlike Tom Weire, who drives with an accidental grace that makes his speed seem almost irrelevant—or Jan and Dean, who simply drives accidentally—Frank is intensely and precisely reckless.

The Zero hums down out of the mountains and onto the road encircling the North Shore. Frank pulls over and announces, "I gotta make the gun. You drive. You know where we're going, yeah?"

I unstrap and get out. I walk around the back of the Zero to Frank on the driver's side. He stands absolutely still, as if thrown out of time, his hands on his hips, looking down the road where headlights in the distance glow like close stars.

The torque from the bullet train motor makes the action of the accelerator delicate. I touch the gas and the tires break loose. Frank says "asshole" and I look over. The Pop Gun is assembled. It's stubby. Part submachine gun, part cannon. I shot it at the beach. It put a hole in a lifeguard station you could walk an elephant through.

Frank says, "You can't drive. Stop, I'll do this," and I pull over, open the Zero's door and get out.

Leaves overhang the road. There is no moon and the leaves are only colorless and approximate. I walk around the Zero and fall back into the passenger seat. Frank starts the car and we take off with a violent jerk.

I figure why worry, Frank's reasonable, he just wants to make a point. We'll drive to August Hona's apartment—a small building, nine glass-fronted units, three across, three stories high, ticktacktoe. Frank will slip the "rip clip" into the weapon. I doubt he even wants to hurt Augie, just scare him. There will be a light on. The drapes will be pulled and the square front window will give off a stark brown glow. Frank will get out of the car and step below Aug Hona's unit. The shotgun will go off in a long jerking pulse of flame, blowing out a window, maybe two, and that'll be that.

We're a mile down the road when the Zero's lights cut around a curve. The high white rectangle of a refrigerator truck's rear doors stand in the night. For an instant I think we're going to smash into an empty movie screen. Then Frank brakes. The Zero slides sideways and he says we're dead.

28 APRIL

In the church the priest says, "Unto thee, O Lord, I do lift up my soul. O my God, I trust in thee: let me be not ashamed, let mine enemies not triumph over me. . . . Remember not the sins of my youth, nor my transgressions: according to thy mercy remember thou me for thy goodness sake, O Lord. . . . What man is he that feareth the Lord? Him shall he teach in the way that he shall choose. His soul shall dwell at ease; and his seed shall inherit the earth."

Jan and Dean and I are sitting in pews near the front. Jan whispers, "Try this on for size. I just two seconds ago talked to a guy at the bank. Unreal news." I say later, but he goes on, "He said I'd probably qualify for a loan. We talk Monday. This could be it. Though," JD sighs, "maybe he just didn't want to shit on my face over the phone."

The priest continues, "Thou preparest a table before me in the presence of mine enemies: thou anointest my head with oil; my cup runneth over. Surely goodness and mercy shall follow me all the days of my life: and I will dwell in the house of the Lord forever."

The funeral is open casket, Maye Hona lies in a mahogany coffin looking like a life-size doll of herself. A coronary embolism. Her two sons, Dewey and August, sit in front of us. Aug's eye is bandaged and his face is bulky with grief.

A bad week. Paramedics torched me out of the Zero after it slammed sideways into the refrigerator truck. The back of the car was cut right off. We spun into a ditch and I looked over and Frank was gone, the windshield shattered, and a face with black feathers for a mustache was peering in, going, "Hey, we got a life in there? You okay? You okay?"

I was but Frank was not. He'd left the five-point harness undone and he's lucky to be in a hospital instead of a mortuary. He's in Intensive though and, who knows, he may make the latter yet.

MAY

1 MAY

I've kicked. Three days curled up sweating through a sheet
sucking my thumb feeling like my fingers were stuck in a
light socket.

I got nightmares while feeling the worst, after Roberta said
she loved me then allowed that, while she must stay intact,
as a consolation prize she'd fire sale me a BJ, and settle for
half cash plus an IOU. But now it's over. Now I know what
I've got to do.

2 MAY

Fire hose this place.

It's night. Under the bomb, Less Nervous looks shot from
the Stone Age. Through the back door I can see Jan barbe-
quing two steaks over a spit he's pieced together on the gravel
lot behind the building. Light from the fire ripples his face,
his hair stands up, electrified. He looks like an angry devil.
"Dewey cut off the electricity and the water."

I say he can't do that and Jan laughs, "Fauntleroy, he owns
this place. It's a miracle he didn't do it before." He flips a
steak on the grill. Fat splashes against radiant coals. Smoke
ascends in a veil. "I talked to the bank today." He says, "No
loan because I'm a quote, unquote, zero, financially."

He forks up the steaks, flops them on plates, carries them

inside, and sets them before Mr. and Mrs. Buddy Walsh. Buddy, the Ford salesman, is under the weather. The new car smell has, I guess, already worn off his heroin addiction. Their table is lit by candles and through their wan light Buddy's face looks made of wax.

A new sign—indicative of the new regime—is up. It reads: NUTRIENT SLUSH—ALL YOU CAN STOMACH $7.99.

On the lam against a sudden chill, Jan stands under it looking out at the street before turning to eye the paintings, broken juke box, posters of Lenin and Marx, pool table, and two old sofas—a lot of it collateral he had taken in exchange for loans to even unluckier business friends. Better to cushion their plops into bankruptcy. It will all be gone tomorrow.

Today at Queens Hospital a doctor who looked hip said, "Fracture of the left tibia. Many, many, many bad bruises and nasty lacerations—flying through a windshield isn't a trip I'd recommend for anyone . . . Let's see, a concussion, a bad contusion, anyway. We're just getting a little hairline on the X rays, but he's real disassociative. He knows where he is but not quite who he is."

"He has amnesia?" I asked.

"Not quite. He can remember, but says he doesn't make sense."

"He can't understand things?"

"It's more literal. He repeats over and over, 'I don't make sense.' He can't read and says I'm gobbledygook, and it's been getting worse. So pretty much we've had to knock him out. Care to go up for a look?"

No. But I do. We go up to Frank's suite. He is sitting up in bed. "We don't really know where he is going now," the doctor informed. Sun must have been coming through Frank's window in a strange way. Because there were two bright dots of light on the wall at the end of my brother's bed, as if Frank's eyes were lasers. But those eyes—while wide open—were, I guess, seeing just about nothing at all.

3 MAY

Firemen using water cannons blow everything out the door except the Love Machines, beer kegs, and Mister Real. They'll wait for their money until I get my insurance check Thursday.

Now, Dewey.

4 MAY

Do What You Look Like. Dark at noon. Paneled with teak veneer and rashed with little starlike lights that are bright but do not illuminate, a clear night under a wooden sky. A floor show sputters along: he-shes introduced by a baby-faced yo-yo in a flowered shirt. "Mister Liz Kennedy! Mister Sereena Montavo! Mister Deborah Diamond!" Some are mannish, others so pretty I can't tell, even as their outfits are reduced to nothing but glittery lines and dabs.

Dewey is tending bar. The hem of his old GEEVE 'EM T-shirt rises above the line of his belt, revealing a crescent moon of hairy stomach. He hands me a Coke. "How's Frank?"

"Incoherent."

"Cut you a deal, Junior, eighty grand and Jan packs his bags."

"Try $1.5 million and the price goes up $500,000 a day until you pay off."

Dewey cleans a glass. "Not to put too fine a point on this, but I can give you legal problems to die for." He sets the glass bottom-up on the bar. "A fresh young thing like yourself could have friends at the state penitentiary right up the ass."

5 MAY

No $1.5 million from Dewey but a knockdown dragout with the insurance guy, a Tahitian yuppie who says Panasonic Fire & Casualty won't pay me off, that no motorcycle is worth $135,000, and no stereo costs $80,000—even when he sees receipts from Discovery Systems with every hand-built item itemized. And he's not jumping for joy at the task of having to replace 8,500 micro CDs either.

I sit outside on the wide lanai of the Royal Hawaiian Hotel, home of the $8 cup of decaf. Though Frank says cash is trash and that money is just an idea we all have agreed to, I've got to get some soon.

No $2.5 million. Perhaps Dewey isn't having any. No matter, I've taken charge. The sandblasters were in today, and though Roberta says it's too middle class for words, and though my master plan is to make Less Nervous a Mecca for the New Stupid, for now I'm going after the less discriminating 'If You Think You Stick' crowd by booking Numb.

But as far as handling Jan and Dean—it'd be easier forging girders from mercury. No electricity and he has signed contracts with acts throughout the summer. I string a line from Roberta's a block and a half away only to provide power for another money-losing triple bill: Shit, Chemistry Headbutt, and I forget the last one. Too bad 250 penniless Piss Poppers who couldn't care less about $10 zombies can't cover the expense of $750 minimums apiece plus 20 percent of the door.

Jan and Dean says he was better off getting blown away in the marine corps. He hated the food and having to shoot women and children, but he's nostalgic for the cash flow. He says expect no heaven, just maybe many penitent reincarnations and with his luck he'll be doomed to spend a hundred lifetimes as an eyeless crustacean scurrying the bottom of the Mariana Trench.

9 MAY

No, Dewey isn't having any. But the remodeling continues apace: the painters were in here this morning, Mister Real excepted, I had them squirt Less Nervous black. They, like the firemen and sandblasters before them, must be paid. With Frank in oblivion I pay a visit to Syntyrsystym, figuring to reach out and touch our empire for a loan.

Unfortunately—I guess because our empire is everywhere—it's hard to see it anywhere. I grew up knowing little about our local holdings—a lot of farmland and real estate, a couple of state senators—and Antiswaq may have robbed me of other essentials: like the reality that no one now works for Frank except software.

Syntyrsystym is empty. Big Store is shut down too and entering Frank's Mind I find it in subacute, experiencing nothing but anger and confusion. Across the hall at Syntyrsystym all I recognize is Frank's stuffed race horse, Shining Path. All his terminals are gone.

☢

I drive Jan and Dean's old Ford out to Blue Villa. It's a ghost town. Nothing is finished. The wood framing still stands on the townhouse foundations like the bars to an invisible jail, and the trenches for the pipe Augie Hona lunched haven't even been filled.

I drive to Frank's real estate office two miles down the road. It's in his unfinished and otherwise unoccupied industrial park.

I park the Ford, walk to the bulletproof, blast-resistant front doors, say the words *A good clap, a fore marriage, a bad wake, tell hell's well. Forever Praised be Providence* and go inside.

Above me, his airship. A 200-yard-long dirigible powered by turboprop engines. Before communism went banko, Air Force Academy cadet Frank proposed 200 of these to be kept armed with nuclear-tipped cruise missiles constantly hovering just outside the USSR like flies over a monster piece of rotting meat.

I call Weire and say Blue Villa's deserted. "Some framing is up, there's tar mopping around the plumbing, but that's it and everybody's gone."

Weire, his voice small over the line, says, "Well, when you don't make your payroll."

I say, "Look, I've got to have some money."

Weire says, "Call the guy at Century Rents. Then call Frank's banks." He gives me account numbers. "I'll see what I can extract, but first find out what's there."

I do that—the accounts are all void—and afterward find myself staring above at the blimp's black pillowy skin, hung on ribbing radiating from its nose like the spokes of a humongous bicycle wheel. I'm in shock.

10 MAY

The beach. Nutted-up Icicles have shot two people in the water and now government surfers patrol the breaks from Queens all the way out to Twos and Threes. Beyond them the long pipes stand like skyscrapers built on top of the ocean. A pickup truck swings off Kalakua. Its tires bound over the curb, the rig shoots toward the shorebreak, wheels spinning up spewing slats of sand.

Tom Weire's skin is shiny with 175. His brown body looks vaguely melted, as if he were made of warm brown wax. He's doing magic tricks. He has me shuffle, cut, and take the top card off the deck. Then he calls it right every time. I say old Jerry Wiler came into Less Nervous this morning to look at the bomb casing again, that he pulled up in a Bentley. Weire says the government pays old Jerry a bundle to not spill the beans on how to build a real one, most particularly Jerry's lifetime dream—a five-stage 2.2-gigaton "mountain buster" hydrogen bomb thirty-eight times the size of the largest ever detonated: it was designed to destroy the Soviets' central command authority buried under the granite monolith of Zhiguli, 500 feet beneath millions of tons of rock in a sphere of concrete and steel. Conventional nukes would have been firecrackers against it. So SAC got the old guy building it in an earth-penetrating mode. But when they got the weight specs they realized that with no Titan rockets left in service they couldn't lift it. They were hot-rodding an MX when Reagan got his notes mixed up at Reykjavik and the cold war collapsed. Leaving old Wiler all dressed up with no place to go."

The truck comes screaming by again. It's filled with pale women in bikinis. Weire says secretaries from the Black Lagoon.

I ask him, "Can they do that? Legally?" He says, "Of course, this is America in the oughts. If you can pay, it happens."

1 1 M A Y

When Vorhaggen asks I tell him the LOADS are nothing but make-work what-if antinuclear proliferation scenarios Frank is contracted to complete for the air force. In his car parked next to a stop light I hear Nirvana scream across a decade from some Tita's zip wagon. Vorhaggen, his hand in a cast, says, "How is he?"

"Frank? The doctor says he's normal and can't handle it, they've had to sedate him."

" 'Normal and can't handle it'?"

"Head injuries knocked out half his ego and without it he can't understand what he's been doing or why he's been doing it. The frustration sparked a violent episode."

Vorhaggen says, "So you're in the driver's seat."

"What happened to your hand?"

"It got stomped at La Femme Nue."

I ask if the police are tapping my phones.

"Tapping your phones? Sonnyboy, we're tapping your life. Let's talk story."

"What's that?"

"Francis Taylor Crawford."

"Is it kosher to drag people off the street?"

Vorhaggen starts his car. "I said get in and you got in."

I'm afraid he's taking me downtown. "Frank's just doing what he's doing. People have a lot of freedom these days. Nothing fishy."

"Nothing fishy? Hoale boy, your brother has motives that would raise the hair on the back of a mako shark."

Vorhaggen says the police believe Frank made miscalculations and has decided the only way to get enough lava is by setting off a nuke under the ocean floor.

When I say, "right," he asks if I can spell patsy and says he's talked with a deputy DA. "There will be no deal on your assault charge or plea bargain to a slap on the hand. You're going to jail."

1 2 MAY

Weire selects a cue stick, lays it against a chair. "I sympathize. I drove by the prison farm this morning and saw all these healthy hearty sorts in denim hoeing weeds out of a rutabaga patch and it looked like fun. But if I was you, I'd just as soon not."

I say I want him to hire independent auditors to assess Crawford Construction top to bottom and Tom Weire replies that would be like hiring Typhoid Mary to deliver serum for the plague.

Through the open front door the sun is at the horizon, a flaming slivery arc. The sea in front of Kanoe's beach glistens like a molten metal foil. A few guys are still out surfing. One gets crunched by a wave. His small board shoots up high above the whitewater and flutters, suspended by the wind, before falling end over end into the backwash.

Weire walks around the pool table, plucks balls out of their pockets, and places them into a triangular wood rack that lays on the worn green felt. "Somebody really got their back up downtown. The cops—and when I say cops I mean maybe even the FBI—want that Egg." Weire chalks his cue. "By the by, care to guess the sticker price of an eyeball these days?"

I ask him, "What was I supposed to do, just stand there?"

He bends into the circle of light above the table and shifts the balls around in the rack. He is wearing white cotton slacks and a shirt embroidered with yellow-and-red fish. "Your word against theirs." He lifts the wood triangle off the table. "Your break."

I pick up a cue stick and say, "You believe me, don't you?"

"At the rates I'm gouging your brother, I can't afford not to."

I take my stick, scrub its tip with a dice of chalk, crack the rack, and sink the two and the eleven.

Weire asks, "Crawford, big ones or little ones?"

I step around the table and drill the five.

Weire says, "Lucky. You know what Frank had in mind with his plans to blow up the Soviet Union, don't you?"

The three ball sits on the lip of the side pocket. I tick it in, line up the one, and tap the cue ball. It strikes the one ball and the ball rolls slowly toward the corner pocket. I say, "Get legs." The one drops and I say, "To incinerate communism?"

Weire says, "In your dreams. He was bucking for top dog in the National Command Authority."

I say, "Come again," and Weire says, "Frank wanted to be the guy who in a nuclear war—when the civilian chain of command is torched off—takes the helm. The Emperor of Oblivion, flying above apocalypse in an SAC 747, ruler of all the glowing dust particles."

I miss the six. Weire lifts his cue. "It wouldn't have been a bad bet. In an all-out war the Soviets could've fired an SLBM on a depressed trajectory and Washington, DC'd be white heat in six minutes. Frank woulda been in the catbird's seat at 50,000 feet. Who'd believe the Soviets would spend two trillion on a nuclear arsenal to let it rust in its silos?"

Weire taps the cue ball. It strikes the thirteen. The ball rolls toward the corner pocket. Weire says, "Walk." The ball drops. "Want to know a secret? What happened to the Egg?"

"Dewey's got it."

Weire nods. "Bulls eye. Do you know what's in there?"

I say, "Infinite riches."

"But not normal, everyday infinite riches. Kinky infinite riches."

I ask like what and Weire replies an itty-bitty hydrogen bomb.

1 4 M A Y

My brother has been stabilized on a many-times-over-normal dose of his own medicine, Antiswaq, and has come around. Yesterday he began to speak and his incantations have, in a day, returned to the terse and concrete from the hyperbolic and surreal, and now, he says to me, "So the yes-sir boy becomes the fuck-you man." I had followed his doctor up to my brother's private suite on the third floor. Laminated with casts and bandages, he resembles the Michelin Man.

Seeing me, he pops the Wall, keys the *Star*.

"Weire's right off the bus from Oz. But just for the sake of argument, let me take you to school. Even if you had a nuke you couldn't use it." Frank sits up in his bed. "They're unusable. They're all salvage fused so if you tamper with 'em the RDX chemical explosive'll blow up in your face, but that's it—you'll just have plutonium scattered for a hundred yards in every direction. To get a nuclear blast you'd need the three permissive-action link codes that arm the thing to begin with plus the 'go' code. And nobody has that. They are lines of random digits long enough to stretch around three city blocks. You'd have an easier time winning the Chinese National Lottery than picking those numbers. So, to cut to the chase, buddyboy, (A) I'm not idiotic enough to go snatch some off-the-wall nuclear device and (B) even if I was there's nothing I could do with it. So do me a favor, Tod, go and deal with Blue Villa, deal with Century Rents, deal with the penny ante stuff, and let me handle the rest of the world."

Frank had a built-but-not-completed office complex he

wanted me to handle. "I called the guy at Century, who didn't want to lease unimproved space. He wanted them decorated before he'd rep them."

"What an idiot. You can decorate half of 'em just by closing the doors. Rental space is rental space. Four walls, electricity, and all the parking they can eat."

I say Century wants a model and ask, "How are we going to build one? I called your banks and they said you'd closed your accounts."

Frank replies that he doesn't need banks. From now on he's his own bank. "What do I have to do, Tod, cross-stitch this on a sampler? It's simple. Pick up the yellow pages, order the crap, and when they're done you say 'bill me,' and if they don't like it tell 'em to rip the shit out."

I ask what about all the people he had on his payroll and Frank says, "I'm not the Job Corps."

The weather has changed again. Once more it has cooled and the sky is crashing down. Rain smashes against the windows of Frank's hospital room. There are green, banana-shaped bruises, iridescent as a pigeon's chest, at the top of both cheeks. "And you better remember again who is the tail and who is the dog. Because we got big problems, buddyboy. Maye Hona had shared deeds and limited partnership agreements that can still tie up everything. Dewey was named executor of her will. A trickster and a pimp. Breaking up a twenty-year-old corporation worth a country can be a bitch. We're going to be people with pruning shears separating Siamese twins connected neck to nuts."

16 MAY

Morning. The skies have blued and the air is fresh and thick. The storm drains have backed up on Kalakua and the street is a lake. From the sidewalk Tom Weire skips a quarter across shallow water flat as a mirror. He pulls open the brass front door to Do What You Look Like. I follow Jan and Dean inside. Behind the bar, big fat Rastafied Ronald Sousee says, "No Crawfords in da club."

Weire says, "Greetings to da kine. Water for me and White Russians for my friends. Chop-chop." Sousee rotates a wet rag over the bar top. Finally Weire says, "We're here to see Dewey."

Sousee plucks up glasses and we sit down. On stage a statuesque he-she begins to strip. Her costume dissolves in a blizzard of pink feathers, revealing a leggy being who has a body like a woman's, but elongated and exaggerated, like a Barbie Doll.

Jan looks around and says, "Thirty people in here at noon. I'd kill for that."

Weire suggests we might attract a larger clientele and be more popular if Jan were more polite.

Jan says, "If I wanted to be more popular I'd join Whitesnake." I see his eyes tick to the stripper. "That contraption has given me a hard-on as big as a baseball bat."

Dewey appears. Grizzle around his cheeks is sparkly under the stage lights. He says he'll give Jan $100,000.

Weire shrugs, blows a smoke ring that wobbles, expands, rips apart, and he says, "Add another zero and change the one to a four."

Then Dewey says, "You guys got three days to get out. Then I'm taking a bulldozer and flattening that place to the ground."

1 7 M A Y

Frank is out of the hospital, normal as the day he was born.

We are at the ribbon-cutting ceremony at the slaughterhouse, big as a stadium, but white and cathedral-like. Across a fence a line of cattle is being led into the butcher bays.

Weire says, "Christ, Frank, you got everything here but the stone soap and Zyclon-B."

1 8 M A Y

The New Island begins. Pinned in the hard light of the bathysphere's three laser spots, the magma looks like a billowing ribbon of glowing intestine shooting out of the earth and coiling into black water. Looped and curled over the ocean floor, a stew of a giant's guts. The lava cooks off the water as it shoots up and creates a ghostly underwater steam around its coils. We watch on an HD color monitor that seems, in this tiny space, as big as a movie screen. The guide for the explosives is complete, Frank's Russian mohole men have drilled three-inch pipe into lava, and though deeper than they had estimated, the vault door is now cracked open.

Paradise in hand, I want up. The bathysphere smells like an underwater outhouse and is making loud, hopefully meaningless pinging sounds. We are 2,600 feet down. Though the bottom crawler's crush depth is 2,400 feet, it has a double hull—titanium on the outside and HY 140 steel on the inside separated by a free flood zone in between—and Frank says the Russians are just rubber-spined about their warranty. He says that the New Island will be here in a week. Frank kills the laser spots and the HD screen goes black. Thinking about what Weire said about the nuke, I see the hot coils again, big dim entrails that give off a grand and sickly glow.

19 MAY

Across the street from the flat green waters of the Ala Wai Canal and still parked in front of the chunked and splintered rubble of the building that it wrecked, Joe Dozer's room-size jaws open and close. They extend from the chassis by the machine's long metal neck and look starved for something to bite, break, and crush.

Jan and Dean is up in the cab dressed in his old orange canvas swimming trunks, one thick furry arm yanking on the control stick. He wears an Outrigger Canoe Club T-shirt and is smoking a fat flaming turd of a cigar. He is not accepting me as the boss. Last night he bought half a stolen cow off the back of some local's pickup truck. Four hundred pounds of Heimlich maneuvers for $600. Now we have almost no cash whatsoever.

I climb up to a cab newly inscribed with the words CRAW-FORD CONSTRUCTION: *We Serve You Right* and say, "Vámonos. Let's roll. Frank's shop closes at five."

Jan says this baby could wreck a city.

I say, "Move over." JD climbs by me, jumps to the ground, whacks absently at the back of his swimming trunks, removes the cigar from his mouth, and offers that "a baboon could operate this thing."

I say, "Perfect." What a week. At least the Honas forgot to bulldoze us. That's just got to be next. I tell Jan to get in the Ford and follow me.

The idea is to drive Joe Dozer six miles to Bernie's shop so his mechanics can drop a bigger engine in before more Japanese executives test drive it. But sixty feet down the block I lose oil pressure and am lucky to make it to Less Nervous without leaving the engine in molten puddles on the street.

20 MAY

Frank says that to shore up an economy imploding due to the $6 trillion deficit—to stop it from collapsing from within—the United States has put itself up for sale. Yosemite's worth of national forest lands have been bought by German timber companies who employ as many lumberjacks as I do. Frank says it took them an extra fifty years to do it, but the Nazis have finally won the war.

Then my brother says he has, no thanks to me, discovered the end of the universe. Amer-Eye has photographed the far plasma at the gates of the infinite void.

21 MAY

Dr. Nyung's new associate is a young, freckled Amerasian. He has a hip, short, concentration-camp haircut and nice clothes. Tattersall shirt and church window tie.

He says that last year through thirteen different banks, Syntyrsystym had drawn $54 million from Crawford & Hona trust and equity accounts, $8 million of which went to purchase a Monk-Stoller 6550000-ME, a German knockoff of the Cray "superfat" computer used at the Atmospheric Research Center in Colorado. I say Frank was probably using it for something in Heaven or above at Amer-Eye and Doug—that's his name—says it was shipped to Maui, 3645 Red Apple Road.

Hyper Mart. I ask what the Monk-Stoller is designed to do and Doug says, "Match random digits in an infinite number of different sequences."

I ask, "What could be the purpose of that?" Doug says, "You tell me."

He says that he'd pulled one of Frank's files and something else popped to the screen. He shows me a piece of paper that reads:

KAENA POINT MISSILE		
TRACKING STATION:	2 X 220-KT MRVS	SS-N-6 SLBM #11
LUALUALEI:	1 X 220-KT MIRV	SS-N-18 SLBM #2
MT. KAALA AIR		
FORCE STATION		
(GROUNDBURST):	2 X 220-KT MRVS	SS-N-6 SLBM #13
PALEHUA SOLAR		
OBSERVATORY:	1 X 220-K	

He says there was more but READ AND FEED appeared on the screen and he didn't have the feeds so this is all he got on speed print before it wiped.

It's a LOAD, but not one of mine. More incoming. Not us hitting them but them hitting us. I could spit to Mt. Kaala and two ballistic missiles packing 220-kiloton warheads would blow my soul to the promised land.

22 MAY

On the bridge of the *Gogol*, minutes before we hit weather, Frank says the universe has been revealed to him as useless, that he's discovered all creation is nothing but a thin tricky gruel of energy, matter, and the infinite void. Thus, he's decided to concentrate his efforts closer to home: to market a computer "entity," Loci, that will change the traditional business management from a pyramid to a needle.

Entities smaller than a human cell will roam computer databases and make management decisions on their own and be answerable only to the programmer. So a CEO will have total control of his whole company all the time and be spared the cost and confusion of bureaucracy.

Secretaries and managers will disappear. Everyone will be in sales or service.

Everything Frank touches changes. Take this thing. Originally, the *Gogol* was operated by the Soviet Navy, then by

KGB coastal border troops. Frank bought it for scrap and re-fitted it as a demonstrator—ripped out the old engine and installed a Perkins diesel—mindful that Third Worlders might want more refitted as antisub, antisurface, antiair, radar picket or target-towing ships. But bored with salesmanship and pa-perwork, he turned the *Gogol* into a pocket *Love Boat*. When lovers proved in short supply, he made it the launch control center for the Proteus.

It took six months to give the *Gogol* its current face. Though aspects of all faces remain. Magnetic anomaly detectors sit beside the stern-mounted high-frequency sonar while mo-hole men sleep eight to a honeymoon suite.

The bathysphere rests at the stern. Its umbilicals of braided air and fiber-optic lines loop over the fan tail.

Rocky thunderheads top the horizon. They cast shadows that turn to darkness over the water. Leaning forward, one elbow to one knee and chin propped on his knuckles, Frank's angular face is rose in the night operation lights. He is bent over a chart table looking at an oscilloscope and a TV mon-itor on which computer-driven seismic graphics move by in a slow stream. It begins to rain and Frank says let's book.

The drops are warm. The deck is as slick and shiny as a dirty mirror. Mohole men are at the aft in long bright orange foul weather gear—Day-Glo togas. I can hear the farting of the *Gogol*'s underwater thrusters, blowing in spasms to main-tain the ship's position within three meters. I go over the side and hang on as I am lowered by the winch. Below, in the dim, three yellow inflatables and a big black Zodiac bob on lines around the bathysphere, which, through the whipping cur-tains of rain, looks as it has looked before, like a huge old-fashioned cartoon bomb.

Frank's hands skid down the line. A flap of skin has slid off his palm at the arc between his forefinger and thumb, the cut wells with blood, he sucks at it and says get below.

Already I'm soaked. Just a little squawl and no big deal but still the bathysphere could be a cork. The *Gogol* is into the wind and the waves roll down its hull in deafening sighs, each roller leaves the white hull's rust, barnacles, and mussels glis-tening. It's like being on a roller coaster where the track moves and the car doesn't.

My feet touch rungs on the ladder and I climb down the hex pattern of the steel mesh deck. Below are the bathysphere's metal guts—its pumps, generators, and electric engine. The bulkheads are scarred with wormy crooked welds. This is no place I need to be.

We descend. There are wandering glows on the HiDi screens but I can't tell what they are. A laser beam puts out a long O of light so white it's a flash across the new and liquid ocean floor. The idea is to let the lava fill this gully then use the flatness of its cooling surface as a foundation for the first long pipe.

We bump down on a ridge at the edge of the rift zone. In the lights the fumarole spews a gauzy curtain of water smoke from the magma that feeds it. Then a scratchy glow on the screen that the Russian engineer says is a hot spot, magma convection currents carried up toward the crust. He is staring at the HiDi screen. "But this is what you call in the USA a motherfucker."

I don't understand. Vent life is dying in the rising lava, killed at its base by the hot liquid rock, but up the walls of the crater a community remains. The monitors show blind, brachyuran crabs scuttling after red-tipped, mouthless, gutless tube worms. Above us are blue and purplish zoarcid fish. The lava is rising around mineral chimneys that until weeks ago stood fifteen stories high.

The mohole men drilled back down the magma chamber. Easy due to the fractured nature of the basalt in the chamber. But something on the HiDi has scared the engineer out of his English, so that he is, suddenly to Frank, screaming gazooki and bazork and Frank is saying, "Just get the lead out."

We seem to be tightroping the lip of the crater, following a track no wider than a sidewalk that's been blown to hill after gully by a monster earthquake. I ask Frank what is wrong. He puts a thumb in front of the pilot's face and makes a jerking motion. We ascend. I feel sick and then there's a sliver on the screen I recognize easily: a marble-eyed lemon shark maybe eight feet long, mouth open in a streamlined grin, and I'm relieved, if for just a second, to bask in the comforting reality of a man-eating fish.

When we reach the surface we can't get back on the Gogol. Hatch open, the bathysphere ascends, tips, descends. I stick my head out. Behind dark, rocklike clouds, a last bloody sliver of sun lights long rolling waves. They look like roofs with churning white water cresting at their beams. Water smashes the tall stem of the hatch. Somebody above drops the winch cable, but it won't work. Frank says I should monkey up the line, pull myself up arm by arm.

Right, and cut my palms to shreds just in time to get slammed to jelly against the hull. I tell him be my guest, I'll wait for the mohole men topside to fix the winch.

Flying back on the Cayuse under a lightless sky I ask what went wrong. Angry, he laughs, "Get smart, buddyboy, just remember to make sure you don't know shit about anything at all."

23 MAY

Art may be the answer.

We host Ikiku Iiiiiio. Japanese, somewhere between forty and fifty, she wears thick round black framed glasses and a little black dress. Ikiku got her start in Piss Pop, but has gone from music to visual art. Her visual art is her daughter, Betty, who stands white, tall, and naked on a pedestal under the bomb. Her breasts are large for a Japanese girl and her mouth looks like a Valentine on her beatific little face. Hiro/Mr. White of the White Gallery had introduced me to Ikiku as a "vivid and exciting young man, the new Frank" and Ikiku, who spoke no English, communicated an invitation.

We do an $800 door and afterward I go to the Kahala Hilton where Hiro leaves me with Ikiku and Betty who, as her station as a statue allows, rides in the taxi clothed in a sheet. I don't know what's up. Looking into the artist's eyes expecting to see insanity I see, instead, business. A phrase in English Ikiku has mastered is "Frank" and she ushers me into a suite where Reagan has slept.

My. She's direct. She hands her daughter a Seen Clean and is gone. My NEG, her NEG, the international language of love. Betty says "Frank," and swings a pale arm to the bathroom as if I am a game show contestant who has just won a shower. I feel lost, confident, and out of control. In the pink stall, she washes me and afterward she feels so delicate and unused. When I enter her she says, "Oh Frank, oh Frank," and her ground zero makes a remarkably sexy little squeak.

Making love to art, clean, expert, the art of decoration not revelation. Betty was art as is the superfine illustration on the orthodontist's waiting room wall. Commercial art (okay, she's a whore). My love for Roberta has been declared to me by my terror of being discovered. A burning desire that she not find out about this has mated with a burning desire to go do it again, and I have, for an instant, the weird fear that in my strange case lucidity may be the most dangerous drug of all.

24 MAY

Roberta says the sky is falling and that before it does we better make our nut. She got hip to Betty alright, just not the way I would have feared or guessed. Roberta wants to be art as well. Her plan: We bootleg Frank's Mind—she says she'll snatch it out of his office above Big Store if she has to—hot-rod the Love Machines and morph up new Robertas as the main attraction. So we'll have tall Robertas, skinny Robertas, blond ones, sad ones, bad ones, a funky soulful Roberta, the smeary lipsticked "white-trash Valkyrie" Roberta, the Bible Belt Roberta, Barbarella Roberta, Roberta in an Azzedine Alaïa catsuit holo-ing the dance floor with the stern, black leather über-bitch Roberta. Patrons will even be able to design their own Roberta—any one they want, even a nude, crude, rude, semi-stewed, lewd Roberta, for a price.

Two mainland college guys come in while I'm on the cellular booking an eighties retro night: I, Me, Mine plus Bulimia Banquet and Why Ask Why. They spent all day on the beach. One smeared himself with Dead Man, but the other is burned purple and has blisters ballooning across his back. His eyes are lines and his cheeks glisten with tears or fluid cooked out of his skin. He says through lips puffed to fat worms that he just needs to get drunk and I tell him he'd better let me take him to Doc in the Box or he'll die. He's got the worst sunburn I've ever seen. I ask why he didn't use any Dead Man and he asks what's that? Dead Man sunscreen, I explain. He tells me because he wanted to get a really good tan.

I lay a bar towel over his head to tent his shoulders and we walk down to Doc in a Box. Someone, an alert art dealer I suppose, has booted the sky with: MONDRIAN. HANDSOME. SICKLY. READY TO ROLL. When I get back Roberta is peering over photos I took at Ewa Beach, as if each were the result of a vital reconnaissance: Roberta in a red bathing suit made of string inscribing the fresh condiments of her adulthood; new breasts and exact little ass. She looks up at me. "Lover, the end is near." She asks if I'll take pictures of her naked so the cockroaches will have something to remember her by.

Then she reminds me that it's time to go hardcore.

25 MAY

Bop tops exploding red, white, and blue under a long pall of brown smoke from engines decades past their prime, state police cars whiz like angry wasps around a line of trucks and armored vehicles that stretch all the way up into the mists of the mountains.

Civilization is having a problem with itself. I stand surrounded by Cut Grunts and rock-faced Koreans shouldering Disney Bulldogs. A cop with a metallic voice and sounding like a pissed-off automaton is reciting the manifest: "190 T-72 and T-80 main battle tanks; 137 BMP-3 infantry fighting vehicles; 190 BTR-80 armored personnel carriers and command vehicles; 18 antiarmor BTRs with 24 AT-5 antitank guided missiles—" On and on.

On the Wall this morning CNN labeled it as "miles of motorized rubbish." All strung from Pearl City to the big airfield at Hickam.

Like the fabled fingernails that continue to grow in the grave, appendages of the Soviet Union continue, in one form or another, to exist if not flourish and Frank has scored big: he's Fed Ex-ing an entire Category-A Soviet-style Motor Rifle Division minus a tank regiment to the African king, whose problem is his neighbor to the north, a former French client state Mitterrand armed to the teeth as protection against Mu'ammar Gadhafi. The neighbor sent four regiments of infantry south to snatch a fifty-mile crook of the king's top wadi, a desert riverbed along his border that is scorched in summer but provides water to half a million people the rest of the year.

A green boat-nosed armored amphibious vehicle mounting what looks like a medieval siege cannon lumbers past. Black smoke spews in a thick billowy flag out its exhaust. Across its steel back there is a familiar advertising logo above a big white Arabian script. I ask Weire what it says and he replies, "Black tar heroin by Anheuser Busch, fortified with vitamins A, C, and B_{12}."

He says the division is to be commanded by the West Point–trained leader of the 17 Devo 3 Gangsta Crips. Bullshit but still. I was up at Hickam this morning. Evidently Fed Ex has put half the United States Air Force on layaway. C-5 after C-5 after C-5 with OVERNIGHT ANYWHERE painted across the two-story-high fuselages loading up you name it: everything from self-propelled 120-mm mortars to armored engineer vehicles with assault bridging equipment.

The cops have pulled over three big eighteen-wheel tractor trailers. Inside, SA-16 shoulder-launched heat-seeking SAM "Stinger-skis," AGS-17 30-mm automatic grenade launchers, and 12.7-mm NSV heavy machine guns are stacked like cordwood.

On the Wall CNN camera crews at Pearl showed Cut Grunts driving armored recovery vehicles and armored artillery tractors through the red lights where the highway crosses I forget which boulevard. Having hundreds of tanks and trucks wait at the light was crazy, so Frank had truck-mounted 122-mm multiple rocket launchers with twin-fifties mounted above their cabs wall off the intersection and when the cops got salty he had a Cut Grunt pot off 300 rounds over the ocean and that led to a compromise: the cops are citing him for 520 failures to yield.

An artillery fire-control vehicle, a house-high box with tires to my shoulders and cracks in the rubber between their tread thick as my thumb, is parked behind a trailer. It has a blown engine.

The guy on the Wall said Cut Grunts are unloading transport, recon, and antitank helicopters, plus "flame weapons" and an AK-74 for anybody who wants to carry one. All this comes with 1,000 former Soviet officers, drill instructors, warrant officers, and long-service sergeants Frank got for a song. A full bird, only twenty years out of practice, SpezNaz colonel goes out the door for just $400 a month plus airfare, hotel, and rent-a-car and everybody is a temp, like typists from Kelly Girl: Frank bills each out at $2,500 a month. All his majesty has to supply is the Kunta Kintes—10,000 recruits he takes off the dole at $200 a month underwritten by the Public Law 680 Military Assistance Program, administered by an agency of a United States Government dying to see him stay in power.

Frank keeps the pink on all the equipment, his Majesty leases the tanks, helicopter gunships, etc., from Crawford Construction the way you would a Volvo. Frank will be in the black in five years for equipment he can charter for thirty. Everybody's happy.

Except the police, who continue to recite.

On the marquee above Do What You Look Like is *Coming June 1st: Anal Mania XVI.*

26 MAY

The ghost of Betty Iiiiiio won't go away. Roberta says forget the cosmos and face reality: I need a career and she'll be it. "With your millions and my me," she tells me, on the sidewalk and staring above us, "we cannot fail."

I look up too. Frank has booted the sky. Against its blue, a message in white: ANYONE ANYTHING ANY TIME. An advertisement for the liberties available on the New Island.

There has been resolution re: my exploded apartment. Panasonic Fire & Casualty has refused to pay cash, offering only to replace what I've lost. So I've taken a new camera, a Nikon Image Maker. It morphs, and the image Roberta reminds me I can make forever, is her.

Frank says that invention is just the line between what you want and how you're going to get it. Mating Loci with Light + Weight, he is putting our fortune into an "asset entity"

able to move at the speed of light. This entity will resemble a computer virus and will be able to "contain" up to $10 billion and will constantly search the global financial network for the next best "nest." It will move from one "interest area" the moment a competing interest rate eclipses that accruing in its existing "nest," and be slowed only at "payoff points" by the speed of market mechanisms. It will also move if anyone attempts an unauthorized audit or seizure. At its front will be an "entry stand" capable, in milliseconds, of applying a near infinite number of "keys" to whatever device is guarding the gates of any new repository.

On the Wall: Dope dealers busted flushing gold dust down toilets of their suites at the Kahala Hilton and the city hysterical re: the red army equipment. The mayor says if Frank launches jet-powered barges from Pearl he'll call out the National Guard.

Do What You Look Like got shut down last night by the liquor commission for selling zombies to a minor.

27 MAY

Gold running the sewers and this is the best we can do? Last night Vince hosted Rump Wranglers Anonymous and when I came in this morning a hologram from Fat Boys in Love hung above the bar, like two fellaciating balloons floating above an X-rated Macy's parade.

I've booked Bulimia Banquet for the weekend and Roberta is angry. "Biggerize your brain, Crawford: Bag Piss Pop. Go hardcore." Probably a moot point. Jan and Dean, who spends hours now playing Uncle Vanya on the lit vids, spent our last $2,000 paying off the thrash Catholics, Pius X Principle. He hates the idea of changing the name of Less Nervous to Roberta.

Someone tried to break in and wrecked the lock. Frank replaced it. He had the code changed from the linear *If you want a picture of the future, imagine a boot stomping on a human face—forever* to the more lyric *When a man takes to his bed, nearly all his friends have a secret desire to see him die; some to prove that his health is inferior to their own, others in the disinterested hope of being able to study a death agony.*

28 MAY

Manna from Heaven. On the stern of the *Gogol*, arced by satisfied mohole men, sits another piece of fabulous ex-Soviet technology. Hanging from a skeletal truss two stories tall is the largest drill bit in the world. Designed to bore "instant coal mines," it hangs above the water, an arrow pointed to the center of the earth. Its tip is an enormous synthetic diamond, a conical dodecahedron. Above that a ring of diamond-tipped secondary drills, a weave of metal snakes made of razors and knives. And finally, above that the 368 round vents of the 25,000-horsepower "external combustion engine" that drives the drill on a mix of burning hydrogen that blasts through the rock, spewing the basalt toward the surface while driving the spinning drill deeper into the earth.

With luck, we won't even need it. Yesterday Frank torched off the string of high explosives the mohole men had lowered into the hole. It was flawless. Though he set off the equivalent of 80,000 tons of TNT in less than five seconds, I'm not sure it even rocked the boat. I didn't feel, hear, or see anything except what appeared on the forty-eight-inch-high definition monitor/simulator mounted on the *Gogol's* bridge. Like the screen on a CAT-scan, the simulator showed the hole, thin as a hair, in relief. When the explosion went off the hair disappeared in a string of flashes and a red worm of lava ticked up the face of the monitor/simulator.

Now we are going down again. As usual, the bathysphere is hot and stinks. New tech. Frank now has a dozen microprocessors babbling at each other in six different computer languages. The "porthole" shows nothing but murk. Yesterday they didn't even touch bottom there was so much crap and turbulence in the water.

During the descent we key to the monitors that run off

cameras equipped with SIT lenses—underwater starlight scopes like the army used in Vietnam and Iraq—but at 2,300 feet Frank hits the laser spots. They create a hallway of light. A fish that looks like a huge eyeball with a snake's body for an optic nerve drifts up through the floor of this corridor. It gives us a singular stare and twitches up through the ceiling. Then, below through the murk I see magma rising like a cloud of filthy growing brain.

29 MAY

To be where he wants when he wants, Frank is taking delivery of a Tu-22M Backfire bomber FOB Vladivostok. The Russians are throwing in attack radar with terrain-following capability, and once Frank guts and upholsters the H-bomb bay the Backfire will fly 44 at Mach 2.1.

Odd what people leave behind. Frank, invited to the old Soviet naval aviation base in Alekseyevka to kick a tire or two, saw this bat plane still flying the colors of the Royal Air Force of West Sudan—it was a repo—fell head over heels and bought it. As if it were just a party favor, it came with a floppy loaded with a full-blown 1987 schematic for nuclear attack on the Hawaiian Islands. Courtesy of a former Soviet air marshal, it's as linear as a grocery list: fifty-one nukes delivered by Yankee-class subs patrolling off the islands and by a single Delta III–class submarine lounging in the Sea of Okhotsk. Just some ex-Soviet targeteer's daydream, Frank put it on his Mind at Syntyrsystym and says once again I panicked over shit.

I flunked my urinalysis, I tested clean. Weire says the state may attempt, in effect, to declare my consciousness felony illegal, and outlaw my natural state of mind.

On the beach tonight, wondering what to do sixty credits short of a B.A. in the history of television, I see a great cumulus mop of blond hair. The beach girl I saw the day I flew back from Mexico: 3-D eyes, Cheshire cat grin, and a body from another, better world.

30 MAY

Frank has fifty Korean bank guards at the docks at dawn. Nine-millimeter Disney Bulldogs in hand, they pace the parking lot. We wait for the National Guard, but nobody shows except a news copter from Channel Eight. The long pipes stand atop the great donut barges. Even though Frank doesn't torch off the engines until each barge has approached open water, the noise from the old B-52 turbofans is so loud it's like silence, so thunderous there is nothing left to hear. I scream and the only thing that tells me I am screaming is the air firing up the bottom of my throat.

31 MAY

On the Wall, I see what I think is a weather report, an aerial shot of a white cloud slouching to one side. Then I see that its source is on the ground and think, my, the volcano on the Big Island blew, so I turn up the volume: Kazakhstan has announced the aboveground detonation of a nuclear warhead in violation of the 1963 Nuclear Test Ban Treaty.

And that's it. I watch forty minutes and all they have on tape is a helicopter crew from Quebec, there by accident covering the Canadian national parachute team, flying around the cloud and saying holy shit in French—plus cuts to everybody else in the world wondering what the hell is going on.

On the answering machine, a message from Frank. Paradise on top. The lava is spewing out of the hole at twice the expected rate, not only filling the crater but beginning to cone.

JUNE

Frank is a patriot and says it might not be a bad idea, before somebody else does, to buy the United States. Not every corner cathouse or ma and pa liquor store—that would be absurd—only the essentials. He figures that 630 publicly owned companies with a net stock value of $26.35 trillion control 68 percent of the economy and all the decline of the American industrial base sob sistering and the Ccrash notwithstanding, if he took the aggregate assets of those companies and placed them against the aggregate cost of the stock it would take to snatch them up, profitwise he'd still squeak by with a cool trillion. Even though there'd be a lot of paperwork he says the concept is attractive. He'd use ignition financing—most of his investment going to just setting up the deal. The money itself would come from banks that, to get their money back, would sell off the country's assets. I ask to whom? Other Americans? Europeans? Venusians? Frank has a subtle sense of humor and maybe he's joking because he says if he does it he'll start micro before going macro—execute a leveraged buyout of Montana, then get the pink slip on a few other wallflower western states, Idaho or Oregon. See how that goes then maybe go wide.

On the Wall everything is still being preempted by the nuclear warhead test in Kazakhstan. The latest news is that it wasn't a test. It was an accident. Frank says, accident my ass.

His right eye staring off at nothing and dressed in the clothes of downward mobility—sport coat, a bent and dented rep tie, and grey slacks shiny at the knees—August Hona is peddling surfboards. They're pop-outs, stringerless boards copied from the templates of more expensive and durable models. He sells them from a Dodge van painted metalflake blue. An explosively detailed mural of the beach had been drawn on the side. Palm trees with luminescent orange leaves and purple trunks frame a green sea topped with surf that appears as rigid as fallen snow.

He tells me he is hurt bad and I am going to pay.

On Maui when I was a boy, the Honas' house was a sprawling junkyard below us. Aug had problems growing up down there. Borderline autistic by nine or ten, Augie was a gibbering idiot, primal in the streets, worse than I—safe on my Ritalin—would ever be. I'd listen to him howl and babble convinced that if I studied him long enough I could learn the secret language of the mad.

2 JUNE

Frank gives me an envelope to give to the president of the United States. He is visiting the governor's home in Kahala. Roberta says: "The president of the United States? The one living in this solar system?" Forget it, I'll never get within two blocks of the place. Somehow she still doesn't get it: here and on the other islands, Frank is considered as powerful as the devil and as lucky as God and, using his name, access should be easy. I've talked to presidents before.

Nevertheless—though sane as Superman, due to the meds, the psychotherapist, and my inability to serve the public—I am, backgroundwise, clothed in the rags of whackosis and I'm surprised it is, in fact, so easy. The street is blocked off in rings: state cops, behind them Korean private police, then the FBI, and finally the new natty Presidential Guard in lightweight charcoal suits. Weire says the new guard is the result of the Secret Service being sold to Burger King. In any event, bankerish G-men relax against a black Suzuki limousine. It's lunchtime and, on a big white-clothed table on the lawn, there are mangos, papayas, and guavas in a wreath around a cooked pig. Whole, he has been, from neck to rump, sliced to discs of ham. The atmosphere is congenial. Fruit drinks and Disney Bulldogs all around. I say my name to a smiling man holding a cellular and, as if entering the stations of a happy hell, I am admitted through security, ring by ring.

The president, made so by six .233-caliber rounds fired into the head, throat, and chest of his predecessor, sits in the governor's kitchen. Squat. I get a handshake that may require an X ray. "Oh yes," he says. "Boy, I've read your tombstone. The New Island and that brother of yours. The shotgun-waving cowboy." His meaty face floods with delight. "Like the poet said, having your head up your ass can be a full-time job."

3 JUNE

Frank says that, like the poet says, the president of the United States is only the guard at the museum gate and then adds, "You're gonna do time."

The sky is white. Frank pushes the Cayuse's joystick forward. The ocean jumps to us and Frank powers out of the dive so low that the Plexiglas in front of me catches a hard whip of spray. The copter screams over long, grey rollers peaked with curls of dirty foam.

Frank's helicopter evolves. He is developing "Attack Packs" that Third Worlders can mount on anything from a dirt clod to a YF-22 and the Cayuse has been fitted with one: a firing platform to launch the Sidearm AGM-122A antiradiation missile designed to attack antiaircraft and artillery radar systems, or just some poor guy's car, if Frank feels like it.

Below us, the city-block-and-a-half donut barges circle the *Gogol*. Their cargo of long pipes stands in the air, each section surrounded by its necklace of winches and casting long shadows across a metal sea. One long pipe is half the height of the others. It is being lowered into the water where it will anchor itself on a floor of soft magma a couple thousand feet below.

I say, "I'm going to jail?" Frank says, "Sure. For assault. The DA won't budge." He sends the Cayuse in a swooping arc toward the beach, wheeling low over the beach at Waikiki. Surfers, their boards rocking like pumpkin seeds, look up at the commotion. Sunbathers gaze up too, some are freaked, others tentative, in their dismay.

4 JUNE

I book back to Jeanie's, break in, and this time really go through the place. On vacation, my ass. And if I'm going to jail I'm going to settle this first.

Jeanie was trying to earn money to buy a condominium. Nobody in her family had ever had a mortgage and I was tempted to forge Frank's signature on a few papers at the bank, except Jeanie was honest and hated to sin. Take sex.

At night after we made love Jeanie would talk in her sleep, she'd say, "No stop it," and, "Get away from me." She'd swing her arms around and once she hit me on the cheek hard enough to bruise. Later that night I'd had my own dream. That I'd hit her. Her nose exploded like a bloody bomb and I woke up with my heart banging in my ears and my sheets soaked and Jeanie lying there curled up, her face a peaceful, pretty mask, faultless and unabused.

Our last argument was about her going to confession every week. I asked, "What do you cop to? Shoplifting? Racketeering? Mail fraud? Cattle mutilation? What?" Then I said, "Hold on, we're not married, so God must be furious about our sex acts." Perfect. I said, "Don't the priests get tired of hearing three fucks and two blow jobs, four fucks and one blow job, two fucks, five blow jobs, and the odd around the world, week after week? Wouldn't it just be easier to clip coupons and mail them in quarterly?"

By then Jeanie was angry about her photos, was sick of haunting car crash sites and apartment fires. No more wearing $3,500 evening gowns to cataclysms, mocking other people's tragedies. She got madder when I told her that her big fault was she just didn't have enough guts to really sell out.

❊

I rifle the apartment drawer by drawer and find nothing to suggest that she isn't gone from the earth.

5 JUNE

The light is unearthly at eighty feet. Mohole men have dropped lamps with lenses six feet wide that cast pale suns around the long pipe. Lasers shoot flat rods of light through water clouded with silver dust. A shiny school of tuna swim in a long diamond ribbon, drifting past the long pipe's immense tipped curve. We ascend toward a frogman and I watch the slow fan of his legs and long yellow fins. He is opening the bladders on the long pipe. Bubbles jet and spill upward. Frank has launched a Campedo video camera so we can see ourselves on a monitor, our bathysphere a vague half moon against the black.

We've been down to the bottom of the cone. It has grown to maybe miles around but our visibility is awful because the water down below was a roiling fog. Something is going on, but no one can tell what.

Frank stares at a monitor tuned to CNN: pictures of ambulances and soldiers in bile yellow radiation suits stand by at roadblocks. Even though it happened at a test site maybe a thousand people were killed. Radiation sails the globe. Frank says the casualty figures are just more tits and ass from the media. The real figure is 150 dead tops. And when a hairy expert on CNN estimates the blast was one megaton Frank laughs out loud.

The Kazakhstan government claims again that it was an accident, but Frank says nonsense—nobody ever sets a nuke off by mistake.

6 JUNE

Today the long pipes go down. Slowly. Frank copters onto the barge and I watch as what looks like a piece of sewer pipe as big as a ten-story building eases into the ocean. The winches and lines make high wheezes, creaks, and pops. The mohole men flood the bladders in the long pipe's concrete. The bladders are as big as houses. As they fill, walls of air fly to the surface and turn the sea around the barge to a white riot of blasting foam.

There's been a fight aboard the *Gogol*. The crew is seventy/thirty Christian/Muslim, oil and water, and the hydrogen bomb going off was the straw that broke the camel's back. Frank says superpower peace is only intermission, that Marxism was a walk on the beach compared to the new Islamic empire that's about to jump out of the woodwork from Morocco to Bangladesh—400 million pissed-off nuclear-armed Pakistanis, Persians, Turks, Afghans, Arabs, and wogs.

On TV an unnamed state department source is quoted as saying that the blast was a "plea for understanding" made by moderate members of the Muslim separatist Kazakhstani Party of God. The idea was to set off a 150-kiloton fission device underground at the now-abandoned Soviet nuclear test facilities near Semipalatinsk. The rock strata there are muffling, the Party of God thought they could torch one off with nobody the wiser but the Russian head of state.

The Japanese-Samoan attorney, slim in a boxed-shoulder lady's pale grey suit, says the Voice Locks, the Slaughterhouse, Joe Dozer—you name it—are "financially insane."

She puts a big glass bowl to her lips. We are in the grotto bar beneath a superblock downtown. I asked her how much was being lost. She tells me Frank's business was none of hers. When I say, "So you don't know," she replies, "That's not what I said."

I ask how much we are losing and she orders another drink. I can't wait for our paradise to pop up. Just for the lunch money. Prices on menus are no longer hieroglyphics and the milky green swimming pools of crème de menthe, vodka, cream, and crushed ice she instructs me to enjoy each cost as much as a traffic ticket. "That's not something I know or even if I did know I could tell you," she says. "Talk to Weire."

Behind the glass walls of the grotto tropical fish glide and dart around us, as if we're all members of the deep blue sea.

Vorhaggen says I'm either the biggest foreign arms dealer since Adnan Kashoggi, or for some personal reasons simply need to have more Main battle tanks than the armies of Italy, Spain, and Brazil combined.

I was at Less Nervous taking a Makita "Junior" Jackhammer to ACTION KILLS FEAR on the front door when he came in.

I say, "I'm a bouncer with $15 in my back pocket."

He orders coffee. When I say I can't serve it, he looks around, says, "Basic black, huh?" He hitches up his slacks. "You folks gonna go hardcore?"

"How low can we go?"

"Sonny, don't tell me I don't know the culture. When we were kids the wife and I had the broken glass sap concession at Altamont." Vorhaggen shrugs. "Hey, I myself saw him amok in Vegas. Scum gets a pedigree. Still, history's the judge. John, E, Keith, Bob, Sid, even Iggy, they pale in comparison. Besides the machines can make anybody. Hardcore'd be easy." The detective taps a hardcore rhythm on the bartop. "Guilty pleasure."

"You're not here to talk about that."

"Sammy, Jilly." Vorhaggen's big and his white shirt is mooned translucent under his arms. "Junior, you tickle me." He puts a finger to his cheek. His skin looks scalded. "Your dad. Talk about low profile. He made Howard Hughes look like Elton John. But the money. Just in arms sales. He made some differences in this world."

I say, "Like what?"

"Uganda." He puts a fist to his mouth, burps. "He sold Idi Amin the six Sherman tanks the bastard used to win the revolution."

I laugh. "Idi Amin took over Uganda with six Sherman tanks?"

Vorhaggen nods. "They were the only six in town."

7 JUNE

Libel. But all I can get is the audio, which I tape: *This guy is the worst-kept secret in town, the ultimate trust fund kid. He's been failing upward forever. He had an office in the White House*

*basement before he was old enough to vote. "Nukes, use not Abuse"
was cross-stitched on a sampler on the wall above his desk. But
Reagan knew Frank was for real because he looked so good in his
uniform. The kid was a shoe-in for sergeant-at-arms in the Nuke
Tehran Club until he got in a wet T-shirt contest with Ollie North.*

*His old man was a new-age robber baron—nukes, bandit aero-
space—he leveraged half South America . . . his boy Frank is a
lethal numbskull with unspendable amounts of money, somebody
who could give craven megalomania a really bad name—*

The Wall is sizzling, nothing but Jackson Pollock. What's
on is the Drunk Pundits, a pro-wrestling–style news show.
Frank is the subject—*a whacko scheme to blow a new island
out of the water . . . meanwhile, he's hired members of U.S. military units to act as his bodyguard . . .*

It gets worse, but Frank is not interested in slander,
"especially if it's all true," and on the phone he says, "Your
arms dealership was four pieces of paper in the back of a file
cabinet. I never even saw any tanks. They were buried fifty
feet underground in a weapons depot in Dolinovka and
could've been 300 railroad cars full of porkbellies for all I was
concerned."

I punch through to Weire, say I've got to know what's up
with my brother. "What is he doing?"

"With what?"

"The nuke. Joe Dozer. My life."

I hear Frank's attorney sigh into the receiver, then, "Joe
Dozer is what he's all about. A neat half-baked idea he could
really throw himself into. Give him credit—Joe does what it's
supposed to do: wreck things fast. But so does dynamite and
so does an earthmover and dynamite and earthmovers have
other uses as well."

"Tom," I say, "what about the nuke? He's got one?"

"Had one. Hold on, I've got an incoming." Five minutes
of dead air later, he asks if it's okay if he calls me back.

Sure it's okay. What else is it going to be?

I'm at home, in front of the Wall, looking for news of the
New Island, but there's nothing on but the renegade nuclear
explosion story. Evidently, secessionist hotheads from the
Kazakhstan Party of God acquired three "boosted fission de-
vices," 150-kiloton composite uranium plutonium implosion
bombs. The plan was to lower the yield on one to 10 kilotons

by removing the tritium pellets that provide the boost and then drop it into an "ignition theater" 200 feet belowground at the old Semipalatinsk test site, set it off, and tell the Russian government that 10 million "Slavic occupiers" had better be on the next stage out of town or the other two bombs would be put to more conventional use.

The phone rings. It's Weire, who says, "The Slaughterhouse. Frank wakes up in the morning, gets out of bed, glances in the mirror, and sees he looks like a cowboy. So, he should be an expert in cows. Right? But where should his expertise lie? Frank likes to kill things so a slaughterhouse is an obvious choice. But the problem is that even to kill cattle you have to know something about them and Frank doesn't."

"The nuke," I say.

"Not over the phone," Weire replies. A moment later I hang up to see I have a message from the governor's office: "Bad news from above."

I walk down to Less Nervous. Roberta says the Canadian copter crew made a deal with Disney Holo to form a corporation as big as General Motors, yet with an anticipated business span no longer than the life of a May fly. All to market this image, morphed to continuous loop. I booted it into the Love Machines and, though it cost a bundle, it has been a godsend. The Drastic Plastics, Icicles, and Gloom Slammers have been stilled and made consumers by holocaust. Mesmerized in front of the Love Machines, they watch the mushroom cloud expand and contract, expand and contract, breathe its way back and forth in time. They drink zombies like water, and stare endlessly at this Möbius strip of disaster that, through its hypnotic horror, kills their lust to fight or perv.

B JUNE

Three dead in front of the Unification Bank. Two Icicles, plus a teenage girl—a tourist there with her folks—who picked the wrong morning to discover that her Visa Platinum wouldn't work in the Moonies' money machine. One of the Icicles survived, but Roberta says they had to stretcher him off in chunks. You'd think the first thing they'd teach you in Bank Robbery 101 is that three tabs of Real Mad, a pair of 10-gauge sawed-offs, and an old AR-15 semiautomatic are no match for four sober Korean security guards packing Crowd Management Bulldogs flipped to sprinkle.

Frank says the first piece of pipe coned perfectly, the second lowered, mated, and should crest by dusk. "By this time tomorrow there should be a magma cone 1,200 feet high approaching the surface at 180 feet per day."

On the phone, a medium through which he will now not discuss any kind of bomb for any kind of reason, Tom Weire says if the current administration didn't want millions of tons of magma to come blasting out of the Pacific a cool 185 miles still inside the country's Exclusive Economic Zone—forget the twelve-mile limit—Frank would be off in a box. When I ask what is the use of the New Island to the government if they don't even own it, Weire says: "Wake up. This is the Pacific Rim in the Oughts. They'll own it the same way they own Massachusetts. A no-customs, no-duties, no-taxes, no-passports, no-questions-asked door to the entire Far East. And it's not just us that want it, but the Japs, Israelis, Chinese, Russians, and all of EuroCom, too. Think of a U.N. where all the delegates are horse thieves. It's as simple as that. Now you and me, we gotta get together downtown."

"Where?" I ask.

"You just be hanging by the next few days, and I'll tell you in the car."

9 JUNE

I wonder how much I should tell her about this. Or how much she knows already. I miss Roberta when she goes home at night, or even at work when she runs across the street, but this isn't smart. It's almost four. Jan and Dean is bartending for about another millisecond and she says she'll hear his Ford pull up below, but I'm not sure. Just out of the shower she's on my bed, her wet black hair combed back like a greaser. She's naked and doing "scientific experiments."

She straddles my hips and just as I began to disappear in-

side her, says, "You jerk," and leaps off as if she'd been bucked
from a Brahman bull. Then remounts and uses me, for lack
of a better word, as a dildo. I'm taken in hand and set against
her, and rubbed across the best place ever. "Good fun," she
accesses, swallowing. The tip of her tongue is pressed between her square white teeth.

Then she's going, "God. Cut it out, Crawford." She puts
the back of a slender hand to her dark brow. "You got it in my
eye." I say I didn't go that far and she squeals it's on everything and when are we going to get married?

Writing ROBERTA + TOD across my chest in jizz, she
asks how long before I'll get hard again. I estimate seconds,
minutes, days, as I feel I WANT YOUR MONEY being
scrawled across my stomach and, too, an itch. On my arm.
And there it is, a que, tiny and black. Smaller than a flea. I
scratch it off, have it on my fingertip. It's metal and I see it
move.

1 1 J U N E

"Crawford," Weire says, "when you get a bunch of ex-countries
who made so many hydrogen bombs that, if they wanted,
they could fill every seat in Yankee Stadium with one H-bomb
apiece, and when all those ex-countries are as poor as dirt and
each one of those things is worth a fortune, it makes sense
that a few of them might have got socked away for a rainy
day. To be sold to the likes of you know who."

"What are we going to do?"

"Did you talk to Frank? He's screwed."

"Yeah." There has been a new hitch with the New Island:
as it rises, the magma is cooling faster than expected. A fourth
pipe has been lowered and secured, but the cooling combined
with a weight of hot rock in the pipe has slowed the rise from
180 feet a day to less than fifty and if it continues to cool
faster than it flows the vein will become its own cork. So,
Frank may need the big drill after all.

Weire and I are downtown, on Hotel Street in front of his
perfect red bubble of a 1965 Porsche. Weire pushes quarters
into a parking meter. "I'm thinking about going to the Feds,"
he says.

I follow Weire into a tiny Indian restaurant. White walls, white tablecloths, and a white-suited waiter. The dining room is empty. Weire says, "This place is so exclusive, you and I are the only ones they ever let in."

When we are seated I say, "I don't understand, if Frank's in so much trouble, how's he going to finagle the island?"

"Ai yi yi, Crawford," Weire says, "the same way he finagled Heaven. The air force had to pay him off."

"Why?"

Weire considers me as if, somehow, I am suddenly lacking more than a brain stem, then says, "Okay, Crawford, a little background music. You know his plan for the end of the world? It violated NATO doctrine but it *was* U.S. Air Force doctrine. That was the dirty big secret visionary Frank was too myopic to understand."

The waiter, a tall brown boy, hands us long brown menus. Weire opens his like a book and says, "So all Frank did was go out and do what they had already done. Except his mistake was he gave his spiel to a goody-two-shoes know-nothing under-under-secretary of defense for policy who freaked out and went to the Wall. Frank sees he's going to get it and screams bloody murder. So Defense decided to kill two birds with one stone. They consider Frank just a good soldier—an example of your tax dollars at work—essentially *harmless*—so they buy him off by creating Heaven, which gives them a place to mothball all these lethal-in-the-hands-of-the-wogs thermonuclear guys and run a technological circlejerk."

I say I still don't understand.

"At the end of the cold war they had tons of nuclear weapons people—not only ours but more importantly theirs—they had to find a place for. Frank provided one. Heaven."

I say, "But I never saw more than ten people there at a time."

Weire says most were just modemed in and paid to keep spewing their research into Frank's computer to create a library full of recipes for new and better dooms nobody would ever use. Supposedly.

"So what are we going to do?" I ask.

"Crawford," Weire says, "for the first time in your life you're asking me a question I can't answer or at least lie about. Guyfriendbuddypal, what are we going to do? I do not know."

✳

On the Wall: the answer to a lesser question. Somebody failed to remove the tritium pellets from the trigger to "downsize" the blast and the bomb blew *x* million tons of Kazakhstan halfway to the moon. Reuters reports 2,500 now dead and five times that seriously wounded. On the home front, four local bikedykelesbopunks have been sentenced to three to five years apiece at the state women's detention center. Though the case against them was weak, they did not appeal. Nevertheless, running a stolen car ring on an island is, if you think about it, probably not a very good idea.

12 JUNE

Weire says, the New Island better squirt out of the ocean tout de suite. When it rains it pours. "A fool and his father's money are soon parted. Frank is broke."

I say, "Horseshit. What about all his assets?"

Weire says. "What assets?"

I say, "Take the Waves. An NBA franchise has got to be worth, what? A hundred million? Push comes to shove and he can just sell them."

Weire looks at me. "Are you telling me," he says, "your brother owns the Waves?"

I say, "It's not public knowledge, but sure. You know that."

"What I know," Weire says, "is that two years ago Frank provided a forty-eight-hour line of credit to Jack Seally who was buying the Waves at forty cents on the dollar from the initial investment group. But what he owns now isn't worth the price of his box seats."

Onstage a woman doffs her panties to show she isn't one. A dick inflates, as if with the blustery assistance of a bicycle pump. The Zen County Hate Ranch. They're Top-40, and I'll admit it: way too middle class. Roberta, disgusted, advises, "Crawford, feast your eyes," and shows me a copy of *Young Y,* a "stroke book for the Pacific Rim." The magazine flops open to two girls. Muffs shaved to valentines and wearing nothing but pale hosiery, they recline in that ancient and honorable position, 69. Roberta says they pay models $12,000 apiece. Crawford, she says, that could be us.

At night it hits me. Under the light of the moon I go through the list, and oh yes, I call Tom Weire and tell him that I know the method by which Crawford Trust companies are being liquidated. I say, "Alphabetically. If a company begins with an 'A,' forget what it earns, Frank'll sell it. If it begins with a 'V,' forget what it loses, he'll keep it for a while. That's Frank's idea of corporate command. He sees a list and starts at the top."

Weire says bingo.

13 JUNE

Jeanie calls. After six months right out of the blue. She says she was arrested at customs at Kennedy and was so surprised she got up and tried to leave and got grabbed so hard her shoulder was dislocated. I say, "At least they didn't kill you," and she says she would've been better off if they had.

She won't tell me what she was carrying. I ask her about bail and she says Frank's dealt with that but she's got to stay put. I say, "Where's put?" And she says, "Go ask Frank."

The mohole men have a death ray. Fifty feet from the bathysphere, deep in the black smoky water and pinned in three needles of laser light, a vicious-looking yellow fish is popped to a halo of bright blue guts. Frank is trigger man.

We have a new pilot. Big. He has a blind man's eyes, a jerky gaze or no gaze at all, a red face, and an untrimmed red beard that makes him look as if his chin just exploded. Below, valhalla blossoms in dull reds out of the earth. The cone looks like a dunce's cap with the dunce's blooded brains spilling down the side.

The bathysphere touches down in hard bumps. The ocean floor is a moonscape pocked with coral that could be heads of lead cauliflower. At the base of the new cone there are tall trees of coral hung with pear-shaped polyps. Coils of bamboo coral pulse with light like irradiated bed springs. Tiny bright fish toss themselves across the big center HiDi screen, forming a shower of green jewelry. As big as it is, the cone will not be enough.

For some reason I don't ask my brother about anything at all.

1 4   J U N E

Night. Frank is forty. Today is his birthday. He comes into Less Nervous and says, "Help me."

I ask, "Are you drunk?"

I've thrown him a costume party, whose theme is the twentieth century.

"No, it's my head. I can't even tell how many of you I see there are."

Frank goes inside and, surrounded by monsters, he seems uncomprehending.

We have gone hardcore: Sinatra. Old Blue Eyes floats above the stage. "Two Feet High and Rising" floods the room. I ask if he wants to go outside. We push through the crowd. The bar is packed, a guy could drop dead in here and take two hours to hit the ground. On the sidewalk he says, "What trash. What godawful trash. Whose idea was this?"

His helicopter is there. He's put it down on the street.

I say, "Weire says we're broke." Lights from passing cars whip and slide across my brother's face. His old bruises look like dirt.

He runs a hand through his hair. "That's because I put the money where he can't see it."

I say, "Where?"

"Everywhere."

He climbs into the copter. It has metamorphosed. A thin latticework of tubular aluminum forms the outline of wings. The instrument panel has been disemboweled, popping from where gauges used to be are curls and twists of red, blue, and yellow wire that gather in tangles and loops. There's a hydraulic sucking sound. The blades begin to rotate slowly above my head and a long gash of flame spits from the exhaust with a scream.

Outside Less Nervous, Weire says, "Frank's the snake who eats his own tail and he never really had any idea what was his to begin with. Your old man did business behind hundreds of different corporate titles and licenses. Crawford & Hona doing business as Atco doing business as Best Oceanic doing business as Profile Industries doing business as on and on and on and on."

He lights a cigarette. We are standing out-front beside the damaged Joe Dozer. Its great toothy bucket is high in the air, ready to rip the skin off what's left of the sky. "Believe me," Weire says, "it's a miracle that Frank lacked the basic accounting skills required to bleed the estate to death before now. It took him forever to figure out how to leverage his own equity. Thank your lucky stars he's not any smarter than he is or you'da been out on the street years ago."

A cab eases around the corner and brakes metal on metal. Its headlights dim and three dark, short women in shredded crepe grass skirts get out of the back and stride toward the door where we are standing. One of the women, her beige palm out, says, "Cab fare," and Weire tells me, "Hula whores." Then he says, "Frank fired me."

"Fired you?"

"This afternoon. I told him he was penniless and he fired me."

A couple appears. A bulbous, tan, tall man in white Guccis and a translucent pink shirt unbuttoned to the rise of his stomach. His date or daughter, a chrome-haired voluptuary.

Weire says, "Governor."

The woman sticks a vial under my nose and says, "Breathe."

I do. I go away, travel to the end of everywhere, and when I come back the world is a different place.

I go back inside. There is a hole in the wall and ceiling above the bar, a ragged hatch to the stars, punched there by the wrecking ball to August Hona's crane. Dazed, it takes me a moment to remember how it got there. Seeing four tall, pale, normal-looking guys standing by the door, I ask Jan, "Who are they?"

He replies, "Man-made men." Then says, "Meanwhile, are you gonna go over and snake Dewey's liquor or what?"

Roberta, in a round black-and-yellow bee suit, says, "Yeah."

"I've got enough problems." A costume party was a dumb idea.

"It's just across the street," Jan says. "We'll be out of booze in fifteen minutes. Nobody's there. It'll be cake."

Still trying to clear my head, I tell Roberta I'll hang and drop, and I do. I say, "Gimme the flashlight and I'll lift you down." She drops through the skylight on Dewey's roof. I try to grab her but she's made out of foam and she falls over sideways.

I say, "Let's not monkey with the wine. Just the hard stuff." Then I say, "Bless me Father for I am sinning," and two minutes later Roberta breathes, "Crawford, feast your eyes, what the hell is that?"

The Egg.

Outside, behind Less Nervous, grabbing a box of Dewey's booze, Jan and Dean says, "It's a warhead designed to wear a lot of hats. The worst of both worlds, Fauntleroy. Weire clued me in: an enhanced radiation bomb with a neutron-kill radius wider than Chicago. Plus, as a special bonus, you can use it to trigger far larger explosions."

Roberta, pushing aside boxes of wine and cases of beer, trying to get at Dewey's hard liquor, had found it in the back of Do What You Look Like's walk-in. I took one look at the thing and said I was calling the cops.

"Why not," Jan and Dean says, in a Godzilla suit and going through the back door into the bar, "slip back in there and take it ourselves. Dewey'd have to pay us a fortune for us just to say 'Beg us and maybe we'll give it back.'"

Dewey, out of nowhere and dressed as King Kong, says he's got a present for me to celebrate Jan's deal. "What deal?"

Dewey says, "Sally."

The gorgeous beach girl appears. Dewey pulls a roll out of his front pocket, hands it to her, and says, "Five hundred bucks to let Tod here try anything that doesn't hurt."

She is standing beside him dressed in sparkling white. A thin red belt pencils her waist. That long sheet of blond hair, perfect face. A fairy princess.

I shoulder my way behind her, through people disguised as Churchill, Manson, Elvis, and Zelda, as GI Joe and the Vietnam War. Tony, of Tony's Ark, in a robe that makes him maybe a pope, bumps into me and says Frank has offered him a bullet train motor to use in his boat which, he says, will deliver him and his children from an end due almost immediately.

I wish him luck. At the bar, Sally asks if anybody ever told me I'd make a beautiful woman.

I say, no, wondering: what deal? and where is Roberta? I ask her how she knows Dewey.

"He popped my cherry."

I say, "Come again?"

"Years ago. I was fifteen and in love. He said, 'Honey, your ballroom days are over,' and that was that."

Then she asks if I've ever had a hot water hum job and when I say, "What's that?" she wants to know if something's wrong with me, don't I go out with grown women anymore?

Vince, a grizzly Shirley Temple, asks me what I want to drink and I reply, "Anything."

Sally asks for water, "I'd invite you back to my apartment, but I had a hurricane in there this afternoon."

I ask what happened and she says, "I hide money then panic when I forget where I've put it. But I've got to give you a hum job. You'll die."

Her mouth is on mine. As big as a world. She pulls back and says, "My place. Yeah, lover, you go right ahead. Shoo. This'll be unbelievable."

I grip my purple drink. I can feel the progress of a joke, but I can't see where it will end.

I ask, "Where does the water come in?"

When she doesn't reply I tell her she has a great body and she says, "I've had to work on it. Listen: I was kidding about Dewey."

She puts a long slender arm across my own. Oh Christ, I look through the crowd and see Betty Iiiiiio, masquerading as a normal human being.

I say, "Kidding what about?"

She laughs. "About popping my cherry." She kisses me and says, "No one has."

I say, "You mean you're still a virgin?"

She says, "My, I do have your attention, don't I?"

I breathe, "No cherry?" and she puts her mouth to the hollow of my neck and says, "No, because I don't have one."

"He sold it!" I turn and see Roberta, in her bee suit, tears irrigating her mascara. "It's all over. Weire told him to cave! Jan and Dean has cut his deal with Dewey: $120,000 and a bus ticket to the mainland. Less Nervous gets bulldozed tomorrow."

I say, "You're joking." But no—there, right behind Roberta, Jan and Dean barks no way and that he's blowing his money on art from Mask of Smiles. "I'm going hog wild into minimalism. No paint. No canvas. Nothing. Forget the answers, just give me the questions."

"Who's this gash?" Roberta hisses.

"Baby girl, you're too kind." Sally's voice drops an octave. "Actually, I've got a cock bigger than most regular guys."

Wiping my mouth, I pull Weire off the dance floor, away from a sexy-looking Mother Teresa, and he says, "Thanks for the rescue. That chick smelled like a harbor."

I say, "You let him sell it?"

He shrugs.

I see Dewey with his brother August. I push by Madonnas, Chaplins, and Stalins and scream: "She was a man!" Dewey says, "You've been watching too many movies. She's no more of a man than you are. I just paid for her abortion." He reaches inside the chest of his Kong suit. "You want to see the canceled check for the coat hanger?"

I hit him. Blood rolls from his nose to form the Roman

numeral II. Dewey steps forward, takes a wild right to the temple, grabs my hair, and by the time the cops get there, there's been a melee, I'm burned on the stomach with a Hot Stick, on the ground, Dewey kicking me more or less absent-mindedly in the ribs. Jan bends over and whispers, I say we snatch the nuke, warts and all.

My stomach hurting like I've been cut in half, Jan and Dean and I go through the back door of Do What You Look Like under fading stars, load the Oman Egg on a dolly, and drop it into the trunk of the Ford. The car stands up like a speed-boat.

The party is over. The world has gone home. I am standing there, my blood black under the sickly yellow of a street light, not knowing what to do, when there is a sound of an engine starting across the street. I see the bucket of a huge frontloader smash through the front wall of Less Nervous. Augie Hona, oblivious in his glee, waves and shouts, "Moving day."

My burned-up bloody shirt flying around me like a bunch of flags, I run after Jan, who has sprinted to the curb, where Joe Dozer is parked above a lake of its own crank-case oil. He climbs high up into the cab, hits the ignition, and slams the machine into Aug's frontloader. It swings back, tips over, and crashes into the wall of Less Nervous. Jan cannot control the motion of Joe Dozer and it wheels forward, its metal mouth pushes into the side of the Nancy Spungeon Room, and in a great poof of dust the Love Machines are revealed glowing, like the tubes of an old-fashioned radio. Aug is screaming that he's going to the cops, going to the Feds, going to have us dead. We jump in the Ford and beat it.

Roberta drives, running traffic lights. The speedometer on Jan and Dean's old Ford palpitates wildly.

I'm shoving the genie back in the bottle, I've decided to take the Egg back to Celestial City where they can sell it to God, Gadhafi, or Zsa Zsa.

But at the airport we can't get to International Flights, a state bull pulls up in a black-and-white with his bop top going off like a siege cannon. Jan and I pull the Egg out of the trunk and tell Roberta to book. Crying, she boots it. I expect the cop to either take off after her or get out of his car and arrest us, but he just sits there with his bop-top lights exploding over and over, red, white, and blue.

Jan and I made it to check-in, dragging the Egg between us. We checked it. I forked over my new ANYTHING card. By a miracle it popped through, and I waited crazy for a plane, my senses so gone I heard a jet about to land on our gate and, expecting it to crash into us, stood there praying to die.

Beneath us, on an ocean bathed in morning light, wind-pushed white caps look like flecks of lint strewn across dark blue, finely crinkled tin. A frigate trailing a white wake cruises off-shore from the green carpet of Lanai, a small island formerly owned by the Dole pineapple company and recently sold to the Japanese, who have already turned half of it into a 738-hole golf course. Low clouds cast drifting shadows across the remaining red ground, interrupted here and there by what little is left of the farmland, a few perfect squares of green.

JD is itching, scouring his chest with the cloth of his shirt. I suggest that we're done for and he wants to know how's my stomach and I tell him, "Leaking."

I feel like I've wet my pants. I lift the hem of my T-shirt and see a big wide drooling red mouth just above my belt line.

Jan and Dean asks if I have my pills and I say, "Forget my pills." The jet begins its descent. We pass over Kahului. A scatter of rusty metal roofs.

The plane banks and the scenery slants toward us. The pilot announces our approach and he bumps the jet onto the runway. We're the last to get off. Maui. I stand on the stairs and watch another airliner drift down toward the runway. Its exhaust forms an elliptical brown smudge against an otherwise clear blue sky.

I walk across the runway, toward an airport terminal festive with cops.

15 JUNE?   *Aloha Estates, Maui*

Tom Weire says Frank was born to kill so maybe this all fits: when he got retired from the Strategic Air Command the Honolulu *Advertiser* said Frank was a dinosaur from the future, the high priest of a failed religion. But I think his plan was just too hip for the room, for all he did was suggest the obvious: a massive, preemptive, any-Sunday nuclear strike against what was then the Soviet Union. While it violated NATO declarative doctrine on the use of strategic forces, his idea—knock out the other guy before he can launch out from under your attack—was brilliant. Begin with an X-ray pindown, exploding nukes one a minute outside the atmosphere above Soviet missile fields to blow the brains out of his communication centers. Then take out the older inaccurate liquid-fueled SS-18 rockets bolt from the blue with one ICBM warhead each. The Sovs still had to warm them up like teakettles before launch. The solid fueled ones would have been tougher to catch because they were much easier to fire and in superhard silos. But the genius of Frank's plan was that he knew the Soviets were so confident we'd never strike first, that some of their warheads weren't even loaded on the missiles, much less armed.

The math was the hard part. Frank had to target all command and control, with three warheads aimed at each site, to be on the safe side, and it took two warheads on the hardened silos where they kept their SS-13s, -17s, -18s, and -19s, plus two warheads each on all the garages at the main operating bases for mobile ICBMs—truck-launched SS-25s and train-launched SS-24s.

So what was the Rx? Use twenty Trident Ohio Class subs for the knockout punch. Novel. By U.S. declarative doctrine they were considered purely retaliatory weapons because, historically, sea-launched ICBMs have been inaccurate.

But each Trident II sub could carry twenty-four missiles

on board and each missile mounts eight to twelve warheads. Frank's plan was to have half the subs launch from patrol positions at sea and have the rest surge from their piers in Washington State and Georgia. They'd download the warheads from eight to six if range was a problem. Well over 3,000 right there. Throw in 100 MX missiles with ten warheads each and that's 1,000. Add 500 Midgetmen, and x number of B-1s and B-52s carrying cruise missiles, plus B-2s with gravity bombs and short-range attack missiles and, boom, the Socialist Paradise would've been the irradiated face of the moon.

I am thinking about this outside Aloha Estates. Down the road an armored personnel carrier spills hippies. Old-fashioned long hairs, young and in combat fatigues. Several are shirtless. The APC has pulled off the road and a hippie wearing a hairnet gets behind the turret-mounted twin fifties above the cab and fires at the sky.

A tank wheels by, really moving, with two young blond men in milky blue suits sitting up on top. Down the road they are making a movie, some kind of 1980s retro funhouse comedy farce, *White Snake Joins the Army*. The plot according to Jan and Dean: the whole band gets trapped behind enemy lines and the drummer gets shot in the hair.

This place is my grubstake. Tom Weire got it for me three years ago. And though it is currently unsalable and technically in Weire's name, it is mine and was a tremendous deal. Some lunatic had blown up half a mountain right above the beach, blasting and carving out a huge chunk of its seaward side to form a grotto. Twenty condos were constructed along its sides. Each unit was glued to bedrock like a luxurious sparrow's nest and had a big view of the Pacific—until the land gave way under heavy summer rains and buried six of the brand-new units outright and knocked twelve off their foundations. What made it worse was that this avalanche was cemetery ground that contained the remains of nineteenth-century Christian missionaries and their royal heathen converts.

As soon as I get a grip and a million dollars I'll get crews out here to right and resecure the lower units to their foundations. Until then they'll remain like vast hollow building blocks tipped over on top of each other. Broken windows face skyward and tons of red earth have fallen in a tongue into the center of the waterless swimming pool. I stand in front of the single furnished unit I plan to use for a model. It's unfortunate that this had to happen, but Aloha Estates is fifty feet from the surf and after the salvage I'd be a fool not to be able to make a fortune from this place.

But now I have a problem. I've been really sick and can't figure out how long I've been here. Days, weeks, years? At the airport I counted twelve state bulls in squad cars, but not a peep out of anybody. Surprising.

Cops were hanging around the freight claim office, so we took a bye on the Egg, left it there, and rented a Honda minivan.

The slender highway between the mountains was sided with high dirt berms and cane fields were burning in lines and so fiercely I feared, because it seemed out of season, the flames were flagging from cracks in the earth. Then the road slipped and swayed along the rocky coast. I held my stomach, praying I wouldn't start spilling out.

In Lahaina my old family doctor put seventy-five stitches in my stomach and when I told him that what had happened was just a fight with my girlfriend all he did was smile, shrug, and blink. The only time he voiced alarm was when I told him Frank had canceled my Blue Cross.

How will we get the Egg, Jan and Dean wants to know. What's with the cops—that's the question I want to ask.

16 JUNE   *Lahaina, Maui*

Literalist idiots at the FBI claiming Frank's Mind is not a computer but a brain, and thus possessed of a soul, have, in cooperation with Lutheran Family Services, petitioned the state to have it removed from Frank's custody and placed in a foster home. Where it can be suitably debriefed, according to Roberta.

Chrome Dolphins hang in the air above Main Street. Metal sunfish, whales, porpoises are suspended in schools. It looks like every arc welder on the island has given himself to Art. When we got here Jan said he wanted to unwind and possibly even socialize. He bought a pint of rye at Ego Liquors. I took a sip and felt like I'd swallowed a comet. When we got to the Pioneer Inn I had to stand out by the moorage and wait ten minutes not to throw up.

I've gone there again. The Inn is a large white-and-green slatwood building overlooking the ocean. I doubt anything has changed here in fifty years. In the bar people sit in old wood chairs under propeller fans. A guy with a beard beats out Fats Waller tunes on an upright piano. His hands jump and trill across the keys.

At a phone booth outside I ask the girl of my dreams where in the world she heard such an absurdity and that it's high goddamn time we start facing reality.

"Unsquawk," she instructs. "From Weire. Whaddaya tell my mom I was in juvie for?"

I reply that when she didn't get on the plane with us I was afraid the cops at Honolulu International had arrested her. So I called her mother and said she better check juvenile hall.

I tell her that I love her and that I wish she were here.

Silence. All I hear is screaming. It's midafternoon and the Inn is filling with teenage sailors from an Australian destroyer moored out by the reef. These guys are kids, even younger than I am, and it's like having a keg of beer at a Boy Scout meeting.

Roberta says, "Vorhaggen called. He says if Frank did what he thinks Frank did and if the government knows what he thinks the government knows you're gonna be lucky to end up married to some 350-pound black guy in maximum security at Leavenworth."

And when I reply, "Yeah right," Roberta says, "Crawford. Augie Hona is dead. They pulled him out of the Ala Wai, nicknerd. Fish'd eaten his face but they could tell it was him. Vorhaggen says he was tortured to death and that the one who did it was Uncle Sam."

"Why?" I ask.

"That's the juicy part, Crawford," she replies, "nobody knows."

18 JUNE

In my dream I am losing my teeth. My gums have become infected, green, bubbling, black, and spongy. I am dreaming that my molars and incisors can be jiggled out by their roots when an explosion wakes me up. The sky outside my window is a brief, violent pink. I think: this is it, there was an H-bomb in the Egg and it's gone off at the airport. I sit there, legs tangled in the sheets, my chest cold as snow. Another, smaller explosion goes off and I hear the crackling chatter of machine guns.

Thank God, I'm hip. I realize that it's the White Snakes down the road. They're filming a battle scene at night. I lay down again and, lulled by detonations and flashing light, fall back asleep.

I wake up at dawn. My throat is sore and I'm sweating. Outside I can hear the unmuffled snarl of a crop duster and through my window see the little radial engine biplane swoop low over the sugarcane fields down the road. I am in the model condo. The units above rest at crazy angles, like collapsed, little houses of concrete cards. It's hot already and the sheets feel soft, moist, and dirty.

August Hona dead. I get up and open the front door. My stomach really hurts. I've been living on stuff I've found in the cupboards: canned tangerines, kidney beans, Spaghetti-O's, and white rice and these foods don't seem to be going south too well. I am crapping water and the stitched smirk on my side is leaking a thin whitish ooze only occasionally enlivened with blood.

I stand here hoping for a breeze.

Light is seeping above the mountains. A semi hauling an eight-wheeled lowboy trailer with a tank on its bed comes booming by, whirling up a long pretty ribbon of dust. I walk outside knowing I am built out of glass. Then I go around back, out by the swimming pool and its cargo of dirt. Frank's car Sudden Death is parked under an adjacent breezeway. It's a beautiful machine, a black 1949 Ford two-door sedan. Thin red, orange, and yellow metal-flake flames snake like vines around the front wheels and hood. It's powered by an old Chevy-454 V-8. Solid lifters, a Crower three-quarter cam, and dual four barrels—carburetors used to drowning in gasoline. A T-85 four-speed and a big Sun tach mounted on the dash. Four-eleven gears in a Halibrand Quick-Change rearend.

I walk around it. Traction Masters. American mags. This is the car Frank used to race along the quick curls and twists of the Honoapilana Highway, rimming cliffs hundreds of feet above the deep blue sea.

Sudden Death's black tuck-and-roll upholstery is cracked with age and the tires split with rot. I notice that the back seat is covered with curled and faded pictures of Frank's old perpetual motion machine, Polaroids from a more possible time.

I have driven to the 76 station in Lahaina, Sudden Death's left rear tire practically on its rim, where George Von Aaronson's Visa Gold was good for $1,550 worth of new German Uni-Royals.

In my condo I raise my shirt. My whole side is swollen. The skin around the stitched smirky gash is puffed like cheeks inflated with air. I got a shot—penicillin at the doctor's. This should not be happening.

At night I sit here under an oil painting of an exploding Vesuvius and look at old Polaroids of Frank: teenage Frank in the sand at Sunset Beach after getting crunched attempting to reverse skeg takeoff on a ten-foot wave. Frank graduating from the Air Force Academy fourth in his class. Frank at NASA Aimes in a pressure suit, and Frank standing by the wing of some black insect of a fighterplane that looks like it could kill standing still.

I dream that Dewey's Doberman, Alger Hiss, is here, his nails clicking on the tile floor. I dream that I am lying there on the bed as, in fact, I am, and the dog comes into the room and sniffs my face. I am terrified. In the dream I get out of bed, back away from the dog, and lock myself in the bathroom where I sit on the can and jet blood into the toilet bowl. In the morning I discover myself asleep on the bathroom floor, curled to a fetal Z.

Why did we leave the Egg here? It seems there was a great reason, but now I cannot recall. When I get to the airport and see no one I think the bomb has leaked radiation and killed everybody. Scared to go inside, I fix my eyes on the Aloha Airlines logo above the distant cab stand and walk. Then in front of the main terminal I see Jeanie standing at the phone and think: *Oh, so there you are.*

But it isn't her. Abruptly I can see twenty people at once. Jesus. I walk to a freight desk and hand my claim check to a little brown moke in a blue-flowered shirt. He looks at it and moments later the Egg is wheeled out to me.

The Egg is heavy and it takes two airport guys to help me load it into Sudden Death. Someone drilled deep dark little craters across its domed top and the broken drill bit still protrudes from its side, a tiny metal stump.

21 JUNE

Asleep on my couch, I hear her before I see her. "False alarm, Crawford. The fish didn't eat August's face, it ate somebody else's. Good news, he's alive and can come here and kill you." Roberta's here. Magically. She just showed up and says my floor's so cockeyed we could ski in my condo, sell lift tickets to my living room. She's just off a plane from Honolulu. I was so happy to see her boom through the front door it is like I'm having an allergy attack. I feel something tickle my cheeks, then there is salt in my mouth and I discover I'm crying. In white tennis shorts and baggy red socks, she runs and slides across my tilting floor. She wants to know where is Jan and Dean and I tell her he has disappeared. I got sick when we left the Inn and he told me he was going after food so I could eat and start feeling better. He's been gone ever since and the smart money says he's in the Kahului lockup diming me off paint-by-numbers style in front of a half-dozen Maui County assistant district attorneys.

I'm on fire. I tell Roberta that I need antibiotics. And $500. I got up this morning and then fell asleep on the living room floor and dreamed I was driving down a highway made of babies.

Roberta wants to know if I know what I've got. I raise my shirt to inspect a stomach wound swollen so smoothly I look pregnant. My stitches resemble a bloody, pussy railroad track. I say it's just a bug and Roberta says, "Get real. We got radiation poison from that fucking bomb. Be an angel and lose it."

When I say that could be penny wise and pound foolish Roberta replies, "Minimind, you're nuts."

Frank says that human evolution is over and the smart hor-rors that prevent the failures among us from reproducing have been eliminated. From now on the geeks and garbage will flourish right along with the best of us.

Roberta puts a hand above my eyes. "Crawford," she says, "I could fry an egg on your forehead." She puts a thermometer there instead. Then she says, "105," and draws the word *shit* out for seconds.

22 JUNE

"My God," Roberta says, "this guy's goo." She holds one of the photos up to better light as if trying to make certain it's real. Then she asks, "How many of these people are actually dead?"

I say, "Search me. None. A couple. I don't know."

She wants to know how I got Jeanie to do it and I say spon-taneously. We are upstairs in the townhouse I was going to give to Jeanie, the only one on the top tier that hadn't slid halfway down the hillside. I didn't have a key so Roberta did something noisy to pop open a window to the little half bath-room upstairs.

She's still looking at the photos. "You had her model all this glitzy shit in front of people with their faces ripped up, their legs busted in half, and their insides spilling all over the highway?"

Roberta holds up a picture of an old man whose face, bearded with blood, rests in Jeanie's lap. She says, "That's hideous."

I say beauty is in the eye, and she says the photos look like the really crummy ones Faye Dunaway took playing a fash-ion photographer in an awful old movie whose name she can't remember.

Roberta takes my temperature again. I've settled down but am still riding high at 102.

23 JUNE

I'm in the men's john at the Pioneer Inn peering into a bathroom mirror. I look more or less dead. A machine is on the wall to my left. A chesty phosphorescent lady decaled across its front offers rubbers. Above her someone has scrawled: SAVE YOUR MONEY. THIS IS THE WORST GUM I'VE EVER HAD.

I go back through the bar and into the dining room. I'm waiting for Roberta to bring me some meds. I watch a girl with a brown face and streaked blond hair walk across the roadway toward the pier, a yawning toddler strapped to her back. She glides out to the docks where white-hulled sailboats and catamarans were parked side-by-side. A huge motor yacht chugs into the docking area between the two lines of sailboats. A giant cartoon of a yacht, its superstructure is stacked so high I wonder why it doesn't just tip over. The girl looked at it too, then stepped onto the deck of a catamaran and disappeared behind a triangle of half-folded sail.

Roberta's late and I'm in trouble. I figure that by now my insides are so septic that my intestines are starting to rot. I'm sitting next to a guy who's talking about spending the summer on Boris Yeltsin's yacht and running for God. He can handle a sentence of thought but not a paragraph. When he gets up to go to the john I ask his friend what's wrong with him and the guy replies, "He's got a blown mind."

"Speaking of which," Roberta says, sitting down, "I got you some Lomotil, but no antibiotics. They said they couldn't read my prescription."

But then a surprise. "Crawford," Roberta says. "Christmas morning." She hands me a letter and I read:

Dear Frank,

One

78576746385976233434967806505483540038776747473765
47857364758363432179445722545464297314589897423453
45465765457655546325425647765312555665356656774752

1242399899327837647352796969683783538346265684 6686
7386838766341337134602079346757235618823656823 6578
4626465638589696979079597968487985467241336553 6567
6989079036515541762539793867944980326662154455 12553
1223856797953276573264675625656365734759694386 9589
6978457367586637698486906794987969387678387256 5857
5696487954523123451323413587090046565216568255 72557
6362556254575365856732875769838756959375968239 52437
5238975349763495741961394763189463674896349867 1349
863148967134956712-3491347

Two

2472398572895734895623490635790854892674625476 2354
5938545723495289759283569456918681969365924685 72985
1891757197529173978574897646430953078538548651 623425
3244668789898574563485723475487783493782905689 4352
3981561298356486347815434236523389549509754086 328-
9498691283653489563427891684219865295649859375 98236
5219856724895629835619856234961295623985289357 23896
5689235698234982368523657238965129865298456296 8468
3563754699462395648965197862356198356123654895 6436
5619296564562194351236529815623879652375623475 2815-
6218757868516753756198581296356218563685632869 572353
6583765928735627656235679464626464896365981368 5322
3453426466797789845342766878988093409567579012 0975
75790208932098555782103895493490575 97-8238790537

Three

3482985307634067340673406734067350785860978609 4763
0752917094132089534957498571209246921365286529 365298
3652865234865281568236528965296734965289652865 3894
6385634876539185629865283496534965349865219562 19651
6459132563186539865295265265275247562275479562 75278
5782165275238756256275378578564387573265478563 87456
8975187572356217421342423452752756275783532785 84686
9862837652856128528652875276527836562578256216 52856
2885237527865287238752362365278323875626542378 28-
7521652781461285218756728462785762563675235625 273652
9527857236527836265237875216852876521656213752 815621
7856263578627527527865256236521865271521387562 156213

78527852378527375237526356237852378627562562 4627856
23785278156236528752785623562752875265623752785 2785
6287356

Go

17852853495629605298528652381965287965029562311 9529
529450629516-293529529356239529529529529579298

The lock, Brudda. It either lets the genie out of the bottle or stuffs him back in. I forget which. You figure it out. Meanwhile, have a bitchen summer and stay as sweet as you are.

Dewey

I ask her where she got this and she says from Frank.
I say, "He gave it to you?"
Roberta says, "I gave it to me."
I say, "How?"
She says, "From his desk in his house."
I tell her she doesn't know the words to Frank's locks and Roberta says who needs words when the windows are open. She says she had her choice of four.

☢

In the tilted condo Roberta is sitting on top of me, nothing on but a little bra of old-fashioned white lace. She's trying to remember useful paradigms from her mother's encyclopedia of sex acts which she says include many ancient Japanese and Chinese love tricks that "sound scary or disgusting at first, but after a second you realize might be way fun to try." But she only remembers one for sure: "Where you come so hard that if they're not careful, both people end up in the hospital."

I ask who wrote it and she says, "Buddhist monks, *Penthouse* pets, beats me."

Legs apart, knees denting the mattress on either side of my hips, she places me where she thinks I need to be.

I say, "Perfect," and Roberta sighs and her long eyes almost close. "There, right there." She swallows. "See, Crawford, a little moderation until we scare up the marriage license and everything'll be fine."

I ask if it feels okay.

"Push just a little harder," she says, swallowing. "Just a little."

I do and then she's on the floor, crying one more move like that and she'll sue me for assault.

24 JUNE

On the phone Frank says, "Go get Grandpa to unravel the codes." When I say, "What codes?" Frank says, "Chances are Grandpa's dead in his house."

25 JUNE

My temperature is stuck at 103. If the fever doesn't break I'll have to go to a hospital, get arrested, and marry the black guy at Leavenworth. I look at the Egg leaning against the tilted wall of the bedroom. Its perfect metal shape has been drilled and dirtied. It could be a beer keg from science fiction. Roberta, in the strands that form her bra and panties, gets up, walks across the room, lifts her purse off the top of the Egg, plucks a letter out, walks back to the bed, and hands it over.

I read, "—courage for the most strange" blah, blah, "visions," "the so-called spirit world," on and on, and ask: "What's this?"

She says she found it at Frank's, clipped to the note from Dewey.

She climbs over me, covers herself with the sheet, and says, "It's cool if you come on my tummy."

I say I wonder what it is and she says, "Know the question nobody ever asks?"

I say, "Roberta what is this?"

She says, "The question is, what's Frank's sex trip?"

I say, "Beats me. I guess like a priest or Superman or the Lone Ranger. When it comes to the essential frictions sex, Frank has gone above and beyond."

✲

In my condo, Jan and Dean, back, says, "This place smells like shot wads." I say it's just musty and ask where he's been.

"On vacation," he replies.

"No," I say, "you've been gone for days. Where have you been?"

"We've got to get him," Roberta points to me, "to a doctor."

"What's wrong?" Jan asks.

Roberta lies on the bed under a lamp that, below its light and shade, was shaped and painted by Jeanie to make a globe of the world. "He's dying of infection."

Jan looks at me and laughs, "Hypochondriac." Then he turns to Roberta and says, "I'm going to ask you one simple question: Are you sucking his cock?"

"Are you—" Roberta twirls a finger around her ear.

Jan says, "I know you're jerking him off."

Roberta slides off the bed and says, "You're not my parents. You're not the boss of me."

JD reaches over and grabs Roberta by the chin and tells her to breathe.

She says, "What for?"

He says, "Because if I smell jizz on your breath, I swear to God, I'm gonna rip his head off."

Roberta exhales and claims, "Colgate."

26 JUNE

Eying the Egg in my living room, Jan and Dean has advice. "Face facts: Hawaii's hired so many weed-eater cops they couldn't find us if we put up a pup tent on the lawn at Honolulu City Hall. God willing, Crawford, we could be stuck here free forever."

We are on my lanai above the cracked and empty swimming pool. A white-eyed cat spills from a window next door, another erupts from the condo's crawl space. I say, "The Egg is poisoning us."

Jan and Dean bites the tip off a cigar: "That means nothing. Because chew on this, Fauntleroy. As long as we got it, everybody else has to dance to our tune."

I punch through to Weire from the phone booth by the Pioneer Inn and say, "If there's a bomb in the Egg, what would it be?"

Weire says, "A Soviet 'Pocket Apocalypse' version of the W-80 200-kiloton warhead normally fitted to an air-launched strategic cruise missile."

"What are the chances that's what we've got?"

"One in 10,000. One in a hundred. One in ten. Fifty-fifty. Hold on, I've got an incoming." I wait ten minutes, then do something stupid: hang up and call Vorhaggen. I ask him flat out what he thinks is up, realizing as I ask that he'll put a trace on the call.

"Best guess," Vorhaggen says, "Frank had you fly the Egg out of Celestial City, but couldn't get it back into the mainland without Dewey. He doesn't trust Dewey Hona, so he pays some Russian an extra $15 to have the Egg coded to self-destruct if anybody tampers with it, and he let's Dewey know."

"So I'm just a fall guy if anything goes wrong."

"Brudda, can you spell dictionary?" Vorhaggen says that he and his figure that Dewey, sitting on his monster computer in Mexico City, knew the codes were relatively simple to break, because their numerical equivalents corresponded to mottos or reasonably well-known quotations. "The good news for Dewey Hona is he can start breaking into the thing. The bad news is that the computer makes enough mistakes to get the Egg degrading toward self-destruction." Then he asks me where I am and I hang up.

In two minutes there'll be enough cop cars here to arrest Tanzania. I climb back into Sudden Death, drive back toward the condos, and call Weire back from the pro shop at the Kaanapali Golf Club. "What would Frank have done if I'd been arrested?"

"Cut his losses. Just like Dewey's gonna do now."

I say, "What's that mean?"

"It means, Crawford, if Dewey doesn't track you down, rape Roberta with a tire iron, nail you both to a wall, and cut your hearts out then you know you're really screwed. The only reason Dewey won't fly over and kill you is if he knows it's a ~~nuke with~~ its fuse burning. Otherwise, he'll just want to be ~~p~~laying pocket pool out of the blast radius."

it's degrading—will it blow up?"

Weire says, "It could go off never or five seconds from now. And next week your glowing atoms will be falling into Indonesia, Idaho, and Italy all at the same time."

Molten with fever I see the bop tops whizzing by, but the police don't know Sudden Death from Mamie Eisenhower. The car is frying. I shouldn't be driving and suddenly can't even remember why I am but see I am, accidently, headed back to Lahaina. I pull a U-ie in front of a speeding Maui County black-and-white and slide sideways off the road. But the cop is so eager to arrest fugitive me in Lahaina for treason and aggravated mayhem he doesn't have time to pull nitwit me over in front of the golf course for reckless driving.

On the radio the station is thirty-four hours into three days of pure piss pop. Chemistry Headbutt, Phkyrslph, Get Not Want, Meat Is Murder, Harriet Morsel, Shit. During a commercial for Japan I punch into a presidential news conference and hear the president say, "Frank Crawford, if he's a renaissance madman, it's news to me. Now, this island. If it invites a cataclysm, we'll snap his dripper good."

Jan has bought a Disney Bulldog at Nine Millimeters "R" Us and has demanded that I go back into town and buy Band-Aids, black powder, and a shortwave radio. He stares at the weapon in his lap, glances at the Egg, and says, "You know what this is worth?"

"The electric chair."

"Tin horn dictators like hydrogen bombs, Fauntleroy. I'd say two or three billion."

I say, "Dollars?"

"Wholesale."

I tell him that's obscene. Nothing's worth this kind of risk. And when I say we've gotta get it to the police before it's too late, Jan says, "Too late for what—we turn a stolen H-bomb in to the cops and you and I will have our rent paid forever." He lights a cigar. "Face it, babycakes: we're gonna end up either immortal or dead." He puffs. "Savor your doom, Crawford. Because face facts, we may have committed the biggest blunder in the history of mankind."

28 JUNE

Lying on top of me, new breasts astride my painfully swollen stomach, her head between my legs and licking off and on as if I were a popsicle of a lesser flavor, Roberta rises and says, "Crawford, get off the dime."

Her perfect downy flower is at the tip of my nose and I'm burning up—an hour ago my temperature was 104—I am about to perform when I hear the loud crackling burble of Sudden Death's exhaust.

Jan has pulled up outside the bedroom window.

Roberta says shit and unsaddles. I sit up and swing over the edge of the bed, begin to stand, and discover my legs have lost their bones. I reach down and pick my tennis shorts off the floor and tell Roberta to get something on.

And then there he is. In a new green shirt, untucked and unbuttoned. The hair around his red face like smoke, Jan comes through the front door.

I pull on my shorts and totter out to the living room. Jan lights a cigar and says, "Did I tell you I got a new girlfriend? I met her at the Pioneer Inn. Impressed the shit out of her."

"How?" I ask.

"I told her that I've got natural organic gonorrhea and all my crabs are vegetarians." Then he says, "This'll pop your psychic zits: I called Dewey. He wants to buy the Egg. Frank's tits up, so Dewey's got the whip hand now." Cigar smoke strings above his head to the ceiling. "So welcome, baby-cakes, to the end of the world."

Roberta says, "Nice shirt, Jan. It brings out the yellow in your teeth." As if it's the new style, she stands by the bed-room door naked.

I stand there thinking *What a body*, then I realize that I'm crying once again.

"What's wrong?" Roberta asks.

Jan and Dean says, "You stupid little gash. He's having a nervous breakdown with all the fucking trimmings."

I say, "Roberta, go put some clothes on."

Jan says, "*You*," and slams me against the doorjamb. He pushes me back into the bedroom onto the bed. One hand at my throat and the other gouges into the stitches across my stomach, he's trying to claw his way inside me and I'm hitting him as fast as I can, using his face for a speed bag but nothing happens until I reach back, grab the lamp, and swing the globe into the side of his head. The world shatters. Jan lets go and jumps up.

Standing up above me on the bed, he kicks at my stomach and face. Roberta is screaming stop and then I hear a locomotive slam through the room and the side of Jan's thigh explodes. He crashes over me, his knees bucking up and down like he's on an invisible bike at the neck-and-neck finish of a madman's bicycle race. He rolls off the bed screaming, "You gash, you gash, you stupid fucking gash," and the room is all smoke and stinks like a fire in an asphalt factory. Meat is all over the sheets and pillows and I look up to a crab nebula of blood on the wall above the bed.

It feels like somebody's poured warm water over my leg. There is blood all over my shorts and I think I've been shot except I don't feel anything. Then I see that the blood is JD's. It's all JD's and it's everywhere.

29 JUNE

The first time I had a terrible problem like this was after I graduated from high school and almost married a fourteen-year-old who'd already had a breast reduction and the second time was when I went crazy in Heaven punching the clock 600 feet underground replanning nuclear war.

A bad time. After Christopher Boyce dimed TRW off to the Russians the feds got nervous about farm club psychotics working at top-secret defense facilities so Frank had to get me ID for eight different people.

My task was to figure out what had happened to the continent incinerating, atmosphere poisoning, 20,000-warhead gigadeath that was to have been almost assuredly delivered to the global doorstep, according to statistical reports by five United States government agencies, by no later than 1995. My assignment from Frank was, in so many words, to figure out what the hell had gone wrong.

Beginning with the "One plane, one bomb, one city" days through Star Wars, I started with our first doctrine, Massive Retaliation. Born in the late 1940s, when we were popping Hiroshima-like gun-assembly atom bombs off assembly lines like Chevy pickups and NATO was helpless against a Soviet invasion, the idea was at least if you blew up the world the mutant Zulus who survived would grow up celebrating May day for all the right reasons.

But in the 1960s the United States switched to Flexible Response, presupposing a holocaust to arrive in increments. They drop a bomb on us, we drop a bomb on them, they drop two bombs on us, we drop two bombs on them, they drop five bombs on us, we . . . tactical nukes, theater nukes, ICBMs, a careful upping of the ante as both sides negotiated toward an earth-frying megaoblivion.

But the Soviets took "measured retaliation" as a ridiculous beard for something far more ominous and, terrified, pre-pared a bolt from the blue first strike by 200 submarine-launched ballistic missiles. Promising. Half our subs would be vaporized in port, two-thirds of our bombers before they could scramble. Fifteen minutes later, 1054 Soviet ICBM war-heads would detonate above U.S. ICBM silos, followed by an equal number of ground bursts. Because of their multiple warheads the attack would have required only 211 of 1,398 Soviet ICBMs. It would take twenty minutes from first warn-ing to impact, during which the president would have had only two choices.

If he did the obvious—retaliate—the United States would be doomed. Our second strike couldn't hope to knock out the one-thousand-plus unused Soviet ICBM silos. While the "counterforce" first strike on strategic targets might kill 20 million Americans, the "countervalue" Soviet second strike on general military and economic targets could kill 100 mil-lion more.

The only rational option would be surrender.

My conclusion: The Soviets should have torched us off the day Ronald Reagan took the oath of office. Frank, support-ive, then gave me a new task: to propose a "counteroblivion," to re-plan the past, to devise a scheme for a better end. So what would I have done? Easy: killed everybody. Nothing else made rational sense. About 1950 I would have used B-29s and B-36s on a "city-busting" spree that would have knocked the

Soviet Union not only out of the nuclear arms race but out of the twentieth century as well.

It was a detailed plan, four months in the making—by my lights I would have incinerated or terminally irradiated 135 million people—and that's when I stopped sleeping, had to leave Heaven, and moved to Waikiki. Where I went to work at Less Nervous, and thirty-two-ounce hardwood pool cue in hand—egged on by a bad case of opening-night jitters—saw in the big, drunk, raving, and musclebound Mr. Owen Cathcart, USMC Ret.—all the Massive Retaliators of the world.

Roberta and I are at the Lahaina 76. Sudden Death is parked beside the gas pumps, the Egg in the back seat. How we got it in there I don't know. In my condo Jan stood up and walked, blood waterfalling from his thigh. It was like he's walking on stilts but he was walking. He said, "Lucky shot, cunt." Roberta reached for another clip. I snatched the Bulldog and heaved it off the lanai. The "Crowd Management" 9 mm spun to the ocean like a boomerang that wasn't coming back.

Then Roberta—like in the story where the little mother lifts big fallen tree off her toddler's chest and saves the baby's life—dragged the Egg to the car while Jan and Dean, sitting on the couch, his blood spilled as thick as paint all over the rug, wrapped his butchered thigh in a bed sheet. Getting into the Ford, I saw him at the door. He screamed, "You asshole, no Band-Aids."

I call an ambulance and Tom Weire from a pay phone and tell him I need money. He says he's got more important things to worry about. Frank has used the drill. "And now he's got a five-foot hole to nowhere." Evidently the drill bored a tunnel straight down through the top of the plugged-up magma cone, but it's still 400 feet from the source of lava. The drill, surrounded by all that volcanic rock, cooked away its essential lubricants and the engine burned out, leaving the tungsten steel chassis melted into the rock. A twenty-ton cork on the highway to hell.

The front door of our green suite at the Kaanapali Hilton open behind her, Roberta says, "Feast your eyes. I brought you a pharmacy. Penicillin, tetracycline. Plus a ton of Anti-swaq."

Coming out of sleep, I say, "Just say no," and Roberta laughs: "Big talk from a raving schizophrenic."

Roberta has got us a great room. How and who's paying for it, I don't know. She says that I should forget a career in photography, that Frank isn't focused enough to have blown our complete family fortune, and that there has to be a spare $500 million stuffed in a shoebox somewhere, and that my job description should read rich guy instead of hack.

I take a pill. Two and three. Around my stitches a bloody blackened Rorschach test has appeared and I'm certain that my insides are completely infected and out of control.

JULY

Roberta says, "Hair," plucks a curl off her perfect tongue, and in long, fearless, and disturbingly professional strokes finishes with a languid, yet bobbing flourish. Her first. She says. I'm touched. But afterward she tells me she's not in this just for the protein and wants to know what'll happen if the Egg goes off. I say, a fireball a mile wide, then a mushroom cloud three miles high throwing off heat hotter than the surface of the sun—tens of millions of degrees. Plus, a crater maybe 200 feet deep and 600 feet wide. Everything within a mile would be vaporized. Anybody within four miles fried and anybody looking at it within eight miles would be instantly blinded by the flash. The radiation alone could kill 100,000.

The Kaanapali Hilton. An eternity of room service and the perfect green carpet of the golf course below us. I want to stay here. But Roberta says no, somebody will add two and two. We climb into Frank's Ford. I fire it up and jab the throttle. The needle on the tachometer jumps. The engine idles roughly then settles to a blub, blub, blub. We drive to Grandpa's. The big old Chevy V-8 snarls as I pull onto the street and accelerate toward Lahaina and past the sailboats in the moorage. We need cash.

Feverish and daydreaming, I miss my grandfather's turn, brake hard, and slide sideways off the road into red dust. Grandpa's unpaved driveway snakes through his cane fields and up into the green hills where his old white house is perched like a poor king's castle.

I pull up to the place. His ancient black Mercedes is parked out front, resting on its rusting rims. The same model as Hermann Göring's. The little mansion is white and three stories tall. It has cracked plaster Doric columns out front and looks as if it's about to be eaten by the jungle behind it. Jagged shadows from palm trees play across the front lawn. The yard is run-down because Grandpa is one of the New Naturalists. Although he was making money in development right through the Credit Crash, these days he's for total return to the native environment. He supports environmental groups either so far right or so far left that they've met around the back. The last time I saw Grandpa was when he threatened to blow up Waikiki Beach. He had stood right here in his front yard with Danny, a bare-chested tattoo gallery with hair woven to six braids hanging all the way down his back. Danny was one of his disciples, a "deconstruction man," and looked familiar. Like someone whose face I have definitely seen before. Probably on a wall down at the post office.

We walk up Grandpa's front steps and knock. Nothing. But the door is open and we let ourselves in. In the foyer I say, "Granddad! It's Tod!" I listen, expecting to hear him upstairs.

His wife, my granny, was the way people used to be rich. The house is full of marble busts of ancient Greece's top gods, stuffed purple furniture, and bowls of metal fruit. Since she died my grandfather has touched none of it. The living room is unlived in, an abandoned museum made of things that made his former life.

I don't know what to do. The swelling in my side has progressed.

Roberta says, "Go upstairs."

I start up the steps, afraid that I'm about to find Grandpa dead. I say so and Roberta, standing by the front door, says, "If he is, his corpse is still getting a lot of mail." She has a fan of letters in her hands and deals them onto a tea caddy by the door. "Oman Crawford, Oman Crawford, Oman Crawford, Oman, Oman, Oman." Then she says if he were dead we'd have smelled him.

The second floor is as spare as the first floor is opulent. A picture of my grandmother hangs on the wall in the hall. My dad's mom. She died at the explosion of the Proteus. Athletic, even in her seventies she strode more than walked. Her father invented seersucker and she could trace her ancestry to Vlad the Impaler, the Transylvanian who'd win a battle, then string his prisoners up on spears and stakes and eat dinner in front of them. When Vlad's butler complained about the stench, Vlad had him strung up too. My grandmother had cancer. Surgeons were plucking tumors out of her like grapes, but at the Proteus launch her delight made her seem healthy as a kid and the rocket's explosion was the surprise end of her life.

She died on the bridge of the *Gogol*. When the Proteus blew up, though it was miles away, a chip of titanium popped the side of her neck off. When it happened I was rushed below, and never even saw her after that first great flash of light.

We walk into my mother's old room. It's austere. Shellacked hardwood floors. White walls and a white single bed. It is where she worked after she and my father got married. Her owlish eyes stare out of a dozen old photographs.

My mother's fountain pen still sits on the table in front of her bed on top of a stack of papers, all covered with her vivid, erratic handwriting.

I pick up a page of her notes and read:

Paradise.
Origins in Homer. A house party in which Zeus, fearing his wife is cuckolding him, plays the ill-tempered host. Lots of music. Harp and wing the central symbols. Always present. Free of desire. No passion except for religious fervor. Fascist summer camp atmosphere.

Before my mother drowned she had begun to write a book, the history of Heaven.

I walk down the hall to another spare room and there he is, my grandpa, seated at an open window, his feet up on the sill, a book in his lap, reading. I say, "Grandpa," but he doesn't hear. I touch his shoulder. He turns slowly, smiles, gets up, and grabs my hand. Grandpa is Frank fifty years from now. The same headlight eyes, the same sharp-beaked look of a meat-eating bird.

The explosion of the Proteus gave my grandfather hearing problems. He wears a hearing aid he keeps turned off most of the time, but now he turns it on. As soon as I know he can hear me, I say Frank needs him because of the codes, and my grandfather, in a starched blue shirt and slacks with creases sharp enough to cut, says, "Of course he does. Frank needs his granddad because Frank doesn't know anything at all."

My grandpa's hair is ice white but as thick as a boy's. He has red scimitars of blood where he has scratched his scalp and his shoulders are snowy with dandruff. He hates heat and inside Sudden Death, there beside the Egg, he's not too cool. I tell him about going to Celestial City, how the Egg disappeared in Mexico City and reappeared in Do What You Look Like, how we sneaked it onto an airplane, and how it comes to be here.

My side on fire, we are driving toward my Aloha Estates, Sudden Death sighing loudly through the gears. On the highway, the blond beach and silvery sea stream by and my grandfather says it was two trains running: Frank went broke buying the leftover brains and bad dreams of the Soviet Union while Dewey blew the Honas' half of the empire on nuclear containment vessels and bad bail bonds.

I ask how Dewey could have lost that much money. My grandfather coughs and says, "Years of inexperience."

A walled stone hexagon looms before us, high as half the sky. A white flag the size of a movie screen, with a red ball in the center, flies above, unfurled, and is kept rippling by a 10,000-horsepower wind machine. It is the Tojo, a coliseum-size Japanese super block, space-age medieval and alone before the surf.

Frank says, "He's full of shit and you better pray, pray, pray, buddyboy, that I'm a happier man when I find you than I am right now, or you three'll fry in hell. Be at the Hyper Mart in—it's eleven now, be there by two."

I say I will. I'm standing in a phone booth while Roberta and Grandpa wait down the street.

☢

Hyper Mart stands across the cane fields, a white block on the horizon at the end of a rainbow. A store where you can buy everything.

Roberta and I are here to shoplift. We drive in shoreside, past Frank's new desalinization plant and its great sausage-shape primary filters. The car cruises across an asphalt sea—the parking lot is a mile by a mile of asphalt—to front doors as high and wide as a two-story house and windows that are slabs of two-inch-thick bulletproof glass-alloy. We get out and walk to the locks.

Under a sign that reads, GRAND OPENING JULY 4, I say *Have you seen your shadow, baby, standing in your mother?* and one slab swings open.

An interior set of doors hum apart and close automatically behind us. Inside, Hyper Mart is immense and empty. Its vast concrete floor is clean and glassy as an ice skating rink, and there is nothing—no food, no hawkable products—for us to steal. But along the back wall I see something that scares me to death: cylindrical steel casings, which I'm sure are to fit around the styrofoam mold holding fusion capsules. Each is above three yards in diameter, tapered round at the top, and it looks like a monster erection surrounded by four metallic cylinders each as tall as I am and about a yard wide.

I say, "What exactly is it?" My grandfather smirks and says, "The top junk on the ultimate trash heap—the arms, legs, and body of a Soviet quaternary hydrogen bomb, with a yield, I'd guess, twice that of the largest nuclear device ever made."

☢

I recite *We have shared out like thieves the amazing treasure of nights and days* and Hyper Mart is full of cars, houses, airplanes.

Roberta says, "Fuck-o-rama. Crawford, give the devil his

due: this puts numbskull Frank up there with the Pharaohs."

"What's the point of the illusions?" my grandfather asks.

"So you can, so to speak, stock huge items like houses and monster yachts." Then I say *When the still sea conspires an armor, true sailing is dead* and Jeanie drifts toward us in an evening gown that seems to be made out of crushed glass. She goes by us, unseeing, I reach out, my hand passes through her chest.

Roberta walks to the door and says, "Let's go see the Marlboro Man." Through those doors I gaze at the horizon. Out on the ocean, full sail and whacking toward Australia through gliding white-topped summer waves, I see Tony's yellow ark. Honest to God. There's no other yellow that bright on earth. Roberta, looking too, says, "It's Frank's problem now."

But it is Tom Weire who shows up, not Frank. He's driving a rent-a-car. Roberta and I watch a red Avis Toyota that looks like a flying saucer across the black asphalt sea. It eases up in front of us, Weire steps out. I say, "I thought Frank fired you."

He says, "Thick is blooder than water, and besides, he's cutting me in for a quarter of the mushroom cloud."

I say, "Grandpa, you remember Tom Weire." They shake hands and Grandpa says, "Oh yes, Mr. Weire, I remember indeed."

Weire says Frank is at a Y in the road: the New Island or Africa. "The king's sitting on billions of barrels of oil buried under a trillion tons of rock."

The sun burns down. I rub number 225 on my nose. "How'd that happen?"

Weire shrugs. "Algae and dinosaurs die and turn into petroleum mush. Volcanoes blow up on top of them until guys like Frank come along."

"So what I flew out of Celestial City could blow a hole through the rock?"

"Not even close. If you want the oil, the only way to get at it is to blow away a huge chunk of the mantle. You got just a little tactical nuke. A relatively junior bomb. The bomb that acts as the primary. Part of a four-stage 'Quaternary' 80-megaton hydrogen bomb that will deliver the biggest man-made explosion in history, 5,000 times the size of the bombs detonated over Hiroshima and Nagasaki."

We are miles down the coast road from Hyper Mart and sitting outside the big white shack that is Water God All Beef Big Dogs. Weire says, "How do you think Frank got the keys to the kingdom?"

I say I don't know what he's talking about and Weire says, "Two years ago, after your grandpa wrote his letter to the editors of the *Star* offering to 'torch off' Waikiki Beach, I explained that unless he turned over management of all Crawford enterprises to Frank I'd have him declared *non compos mentis.*"

"And he fell for that?"

"I don't think your grandfather falls for anything. I think he just got tired."

I glance across the drive-in restaurant's parking lot. Grandpa doesn't eat in public. His food is delivered by Charlie Wha's ptomaine wagon. Right now he's sitting turned off in the back of Weire's rented Toyota with the air-conditioning going full blast.

Roberta's across the street at a grocery buying steaks and pop and Weire and I are eating outside in downtown Kahului. Teriyaki wieners, with macaroni on paper plates. He says if Frank picks the king over the New Island he'll get half the country's oil revenues.

"So who actually sets the thing off?"

Weire says, "The bomb? Frank."

"He sets it off personally?"

"You don't think he'd give some preppie spade that kind of validation do you?"

I say, "Then what'll everybody do?"

Weire wipes a comma of teriyaki sauce off his mouth. "Line up at the pump."

"That's all?"

"Once it's done, it's done. What are they going to do, spank him?"

I tell him he doesn't sound either surprised or appalled.

"Why should I be," Weire says. "The whole thing was my idea."

☢

My grandfather sits behind me in Sudden Death beside the
Egg. We drive up toward Mt. Klu and Makawao. Cowboy
country. My hometown. One of them, anyway. Low dusty-
looking buildings. A tall transvestite wino in a granny dress
stands in the middle of the main intersection. I stop for gas
at a station where a yellowed grimy sign twenty-five years old
still hangs in the office advertising: Back Hoe for Hire: Call
Frank Crawford.

Looking across the street, I see Frank's helicopter in a grove
of palms behind the long white wood building that is the
Longhorn Bar & Grill. The machine has further metamorphosed. The fuselage has been painted with soft, muddy swirls
of blue and grey and has the silhouette of a shark fitted with
a 50-barrel 20-mm automatic cannon.

Inside, Frank, in jeans, a white T-shirt, and lightweight
lime-green air force flight jacket, sits at a table, fenced behind a line of Miller talls. He tries to give Grandpa a hug but
has to settle for a handshake. Then he turns to me and says,
"Problems." He hid our $6 billion in plain sight all right. Elec-
tronic G-men tracked our Light + Weight "asset entity" energy virus to the Federal Reserve Bank in Arlington, Virginia,
and FBI agents with warrants took fire axes to the Reserve's
modem lines and killed our money dead.

Frank says a hydrogen bomb is simply a commodity whose
value is expressed not by use but lack of it. A hot dog or a can
of beer in reverse.

Weire sits in the back of Sudden Death as Frank drives up
above Makawao. Roberta is behind us with Grandpa in Weire's
Toyota. Eucalyptus trees with ragged white bark curling off
their trunks crowd the narrow twisting road.

Weire says, "Thank you, Herman Kahn."

Both cars pull up in front of our gated family estate and Frank
asks me if I can remember the words. I say, "Sure."

I get out and approach the gate. It is windy. The thick green
leaves of the monster banyan tree across the road sway up

and down. The whole place is surrounded by a high concrete wall. I recite both the Lord's Prayer and a Hail Mary but nothing happens. Suddenly, though, I remember. My father, renouncing Christ, changed the code. I say *Klaatu, berata nikto* and the gate swings right open.

Frank drives in. I walk through the huge stone pillars and stand before a house built on a precipitous fall of land. It's beautiful, originally two stories, but before his drowning my dad added a third and fourth, so it rises up like the superstructure of a great wooden ocean liner.

Roberta, climbing out of the red Toyota, says, "Who designed this place, Tim Leary?" I say, "No, my dad," and hadn't she been here before?

"Not in this lifetime."

I say, "Well, he was a genius."

Frank approaches. There are deep lines around his eyes and for the first time ever I can see him as old. He says somebody has tried to trash the mausoleum so all of us go down to check out the damage. We walk down behind the house to a small structure that looks like a Japanese teahouse made of concrete. Someone has filigreed CASH IS TRASH across one wall.

The Pacific Ocean is an endless pale blue far below us.

I ask Frank if the mausoleum is still locked and he nods, then pulls a slip of paper from his jeans, and reads:

Oh space!
Change!
Toward which we run.
So gladly.
Or from which we retreat.
In terror—
Yet that promises to bear us.
In itself.
Forever.

We file in. No damage. My parents look the same. Under glass, side by side, my father is slender-faced and handsome

in his tuxedo and my mother is lovely and only a little stu-
dious in her wire-rimmed glasses. They appear burnished in
their separate coffins. The effects of embalming appear to
have been a tonic. Both look younger, in better shape, and—
though dead—perfectly vigorous. They seem happy and as if
they are about to wake up and go do something. I say, "False
alarm," and Roberta says, "Those are your parents?" Frank
peers into the glass and says, "They look okay to me. Pretty
good, I'd say." Holding Grandpa's hand, I turn and see tears
slide from the side of his eyes. "Pretty good," my grandfather
says, "my ass."

We lug the Egg out of Sudden Death. It is very heavy and
falls on the driveway and starts making a whirring sound. The
bomb is pissed off. That's Grandpa's prognosis. Dewey or
August or somebody reefed on it so much and so unsuccess-
fully that it's ready to go off. We heave it back into the car
and walk back up to the house. I'm scared enough now to vi-
brate. I just want to get rid of the goddamn thing.

Frank says *Fuck 'em all*. The door sighs open and we go inside. The air smells ancient. I follow Frank past the huge windows in the living room and we go into my father's study. On
the tables beneath his books and paintings—Motherwell's *A
Strange Kind of Music* and *Grand Paysage avec Vache* by
Balthus—are my father's blueprints. Diagrams for the anti-
gravity bus and the Great Walled City.

Frank is in the living room, shoving shells into his automatic shotgun, when I tell him that for my money whatever
he figures is going to happen here isn't, and that whatever
plan he's got, it's a bad one.

Frank says, "A bad plan's better than no plan at all."

Roberta says, "Too bad Jan's not here for the real carne
crudo. Your bozos against their bozos at last."

Frank pulls a cigarette out of his pocket. It's a vague white
stick in the dim. He lights a kitchen match. It glows against
his dark hawk face as he puts the drip of flame to the tobacco.

"Grandpa," he says, "just one question: Can you get into
this thing and stabilize it?"

My grandfather grins, scratches his white head hard enough

to draw new blood, and says, "Tomorrow morning we're going to find out."

"It won't go off tonight?" I ask.

My grandfather says, "Probably not."

3 JULY

Off again to the Promised Land. Heaven. Where my next to final job had been to retarget strategic forces. I went to Frank and said, "Why would the U.S. Government have some college dropout retarget missiles capable of killing millions of people?"

He said not to worry. I existed simply as part of "the mix," an "entity working for an institute contracted to postulate strategic planning." My information was poured together with everybody else's into a stew being stirred at JSTPS, Omaha. Frank said that half of these "kill-point scenarios" could be coming from wetback hackers on their off days from Taco Bell for all he knew.

"But," I replied, "this is blue on blue. The FAX I got says to select targets across the United States." He said that everybody who's anybody in strategic targeting has to do that and, "It's an exercise in countertargeting. They want to know what a smart adversary would think. Either that or the whacko in charge wants a dry run on thermonuclear civil war."

So I set about identifying every worthwhile target sea to shining sea. Frank seemed to like it all until he saw that I had designated a 550-kiloton "bunkerbuster" for Heaven itself. He looked at me, a spark of genuine horror and then anger in his eyes, and said, "What are you trying to do, get me killed?"

Roberta told Frank to get the Egg underground where if it goes off all it can obliterate is us and rock and I'm amazed: he did what she said. The two of them took off for Heaven at dawn and now Weire and I are in his rent-a-car, Tom driving, me sweating and examining my palm. He asks what's wrong and I say I cut my hand but I don't know how.

Weire looks at the cut and says, "Gee. Get another wound like that and your photos won't develop." Then, "Crawford, tomorrow's my birthday. So don't forget: Thirty-eight regular. Neck fourteen and a half, sleeve thirty-one, inseam thirty. Shoe size nine B."

Grandpa's in back turned off and aggravated. We drive through a winding hall of eucalyptus trees up to Mt. Klu. To a gate marked ABSOLUTELY NO TRESPASSING. *United States Park Service.*

Weire gets out and says the words *The most common of all follies is to believe passionately in the palpably not true. It is the chief occupation of mankind.* The gate is on a motored hinge. It swings open and we drive through.

A quarter mile up the road we come to the steel door leading to the tunnel under the crater wall.

The tunnel is three miles long.

Eden. It took my father $50 million and eighteen years to complete. He trucked in 400,000 tons of dirt and seeded it with flora and fauna native to the islands before the arrival of man. It is a beautiful, self-sustaining jungle paradise.

The lava dome is at the center. On its top is the observatory. Then 600 feet below the observatory lie the bowels of Heaven. Once a very exclusive club. Admission by retina. You'd pass a photocell that had a map of the back of your eye and if it didn't match up then you weren't you and you didn't get in. Anyone with a regular job there had been through incredible scrutiny. But what was hard was getting people down in there in a hurry if you had to. Frank had security to watch the electricians do electrical when they were building during Bush and Star Wars. One security guy per electrician. But Frank had to have people in there twenty-four hours to finish. The security people were all union and would only work daylight nine to four and if you wanted security any other time their rep would be happy to sit down and talk about it for a month or two. So if he could do electrical, Fidel Castro could have gotten a job here working swing. No wonder I made the mix.

Under the great curved mirrors of the telescope the observatory is empty. Weire says, "See, what happened is the guys discovered the end of the universe and said, 'Looks like our job is over, let's beat it home to the wives and kids.' "

We take the elevator down. Heaven is built to Soviet-reinforced concrete standards married to U.S. ICBM launch control center specs. The exterior has been hewn out of basalt. We go through the outer vestibule. It has twin-blast airlock doors made of the high-yield steel used in submarine pressure hulls and is insulated by a high-tensile ferro concrete shell five yards thick designed to withstand a blast overpressure of 2,000 psi—the equivalent of a near miss by an earth-penetrating 550-kiloton warhead. All 2,200 square feet of Heaven are mounted on one-inch-diameter high-tensile springs and surrounded by a two-foot dead air space to allow Heaven to ride out shock waves strong enough to shatter rock.

We step out of the elevator and are bathed in cold air that smells like medicinal alcohol. The white ceramic walls sweat. Clean and dark, like being inside a huge refrigerator whose power has been turned off. Frank installed an external filter using activated charcoal that's good against both chemical and bio agents and nukes. There's a freshwater aquifer under the facility with a well lined against contamination from underground explosions. Power comes from a little nuclear reactor, an upgraded model taken from a Trident sub with a fossil fuel backup system that can run off methane created by recycled sewage.

The walls in the control room are misted with condensation. Frank and Roberta are eating spaghetti. Frank spears a meatball, looks up, and says, "Rain or shine, we're unlocking the Egg tonight."

Weire says, "Frank, I've a better idea. Whaddya say we go out, get a bunch of hydrogen and oxygen, get 'em to react, and call it the sun."

Frank says, "Shut the fuck up," and then that the whole thing's already armed past the "go" codes and since the Hona brothers reefed on the tampering device it's ready to blow sky high.

Frank surmises that the life of African oil trillionaires could be sweet, but we're in a use-it-or-lose-it position, so we'd best take the bird in hand. We'll make the New Island. He says two thirty-megaton blasts, one after another, would be ideal—the first to create the initial crater and the second to make the deeper one that will reach the magma. But we only have one trigger, so Frank tells Grandpa beggars can't be choosers, he'll have to assemble the one big bomb, lower it through the hole to the top of the burned-out drill, and torch it off. It may violate the Law of the Sea, but the deep thinkers at the World Court can read the fine print later.

Grandpa says he's crazy, the blast will be catastrophic. "Four megatons is the most you would need."

Frank says, "Based on what?"

"Calculations for bursts down to 2,000 feet. If the primary is 100 kilotons and the fusion capsules are of the dimensions they appear to be, then a three-stage device would yield ten megatons. Twice what's smart." My grandfather suggests Frank save two fusion stages, put them in his hope chest, and remove the uranium sleeve from the second capsule.

Frank says, "Your numbers are wrong. Crater and 'chimney' formation by detonation below 2,000 feet are incalculable." Then he tells Grandpa, "Besides, better safe than sorry."

My grandfather puts a hand to his forehead, scratches, and blood flames his white hair. "You're full of shit, sonnyboy. Fitting the bomb into a ten-foot-wide hole will up its yield by containing the nuclear reactions longer than *any* steel casing alone could do."

But Frank isn't having any—he says the weight of the overburden will cause the cavity his bomb makes to collapse, so he needs more energy. Then he says to Weire, "The envelope."

Weire replies, "This goes on forever." My grandfather tells Frank to just say the words.

Frank asks, "Can you do that if it's already deep into degrade? Won't that set it off?"

My grandfather says, "If it goes, we're gone. Read it."

Frank says *This is at the bottom the only courage demanded of us: to have courage for the most strange, the most singular, and the most inexplicable we may encounter. That mankind has in this sense been cowardly, has done life endless harm; the experiences that are called 'visions,' the so-called 'spirit world,' death, all those things that are so closely akin to us, have by daily parrying been so crowded out of life that the senses with*

which we could have grasped them are atrophied. To say noth-
ing of God.

There is a loud chirp, then the top of the Egg spins and
rises. Grandpa lifts it off and sets it on the floor. Frank looks
at him and says, "What's the verdict?"

Grandpa peers into the Egg. "Perhaps," he suggests, "reading that particular passage wasn't such a good notion after
all."

Frank says, "Meaning what? We're still here, aren't we?"

"My guess," my grandfather says looking into the open
Egg, "is you've got a digital readout just coming off zero and
numbers climbing at about two a second toward I don't know
where. Looks like your Russian friends set this so that once
the code was read the bomb would go off after it reached a
certain number. It's a simple variation on a system your old
man and I worked out twenty years ago. But it's completely
eccentric."

Frank, his voice rising, says, "When'll it go off?"

My grandfather shrugs. "Now. Two days from now. Maybe
never. It could be jammed or completely inert."

I give Frank Dewey's letter. Ask what he thinks it is.

My grandfather looks at it, says, "Garbage."

"It's the safety," Frank says.

"No, it's not," my grandfather replies. "It's just a bunch of
random digits."

"It's the safety code," Frank says. "It's not random at all."

"You're right, sonny," my granddad says, "because there is
a pattern to the randomness: it's the pattern of someone just
banging away randomly on a word processor."

"How the hell old are you, old man? One hundred?"

"You load that into this Egg and all you're going to do,
Frank, is make it twice as unstable."

I want out of here.

Frank folds the letter in half, folds it again. "Can you control it? Slow it down?"

Grandpa looks back into the Egg. "If it's ticking? Maybe I
could slow it down. There's an encrypting device on the side."
He reaches into the Egg and seems, with one hand, to be typ-
ing. After a minute, he says, "There."

Frank, looking into the Egg, says, "It's out of degrade."

"Maybe," Grandpa offers.

Frank says, "The numbers have stopped ascending. It's not going to blow up until somebody tells it to." He looks at Dewey's folded letter, says, "Banging away randomly, right."

Roberta says, "Tod's sick. We're going."

"Where?" Frank asks.

I say, "The house. Frank, let's just all split, if this thing goes Vesuvius—"

Frank says, "It won't do anything until I tell it to aboard the *Gogol*."

"If it torches off on the water," my grandfather says, "you'll have a tsunami, a 200-foot tidal wave that'll throw enough radiation to kill anybody it hasn't drowned."

Frank laughs. "Come on."

My grandfather says, "That is, if you can get it out there. The trigger's been jimmied so bad it could still be destabilized. If you know what's good for you, you'll cut your losses and dial 911."

Frank shakes his head and Weire hands me a small automatic and Roberta the keys to the rental.

I ask, "What's this?"

Weire says, "I call it a gun."

Then he hands me a silver rectangle.

I ask, "What's that?"

Weire says, "Another clip. Who knows who's out there. If you get into trouble, you may need extra ammo, in case you gotta reload."

4 JULY

Dusk at my parents' house. I'm sick and getting sicker. All day in bed staring at the ceiling. Roberta was up with me half the night putting ice on my forehead and cold towels around my pregnant stomach. I managed to sweat through the sheets, probably the mattress, and maybe the floor.

But sick or not, I bet I'm still stronger than Frank. Perhaps I should hop into Sudden Death, go back to Heaven, and kick his ass. Or maybe not. Chances are, the bomb is stabilized. Looking out the living room, I can see the *Gogol* on the horizon.

I glance toward the misted cup of the valley below. Hyper

Mart is ten miles away, but huge on the horizon. Frank claims it's the biggest building ever made.

We're sitting under the red plate of Willem de Kooning's *Valentine*, watching a rerun of *Married with Children*, the episode where the Bundys' house burns down and Kelly dies in the blaze. I know I should have done something, but what? Frank's Frank. He does what he's going to do. Roberta says, "You're holding my hand so hard it hurts. You gotta get some sleep."

I go to sleep and awake in the dark to the sound of my own screams. Roberta is still there above me. She says, "Crawford, unsquawk. You're sweating a river."

In my dream Frank knew that the rocket would blow up and he detonated the Proteus just to kill my father. The reason he'd had me pick out all the targets in the United States was so he could kill his past and learn to have sex with Jeanie— he had her out of jail and stashed in luxury. When I woke up it took me minutes to forgive him.

I ask Roberta what time it is and she says, "Night."

Above us small airplanes hang from the ceiling in attitudes of aerial combat. Cotton strung in puffs twenty-five years ago droops from fishing leader strung from a plastic Me-109, the decaled swastika on its tail meticulously mutilated. This represents smoke and machine-gun fire coming from a new model. A scary black jet. Yesterday there was a blind item in the *Star* saying that Frank, who shot down a Mig and a half over Iraq, has designed a new killer airplane held together with Velcro. This could be it.

Roberta holds a pink capsule above my head. "Five hundred milligrams of Antiswaq just to keep Shiva in her box." She climbs into Frank's bed with me and says, "Swallow and I'll show you a little trick I learned in the army."

From somewhere I hear music in a smooth sibilant string. Bye Bye Master singing "All the Answers."

She gives me a kiss and we begin to neck. Things progress, until she backs away a little and smiles, her mouth as big as a movie screen. Then she whispers, "Are we really gonna get married?"

I say, "Yeah."

She says, "Okay, then let's quit fooling around."

In the dim I see her slip off her shorts and panties. A little later I ask if it hurts and Roberta breathes, "Yeah, but," I see her swallow. "I get the message." She swallows again and says, "Good fun, Crawford, good fun."

Then a whack of light, bright then almost instantly brighter, rising like a hot air balloon.

Roberta sits up on the bed and says no. I pull her down and in the searing light I see the spray dome, a cloud below the mushroom cloud, and below that, miraculously, though it may have been an illusion, I see my brother's lava paradise spilling out of the boiling sea. Then, whipping my eyes away from the neon roil, I look to Frank's perpetual motion machine, the one he invented in high school. It is here, in this room, and I am astonished to realize, in this brightness, its gears are turning and whirring still.

? JULY

So strange. If the *Gogol* made it back to the long pipes and submerged the nuke we shouldn't have even seen an explosion, unless it was of a size beyond reason.

Now at the center of a gory horizon, strong light, a dirty sun shines through steaming mist. The news isn't too good. The island maybe is under water. My fingerprints are falling off and I can pull my hair out in ponytails. At first there was television and talk of evacuation, but now there's no power. Most of the time I just hold Roberta. She's shocky and blind. She says man-made men will rescue us. I love her so much. We're both in pain, pain that is shooting out of our bones, and if it gets worse I still have the gun and I'll do what is right. The last thing I heard on Robot Radio besides static and a woman reciting the Lord's Prayer was some dying crybaby from Greenpeace claiming that the earth had been punctured like a big balloon.

It's been some kind of a first day of the rest of my life, that's for fucking sure. We remain optimistic, however, and have decided to get married. We love each other and Roberta says forget porno, time to be a mom. I ask her how we're going to do that if we're both going to end up dead or in jail, and she says, easy, if we're dead we're dead and if we're not and there are still jails worth going to, all I'll have to do is mail her a jizz-o-gram and she'll have a friendly bikedyke-lesbopunk squirt it in with a straw.

ACHNOWLEDGMENTS

I would like to thank my editor, Gary Luke, for providing excellent focus, over and over and over again; his assistant, Saul Anton; and Isolde C. Sauer, the indefatigable copy editing supervisor who had to wade through my changes more than once; and the magnanimous Suzanne Donahue. I would like to also thank David Kelly and Doug Holm. I do not write anything more complicated than a check without showing it to one or both of them. I likewise owe a debt to several great writers—among them Kent Anderson (*Sympathy for the Devil*), Tom Bates (*Rads*), and David Noonan (*Neuro, Memoirs of a Caddy*), and John Strawn (*Driving the Green*)—for their vital advice.

John Tillman (author of *The Sixth Battle*) was very helpful as well, largely because he knows everything.

Were it not for my wife, Deborah Wenner, and her strong sense of narrative reality, this book might have been little more than a typed-out hookah dream.

Last, but light-years from least, I'd like to thank my life-long friend and agent, Richard Pine. Erudite, tireless, wily, he did everything but hire Roberta and torch Maui. Working with him on *Aloha* was great from beginning to what I pray now (for both our sakes) may finally be the end.

The poems, epitaphs, sayings, and treacle that provide the "codes" for all of the Crawfords' locks have been taken from the public domain, with one exception, "Miss Universe," written by my ex-cousin, Marty Christensen. Marty, the most significant poet writing in English, dashed "Miss Universe" off between King Cobra aperitifs on the porch of his summer villa overlooking the heart of the light industrial district of Portland, Oregon. For this effort, I am profoundly grateful.